Priceless Lost

by

Alexandria May Ausman

This book is a work of fiction. Any references to historical events, real people, or real places, are used fictitiously. Other names, characters, places, and events are products of the author's imagination, and any resemblance to actual events or persons, living or dead, is entirely coincidental.

Book cover design by Alexandria May Ausman
Editor: Jon M. Ausman

Library of Congress Control Number: 2023924410

ISBN: 978-1-963335-03-3 (ebook)
ISBN: 978-1-963335-02-6 (paperback)

Published By:
Ausman & Cousins LLC
1700 North Monroe Street
Suite 11, Box 284
Tallahassee, Florida 32303-0501

For author interviews: ausman@embarqmail.com

Das Kaiser Haus Series

The Rise of the Priceless (Chapters 1 to 10)
Metal Illness (Chapters 11 to 19)
Jonas the Vampire (Chapters 20 to 29)
Prince of the Elders (Chapters 30 to 40)
Leo's Lamb (Chapters 41 to 50)
Mastermind Malfred (Chapters 51 to 58)
Priceless Lost (Chapters 59 to 66)
Broken Silver (coming soon Chapters 67 to 73)

The Collar King Series

Return to Das Kaiser Haus (coming soon)
Felicity's Child (coming soon)

The Psycho Series

Cemetery Kid (Chapters 1 to 20)
Stop Calling Me Psycho (Chapters 21 to 33)
Motor-Psycho (Chapters 34 to 44)
Delusion of the Collar and the Key (Chapters 45 to 53)
Brutality's Prisoner (Chapters 54 to 64)
Aesthetic Akathisia (Chapters 65 to 74)
Metallic Burden (Chapters 75 to 83)

27 Masters Series

Anita the Benevolent (Chapters 1 to 7)
The Beast and the Witch (coming soon Chapters 8 to 16)
High Priestess of Schizophrenia (coming soon)

Book 7 Characters: Priceless Lost

Abelard: an apprentice black collar stable hand
Agnette: a Haus FemDom
Alexie: a Haus FemDom
Anna: a Haus FemDom
Annette: a Haus black collar
Audrey: a Haus Femdom
Barnum: a deceased Elder of the Haus
Bernt: a young Haus Dominant
Bladrick: an Elder of the Haus
Briton: a deceased House doctor
Bruno: a young Haus Dominant
Byron: a Haus Dominant
Christian: the anger and lust shard
Christian Axel: a Haus submissive, the Priceless
Claus: an Elder of the Haus
Cora: a FemDom of the Haus, the Fur Queen
Darrell: a deceased child molester
Debbie: Meine Liebe's sexual psychopathic and sadistic mother
Der Goldene Hund: the Voice or the Boss shard; the Conscious shard
Der Makellos: German Shepherd named "The Unblemished"
Drexel: a deceased Elder of the Haus
Egon: Haus seduction Master and trainer
Elsa: a Haus black collar
Fiona: a young Haus FemDom
Friedrick: a Haus Dominant, friend of Byron

Fritz: a young Haus Dominant
Gerard: stepfather of Christian Axel
Gisela: a Haus FemDom, friend of Rolf
Grisham: a deceased Haus Dominant
Gretta: a Haus Elder, the Silk Queen
Gustov: a deceased Haus Dominant
Hedy: a young Haus FemDom
Heidi: deceased Dungeon Mistress; sister of Helga
Helga: deceased Dungeon Mistress; sister of Heidi
Humphrey: a child molester with a fetish
Ivar: a black collar Torture Master
Jasper: a child molester with a fetish
Jipsum: Malfred's half brother
Jonas: an Elder of the Haus
Julius: a deceased Haus Dominant
Karl: a Haus Dominant, father of Ryker
Leo: a Haus Dominant
Louis: a low level Haus Dominant
Mad Max: the sadistic shard of Maximillian, aka the Heart and Judgment
Mad Maxx: husband of Meine Liebe; a Haus Dominant
Mad Maxx: the masochistic shard, aka the Brain and Guilt
Magnas: a young Haus Dominant
Malfred: a Haus Dominant
Matz: a young Haus Dominant
Max: the Soul shard
Maximillian: the submissive name given to Christian by Peter
Maximillian: the seductive shard, aka the Libido
Maxximillian: the submissive adopted by the Elders
Meine Liebe: submissive and spouse of Mad Maxx

Mila: a Haus FemDom
Nelda: a low level Haus FemDom
Olaf: Haus black collar door guard
Oswin: a young Haus Dominant
Peter: a Dominant of Der Kaiser Haus; best trainer of submissives
Roland: a young Haus Dominant
Rolf: a Haus Dominant
Rudolph: a black collar stable Master
Russell: spouse of Debbie, a switch
Ryker: deceased Haus trainee
Shelvey, Mrs.: a school teacher
Sigard: a Haus FemDom, friend of Rolf
Sofie: a deceased schizophrenic sister of Leo; known as Maus
Sonny: a child molester with a fetish
Stefan: a deceased Haus Dominant
Steve: husband to Debbie
Tamina: Malfred's former silver
The Lambs: Abelard, Annette, Geraldine, Milo, Ryker
Valintin: a young Haus Dominant
Vilber: Haus black collar door guard
Whiskey: a child molester with a fetish
Wolf: a Haus Dominant
Xavier: deceased Fur King of the Haus

Prologue

In book seven of Das Kaiser Haus, Mad Maxx is forced to make several difficult sacrifices. His Elder Masters believe they have neutralized Mastermind Malfred's power, but have they? No one in the House believes this slippery foe is going to take their insult without an attempt at revenge.

Unfortunately for the Max brothers, Taube, and Christian, Malfred's retaliation proves to be nearly fatal for them. In more ways than one.

Severely injured, traumatized, and relentlessly pursued by dangerous enemies the Mad Maxx shards make hasty alliances they quickly regret. Just when it seems all is lost, including his sanity, the boy is granted the mercy of Felicity.

Only six months to go until the Priceless must pass the collar selection test. With Der Hund still missing, the shard Mad Maxx in a deep catatonic stupor, and Max fading fast, the remaining shards are running out of time, and options.

Language in italics is a conversation between the adult male Master Mad Maxx and his female submissive Meine Liebe.

Chapter 59: Sacrificing the Lambs

"I returned to Master Leo's side thinking about Elsa's gorgeous eyes and her other finer points. He smiled as I took my seat, then patted my hand as I put it on tabletop.

"Meine hase (bunny), you need to eat something. I swear your thinner than a rail. What could I trade you to get you to nibble on a bit of dinner?" He reached over and pushed my hair out of my face. I had not been keeping up my hygiene so my long hair on top was a real mess I am ashamed to say.

I shrugged. "I have no use for anything you possess, Master. The only thing I want you already deny me."

Master Leo frowned at that. "Christian Axel, I am fixing what I broke. You saw that this very night. All things come to those that wait."

I chuckled. "Oh? The sonofabitch that said that never wore a Gott damned collar you can be sure of that. Can we go see the lambs in the morning? I need to see if Geraldine cooked for me. I will eat whatever she makes for me. That lamb works hard you know."

He nodded. "Ja meine hase, we will go see the lambs in the morning. when we get to the apartment I want you to come to the bedroom with me immediately. You owe me a service and I don't desire that Jonas or Malfred block me from it. I think they would likely try to keep you for themselves if I don't move quickly, ja?"

I watched Elsa picking up plates from the empty tables. "Leo be nimble. Leo be quick. Leo snatches the Priceless from the evil dicks."

Master Leo began laughing hard. "How do you do that, meine hase? You manage to rhyme the nursery saying within moments. I swear your mind is amazing. I wonder if even Jonas realizes just how bright you really are? Never mind. I suppose no one around here is interested in your brains."

I nodded at my Master but was caught in a trance staring at that beautiful Elsa. "The fastest route for freedom is not the straight line for the forbidden silver Master. This little cocksucker works for his supper. Does that matter? They don't care about the fucker. How shall he pay them back without using a knife? How can he ever find happiness? when all he wants is a wife?"

Master Leo groaned. "You are slipping off more and more often, meine hase. I worry you will never make it to the collar selection vote at this rate. Please Christian Axel, listen to me. You must try harder to keep that madness at bay. Can you do that?"

I glared to him. "Huh? I am not mad. I don't know what you are requesting of me Master. Can you ask Jonas about that stereo? I will go crazy if he insists on playing it so damned loud. Doesn't it bother you? It seems no one else minds it. Is that something that I will eventually get used to?"

He shook his head. “I do not hear this radio of which you keep complaining of, meine hase. That is the insanity of your disease. Only you can see or hear some of the things you tell me about. Can you understand what I am saying? You hallucinate and believe things that are not truth.”

I nodded and laughed. “Ah, you are right on that one. I once thought many things that turned out to be lies, Master. This was ignorance not madness. I have recently awakened. See that girl over there? She wishes to seduce me. The idiot Maximillian would have fallen for the trick, but the enlightened Mad Maxx knows she is up to no good. Hex wrenches and desperation for being loved has schooled this dumbass painfully well. Can you tell me of this female? Her name I have heard before but for some reason I have forgotten the story.”

Master Leo narrowed his eyes as he examined Elsa from afar. “That black collar girl is trying to seduce you? Ah, you are hallucinating, Christian Axel. Black and silver affairs are forbidden. She surely wouldn’t be so stupid. You are showing delusions of reference. This schizophrenia is starting to deepen.”

That pissed me off a great deal. “Don’t believe me then, Master. I could care less what any of you no nothings think. I wish you would never think of me again in fact.” I yelled out feeling rage fill me.

He reached out and snatched my chain pulling it hard. “Stop that this minute. That is a directive. You shout at me again I will not take you to see the lambs in the morning.”

I looked at the table and wrung my hands. "I shut up as you demand, but I am not schizophrenic, Master. That fucking girl is trying to injure me for some reason. You may not believe me, but it is the Gott damned truth of it."

Master Leo nodded. "Okay, then we will have to agree to disagree, Christian Axel. In both your statements. You are mentally ill, and that girl is not bothering you. Come on, we are leaving. You obviously have had enough excitement for this day. You will come to bed with Leo, and sleep. I have the orange drink coming from the waiter for you since you refuse to eat. You drink that then we go."

I growled. "I don't like the orange juice, Master."

He jerked my leash harshly again. "Tough, meine hase. You will do what you are told. I realize I risk your hate for all that I must do, but that no longer matters to me. I vowed to save you from that fucking collar and these foul men surrounding you. By the time I am done doing what must be done to make that happen, you may want to never speak to me for the rest of your life. It is the risk I am willing to take. You reminded me that to love another for truth, you must be willing to do what is best for their happiness even giving up your own. You do what I tell you or find yourself sorry for it Christian Axel. You're no longer capable of good judgement."

I shook my head. "I cannot be any sorrier than I already am, Master. You can try if you like since I am trapped here with you. I would be careful what you do to me though. One they when I am free, I make all of you pay."

Master Leo glared at me with much anger. "I said enough, Christian Axel. There is the orange curative. You drink that and we leave. I give a new directive this minute too. You be silent. I better not even hear a fucking whimper out of you. I have let this get out of hand by taking the words of the insane seriously. Well, no more of that shit. From now on, you do what you are told without any commentary to your Master Leo." The black collar waiter put the orange juice in front of me.

I sat there wringing my hands, staring at it with bile rising in my mouth. I shot a look at Master Leo. He had his arms crossed and a look of sternness on his face. My eyes searched the Hall until they come across Elsa. She was pretending to not be paying attention to our table. My Master pulled hard on the leash once more and pointed at that glass.

I snorted but drank the nasty stuff. I knew better than to test his resolve to punish me for ignoring his command. It sucked to be the one on the bottom. Believe me, I had learned that to the hilt since my twelfth year. There was nothing I could do about it. These foul men had my number. Christian Axel had to do what he was told or find more damned brands, scars, or worse on the boy's flesh. It was pretty obvious I would have to deal with Elsa's conspiracy, whatever it may be, on my own.

When I finished that crappy drink, Master Leo dragged me back to his apartment. I was already feeling sleepy by the time we reached his door. We entered to find Master Malfred and the Vampire Jonas listening to Master Leo's records. He appeared angered at their going through his things. but he said nothing.

Instead, he tried slipping off down to his room hauling my ass behind him. The Dominant brutes tried to argue that it was not his turn on the clock as it was Master Malfred's time, but he ignored them. I followed behind him yawning, doing my best not to close my eyes. I was just so fucking tired. It seemed I needed a nap. It had been a long day.

He pulled me into his room and began stripping off my clothing. I was too fatigued to argue about that. If he wanted the special services, then he would have to take them without my consciousness. I found myself nodding off before he even reached my boots and breeches. I don't even recall anything after he took off my left shoe.

That night I had this weird dream that I flew through the room onto his bed. Then these butterflies kept landing on my forehead and chest. I tried to swat them off me, but my arms were stuck to the mattress. I heard Master Leo's voice tell me to be still several times, but I couldn't see him anywhere. I found that whole scene very odd, but then again that orange drink always made me have the strangest visions in my slumber.

When I awoke the next morning I found myself snuggled in the arms of the Vampire. I trembled with fear unable to recall how the hell I had managed to end up with this madman. I carefully rolled to get away from him only to find my path out of the bed blocked by a slumbering Master Leo.

That caused me quite a start. I nearly screamed in terror at the idea these two had teamed up against me. Master Malfred and Master Jonas were bad, but if Master Leo was their bosom buddy, well Christian Axel was screwed, literally.

I did my best to calm my anxiety over this latest nightmare discovery. I sat up slowly to see if Master Malfred was in the fucking bed too. I almost let out a sigh of relief when I found only the two of them were holding me hostage. I admit I was sweating it, sure this was a worst case scenario of all three of these men working against me.

My stomach rumbled with hunger causing me to hazard an attempt to awaken Master Leo without stirring the Vampire Jonas. I needed to feed my Geraldine and be fed back for my efforts. I decided I would have to worry about the frightening possibility of a foursome later. Though I have to say I had determined I would fly off that banister before I would let that happen.

Master Leo was easy to prompt back to alertness. He stared at me while I silently mouthed I desired to see my lambs. He shot a worried look at the snoring Master Jonas then nodded. I winced as he attempted to get out of bed quietly, and immediately smacked into his nightstand making much racket.

Master Jonas jumped up with a start. "What the hell. Leo, the boy is trying to escape. Grab him." I let out a yelp as the Vampire tackled me just as I slid off the bed behind the schwuler Elder.

We both fell onto the floor with a loud thud. “I got him. Get the rope. He is psychotic,” screamed out Master Jonas.

I gasped in fear. “Nein, please Master, mercy. I was only getting up for breakfast, I swear it. He pulled my arms behind me and put his knee into my back forcing me to a painful silence.

Master Leo comes rushing toward us. “Jonas! Let Christian Axel go. He was following my command to get up for dressing. I am taking him to the barn to see his pets. Christ man. What the hell is wrong with you? A bit jumpy maybe? I have to ask who the fuck is the psychotic one.”

Master Jonas groaned. “Shit. That scared me to death. Gott damn it Leo. Why didn’t you just say you told the boy to get out of bed?” He lifted his weight and pulled me to my feet appearing apologetic. Too late, I was already bruised from that man’s rough handling of me.

Master Leo growled. “I didn’t realize I had to announce my every move in my own haus. Dammit Jonas, you need to relax a little. I told you last night this whole mess is almost cleaned up. Soon the boy will be all yours once more. Until then, you promised the mercy of allowing me to enjoy his company while I can.”

Master Jonas sat down on the side of Master Leo’s bed. He grabbed my upper arm and pulled me into his naked lap. I shuddered while he wrapped his arms around the boy and pulled my head into his neck snuggling me closely.

He breathed in my ear sounding relieved. “I admit Leo, when you came to me last night with this plan I thought you were funning me. However, this morning I hold this treasure in my arms with the understanding that soon I won’t have to share him with anyone ever again. I don’t know how I can thank you enough for your sacrifice and perfect plan.”

Master Leo bemoaned. “Well, you could be kind and share once in a while, but I realize that will not happen. You are far too selfish, and soon meine hase will be free to choose. He will never be with me once he is without that collar. Only you will be capable of forcing yourself on him for all his days. I do hope you will take into mind that it is not love when you don’t grant him the right to say nein.”

I stared at Master Leo from my wantage in the clutches of the Vampire confused by this strange discussion. I wanted to ask what the hell Master Leo meant about only Master Jonas being able to call special services, but I dared not utter a word. I knew that to interrupt Dominants when they are speaking is a thudding offense. I will say though, that their talking like soon I would be out of my collar filled me with joy. If I could overlook that sinister shit about being stuck in the Vampire’s bed for all my days.

The vampire chuckled. “You know what Leo. You draft that law and get it approved, then I swear on my honor I will work out an arrangement with you regarding the boy. It is not often in this Haus of backstabbers and selfish pricks one can find a loyal friend. Do not assume I am so wealthy I can afford to toss such a rare gift so quickly. I have been selfish all my life, but your generosity and self-sacrifice in this matter has helped me see their can be thrill in return of such a service. Besides, Christian Axel is fond of you. Perhaps it would aid my bid to reach his heart if I allow for his interests by curbing my own." He kissed the top of my head.

Master Leo's eyes went wide, and his jaw dropped in shock. "Seriously? You mean this for truth, Jonas? I, uhm, don't know what a say. Thank you from the bottom of my heart. I am flattered that you think of me so highly, and I am honored to call you my true brother."

The Vampire scoffed but shot a wicked smile at him. "Well, I am not ready to move in with each other and call you my man Leo. Stop fawning and get this boy down to see his lambs for his breakfast. I can hear that belly of his rumbling. He needs some meat on his bones. Nothing worse than a scrawny lover, ja?" He squeezed me tightly then pushed me off his lap and swatted my backside demanding I dress quickly.

I put back on my clothes with a great deal of wonder as I listened to the two of them discuss a new Haus law. I recalled Master Peter telling Master Leo he wanted a draft for one that would untrap me from my metal. I did my best to understand their speaking and plans, but my stomach hurt so badly with hunger I could barely think much less comprehend their coded language. It was clear only that even Master Jonas seemed to believe this plan of my father's was going to set me back on the path for the sacred bolt cutters.

Master Leo insisted I put on a coat even though Master Malfred forbade me the blouse. I was happy to cover my naked chest but did notice the brands were all leaking pus and blood. Over the night a skin infection had started to onset. The two Elders saw this and grumbled about my killing the Haus doctor. Master Jonas told us to go on without him to the barn while he hunted down another sawbones to attend my latest difficulties. Difficulties that were their fault, for the record.

I was relieved that the Vampire would not be making the trip with us. That joy was soon crushed when that hideous Master Malfred, who had to sleep on the couch all night, insisted on joining us. He grumbled the whole trip about my getting to wear a coat against his directive, and about Master Leo's lumpy sofa. I wanted to beat the man myself long before we made it to the barn for behaving like the bitchy old woman. He was quite the complainer when his wishes were minimized, damn.

I managed to keep my mouth silent the entire time from getting out of the bed all the way to the stables. I suppose after being ignored when I asked for aid against Elsa, I was a bit miffed at Master Leo. Bothering to speak to the Vampire and Master Malfred had never been fruitful. All I ever got was beaten and ignored.

It seemed there was no sense in wasting my breath around any of my Masters. Not like they ever protected me from a damned thing anyway. I was definitely on my own when it came to these intra-haus plots and threats to my life.

Hell, to be brutally honest, half the time the fuckers were either in on them or even the Gott damned mastermind.

I found my lamb family excited to see me as usual. I was more thrilled than them this time. I held each tightly with many hugs and kisses, saving Geraldine for last. when she come to me for her well-earned affection she leaned in to speak to me privately.

I shot a look at the Masters to make sure we had no eavesdroppers. Master Leo was off to fetch Geraldine's breakfast for me. Master Malfred was hanging around the gate but seemed distracted by a loud black collar berating one of his younger apprentices.

I whispered in her ear, "Got Ivar, well I didn't actually get him myself,, but he is dealt with. I am ready for the next target meine heart."

Geraldine licked my ear then said, "Good job, Mad Maxx. You have earned your meal. You must make plans to destroy Karl, Alexie and Mila, but beware of Master Malfred. He will not take kindly to your killing his brother. He is blind to the man's evil."

I nodded. "Then I will kill Master Malfred if he gets in the way. I hate that man anyway."

"Christian Axel, which is it. You plot with that fucking lamb. I heard you speaking to it," shouted out Master Malfred.

I was startled and let Geraldine go. She tried to get into my lap, and I pushed her away. Master Malfred stood their glaring at me with the fires of fury in his eyes.

"I heard you boy. You are taking orders from that Gott damned animal. Did it tell you to do what you did the other day? Is that why Jonas is on the phone seeking medical aid this minute? It is, isn't it? I know you fucking schizophrenics. These lambs are a threat to our lives. Leo, get over here. I want to speak to you. Come, hurry." He motioned with urgency to the Elder that was returning with a plate for me from Geraldine.

I stood up and stared at the ground wringing my hands. I felt my heart speeding up. Sweat began to break from my brow. I watched my happy family nudging me gently begging that I rejoin them in the cuddling. I had trouble breathing when I heard Master Malfred tell Master Leo he was certain I was taking orders from the lambs.

Master Leo laughed. "That is insane Malfred. The lambs cannot speak. Christian Axel is not speaking to them. Tell this deranged man you hear nothing but baa-baa from these animals, meine hase."

Master Malfred sneered. "He will lie Leo. That nut killed the fucking doctor over his perception that he must because they said to. You get rid of these animals. I mean this. You send them away. settle this peacefully or I will have no problem fixing this matter with the rifle I have back at my apartment. I am happy to find myself enjoying lambchops for my dinner."

"Nein, this is not their fault, Master. Please, mercy. Don't let him kill them. If you shoot them then I go too," I screamed out in terror, then began to try to drape myself over the group of my family.

Master Leo groaned out. "Gott damn it, Malfred. You have set the boy off. Stop this madness right this fucking minute. What the hell has gotten into you, fool?"

Master Malfred shook his head. "I tell you what Leo, this is indeed madness. You know I am telling you the truth. Leo, I am not funning you. If you insist on ignoring my demands I will attend this matter with my own hands."

I fell to my face on the ground begging with all I had that Master Malfred leave my lamb family in peace. Master Leo did all he could. The Dominant would not relent his threat to shoot them all if I were permitted to keep them for myself. The schwuler Elder was beyond angered at this situation with both of us throwing fits demanding their way.

Master Leo finally called Rudolf the black collar barn animal attendant to aid him in this dilemma. Rudolf listened as he informed him that the lambs had become an issue, after warning me several times to stop my vailing or he would let Master Malfred have his way with my family.

Rudolf rubbed his chin deep in thought, then said, "Well sir, I think there is an easy way to solve this issue. The shepherds will be coming through here in about thirty minutes. If we gather up these lambs in a hurry we can catch the sheep herd and release them into the flock. The lambs are old enough, and they are in no danger of being killed for food. Those sheep are the wool animals. They are not for the slaughtering."

I heard that and yelled out, "Ja, please Master Leo. Let them go be with their brothers and sisters far from the supper plates. I want them to be free." *I said that but to be honest Meine Liebe, I could feel my heart breaking at having to send my friends far away. I knew I would never see them again the second that shepherd took them. This was desperation speaking. I was willing to lose the joy of touching them to assure their safety from these hateful Dominants for all their lives.*

Master Leo looked at me with sadness. "Are you sure about this, Christian Axel? If I let Rudolf take them to the flock, you will never see them again."

I sniffed back my tears and rose to my kneeling. "I am sure Master. Let this man take them to be with their own kind."

Rudolf had an expression of softness in his expression, which surprise me. "Sir, forgive me for suggesting this but there are four of us. I can get one more to aid and we can take the lambs to the shepherd ourselves. That way the Priceless can say a final good-bye and see that his lambs are going to be contented in their new surroundings."

Master Leo smiled with bitterness. "That is a wonderful idea, Rudolf. Ja, fetch one more to aid us. We will follow you unless you have a problem with this Malfred?" He shot a hateful look at the cruel Dominant.

Master Malfred smiled with feigned friendliness. “Nein. I am fine with it. As long as these animals are where this boy cannot ever have access to them again, I am happy to aid in this task.”

I looked at my lambs all crowding me with loving expressions on their soft little faces. I felt the tears breaking out on my cheeks with the realization I would never see any of them anymore. My chest ached with the pain of losing them. I grabbed each and hugged their neck quickly while explaining the situation as best as I could given the short time I had before Rudolf returned with his apprentice.

Master Leo picked up Ryker, Master Malfred took Geraldine (he wouldn’t allow me to have her for my own), Rudolf grabbed Milo, the apprentice black collar managed Abelard, and I held Annette. The five of us walked the many yards behind the barn to the fields to await the flock being herded by the shepherds.

My lambs were frightened and called out to me the whole trip in their panic. I kept my face buried in Annette’s neck so the men wouldn’t see my sobbing like a kid. I thought for sure I would die of the heartbreak. I recalled the day I said good-bye to my Annette and Ryker. Believe me when I say the pain was the same this time too, it had not diminished a bit.

I saw the brown field turn white far as the eye could see. The sounds of hundreds of sheep called out through the air. My lambs became excited and called back, all them struggling to get loose of our arms, ready to join their own species. I squeezed my Annette one final time then put her to the ground on her little legs.

She took off bucking and celebrated her freedom to run. I watched as the Dominants and black collars released the rest of my family. All the lambs followed Annette's rushing to join their flock. Within only a few moments, I couldn't tell my babies from the mass of animals rapidly moving past us.

I stood there feeling lost and hopeless as the shepherds went by not even stopping to speak nor taking notice of our addition to their ranks. Within a few moments more, My lambs were nothing but a large white pattern in the landscape moving on to greener pastures. They were home at last, and Christian Axel was alone once more without a single friend in the world that wasn't forcing me to pay with my flesh for their attentions.

I covered my face and wept openly, no longer caring that the others could see me doing it. I hated no one as much as I did Master Malfred that morning I said farewell to my lambs. I would never forgive him for taking away my only joy and still don't.

Master Leo come forward and took up my leash. "Don't cry, meine hase. The lambs are happy with their family. You did a beautiful thing for them. Your love saved them, and now it has set them free. They will never forget what you did for them. I know that with all my heart."

Master Malfred scoffed. "You see Leo that is the problem. You are the reason the boy developed that fucking belief in the first place. He is simple. You put ideas into his head that the lambs are like people. They are filthy, stinking animals. I can see why he was taken with them. Like his kind, they are here only to serve their betters' appetites, but you made a terrible mistake giving him the impression they were capable of giving any comfort. The only thing that a lamb is good for is the dinner plate, and the only thing a silver is capable of is serving his Master. That is the truth of it plain and simple."

Master Leo pulled me to his chest hugging me tightly while I grieved deeply. "You are a pig, Malfred. The boy just lost his pets. There is so little joy for him in this lonely life he is forced to endure. You could at least show sympathy for his pain, or at the very least shut your fucking narrow minded mouth."

He laughed loudly. "You baby that boy Leo, like you fed him from your own breast. Stop acting like a worried Frau and let's go back to the apartment. I am interested in calling on his services and then I wish to take him swimming with me. He will forget all about those nasty beasts once in my bed, then in the water."

Master Leo squeezed me tightly. "I seem to recall you worked out a service return with this collar regarding his getting to see his lambs every morning. You can no longer keep your side of the bargain since they are where he cannot gain the benefit of visiting his pets anymore thanks to your threats. As for going swimming, you know damned well he is hydrophobic, also partly your fault. I can thank your stupid ass for his not eating a fucking bit of his breakfast. I vowed to protect and defend this collar he wears. Therefore, since you seem to be injuring the Priceless left and right, I am forced to punish you. This morning I called in my rights to send him to a secure place for his best interest. Claus and Bladrick have been notified that he will be beginning their clock the moment we get back to the Haus. They are already awaiting his arrival."

Master Malfred let out a roar of fury, "You prick. You cannot do that."

Master Leo chuckled with evil in his tone. "Ja Malfred, I can. I called Jonas, his other man, first and gained his approval for this early switch. He agreed without quarrel. Claus also voted that you be separated from the Priceless for a few days, for your own best interest as well as for his own. I think you better consider you are not on his list of those he wishes well at this moment. We both are aware of what happens to the idiots that dare to slight this beautiful boy. He holds grudges, fool. Now, Christian Axel, wipe away your tears. You are to pack and leave for your Masters Claus and Bladrick right away. I will see you in a few days, ja?"

I nodded as I did as he ordered sniffing back my tears. "Thank you for the mercy, Master." *If I were being honest, I would have killed Master Malfred had that rat bastard tried to touching me that morning. Master Leo was wise to send me away to stay my homicidal streak.*

Master Malfred bitched and moaned all the way back to the apartment that he had been "robbed of services" by

Master Leo's going behind his back with my other Elders. There was nothing that he could do about it though. It was not even close enough to make me feel better about losing my lamb family thanks to him.

I won't lie and say I didn't feel immense gratitude to Master Leo for causing Malfred at least this minor discomfort even if it meant the piss and blood London Bridge. That hateful Dominant's bed would be cold without my ass in it for at least the next two days and it was really pissing him off.

I would soon find out that my Master Leo planned to extend that chilliness in that man's love life for a much more extended time. It turned out that clever schwuler was not someone to anger nor would he tolerate being pushed around by the likes of Master Malfred.

To my surprise Master Jonas had already packed up all my things. He was standing at Master Leo's door holding my canvas bag when we all came inside. He shoved it at me and told Master Leo to take me immediately to Master Claus's place. I was more than a little confused by the Vampire's rush to see me off into another's lustful clutches. He pulled me into a deep kiss but kept it unusually brief.

When Master Malfred reached out to grab me for his own farewell affections Master Leo jerked my leash with much brutality and pulled me out the door with strength. I again was shocked at this apparent "team effort" of Master Leo and Master Jonas to block Master Malfred's undeserved services from me.

I didn't ask questions, but I was more than a little surprised by it. This was the first time I ever saw my Elder Dominants actually punish the offender for their bad behavior. Normally they make my flesh pay for it.

When I arrived at Master Claus's apartment I was met by the "new Haus doctor." This man was middle aged and appeared more affable then the last one had been. The oldest Elders allowed Master Leo to stay for the examination. I was promptly put on antibiotics, for like the thousandth time, and I was given a stiff warning to return to my hygiene rituals.

The doctor left and the three Elders surrounded me, all of them berating me for neglecting my cleaning duties. I was reminded that attending to my flesh was part of my job as their pleasure submissive. I did my best to point out the contamination of the water.

None of them would hear my explanation. I was threatened with thudding, isolation, and Master Bladrick even went so far as to say they would hand me over to Master Louis and Mistress Nelda for their pleasures if I continued to demonstrate poor grooming.

Nothing they said nor threatened worked. With my lambs gone I felt empty and forlorn. As far as I was concerned they may as well hold me down then douse me with the radiation. I sat there staring in a depressed trance while they stood around complaining loudly of my lack of compliance.

Master Leo took a seat next to me and reached out grabbing my chin forcing me to look at him "Meine hase, listen to me. You are endangering yourself. How do you plan to break that collar if you are dead from infection? You need to take up bathing, and all your other cleansing tasks like you were trained to do. I swore to you I never would call special services in the water again, and none of your other Masters will either. when you are in the bathroom your privacy will be honored. Are you listening to me? We all swear to this."

I shrugged. "Thank you for the mercy of it, Master. That doesn't change the fact that the water is radiated, now does it?"

He sighed loudly then shook his head. "I told you I have the antidote. You need only spray down with it before each shower, and you are protected. See you used it last night and you are not dead today."

I nodded. "It takes a bit for it to kill, Master. You don't understand. I cannot come back from the dead if I am killed in this place. Then I will never have my lambs back. I will be trapped haunting this horrible place like Casper does. I don't want to be stuck here with him."

Master Leo shot a look of concern to Master Claus and Master Bladrick. "That antidote comes from the mystics, Christian Axel. It is guaranteed to protect you from that contamination, I swear it. Is there nothing I can do to get you to believe me?"

I didn't respond to him. I no longer felt like speaking to any of them. They only care about what they put into my mouth, not what came out of it anyway. I looked away from him and shut down. There was plenty going on inside the wheel room to distract me from the outside existence anyway. I threw the flesh into auto pilot and joined my brother shards in the inner world.

The boy attended the lust of his Masters Bladrick and Claus without quarrel but did not much else. when not being used for their pleasures he sat quietly staring in a corner without expression or much movement. He refused all food and barely drank liquids. He would not utter a single word nor make sounds other than the occasional yelp when one of the Masters got too rough with him.

This sudden withdrawal from interactions appeared to startle the Elders at first. They called Master Leo and Master Jonas several times that first couple days trying to get the boy to respond to their attempts to stimulate responses. The Vampire even went as far as a mild thudding with the tawse. All he managed to elicit was a mindless wail when he struck the flesh. The boy didn't even beg him to stop.

The flesh was immune to all their fruitless attempts. They could make the boy lay there and take their abuse but there was nothing they could do to make us give them the gift of our attention, whether positive or negative. when us shards work as a team to ignore them, then you can be assured the results are a lifeless lump of skin and bones without any cares.

By the end of the second day, Master Claus and Master Bladrick had stopped molesting the flesh and left me to my quiet solitude in the corner of their living room. They found no sport in the mechanical boy that was mirroring their own bad behavior. They were treating him like a machine without the capacity for feelings.

Taube reflected back the Masters' definition of the boy, while Maximillian and I dreamed of a world full of lambs, beautiful girls that adored us, and green wide open fields without walls as far as our eyes could see.

It was a dark time for all of us despite the thrill of imagining our hopes had come to truth. You see Meine Liebe, living inside your mind is not a fulfilling life. The fantasy world we create for ourselves to escape our pain is never capable of healing the wounds of reality.

In many ways, it makes the brutality of our existence even harder to endure. It was pretty clear that if something didn't give soon, Mad Maxx would slip away into the land of the dead for good.

I had not bothered to meet with Elsa in that closet as we had agreed. I did think of it that night of our date. I watched the clock turn to one. The Masters were deep in their slumber, and I was quite capable of picking their door locks. I had been so nonresponsive and non-combative, no one had bonded me for my safety.

I could have gone but I didn't have the desire to see the girl. She could have been honestly interested in coupling with me, though I seriously doubted that. I decided not to find out. I had no will to act on my own interests any longer. I simply sat there trapped within my deep inner thoughts of despair. I didn't even regret that I may have lost a chance to engage in sex with the gender of my preference.

At the end of the third day of my silence and lack of interaction, Master Leo came to the apartment to check on my welfare. He found two very worried Elders and a despondent boy almost too far gone to save.

"He could not believe that I had not snapped out of my grieving. I suppose for us sub-humans we are not capable of mourning for more than the couple of hours that our tiny minds are capable of comprehending?" Master Maxx laughed with much bitterness at that statement.

I chuckled too thinking of how stupid his Masters were to not expect he would be so deeply affected by the loss of his only happiness in his harsh life. It seemed beyond my imagination that even Master Leo seemed unable to have empathy for him, but then I thought of Mrs. Shelvey, and the many other so called well-meaning normals in my own dark world.

I nodded and hugged his big arm.

He chuckled then ruffled my hair. "Ja, you understand Meine Liebe, don't you? Well never again. I do know you grieve and sadly that is the fuel that runs your wheel for all your days. You see you must learn to wear a fake smile, laugh without feeling and pretend it is all okay. The normals do not like to hear the truth of the hell we are trapped in. That is too much for them to bear, though they expect us to do it without complaint. They will call you strong, but the truth is you are anything but such a thing. The ugly fact is you will spend all your days attempting to hide your inner weakness and vulnerabilities. Don't you ever fall for their lies that they never judge you for the things you have done and will do to survive. Be smart and you give them your silence. The normal will never understand you. You must learn to pretend you are one of them and feed them the lies that make them feel better. If you dare to show them the true you, then be ready to spend all your days with a monster they will thrill to hunt you. You are already mortally wounded, meine Frau. If you let them smell blood, be ready to be devoured in their shark-like feeding frenzy. Now don't worry, meine heart. I will teach you to laugh when you want to cry, and joke when there is nothing funny about the situation. Only one of us will see that the size of your smile is equal to the girth of your terror. Even then, when you find that kindred spirit, beware. The injured and scared are just as likely, if not more so, than the blessed to rip you apart to get out of their traps. I need not point out that you were raped by your very own man the first time you were left alone together. I may be sorry for that horror, but I will never be able to undo it. I didn't take my own good advice and we both must pay for that for all our days, ja?"

I narrowed my eyes then turned to look at him. "Does it really matter what you did that day, Master? I love you now, and I do understand why you did it. There was no other way."

He smiled at me and shook his head. "Meine Liebe, there is always another way. You see I did to you what had always been done to Mad Maxx. I punished the victim instead of the criminal. I should have busted Debbie and Russell up, not you meine heart. I was so hell bent to make you my own and pay them back for betraying me. I forgot that there was a little girl that would have to live with the injury I caused her. You must work harder than others to prevent yourself from continuing the cycle of terror from which you were conceived. I forgot myself only a moment, and now I must live with that being the first memory of our love for one another. I deserve it, but you meine heart, do not. I am not a good person, meine demonseed Frau. However, I refuse to be the worst person. We can never change our past, but we can be Masters of our future. This you understand?"

I nodded., "Yes, I think so Master. I don't want to be like Debbie and Russell, or Master Peter either. You can help me not become a monster like them?"

Master Maxx laughed hard. "Ah ja, Meine Liebe, I can. Unfortunately, I cannot prevent the monster that already lives in you. That beast is one you alone will have to learn to control. I think ultimately, you will win your inner battles. I see a fierceness in you that only one of your blood line possesses. I may not have been thrilled at my interactions with your relatives, but one thing no one can deny about a Krause is that they are made of the stronger stuff. Not the wars of the world, Hitler, schizophrenia, nor splitting of our Motherland, eradicated them from the world. That uncle of yours did manage the unbelievable and your father nearly sent me to my grave. You have the pedigree and the intelligence to survive, but I see that you were gifted with so much more. Your heart is made of an unbreakable material unlike anything I have ever seen. This is the thing I love about you the most, and to be fair, fear even more than that."

I scoffed. "You are not afraid of anything, Master. You are big enough now to beat up anyone. I can't wait until I get big too. Then I will show Debbie and Russell what happens to people who mess with me."

That statement made Master Maxx howl with laughter. "Ah, Meine Demonseed Frau. I am afraid of you. You need not be the giantess to bring this dumb man of yours to his knees. You must always remember the Lion may look impressive, but it is the lioness that is the truthful threat to all those that threaten her pride. Now on with the story, ja?"

I nodded but to be honest I had no idea what he meant by that statement and wouldn't understand it for many years to come. But for the record, he was right.

Master Leo come over and sat next to the deeply depressed boy with a smile on his face, "Meine Hase. I am told you refuse to eat, speak, or move unless ordered to attend your Masters services. Well, that is not a good thing. I want to say I am disappointed by your passive resistance, but I do understand why you are behaving this way. You are saddened at losing your lambs, ja?"

The boy said nothing. He only stared at the wall, but we the shards listened to the schwuler Elder ever vigilant for commands. We assumed he was there to retrieve the boy for his clock with Master Malfred, the Vampire and himself.

My Master frowned at my lack of response. “Ah, you are upset with your Master Leo as well. I want you to know I only did what you asked me to do. Make sure you do not punish me for the actions of others.”

I turned my head and glared at him with anger but maintained my silence. I realized he was baiting me to say I was merely returning the service they all had given to me. Master Leo didn’t brand me like the others did nor had he been the one to suggest sending my lambs away. I was aware this was a trick.

He looked deep into my observably furious expression. “There is still the boy I love in that head somewhere I can see him. I had come by to take up your leash to return you to your man Jonas. However, if you would rather, I can send for him to claim what belongs to him exclusively. Your good health is no longer my concern, unless you wish it to be. I am maybe too eager to believe deep down you still have feelings for me and would desire I continue to be a part of your life in the Haus.”

I raised my eyebrow at that weird statement. “You speak nonsense, Master. I beg your mercy to not torment me with mind games. I go with you if this is your wish. It matters not to me, one of these men or you. All the same to me."

Master Leo chuckled. "Did you hear that Claus? The boy does have a voice. I had almost forgotten what he sounded like."

I shrugged then went back to staring at the wall no longer interested in anything Master Leo had to say since he found it so damned funny that I bothered to speaking.

The Elder suddenly looked up with an expression of seriousness. "Christian Axel do not shut me out, I beg of you. I come here to give you news you may find comforting."

I turned to glare at him again. "Oh? Did my mother die in a painful accident? Or maybe Master Malfred fell from the banister? If not any of those things I find no joy in anything you have to say to me."

Master Claus and Master Bladrick gasped but Master Leo put up his hand demanding silence of them. "Nein, your mother and Malfred still thrill at their fine health. However, I don't believe Malfred will be happy that he didn't fall to his death when he gets the information I am about to deliver to you, meine hase."

I snorted. "I am all ears Master. Anything that brings that bastard pain, I am most happy to hear it."

Master Leo nodded. "Well, I drafted a new Haus Law that would permit only a blood bonding of two partners to a single silver. One must be male and the other must be female. The law went on further to include female to female bonding be recognized from this point on. Cora, Jonas, Bladrick and I have signed this law. Gretta has passed the thing this very morning."

I shrugged. "So? What the hell do I care Master? It is too late for my ass now isn't it?"

He shook his head smiling bitterly. "Nein it is not. I had this law retroactive for the last year. That means all blood bondings past the single one with Jonas are no longer recognized by the Haus. You never blooded with a female, so you are no longer trapped in your metal meine hase."

Master Claus let out a loud wail. "You better be lying, Leo. This cannot be. Brother Bladrick, is this truth? Did you betray me. Surely you didn't help this idiot undo my blood bond to the boy. Why the fuck would you do that?"

Master Bladrick scoffed. "I didn't betray you brother. I did what was right. I was asked to sign a law that would free this boy to make an honest run at the bolt cutters. He was robbed by your cruel punishment for a crime you set him up to endure for your benefit. You used that loyalty to take more than you had the right to take. If you want that boy to love you, then give him the dignity of choice. He has more than earned it. Don't be an old fool Claus. The boy comes here without quarrel and allows our foul interests in him. He has never failed in doing what no one else ever would. Personally, if I were in his boots I would have flung myself down the stairs to avoid such a nasty fate. He may fail to break that collar of his, but if he does it will be on him, no you, not Malfred, and not Leo."

Master Claus shot a look of confusion at Master Leo. "You did this Leo? What the hell. Why? You surely know that bat Jonas will block you from your services from the Priceless now that you handed him the right to do it."

Master Leo nodded. "Ja, normally he would. However, I am with Bladrick. The boy deserves his chance to prove himself Dominant. I had no right to take that from him, and neither did you or Malfred. I gave him back the thing I stole. I am sorry brother, but I love this boy. I would give up all I have or ever will to see him happy."

Master Bladrick smiled with warmth. "I couldn't have said it better myself, brother Leo. Now, Christian Axel. Get the hell out of here. It has been a true pleasure. Thank you for giving this old codger one last vision of glory while his eyes can still see."

I looked at the floor unable to comprehend the words that Master Leo had spoken. "I don't understand, Master. This means that I never have to grant the special services request of Master Malfred or any of you?"

Master Leo smiled then ran his hand down my cheek. "Jonas has granted you the power to choose if you shall grant privileges to your other Masters. If you say nein to any of us but him, your word is to be honored. You cannot be punished for it. Only Jonas is the legal man that can enforce your compliance to his lustful interests. The rest of us are left to do their best to try to curry your favors best we are able."

Master Bladrick snickered, "Well, that leave me out. I have nothing worth having in return for the amazing gift he can grant to me."

Master Claus scoffed. "Neither do I brother. Fuck you Leo. I never liked you much but now I really hate you."

Master Leo giggled. "Ah, you know if you keep talking dirty to me brother, I may offer to take up the slack in your bed."

Master Claus rolled his eyes. "Yuck, let me say that again, yuck. I am glad you said that though. Now I need no one. I will never be able to get it up without thinking of your ugly face Leo."

I shook my head with the news Master Leo finally sinking into my hard head. "Wait a second. Master Claus you do have something to bargain with me and so do you Master Bladrick."

They both sat there with their mouths with open, then Master Bladrick found his tongue. "Well,? Are you waiting until the buzzards light on my head for their supper of me before you speaking what we can give to keep enjoying your adoration boy?"

I glared at Master Claus. "I demand you stay the hell out of my way with the Voting Council. Stop trying to lock me in my collar and withdraw your interest in using me in any fucking plots you are involved in or will become involved in. If there is so much as a whisper that your attempting to bring me into your dark games again, I will turn my back on you for all time. You treat me with honesty, then I come here as if there was no law that frees me from your bed. I will further sweeten this deal by adding that this arrangement will continue past my breaking of my metal. I realize your attempts to trap me were done because you feared my leaving you soon. Well, stop trying to steal my right to freedom and I grant you my undying loyalty until the end of your days for it. Do we have a deal ja or nein. If you do agree, I want it in writing this time Masters, I say that with respect."

Master Bladrick closed his eyes with a huge smile on his face. "I never believed in Gott until this minute, Christian Axel. Now I feel both elated that there is a heaven and frightened because that means there is also a hell. I agree to your offer and ask Claus to call for a car. I need to get to church right away. I need to speak to the creator and see if I still have time to bail my sorry soul out of damnation." He laughed but to be honest he wasn't kidding. He actually did rush to church to beg forgiveness that very day.

Master Claus looked at the floor appearing to tear up. "You would be willing to do this despite all I have done to you, Christian Axel? I admit I am a selfish and lonely man. I need not tell you as you apparently have recognized that. I will also take your agreement with pure respect for you and with shame for my own bad behaviors to one that never deserved it."

I shrugged. "What has been done cannot be undone can it, Master? I worry about yesterday when tomorrow isn't threatening to be my last on Earth. You draft the agreement and I see you in five days for the blood signature. I will never fail either of you, be sure you return the service and never forget that I have always been reasonable even when you were not."

Master Leo let out a small gasp then wiped the tears from his eyes. "You move me to tears, meine hase. I would dare to ask you if you offer me the same deal, or will you shut me out as I know you will Malfred. Both of us deserve your disdain much more than Claus or Bladrick."

I wrung my hands. "I swear I will never allow Malfred to touch me again. I will had my man Jonas kill that fucker if he dares to rape me as he always has done. He took what was never his to begin with. The man stole my family and views me as nothing more than a cock warmer. Well not his any longer. Master, that is more complex. You betrayed me, but you have corrected that by giving up what you also stole from me in the first place. I want to forgive you for all you have done, but I cannot forget all you have also done."

Master Leo nodded with a sadness in his expression. "You are right, meine hase. Maybe it is for the best that I suffer the same loneliness that Malfred will. Elders can own no collar but the Priceless, and Dominants do not like to leash to us. Condemnation to an empty bed is fair for the nightmares I caused you. I realized the brands you will wear for all time are the result of my allowing Malfred to sneak onto the sixth floor. I should have warned you that I was sending you to flush him out. I didn't know they were going to rape you into a blood bonding, nor did I know that they would get the drop on me, but there is no excuse for sending a boy to do a man's job." Suddenly Master Leo's shirt began whimpering.

I nearly jumped out of my skin as my shocked eyes focused on the source of the noise, a lump in the front of his jacket. I shot a look of fear at him then looked back to see it was moving around by itself.

He began to laugh. "Okay I admit, I went and collected Der Makellos early from his mother in case you were unreachable this morning. I was hoping to talk you into a bath and breakfast to hold him for a few hours."

I smiled with glee and held out my hands. "Deal, please mercy, Master. Let me hold him." I would have agreed to almost anything to have that puppy for even five fucking minutes.

Master Leo unzipped his jacket and handed the squirming baby dog to me. I squealed with thrill holding my friend to my face. He licked me with vigor and struggled to get closer to me still. For that moment I forgot anyone else was in the room. Only Der Makellos and I existed. My Masters sat on the couch speaking quietly while they watched me play with my puppy. They seemed humored at our silly antics there on the crossdresser's living room floor.

Der Makellos would furiously jump and yip at me and I would roll away feigning fear of his brave mock attacks. I laughed until I was near tears at the faces he made when he would trip over his oversized paws.

I was consoling my little friend after he had failed to frighten me with his tiny barking, when a knocking began at the door. Master Leo opened it to allow the Vampire to enter. He spoke in whispers to Master Leo while I kept a baleful eye on my man. I had been so thrilled to hear I would be able to deny Master Malfred. I had forgotten how much I feared and hated Master Jonas.

Thanks to Master Leo's new Haus Law, I was trapped with this monster for all the rest of his days, broken collar or nein. I would never be able to deny his demands for the privileges granted any spouse nor could I gain a legal divorce, yikes.

The Vampire come over and knelt down next to me and Der Makellos. "What do you have there, Christian Axel? Ah, he is a fine hound. Leo says this is your pup that you chose to be your buddy. Well, he is welcome in our home. It is time for you and me to get back, ja?"

I looked up with fear gripping my chest. I realized it had been two weeks already and the Vampire would be looking to feed. "Uhm, I need to go to Master Leo's to get our puppy settled in Master. Forgive me, but that is my responsibility. This is not my hound exclusively. Master Leo got him for he and I. I beg you allow me to attend my duties to Der Makellos and Master Leo first? I believe I also owe my Master a shower and eating my breakfast as agreed."

Master Leo grabbed his chest and tears broke out on his cheeks. “Ah, ja, Christian Axel is correct Jonas. The hound is our baby together. He made a promise to attend his hygiene and eat his breakfast for me if he could aid in getting the pup settled in our apartment. You wouldn’t interfere with his promise to me would you?”

The Vampire growled. “Okay, let’s all clear the air this second. I want to know the schedule of sharing my treasure with you buzzards. I am a reasonable man, but I don’t like sneaking or surprises.”

Master Bladrick chuckled and crossed his arms. “Boys, Jonas is right. If I were in his position I would not be so calm about this. I for one say thank you Jonas for being a good soul.”

Master Claus sighed. “The Priceless has agreed to grant Bladrick and me privileges. I do not have an exact timing yet though, but the price is settled and will be put in writing as per his request.”

Master Jonas nodded. “I can help you with that detail brother. Before he became our shared silver you and he had arranged for Thursdays at one. I think this shall stand until the end of your contract. If you and Bladrick agree that is.”

Master Claus smiled with understanding. “You are a wiser man than I ever gave you credit for Jonas. Bladrick and I accept that day and time without quarrel if the Priceless is well satisfied this is a fair price for what he receives in return.”

I nodded while snuggling my hound closer to my neck and singing him a nursery rhyme under my breath.

Master Jonas nodded then shot a look at Master Leo. "And you brother? Have you and my man come up with an arrangement as well?"

Master Leo wiped his eyes. "I would love to lie and say ja, but nein. I was unable to secure privileges with the Priceless."

I shook my head. "Master I think you maybe misheard me. I say to you I grant my favors upon your request for the price we originally agreed upon many weeks ago. You already forgotten the price I asked of you?"

He smiled brighter than the sun. "Nein, meine hase. I never forget what I swore to you. Jonas I was mistaken, our agreement is also solid. You and I can work out the details as time goes on?"

Da Vampire groaned. "If that pup is living with you Leo, then I think I will always know where to find my man when he is not in my bed." That statement caused all the Masters to laugh.

When they all had stopped their mirth, Master Jonas gave me a stern look. "Well, how about your Master Malfred? Am I to assume you worked out an agreement with him regarding special services as well."

I shot a look of fury at the Vampire. "I would suck the devil's cock in the deepest pits of hell for the lifespan of the sea turtle before I would allow that Dominant near me again Master. I thank you for the mercy of it."

Master Jonas grinned with wickedness. "That is my boy, good. Then I am at peace with these arrangements. I say we send the boy to Leo's for his shower and settling the hound, then we all go to the Great Hall to celebrate the first change to Haus Laws in over twenty years."

Master Leo nodded taking on a dramatic expression of concern. "Jonas, I think you should make sure to invite Malfred. I want to be there when he is told of this amazing news. I think it wouldn't be right that he hears of it from anyone other than his brother Elders." He had to stifle his thrilled giggle at the idea of sticking this victory right up that man's tailpipe, in that Malfred would never again get to take a thrust at my own.

Master Jonas shot a look of humor at Master Claus and Master Bladrick, who grinned back with evil at him. "I wouldn't neglect sharing this wonderful news with our dear brother Malfred. Come on boys, put on your finest. Let's show our Priceless collar how old dogs can teach young pups to never underestimate the power of years of wisdom."

Master Jonas followed Master Leo, Der Makellos, and me back to the schwuler Elder's apartment. He had brought with him his favorite vampire outfit for me to wear, and my make up case. I was unhappy to not only be forced to take that fucking shower but to dress up like a freak as I have in the past.

When I balked at such frivolity Master Leo reminded me that if I forced him and the Vampire to punish me, Der Makellos would suffer with me because I would be too thrashed up to attend him properly. I whined a bit but took the outfit and makeup case and headed to the bathroom while Master Leo put the baby hound into his puppy crate.

I stood dare staring at that shower trembling for many minutes. Master Leo come into the bathroom when he still had not heard the water running in many minutes. He offered to spray me down with the antidote to aid me in attending my frightening task of bathing. I finally relented and allowed him to dose me well with the oily stuff.

Master Leo started the water as I braced myself. The Vampire came through the door with a new razor and "pleasure submissive kit." He gave me a lecture about my duties to my Masters to keep myself and them safe from the dangers of special services when hygiene is neglected. I stood there shivering from the stress of enduring the horrors of constant shaving, enemas and keeping my flesh sparkling clean for their pleasures with the boy.

In the end, I got into the shower and attended all my duties as I had been trained to do. I did it for my best friend Der Makellos and for the hope of my freedom from this nightmare that seemed closer than ever. If I could find the strength to battle just a bit longer all I ever desired was around the corner.

I wisely decided that angering the two men that had managed to unlock my metal, and save me from Master

Malfred's lust, was not a smart move to be making. I decided to do my best to keep them placated until I could at last run away through the front door.

When I finished all my hygiene rituals and was at last dressed and made up I had to endure the many compliments and thrills of my Masters. You would have thought they had never seen me clean, and my hair brushed before they way the two of them went on. Master Jonas took up my leash with his chest puffed up in pride.

Master Leo and he had put on fine outfits themselves while I had been enduring the many tasks of my own sad station. They stood there offering each other nice words while I pet and did my best to comfort my whimpering little hound. He was already missing his mother and siblings. Master Jonas and Master Leo assured me that in a few days he would no longer wish to be with them. His own world would be all about his buddy Christian Axel.

I felt bad to be stealing him from his family to cure my own selfish loneliness, but my Masters told me if I had not taken him he would be stuck in a pen training to eat runaway silver collars. I gulped at that thought and followed my Masters out of the apartments promising myself I would never give Der Makellos cause to chew me up for his supper.

Master Malfred, Master Claus, and Master Bladrick were waiting by the back stairwell for our arrival. I could see their eyes all light up when they noticed I was cleaned and well-groomed for the first time in many weeks. Master

Malfred come forward to try and grab my hair to force me to kiss him. I backed up until I hit the end of my leash.

Master Jonas reached out his arm blocking the Dominant from reaching me as I pulled hard trying to escape him. “Back up brother. Leo and I just had to hold this boy down kicking and screaming to get him cleaned up. He is agitated to the hilt. If I were you I would keep your distance or maybe find yourself flying without wings, ja?”

Chapter 60: Admitting Madness

Master Malfred shot a wanton look at me but nodded. "Ah, of course. I should have known that he wouldn't look that nice without a bit of violence. No hurry. I have been waiting for the last three days to enjoy my man. What is another couple hours? I would rather he calm down anyway. I normally would offer the right to join in my thrills Jonas, but today I have decided to be selfish. You can have what is left of him after I get my fill." He chuckled with wickedness in his eyes causing me to look at the floor with my heart speeding up in fear.

Master Jonas looked back at me with a "knowing" smile on his face. "Tell you what Malfred, let's discuss this over dinner, ja? I am starving. Come, meine love, time to follow your man to the Great Hall. You behave yourself and keep that pretty mouth shut until you are told otherwise. That is a directive."

I glared with open hatred at Master Malfred. He paid my resentful expression no mind. Without another word he went forward and joined Master Claus and Master Bladrick. Master Jonas and I took up the rear of the group. The Elders then trooped together down the stairs headed for the Great Hall.

Once we arrived, the black collar attendant quickly led us to a large table. I pulled out the chair for the Vampire, then was commanded to take the seat between Master Leo and Master Jonas. Master Malfred's protested loudly that he wanted to have easier access to touching his Priceless prize. His constant bitching and foul statements about his interest in molesting me caused me great anxiety.

Master Jonas had to warn me twice to stop wringing my hands as I rocked in my seat. I thought for sure I would end up thudded because I kept forgetting he told me not to be doing that in the public. after the Elders had turned in their food orders, Master Jonas tapped on his water glass with his spoon demanding the attention of the Elders.

He cleared his throat then with much thrill announced. "I wish to congratulate our honorable brother Leo for the beautifully drafted law of his. It is with great joy that I report that our beloved Sister Gretta approved it as the new Haus rule this morning. Leo, I dare say this is a spectacular move into the modern age. We all agree that the FemDom has long been neglected by her brother Dominants. Well no longer. Let us all give Leo a round of applause for his amazing work on this groundbreaking project."

Master Jonas and all the Masters but Master Malfred broke out in clapping. Master Leo dramatically grabbed at his chest, blew them kisses and batted his eyes as if he won the Frau beauty pageant.

When the excitement calmed down Master Malfred pulled on his tie nervously then leaned forward toward Master Jonas. "Uhm, excuse me brother, but I seem to be at a loss. What is this law that you say Leo got passed in the Haus? I uhm, was never told that anything was to be considered by the honorable Gretta."

Master Leo smiled with evil while Master Jonas wiped his mouth with a napkin. "Oh? well gosh Malfred I thought your spies, I mean, friends surely told you of Leo's Law. That is what they call it. You will love it Malfred. You see, it allows for the FemDom to legally blood bond with another from 1972 onward."

Master Malfred narrowed his eyes appearing confused. "I don't understand. I mean sure it is great that the FemDom be included in blood bonding rights with the lovers of her choice but why for 1972 forward? I was not aware of any FemDom that was denied she had properly blood bonded last year. In fact, how the hell can a female blood bond anyway? She has no penetration ability."

Master Leo grinned, then glared right at Master Malfred. "Ah, you see you misunderstand brother. This law was not acted from 1972 onward to legitimize an illegal female bonding. It was done to delegitimize several legal male ones. From January 1, 1972, forward only two blood bondings per submissive is recognized and allowed in this Haus. One male and one female."

Master Malfred nearly choked on his spit at Master Leo's words. "Wait, nein. This cannot be accurate. If this Law is truth then that means…"

Master Jonas interrupted with a huge grin on his face. "That means you are no longer married to the Priceless, nor is Leo, or Claus. Christian Axel exclusively belongs to me since I blood bonded the boy in the winter of 1971. He only has the open bonding for his future Frau, the female

Priceless mate of his choice, Malfred. Oh, and this also means I own exclusive rights to his special services. I have decided that despite your past generosity of sharing my truthful man with me, I will be selfish in return. You are never to touch my Priceless collar again. You lay a hand on him I will call it theft and see you exiled from this Haus immediately. Good luck collecting the leashes no one grants the Elders, since other than the Priceless collar you can hold no other silver of your own. Welcome to the sixth floor, Malfred. You won your spot among your betters through theft. Well now you can enjoy it with an empty bed. Since you are an old man that shouldn't bother you too much, oh wait, but you are not elderly are you Malfred? You forced your way into the position before the rightful and mature age of fifty-five. You must have known the reason that season in the lifespan was selected because this is when the sex drives are less bothersome and can be overlooked easily. Elders were meant to be settled down in their vices so they could engage in wiser reflections without lust driving their every move. You have only just turned forty-one, ja? Ah, I bet that the extra decade and a half of bachelorhood will be a burden for you."

The table of Elders broke out in laughter as Master Malfred glared in fury at them. "You rotten, dirty, bastards. You motherfuckers tricked me. I demand to speak to Gretta. You cannot prevent me from holding the Priceless collar for my own. He is community property of all the Elders. Denying me right to all his services, well, that is robbery."

Master Claus crossed his arms still chuckling. "Ah, you should know all about stealing from your brothers. You are the biggest thief in this whole Haus and that is impressive given this then of scum. I for one will not dispute Jonas's claim of truthful possession to this boy's sexual artistry. However, if you wish you may go speak to Gretta all you like to complain. She will not listen to you of course because no one is saying you do not own your piece of the Priceless, Malfred. You can look at him all you like. You can even call any superficial service you want from him. Go ahead and command him to speak to you in a way that makes you feel good about yourself. He won't deny you. The simple truth is you just can never taste his metal without his man's approval is all. Didn't you get your seat at this table by reminding all of us that the right to a silver's intimate service is exclusively at the discretion of his blood bonded partner? Ja, I believe that is correct. Therefore, if Jonas says you are to keep your hands off his legal lover, then that is his right."

Master Malfred stood up so abruptly he knocked over his chair and sent me to my face in terror at Master Jonas's feet. "Fichen dich, Claus, and all of you can suck my cock. You will not get away with this. I will fight the law. You will be sorry when I get that boy back on my leash. You cannot beat me at this game. I fucking created it, and I created the Priceless too. He belongs to me. I demand you give him back to me immediately."

Master Jonas reached down and pulled me into his lap. I buried my face into his chest trembling in fear caused by the loud yelling of Master Malfred. I felt the Vampire wrap his arms around my waste then whisper in my ear to be calm that he would not allow Malfred to get to me.

I clung to my Master praying he was not lying to me like everyone always seemed to be. I was beyond scared that Master Malfred would drag me off to do Gott knows what. Master Leo leaned over and without a word put my head set over my ears. I heard Master Jonas grumble a thank you to him and Master Leo mumbled back a polite you're welcome.

Master Malfred continued to rail loudly threatening to do terrible things to me the second he had me back in his clutches. This horror continued for many minutes. The entire Hall had stopped everything to watch and listen to this drama unfolding at their Elders' table.

Master Jonas finally tired of the Dominant's bullshit and bellowed out. "Shut the fuck up, Malfred. You wanted to be an Elder. Well, you are one, motherfucker. As for your saying this boy is of your creation, are you claiming paternity? If you are, then may Gott help you. There are laws in this Haus against such unnatural acts with their own kinsmen and kinswomen. If you are not the father, then exactly how do you think you are entitled to my submissive spouse's favors without my approval? I am all ears to hear how you can justify taking my own mad out of my bed." He chuckled with great mirth at the hopeless predicament Master Malfred had found himself in.

The angry Master paused his rant. He realized, at last, he had been beaten at his own game of manipulation.

He stood there appearing unable to think of anything further to say when at last he took a deep breath/ "I find it hard to believe Leo wrote this law that goes against his own favor," he snorted.

Master Leo laughed out loud. "Ah, well it is true it shuts me out of my marriage with Christian Axel and my ability to enjoy him in my bed if Jonas were to wish it. As it stands, he and I came to an agreement. I made sure to get the signatures, and he offered me a taste of his precious metal for my sacrifice. However, I cannot take the credit for the idea of this Law. That honor belongs to your man. You know, the one you fucked over royally in your rush to obtain what was never yours to have. You see Malfred when you climb up the back of others to get where you are going, sometimes they resent your forgetting how you got there."

Malfred's eyes nearly bugged out of his head as his face turned bright red in anger as he yelled out the name Peter. Without another word he stormed off leaving the Great Hall. I assumed he had gone seeking his old associate, My father, to take out his wrath over his compromised position within the Elder ranks.

Everyone at the table broke out in loud laughter. The sounds of these hateful men's mirth felt like stones being pelted at my flesh. I whimpered in terror and squeezed the Vampire more tightly nearly crushing my face into his chest. He silenced his sounds in response to my clinging behaviors.

Master Jonas leaned toward the still chuckling Master Leo and hailed him to speaking. "Leo, the boy is behaving like a scared kid hiding in his mother's skirts. What the hell is going on with him? I mean I am enjoying the affection, don't get me wrong but something is strange about it." He grabbed the Elder's hand and laid it on my back to allow him to feel my trembling.

Master Leo gasped. "Uh oh. Okay, I am not the expert, but I think Christian Axel is demonstrating something called Regression. That means he is behaving like a little kid because his mind is overwhelmed so it has returned to a simpler state of being. I read in one of my books. They say this happens when someone is severely traumatized. It is most likely that Malfred's violent gang rape and all this loud noise with excitement has set off this nasty reaction. I believe we better get him out of here Jonas. If we don't lower his stress immediately, I understand it can get much worse."

Master Jonas nodded. "Shit, we don't need that. You handle Claus and Bladrick. I will head to my apartment with the boy this minute."

Master Leo grabbed his arm before he could stand up. "Wait. Take him to my apartment. We let him spend time with his puppy. That book also said that pets will rapidly lower stress and are good therapy for those with troubled minds."

Da Vampire grumbled. "Ja, alright I will meet you at your place. This better work though, Leo. I find out you are filling my ears with pop culture psychology I swear to Gott

I will feed you to Malfred." He held me firmly to his chest and stood up with a groan over his maintaining my weight.

Master Claus chimed out, "Jonas? where are you going? Aren't you a bit long in the tooth to be carrying around that boy like a baby?" He chuckled nervously.

Master Jonas flashed a look of anxiety at Master Leo. "I leave my brother to explain Claus and offer my apology for this early retiring from our celebration. I see you both another time. Thank you for the pleasant company this evening. It will always be in my memory and will grant me a smile." He quickly took off never letting me go from his arms as he rushed from the Great Hall for the stairwell.

I hummed nursery rhymes to myself as the Vampire moved with speed up the steps. I continued to shake like a newborn calf unable to gain a grip on myself. My stomach rumbled angrily at my continued neglect of filling it. I never pulled my face away from my Master's chest feeling I couldn't deal with all the light nor sounds in that place, not even to calm my deep hunger. Master Leo had been right. I had gone simple.

The truth was something inside my head had broken. I had become incapable of thinking of anything other than I was going to be injured, hurt or tortured at any moment. I clung to the Vampire believing him to be my savior. It was quite strange that I could not really understanding this was one of the men that had done all those things I was so afraid of. This was also the very person that was going to do them all repeatedly throughout the rest of my life. Y*et, there I* *was, believing he was saving me from the pain of my existence. To this day, I still have no idea what the fuck happened there. This was maybe one of the weirdest experiences I ever had in the land of the dead.*

The Vampire put me down on my feet when we arrived at Master Leo's door. I stood there but continued to hold on to my Master doing my best to cover my head with his long jacket. He chuckled at my childish actions and constant whimpering. He patted my back telling me I was safe but somehow I knew better. All I could think was bad things were coming for me, and there wasn't shit I could do about it.

Master Leo arrived to find the scene not much different than the one he witnessed in the Great Hall. He attempted to capture my attention by calling my name while he opened his door to let all of us inside. I responded by nearly crawling up the Vampire Jonas in terror at hearing someone appearing to be looking for the boy. I could hear my Master demanding Master Leo stop upsetting Christian Axel and to be quiet.

Master Jonas dragged me inside the living room by force. I attempted to keep from entering by taking off on a blind run at the last moment. Don't ask, I have no fucking idea what the hell I was thinking. This only managed to further disturb my already disrupted Dominants. The sound of our coming into the room and the lights coming on caused my pup to stir.

I heard his whimpering and lonely vails. This abruptly brought me out of my wild panic. I stopped trying to get away and tore inside to attend my baby hound. I grabbed the little black bundle and cuddled him to my neck hushing the frightened Der Makellos. His sounds of distress calmed immediately which caused me some relief.

I sat down next to his crate and rocked with him mindlessly singing, "I do not like dee, the doctor fell. The reasons why I can never tell. But do know this, do know it well. I do not like dee, the doctor fell."

Master Jonas and Master Leo took to the couch and watched me consoling my tiny hound in my trancing. They appeared very concerned over my attempts to get my nervousness under control. I could not shake the belief that Master Malfred would not take out his displeasure on the ones behind this new law. It had become the habit to expect all retaliations for perceived slights would always roll downhill.

I was painfully aware that Christian Axel lived at the bottom. My thoughts on this threat were not without precedent. My flesh was infected by it and my dignity stolen more than a dozen times in only the last few weeks thanks to this Master Malfred. My fear of his retaliation was further proven by the things he had loudly announced in the Great Hall to do to me the second he caught me without protection.

I could go further by adding that I had recently recalled the reason I knew the name Elsa. That nasty orange drink had caused many weird dreams, but one in particular stood out. I was walking down the hallway, and someone tapped me on the shoulder. I turned around to find my eyes and mouth polluted with pepper spray. This would seem to be a memory, but in this scene I could hear that horrible cook Evelyn on the phone in the background. She was speaking with her and Felix's daughter, Elsa.

That odd background recall led to my realization that the black collar no doubt had come to the Haus for a singular sinister reason. She was obviously seeking out the one suspected in the deaths of both her parents. The identity of the alleged guilty just happened to be Mad Maxx the Priceless.

Her eagerness to coax me into a private meeting with the promise of a couple with her could easily be explained with this information. To my dismay, it wasn't because the girl thought me irresistible. My understanding that I was now the target of a vengeful family member seeking justice for her losses added panic to my already horrific situation.

It was not likely that Elsa would listen to my believing both Evelyn and Felix were a threat to my life. Nor did I think she would believe that I had pled with her parents to leave me in peace many times prior to engaging in what I viewed as self-defense attacks.

Please do understand this meine Frau. I did all that I have done because I wanted to live. All my behaviors while I wore that collar were because I was either too stupid to find a way out of my predicament or there was no other choice for various reasons from bondage to do it or die for hesitating.

I don't like killing any more than I enjoy being used as the pincushion pleasure submissive. I would have done almost anything to avoid both of those sad facts of my survival in the Haus. Not a single moment day or night passes where I have not wished a thousand times that my memories were all hallucinations and delusions of a madman.

However, a frog can desire that he can be a horse all he likes. That won't change that he will never graze a field nor pull the farmer's cart. Nein, you listen to me closely Meine Liebe, wishes are not horses. What they are is a waste of time and fuel for depression. My advice to that fantasy frog would be to learn to swim well enough not to drown and remember at least he is not the worm. Things can always be worse and sometimes they really are.

That all said, you must be aware that any action you take, even if it is unavoidable in your bid for survival, will have serious repercussions. Sometimes, no matter how well you plan, the side effects of your attempts to escape the grave, or worse will be unexpected. They can be worse than if you had just laid there and took whatever it was you were attempting to avoid.

The honest truth is that Evelyn and Felix came after me first, and I responded only after many months, even more than a year for one, of trying to find another way to get them to stop doing things meant to end my days. Elsa was the unexpected consequence of ending those two.

I suspected, rightly so too, her sudden appearance in the Haus was for the sole purpose of making me pay for the crimes I had committed in an effort to save myself. I think part of my nervous breakdown that day may have been fueled by my fear that if this female persisted in attempting to gain vengeance, I would have to kill her or be killed.

As I said I don't like killing. I hate it in fact. No matter how necessary it may or may not have been, I am far from blood thirsty. I found that it is barely tolerable when in self-defense and horrible when done to prevent a worse personal outcome if I had hesitated.

In the case of Elsa, it was the worst case scenario. She had never harmed me in any way, yet, and her anger with me was without a doubt justified. That didn't mean I was going to lay there and let her slit my throat. That didn't make my task of preparing, if need be, to end this beautiful girl's life or face growing a tree for failing in my efforts, any easier.

So, we continue with the story.

"I was feeling oddly disconnected and lost despite the warmth of my buddy Der Makellos. I chanted my little verse faster noticing I was unable to blink for some reason. I rocked back and forth almost as if stuck in a repeating loop. This strange sensation was deepening, causing me to panic even more.

As the anxiety level rose within the boy, the louder the Vampire's radio seemed to get. I had on the head set but the spies were off on a coffee break. I could hear the songs, and DJ's wailing from every wall and the ceiling. It had increased from a soft background sound to a roaring storm of deafening noise in only a matter of minutes.

I gently laid my now peacefully snoozing pup in my lap. Then I covered the ears of my headset with my hands pressing them with all my strength. I was secretly hoping I could get enough pressure on the sides of my skull to crush it like an egg. I was beyond frantic to stop the endless noise you know. I suppose I thought it would hurt less if I imploded it rather than have it explode, but that was likely silly thinking. Either one would have been pretty ugly.

My Masters were witness to my obvious struggle with my meltdown. Master Jonas went to rise to come to my aid. Master Leo grabbed his arm and warned him that I was psychotically agitated. He told him it was best to let me ride this out. I heard him tell the Vampire they should be quietly vigilant in case I got violent but not to interfere otherwise.

I was angered by that bullshit calling me psychotic like that. "You shut the fuck up. Stop telling all your friends that I am psychotic. Gott dammit. Oh, and stop pretending you have any friends to begin with. They tell you lies. Everyone hates you. There, listen, you hear that? It was just on the fucking radio. Deny that I dare you. You call me paranoid, but it is you that is deluded Master. They cannot be untruthful on the airwaves, you know. That would be illegal." I crushed my ears tightly and winced against the blasting sound of that Vampire's crazy music.

Der Makellos wriggled when he heard my shouting like that. For a moment, his welfare caught my attention. I dropped my hands long enough to lay him safely on the soft rug next to his puppy box. I then turned my hate back at Master Leo and Master Jonas.

"Did you hear it? They reported on the weather forecast that the Guard is coming from the east. There will be flooding and some thunder. What did you do this time? You shouldn't go raping little boys and girls, you know. There is a law against such things. I knew that. I read it once in a magazine. This Haus is the high ground of hell, isn't it? I have been dead all this time and you both lied to me. I know better. Why the fuck are you sitting there laughing? There isn't a Gott damned thing funny about being a child molester. I will get out of this maze sooner or later. Then I kill all of you." I covered my ears once more and rocked harder in place yelling at the weirdos on the couch that called themselves human beings.

Master Jonas growled out, "Enough, Christian Axel. You stop that shouting right this minute."

I shook my head. "I haven't said a fucking thing, Master. You are hearing voices. Master Leo, the Vampire is psychotic. He is speaking to the walls. You better run for your life. He will suck out your blood and then fuck you. That is morbid, you know, but that is the rumor."

Master Leo put his arm out to block Master Jonas from getting up to pummel me for saying that. "Jonas, ignore him. He has no idea what he is saying. The boy is mad."

The Vampire glared at Master Leo. "No kidding, Leo. I can hear him, shit half the Haus can hear his crazy speaking. Do you have a gag? If he keeps screaming someone may call and complain. This insanity will get around the hallways, then our Priceless won't need to be worried about how many blood bondings he has. The dead have few troubles. We cannot just sit here and let him wail like he is. Be reasonable."

Master Leo sighed loudly. "Christian Axel, listen to me honey. You must lower your voice and calm yourself. Otherwise, your Master Jonas will tie you up and get his gag."

I groaned out in pain. I was really hungry by now. "Don't let the Vampire near my puppy. He will catch fleas from him, and I have no money to pay for the flea spray. Please Master ask him to turn down his radio. My head is aching from the noise. He will bring the Guard if they hear all that racket. Did you get any letters from Geraldine yet? Did she send the cookies she promised? That lamb works hard you know." I leaned my head back into the wall and closed my eyes trying to brace against the incredible agony that was spreading through the boy faster than a fire would a gas station.

Master Jonas bellowed out, "The lamb cannot speaking or write Christian Axel. Nor does she cook for you. I do not have fleas. There is no radio playing. If you want cookies Leo or I can get them from the kitchen. Stop talking this nonsense, which is a directive."

I moaned loudly. "Monday I am told I am fair of face. Tuesday the Priceless was full of grace. Wednesday Mad Maxx was fill with woe. Thursday my dignity was bought and sold. Friday I was called loving and giving. Saturday I always work hard for my living. Sunday has now come and gone, but no matter what I do it is always wrong."

Da Vampire shot a look of confusion at Master Leo, "What the holy hell is this boy rambling about? Leo, this has to stop. Give him the orange drink or call the Haus doctor. I cannot take any more of this crazy shit."

Master Leo crossed his arms and shook his head. "Jonas you married the boy. That means you must deal with him as he is. This is what mental illness is all about, crazy speaking, and illogical decisions. All his life, and yours, this disease will rule your world. Nothing you do will be possible without making provisions for the possibility of Christian Axel's symptoms. You better get used to it. He is only fourteen years old, and schizophrenia is progressive. That means over the years he will get worse, never better. I guess you snatched up this pretty boy for your lustful interest without considering the consequences of taking him without knowing him first?"

Master Jonas looked at the floor appearing mildly shameful. "Ja Leo, you have me there. I saw only the beauty and youth of this legendary silver. I assumed I knew enough about him and his illness to think I could handle the demons that swim inside his blood. I admit I never expected it to be so difficult. I just assumed he would fear my anger so much he never could deny me what I command of him."

Master Leo clicked his tongue. "Well, you see Jonas, the definition of insanity is foolishness or irrationality. You cannot reason with one that has none. I suppose if he had been retarded you would have assumed you could beat him into knowing his left from right or if he had cancer you would give him a directive to stop being ill. There is no controlling this disease. You believe in myths like most swear by provable science. Well, I can say for certain that boy's demons do not live in his blood. They live in his head and heart. I won't point my finger at you without pointing four back at myself brother. I am just as guilty of thinking all it would take is love and patience to bring the boy back from the hellish place he is trapped. I of all people should have known better. My Maus was never the same after she got sick. She nor Christian Axel can help how they act. It is up to us the non-afflicted to change since they never can."

Master Jonas shot an expression of thrill at Master Leo. "Ah, you are right Leo. The boy is mad, and cannot turn it off nor on at will can he? That would also mean he cannot return to a place of perfect rationality, not ever again. It had not occurred to me before this moment, but Christian Axel will require a guardian for all his life. He will never be capable of living beyond these walls in the world. That would be the case even if he breaks his metal. If he were cut lose to full freedom then very bad things will happen to him or others that cross him. Outside this Haus, society is not so ready to overlook such a thing as doctors falling down stairwells. Hmm, I have been looking at this issue all wrong Leo. This schizophrenia is not a curse at all. It is my salvation. I won't ever have to give up meine heart because he can never leave me. I am his only truthful hope of survival. This is wonderful news. I thought I would have to keep the boy on a leash and follow him around after he is judge Dominant, but I think that in reality I need only apply for control over his welfare. That legal right will hold Peter at bay and keep the boy in my clutches for all time. when he chooses his mate he will bring her back to live with us without quarrel. He has no choice. She too will be afflicted with the same demons."

I opened my eyes in full on terror. "Nein, I can hear you, Master. I will not stay here with you when I break my collar. I am running away with my hound and my lambs. There will be nothing you can do to stop me. I am not schizophrenic. You are the one insane. There are no such things as vampires or demons. Let me out of this Haus right this minute. You hold me hostage here. It is illegal to keep me kidnapped like this. You call those door guards and the snipers. Tell them all to stand down. I want out of here. Someone let me out. You hear my crazy man? You are a criminal," I vailed at the top of my lungs.

Master Jonas come off the couch ignoring Master Leo's begging him to let me be. He grabbed my leash near my collar and dragged me across the floor, thankfully away from Der Makellos that was sleeping next to me. Once he got me to the corner he backhanded me into silence.

I wept loudly while he shook me with much anger. "You will be stop this insolence immediately, Christian Axel. If I hear you ever call me names again I will beat you until your so brain damaged all you will be capable of doing is laying in your own piss when not sucking my cock. You hear me? You are not leaving this Haus, not ever. For starters you belong to me for all my days. I do want you to love me, but I won't put up with your constant fighting with me. I don't give a fuck if you are schizophrenic. Who you are, boy. I demand you say that you are the schizophrenic. I want you to hear this coming out of your own fucking mouth. Then you will understand without me you are condemned to a prison cell or worse. Christian Axel you say it right now Gott damned you, do not test me." He struck me again with force.

I shook and did my best to cover my head from his blows. I refused to confess to a lie no matter how many times he hit me. The Vampire became so overblown angered he knocked my headset off and grabbed the sides of my head forcing me to look into his furious eyes.

"Say it boy. I swear I will rip your ears off if you don't. I want you to yell it." He clawed the side of my head making me wail in agony.

I took his abuse for several minutes before I realized he was really going to disfigure me if I continued to refuse his command. "I am the schizophrenic, Master. Please, mercy. I beg of you to let me go," I shouted at the top of my lungs. *Look don't judge me on this until you been held in the air by your ears. I would have said I was a fucking teapot at that point, those claws of Jonas's hurt.*

Master Leo had jumped up from his couch and grabbed Master Jonas. "Let the boy go, Jonas. You have completely frightened him and likely set off a major psychotic attack. Good job. I will go get the fucking ropes. He is going to hurt himself for sure now. You are a bigger idiot then Leo and that took work, fool." He took off down his hallway to gather up his restraining tools.

The Vampire dropped me to the floor. I rolled up into a ball trying to cover any part of me that I couldn't afford to lose. My Master stood over me chuckling with an evil sounding tone. He was enjoying his beating me down into my place at his feet once more. I was in no mood to push him further. I was more than happy to grant him the victory after that attack. I'd had enough of his brutality. Too bad he didn't think he had received his fill of it.

He reached down and grabbed my leash. "Get up. Come with me or pay for it with your hide." He kicked me in my backside roughly.

I yelped and got up but kept my arms over the top of my head in a cower. Master Jonas took off down the hall after Master Leo. I was helpless to do anything but run along behind the rushing Vampire. He barged into the schwuler Elder's bedroom. Master Leo was digging in his closet when we came through the door.

"Bring the ropes Leo and hurry the fuck up. Christian Axel, you strip down boy. Do not argue with me. I mean it." He jerked hard on my leash.

I went right to work removing my fancy vampire outfit while Master Leo shot a look of concern at Master Jonas. "What the hell are you doing Jonas? It better not be what I am thinking. This boy needs rest. Your lust can wait until he is feeling bedder."

Master Jonas shouted in fury, "Leo, shut up. This is my man not yours. I will do with him as I please."

Master Leo put his hands on his hips and snapped, "He may be that, but this is still my fucking room Jonas. That over there is my bed. You will not molest this boy in my fucking apartment. I forbid it."

The Vampire smiled diabolically. "Oh? Is that so? Well, no problem then. I take him home to our own apartment and he can stay there far away from you Leo. Either way, fine by me. Christian Axel, get up, follow me. Get up, follow me. We are leaving." He pulled on my leash near dragging me to the bedroom door with one boot on and half my clothing in various stages of removal.

Master Leo shouted out sounding desperate and frustrated. "Stop, Jonas. Okay, forgive my momentary forgetting my place. He is your man. I have no right to interfere with your rights to his services. I will leave you to it if you agree to stay here with him tonight. You may need aid with the boy. Don't be foolish Jonas. Please accept my apology and offer to help you keep him safe." He shot a look of sadness at me.

Master Jonas grinned. "Now we understand each other, Leo. I will forgive your rash, unthinking demands. You can talk me into staying the night with my man if you would grant a favor in return. Christian Axel is rumored to have found sexual interest in your touching in past encounters with him. I need him to be in a lustful state for my fetish feeding. He is at this moment angered and full of madness. Could I request you attempt to bring him to penetration ability without setting off his apex? If he could find that state of mind he would be ripe for my special interest in him."

Master Leo's eyes went wide, and his mouth hit the floor. "What the holy hell. Are you serious? You want me to get the boy up so you can go cut on him, then suck out his blood? Jonas, that is disgusting."

I began to attempt to slink away hoping that the Vampire was distracted enough that I could escape. I knew it was nearly time for his horrid blood thirst. This was turning into a true nightmare rapidly. He felt my chain tightening in his grip.

He flashed an agitated glare at me with fury in his eyes. "I told you to strip, Christian Axel. You make another move for that door you know what will happen. Leo, make up your mind. Help me ease his pain over this necessary task he must endure or give me the ropes and get out until I am finished with my intercourse with him." I sat down and went back to removing my shoes as commanded taking slow shallow breaths to brace myself for this horror.

Master Leo looked from me then back to the Vampire. “I uhm, don’t think I could do what you ask even if I wanted to Jonas. I am sorry to admit the boy has found no interest in me since the gang rapes and blood bonding in the Great Hall. I guess you will have to wait and engage in this, uhm, fetish of yours another night. There is no way you will get Christian Axel to feel anything but resentment, agony, and hate in the mental state he is in.”

Da Vampire chuckled. “You won’t even attempt, Leo? Let me say this to you, I am taking my feeding from him even if he is not complete. I already am behind by several days thanks to the bullshit with Malfred monopolizing the boy’s special services. It is more traumatic if he is not distracted by a fantasy lover. You could fill that position for him this time, see if it works out. Otherwise, he can just cry and scream when I drink from him like he always does without that comfort.”

Master Leo grabbed his chest as if he had just been punched in it. “He screams and cries when you do this to him. Jonas, Christ, have you no heart? He is just a little kid.”

Master Jonas pulled on my leash roughly as I had finished undressing as ordered. “Get into Leo’s bed and be still. You will wait in silence for my pleasure, Christian Axel. Leo, listen you don’t bother to notice his age when you enjoy the special services with him, so stop trying to preach to me. I will do you the favor of keeping you from sounding like the hypocrite you are. I am the Vampire. Unlike you I make no excuses for my cruel nature. This boy's youth is part of the attraction I have for him as it is for you too. Don't even try to lie to me as you do to yourself. I have my dinner and desert waiting for me, so you either take my offer or leave, or hell, watch if you want. Maybe I convert you once you see the beauty in the blood feeding."

Master Leo began to leave but stopped at the door and took a deep breath. "Fuck, I will hate myself for this, but I cannot leave meine hase to suffer your interest alone. What the hell do I need to do Jonas and say anything other than instructions for this abomination I will punch you in the mouth." He said without turning around.

Da Vampire chuckled. "Well, you need to strip down, then see if you can make the boy desire a rut with you. It is that simple Leo. Oh, but I warn you again, do not allow him to reach orgasm. You are only here to excite him, not release the very thing that gives his blood its talent to keep me young."

Master Leo turned around and began unbuttoning his shirt glaring at my Master. "You know, I think Christian Axel may be right. You are insane Jonas. The only thing in his blood is what is in mine or yours."

Master Jonas shrugged. "As you say, Leo. Shut up and get to your task. Christian Axel, I am not going to bond you this time unless you try to fight me. This is not our usual ritual spot, and you are agitated enough without the bondage I believe. You be still and do as you are told. That is a directive. If I have to stop and tie you up, I will make you sorry for it. Do you understand me boy?" I closed my eyes and nodded doing my best to keep from weeping over this dishonor.

Meine Liebe I will stop here to say, I hate being that Vampire's blood doner to this very day. He always tells me I will get used to it, well he is full of shit. One can never get over being another man's dinner and unwilling lover. when your time comes to deal with this monster, we will need to work hard to prepare you for his disgusting habit. Until then, try to remember, after all these years of dealing with this practice of his twice a month I am still alive and well. I want you to trust me when I say you may hate it like I do, but you are strong enough to handle it, probably better than I ever have. I mean you endure that Whiskey guy. Even Jonas's isn't that gross, yuck.

I turned around and glared at him but said nothing. He was well aware of how I felt about the fetishers like Whiskey, Sonny and Jasper, double yuck..

Master Maxx feigned a look of embarrassment. "Yikes, if looks could kill, ja? I apologize for hitting that nerve meine Demonseed Frau. I was merely saying there are worse people out there than the Vampire Jonas."

I snorted. "That Vampire man better watch out, Master. If I ever get the chance, I am going to stab him in the heart with a stake. I don't like him for what he did to you already. I think he may want to stay the hell away from me. Hey, fire kills Vampires too, right?"

Master Maxx's eyes went wide in shock as he drew in his breath. "Uhm, Meine Leibe, I didn't want to say anything, but you seem to be obsessed with burning places down. I hope that wasn't caused by anything I have told you. Don't forget my little fire bugging got me put in the mental hospital at eight years old and got our brother Ryker killed." He kissed the top of my head.

I grinned with demons rising in me. "Nein, I like fire because it destroys everything it touches. I am not like you Master. I don't care if they put me in a mental hospital or even prison. At least there I hear you get fed once in a while, and finally I would have friends too. The best part is burning hurts a lot. Humphrey taught me that. If someone makes me cry, then they deserve what they fucking get. Let the police come get me. At least then maybe someone will fucking listen.

Master Maxx swatted me with the cane. "Enough, Meine Liebe. You need to stop that anger demon in you. Shit. If I don't watch out you will be a bigger killer than you man. I want us to have a normal life with our children, lambs and hounds. We cannot do that if the two of us go around murdering everyone that ever pissed us off. This you understand, ja?"

I rubbed my leg, that cane fucking hurt. "Yeah, I know Master, but I am going to kill a few people, so I think you better teach me how to not get caught. Otherwise, I will see you when I get out. Ha, bring bail money." He swatted me again.

"Christ, meine Demonseed Frau. You scare the shit out of me sometimes, you know that? I often wonder if they had managed to get you to the Haus, what kind of monster would you have become? You do have that Krause blood in your veins. Trust me, your Uncle Malfred and father Karl are some of the meanest fucking creatures to ever walk the Earth." He looked deep into my eyes as if trying to see the demons that lived inside my head.

I giggled. "Well, I can say this Master. If I ever do go back to that Haus, I would kill them all, except Master Leo. I think he is worth saving. He seems to love you a lot even if he did mess up. We all mess up, right? I have decided to help you burn down that horrible place. Soon as I am big enough, I will be ready to help you send every one of them to the devil where they all belong. I would go right now if you will take me."

Master Maxx rolled his eyes. "Oh hell no. Not until you learn a little self-control, meine Demonseed. At this point I fear sleeping in the same room with you, and I know you love me. Shit, if I let you out of here, I think more than Das Kaiser Haus will burn. By the way, I didn't think I ever needed to say this, not killing a Master is a prime directive. That includes Peter. Are you listening?"

I smiled with evil. "I am, Master. However, Peter is not my Master, now is he? He is yours, but not for much longer." Master Maxx swatted me a third time.

"Okay, we go back to the story. I fear if you see me piss myself in terror I will never be capable of re-gaining your respect for me. You know what? You keep that mouth of yours shut. That is a directive."

"Fuck, Mad Max, what the hell have we gotten into? Our Frau is insane. You mark my words, we will suffer for loving this female."

"She is definitely worth it. No matter what we must endure Maximillian. I mean look at her. She is everything we ever wanted in a Frau."

"I will remember you said that, after we are fried extra crispy by this demonseed. Mad Max, face it, you have always been a fool for a pretty face with a dark heart."

I giggled at his talking to himself and got swatted by the cane a fourth time. I turned around to sulk while he continued his inner dialogue for another few moments.

Master Maxx/Christian Axel is one crazy motherfucker, oh I mean, one crazy fatherfucker.

I am the crazy motherfucker, right Simon?

Hey man, wait, don't answer that. Aren't you the one who always says never admit to that shit on paper?

Yikes, we totally deflected that disaster didn't we Dude?

All I am saying is people who talk to themselves like he does, you probably should let them cut line and keep your distance. They are off balance.

"Anyway, as I was saying. Master Leo stripped down then crawled in the bed next to me. I stared at him wondering what the hell he thought he was going to do other than piss me off more than I already was. The last fucking thing I wanted to see in bed with Master Jonas was another Gott damned man.

As the Vampire removed my chastity device, I laid there wondering how the fuck I managed to get so lucky in life? I am not only the straight man that hates penetration sex, but I have handfuls of the wrong gender wanting to fuck me any chance they can, even under the worst of circumstances as Master Leo was proving that night.

Master Leo pulled me into deep kissing and whispered many romantic things into my roughed up ears. They made me leave my headset on the floor where Master Jonas had knocked it off. I was not the least bit interested in anything he had to say nor in his gentle touching neither. I just wanted the Vampire to get his horror over and done with me. The burden of enduring that male lust business still bothered me more than I can say in those days.

Okay, ja still does but sucks to be me, ja? At least I have my demonseed Frau to cuddle and have natural sex with now.

I moved my booty further over on his thigh. I had gone as far as possible from his boy part at those words.

He laughed loudly and pulled me back to my original spot. "You stop that Meine Liebe. I waited a long time to have my female and I intend to enjoy her often."

I rolled my eyes at that, making sure he didn't see it. I hated that fucking cane.

When after many minutes the only cock rising in that bed was Master Leo's, the Vampire sighed. "Okay brother. Give it up. Christian Axel is as interested in sex with you as he is with me. Shit, this is both good and bad news for Jonas. I am happy he isn't in passionate love with you. Though I apologize for admitting that out loud. However, his lack of lustful intent will thin the blood feeding. I will have to increase my intake if I don't solve this issue soon."

I heard that shit loud and clear. There was no fucking way I was willing to endure more of this cutting and sucking crap.

I turned my head to stare at my Master with fury in my eyes. "Forgive me for speaking without being noticed, but Master you never asked me if I could do what you require for this fetish for myself."

Master Jonas smacked my face harshly. "That was for disobeying my silence order. Now as to your inciting your own interest, you can do that?"

I narrowed my eyes while rubbing my sore face. "With a few moments of privacy, the right visual tools of the female, yes, I can. I am capable of masturbation though you don't ever allow me to get any fucking relief."

He slapped me again. "Watch your tone, Christian Axel. Ja, well to be honest I never thought of it. Hell, if you can find your sexual thrills with only a girly magazine, that would solve having to seek women to tease you with."

I growled. "I would rather have the females than their photos, Master."

He laughed. "Too bad for you. Leo, do you have any of the Playboy magazines around here in this haus?"

Master Leo scoffed. "Uhm, sure Jonas. I keep them right next to my tampons, and nail polish. Fuck no, I don't have stuff like that around here. I am pure schwuler Jonas. I don't find interest in the girl's flesh."

Master Jonas groaned. "Well, shit, okay I have one or two old ones in my apartment I believe. Can you loan me a robe and keep an eye on the boy while I go get them?"

Master Leo nodded., "Ja sure thing Jonas. Just hurry back would you. This whole thing is creeping me out."

He rushed into the bathroom and threw on Master Leo's robe to cover his nakedness then headed for the door turning back only a moment to say. "Oh, keep your hands and cock to yourself Leo. You can have him when I am finished but not a second before. He must be unmolested for at least twelve hours, or the blood is no good to me." The Vampire took off to seek out the X-rated magazines.

I glared at Master Leo as he smiled at me. "Well, I suppose I could ignore Jonas and fuck you really quick. Then he wouldn't be able to slice you up, meine hase."

I growled out. "Needles and pins, needles and pins. when a man marries, his trouble begins."

Master Leo scoffed. "Isn't that the honest truth. I can never apologize enough for this life you endure Christian Axel. I am going to remove myself from this bed and go attend our baby Der Makellos. I admit I am too chickenshit to witness the foul thing Jonas is going to enforce upon you. I will also confess I am a jealous lover. I cannot be in here when he has his way with you. I may get homicidal over it. I not only don't care for sharing my lovers, but I also don't believe in having more than one at a time. The human heart is a vast space meine hase, but for Leo, it is too fragile to be twisted in more than a single direction. I would like to be with you tonight, but you are not well. I wish Jonas would relent, but if I push him, he will block me from ever seeing you again. I think this sanctuary and Der Makellos are too important to risk over something I have no power to stop."

I sneered at him. "You need not apologize to me Master nor withhold your desires for my good health. Do you really think it matters that there are two cocks instead of only one? I obviously don't desire either of you. That never has stop any of you from taking what you want and calling it your right. Do whatever you want to me Leo. I will think of a beautiful woman, a sunrise, my lambs, a world where this Haus burns down to heated dust. At the end of the day, none of you will ever break me from seeking the happiness thus far denied at my every turn."

He looked at the bed near tears. "Do you hate me for truth? Please don't lie to spare my feelings. I need to know, meine hase. I honestly don't desire to injure you further by forcing my fantasy on a boy that wants nothing more than see me dead."

I rolled my eyes. "I will tell you I forgive you for lying to me. I think you do love me with all your heart, Master. I will not lie and say I don't love you back. If I didn't then I wouldn't be so fucking mad at you this minute that I could rip your eyes out. A heart can only be broken if you truthfully cared for the one that did it. I told you I am not fickle. My love is forever and not lost over a mistake. I swear I will kill you if you ever hurt me like that again. You call on my special services, I will grant them without quarrel. Better you then that fucking rough Vampire, or the brutal intercourse with Claus. At least you're gentle about it."

He groaned. "Ja, well I suppose my competition isn't exactly tough to beat in the sack. I shouldn't ask this, but does this idiot really cut you open and drink your blood, like with a knife?"

I pointed to my chest below the M brand and to my right upper thigh. "The scars prove that, Master. If you want, stay and watch the madman. Maybe then you would feel compelled to tell him to turn down his fucking radio shit. If I am forced to listen to that song one more time, I am taking a bath without the antidote. I hate that song."

Master Leo frowned. "What song do you hear meine hase?"

I winced. "The DJ says it is called "Old Man" by this fellow named Neil Young. The singer talks too much, and I am sick to death of old men," I shouted as I began wringing my hands with agitation.

Master Leo flinched. "Ah, ja I know that song. I had enjoyed it, but I can see why you would not find much pleasure in it. Please meine hase, you need to calm down if you can. If you get upset again then Jonas will hurt you more. Your face is already turning black and blue from his angry blows."

I yelled out, "So what? I noticed he didn't bust up my mouth. That means I can still suck your cock, Master. Get out. Get the fuck out. All of you stop crowding me. Do you not see I am working here? Motherfuckers, the whole lot of you. Where the hell did I put that stupid headset? I am missing the spies information. How can I find out what Elsa is thinking about without it? She is trying to kill me, Leo. You better call the Gott damned police, or she will end your fun really quick."

Master Jonas come into the room to find me shouting again. He slammed the door which sent me to immediate silence. I kept my eyes out of his gaze as he stormed over to the bed and threw a girly magazine at me. Master Leo had already left the bed and went back to the wall granting me space to piss my fit.

"There is your woman, Christian Axel. Shut the fuck up and get to it or find yourself with a reason to be shouting. Leo, come with me. We give the boy some privacy for a bit." Master Leo nodded then followed Master Jonas from the room.

I sat up and picked up the magazine. I could hear the two of them arguing about my mental stability in the living area. I closed my eyes and took a deep breath. I opened that pornographic magazine and found no pleasure in looking at the girls displayed. It was no better than I often was for my master's lustful appetites. I groaned as I realized I was actually turned off by this disgusting exploitation of the female form.

I tossed the magazine off the bed onto the floor feeling hopeless. I knew if I couldn't demonstrate my eagerness for the mount Master Jonas was going to beat the hell out of me for sending him on a fool's errand. I closed my eyes and recalled my beautiful Annette sitting next to me in the green fields.

She was wearing a pink dress and a peaceful smile. The loving calls of my lambs filled the air, and I could hear the tiny yips of Der Makellos as he attempted to chase the butterflies around. Annette was making sausage for my dinner, the heavy smell of it blanketed her as I leaned in to kiss her deeply.

She leaned into my ear and whispered. "I will make love to you here in the tall grass Christian Axel, but we must hurry before our infant daughter awakens from her nap."

I opened my eyes and smiled as I saw I had gained my lustful interest. To my relief, my imagination was far better than any gross photo wearing a fake smile. Master Jonas returned to find me ready to provide him the service I had been perfectly trained to do. He didn't hesitate to push me back to the mattress and cut open my flesh just above my right wrist.

As the Vampire fed from me, I closed my eyes again. I did my very best to join my Annette in our fantasy world of freedom. It worked to calm my nerves as he sucked at my wound but when my Master finished his meal I was abruptly pulled back to reality by his over eager demands for the special services.

You see the problem with my escaping Master Jonas's lustful interest was the man has many proclivities. Besides that, vile blood drinking, he always commands me to look at him when receiving oral services and even when engaging in penetration intercourse. It doesn't matter if he is behind me, under me or over me, he insists on seeing my eyes gazing at his own. I have no fucking idea what that is all about, but if he ever demands you to do that, then mind him Meine Liebe. That motherfucker has a wicked backhand, and he isn't afraid to use it liberally.

I groaned. "I hate it when the customers want that Master. It is not only stupid, but it also makes the job harder."

Master Maxx nodded. "Oh, I agree with you one hundred percent. Nothing worse than having to see the bastard that is raping you. I think maybe that is the point. It is another way to enjoy the power they wield over you, ja?"

I shrugged. "I guess so Master. I always thought it was because they think if you are focused on them, you can't be looking for a way to escape. They know they are creeps and that I want to kill them."

My Master paused a moment then chuckled. "The next time I call the special services maybe you better keep your eyes on me, just in case."

I laughed like a little girl because I was one., "I already do Master. You are gorgeous."

He squeezed me tightly while chuckling., "And you, meine demonseed frau, are brilliant. A seductress of the highest caliber already. You're not even a fully matured woman and that tongue of yours is more silver than your Priceless collar. I am surely a dead man."

I stopped laughing. "Only if you ever betray me Master. Otherwise, I will love you forever and do whatever it takes to make our dreams come true." I waited for the cane swat, that never came.

Instead, My Master pulled me into a deep loving kiss that lasted for several minutes. Had he not had to empty his bladder; the story would have most likely had to be paused for a passion filled tryst, on that nasty mattress. Yeah I was nine in every way but the ways of sex. In that realm, I was already light years beyond most woman of menopausal age. Guess it sucked to be me as badly as it sucked to be the submissive Mad Maxx.

When Master Jonas had finished using me to sate his pleasures, he called Master Leo back. He offered to give him the privacy of requesting his own special services from me. I kept my eyes to the floor giving my Master neither quarrel nor approval over any decision he wanted to make.

Master Leo was not a fool as I had hoped he would be. He was aware of the Vampire's moody nature and tendency to withdraw offers. He decided to accept Master Jonas's generosity and I had to endure a second round of the blow job followed by the unwanted buggery to fulfill his lustful interest in me.

My only consolation was that, as always, Master Leo was a gentle and conscientious lover. Not that it helped much since Master Jonas was a brutal one. As you are already sadly aware, meine heart, once you are sore, a feather used with much care is uncomfortable as hell.

I was allowed to play with Der Makellos for a bit as a reward for servicing my Masters with only a few tears, that they knew of anyway. I enjoyed my little hound's affections and couldn't seem to get enough of petting his soft fur. My troubled mind found peace in his dark brown eyes. He made all the humiliation go away the second he showered me with his loving attentions.

Da Vampire and Master Leo decided to defend against my sneaking out of the apartment by forcing me to sleep between them as they had the night before. I was sickened by that idea and got into a little trouble for trying to slip my puppy into bed with me. I wanted to cuddle with him, not the foul men that tended to awaken in the night to further molest the boy.

I was told to hold still to endure Master Jonas reaffixing my chastity device as the Masters prepared for bed. Master Leo crawled into his bed then looked at me with a bit of pity in his expression.

Master Jonas noticed it and groaned. “What now, Leo? Don’t you dare say a fucking word about my keeping the boy chaste.”

Master Leo shook his head. “Nein. I was not going to. However, I must ask, are you sure about using Peter to train the boy for his final section of the Dominant testing?”

I nearly choked on my own spit as I threw a look of terror at the Vampire. “Master? Is Master Leo speaking truth?” I held my breath unable to comprehend this latest nightmare situation.

Master Jonas chuckled. “Calm down, Christian Axel. Peter volunteered for the task of teaching you proper thudding techniques. Besides the man is the only Dominant in this Haus that has as much to gain or lose if you fail to break that metal of yours. That alone causes me to trust him. Besides, he is your father, and we need his and your mother’s vote in the collar selection. Granting him this favor will help assure that goes smoothly. You don’t realize this but every cocksucker in this Haus, including Malfred, is looking to get you alone. None of them will care if you say nein nor will they be fearful of retaliation this late in the game. Only your father can be trusted to keep his mouth off my metal." He stood back and pointed to the bed motioning me to get in it.

I looked at the floor as I followed his order. He was so damned wrong about Peter. He had accidently chosen the one Dominant in the whole fucking Haus that not only was looking to taste his metal but had the right to do it by agreement with the Priceless himself. If he could find a way to call on his rights without setting off suspiciousness that is.

Well, Master Malfred may have come up with a plan to become an Elder at forty-one, but my father Peter is the true Mastermind. I was screwed literally.

On the bright side, maybe Master Peter could help me with a little issue that spanned back to the days of his own reign, before Elsa could manage to get me into that fucking cursed storage closet on the first floor.

Chapter 61: Geraldine's Mercy and Malfred's Revenge

I got into the bed and held back my groaning best as I could. The Vampire pulled me to his cuddling and Master Leo stared at me with a look of pity. I wish I could say that sleep found me quickly but that was the hell of my situation. I found myself fatigued all throughout the day but alert the second the sun went to his slumber.

The only thing worse than insomnia is not being capable of unconsciousness when being held hostage in a mean old Vampire man's spooning. I do believe I told you Master Jonas snores like the chainsaw, ja? Well, if I forgot to say it, then be assured that bastard does.

On more than one occasion I have desired to smoother him with his pillow just to get him out of my ear with that fucking noise. This night was no different. I felt like I was sure to blow to pieces when he began his thunderous loud breathing within only a few minutes of the lights going off.

I laid there thinking of all the mistakes I had made like I usually did in those days. I tried to imagine what other people in the world outside the walls were doing right that minute. I wondered if Annette ever thought of me the way I did her. I even spent some time imagining what my lambs were doing in the darkness with their new family.

I did my best to focus on how I would handle this new twist of dealing with Master Peter. I also, attempted to make a plan to avoid having to kill Elsa, or Master Malfred when either of them come looking to take their vengeance on the boy. I knew that it was likely nothing I did was going to stop the inevitable murder or be put to the yard scenario, but I really hoped to prevent it, you know?

Then I spent the rest of the night weeping like a little child. I was just so damned sick of all the bullshit. It seemed like it was never going to end. Several hours into my crying jag, I felt Master Leo attempt to hijack me from Master Jonas's grip for a cuddle of his own. He managed to pull me into his embrace, only to have the Vampire awaken slightly and drag me back into his own cuddle.

I held as still as possible pretending to be out cold. I knew if either of them found me alert they would want seconds on their earlier sexual assaults. That tended to happen often in my early tenure with the Elder Masters.

By this time Christian Axel had learned to fake sleep. Not that it would always keep them from their interests with me, but it would work at least a few times when the Dominants tried to molest me in the darkness.

Master Leo's attempt to steal the boy from the Vampire's claws was a major blunder if he didn't wish to be around when Master Jonas enforced his rights with me. That night, My playing opossum did no good.

I did my best not to be angered with him over his stupidity when I was harshly rousted then brutally forced into full special services in the wee hours of the morning with the Vampire. He didn't care that Master Leo was trying to sleep nor me neither.

When I began to wail during Master Jonas painful coupling, Master Leo who had rolled his back to that rape scene, got up and stormed from the room slamming the door behind him. Master Jonas didn't miss a beat. He merely continued his intercourse while chuckling with humor that he had managed to steal the Master of the Haus's bed and from him.

The Vampire gained his orgasm and let me free of his grips. I moved as far from him as possible across that mattress as he returned to his slumber.

After I was sure he was back in the land of dreams, I slipped from the bed with much stealth. I wanted to visit with Der Makellos, and to be honest, cry some more. I was never going to sleep anyway with that sex fiend laying right there only inches away.

I suppose I assumed Master Leo had gone to the second bedroom in his apartment. To my surprise I found him in his living area playing with the excited puppy. I stopped in the darkness of the hallway unsure if I would get thudded for daring to be out of bed. *Insolence for Master Jonas's command you know.*

I watched in silence for several moments as my Master giggled at Der Makellos chasing his hands as he teased him. My desire to engage in that fun looking game overwhelmed my good senses. I came out of the shadows without a word and sat down next to the puppy box for a better look. I kept my eyes down and wrung my hands waiting for Master Leo to chastise me, then demand I return to the bedroom.

He snuck a glance at me but didn't end his funning with the baby hound. I took slow, shallow breaths, sure that at any moment he would become angered and send me away. Then Der Makellos saw me sitting there. He fell over his big paws as he eagerly came running to welcome his partner.

I scooped him up the second he got within my reach. He licked my face and whimpered with thrill. I giggled and kissed him back. In those moments, all my troubles went away. I could forget the pain in my flesh, the agony of my situation, and the hunger in my stomach. That puppy was a cure for everything ugly in my life, and I loved him for it.

I laid him back down in the floor and rolled up around him enjoying his vigorous adorations. I had briefly forgotten that Master Leo was watching. It didn't even occur to me that I had stolen his playmate's attentions the way Master Jonas had stolen his hase.

He cleared his throat then said softly, "You okay, Christian Axel? I mean, Jonas didn't hurt you did he?" Master Leo looked at the floor and sniffed as if about to weep.

I nodded without looking away from my playful pup. "Ja, I am always fine Master. Are you going to tell on me for being out here instead of in the bed?"

Master Leo shook his head. "Nein, meine hase. I am glad to have this time with you and our baby in fact. I want to apologize for not being capable of stopping this horror for you. I feel so Gott damned useless. I mean it had to be done to end Malfred, but Jonas is just such a, never mind. It is bad manners to discuss such things about your Dominant in front of you. I will only say I am grateful for this little mercy, ja?"

I smiled as Der Makellos tried to nibble on the end of my nose. "I thank you for that mercy Master. Can I do anything for you in return?" I didn't look at him when I offered a service return as is the proper protocol for his not alerting Master Jonas to my rule breaking.

Master Leo chuckled. "You are already doing what I wish you to do. I would ask that you share the pup with me a little though. Can you and he come over here or should I go to you?"

I picked up the squirming pup and moved both of us within reach of my Master. Der Makellos was immediately in doggy heaven with two parents offering to play with him. He rolled, yipped, growled, jumped, flipped and licked for the next hour as Master Leo, and I roughly housed the pup. He couldn't seem to get enough of the affection lavished upon him.

Then, at last, he yawned and whimpered. Der Makellos was only a baby back then and his energy level, though high, was short lived. He needed a nap to re-energize for the next round of thrilling games with his humans. I smiled with joy when he come over turned around three times, then curled up next to my naked right thigh for his slumber. I petted him as he drifted off to dream of chasing fast moving objects and Master Leo's hands.

Master Leo leaned back against the wall and closed his eyes. “That was a lot of fun, meine hase. I had forgotten how great it is to have a pup around. They can wear out an old man quickly though. Damn, I think Der Makellos has the right idea. A nap is exactly what I need too.”

I giggled. “The Vampire is snoring Master. You could easily slip into that bed but beware not to wake him.”

My Master frowned. “Ja, Gott help me if he mistakenly thought it was you instead of me next to him. That man is the pervert. I think maybe I take my rest on the couch just to assure my safety.”

I sighed. “I wish I could stay on that sofa too. I suppose I better sneak back before I get caught and thudded. Again, thank you for the mercy of not telling on me.” I kept my eyes on my snoozing baby as I said that.

Master Leo scoffed. “I would never tell that bastard about anything you do to find relief from that nasty shit he does to you. I always imagined it was bad, but shit, it is worse than I ever thought. Now, he has handed you back over to Peter as well. Christian Axel, I must admit I fear for your mental health and worry you are in a lot of danger. Please tell me, is there anything I can do to lessen your burden?”

I snorted. “Besides taking my place as the sex partner of Master Peter and Master Jonas I cannot think of a single thing. You already gave me Der Makellos and disposed of Ivar. That is more than anyone else has ever done for me. I thank you for the mercy of it.”

Master Leo laughed with bitterness. "You know there was a time when I would have been happy to try to coax Peter to look at me the way he does you. I even did try, but the man is also a top. That was of no use to either of us. A zebra cannot change its stripes. As for the Vampire, yikes, I love you more than you can know but that man's fetish is disgusting. I would puke and end that romance quickly. You have my respect meine hase and my pity too."

I shot a look of anger at him. "You can keep that last thing to yourself Master. I don't want you to feel sorry for me. Hugs, sweet words of love, and cuddles are as useless to me as a mother that would kiss the mortal gunshot wound of her son's chest thinking it will make the pain go away. What I need is action not fucking useless emotions of regret for my shitty lot in life. You slit that Ivar's throat, and that aided me. You helped me seek out Master Peter's help to unbolt my metal. You made the sacrifice by passing that law too. If you really love me, then you will keep doing and stop the useless feelings. That is how I have survived this hell for as long as I have memory. I was born into this nightmare Master. I don't know anything else. However, I can imagine what it would be like to not have to endure abuses of every kind, be afraid all the time, and go to sleep without fear of rape. That is really all I want. If you desire to earn back my affection, help me get there in one piece, ja?"

Master Leo's mouth twisted into a peaceful smile. "There is hope that you will adore me again then. For that meine hase, I would even let that nasty Vampire cut me open then fuck me."

I almost choked, I laughed so hard at that. “Nein, you say that, but I know better. You are not fucked up enough to endure such a thing. You would have to be under threat of death like I am to make it even once in his intercourse. I may hate sex with the man, but I can say one thing for truth. I would choose you or Master Peter any day over any of these other perverts. You are gentle about it, and my father is mostly normal in his desires. Though his being my father is beyond fucked up. All the others are either twisted or brutal in the way they like to take their special services. You know Master Peter once told that idiot Maximillian that one day in another man’s bed would make me appreciate his kindness within his intimacies with me. I can recall I laughed at that thinking there is no such a thing as kindness when it comes to unwanted sexual assault. Well, I hate to admit how wrong I was to not heed his truthful statement. Rape is rape don’t get me wrong, but what Malfred, Claus, Jonas, Xavier, and many others have done is far more than just forced sex. They violate my mind as much as they do my flesh. I could just wash away Master Peter’s nasty lust, or even yours, and be assured I would survive the humiliation of it to fight on another day. There is no amount of soap, nor water, which can cleanse away the psyche when your rapist takes away the belief you will live through their chronic attacks. I fear that one day one of them will beat me too hard, puncture something that will debilitate me for life, cut too deep, or worse where a Master keeps me from ever finding a safe place to hide even within the deepest places of my head.”

Master Leo looked at the floor. "You know I never thought of that before. I guess I just assumed if no one judged you for doing what you must, thanks to the collar, you would eventually get over your disgust with same gendered intercourse. I suppose I am the moron for never considering what it would be like to never know when a Master decides to go too far or forgets himself in his lustful interests."

I shrugged. "You never thought of it because you have never been raped, Master. Those so lucky to be able to count all their sexual encounters as willing can only understand that forcing such a thing would cause humiliation. Well, let me tell you something, that is indeed a horrible thing to have to live down. However, it is not even close to the truthful terror of sexual assault. I think I am done speaking with you about this subject. I hear my words being broadcasted on Master Jonas's radio. If he awakens and finds out I dared to say such things, I will get more than a thudding for it. I have no idea how he can even sleep with it turned up so fucking loud like that. I would like to ask if Geraldine wrote to me, and if you are hiding her letters for some reason? I need to know where she will leave the meals she is cooking for me Master. I won't live long if I don't eat something soon. She is a lamb of her word you know." I wrung my hands and rocked a bi feeling anxious that Master Jonas heard everything I said about him, and others like him.

Master Leo blew out his breath then slowly said, "Uhm, well she told me that she would leave a plate for you at my door in the morning. I can bring it in for you if you want me t."

I nodded. "Thank you for the mercy of it Master. I knew she wouldn't let me down. I did everything she wanted me to. She is an honorable service for service lamb. Do you hear that Master? Can you ask them to stop calling me the schizophrenic? I don't think the Guard will find that a funny rumor. If they keep broadcasting it through this Haus I am a goner. Can you call the radio station and ask them to stop speaking about me? Bad enough they watch my every fucking move. I grow weary of dare constant criticism. I would like to see them do better. Fucking hypocrites, the whole lot of them. I happen to know they let this Haus exist and never report a Gott damned thing of what they do here to the innocent children. They have a lot of nerve you know?" I got up without another word and snuck back down the hallway to get back into the bed before the Vampire awoke to find me missing.

I had left a startled appearing Master Leo still sitting in the floor next to the sleeping Der Makellos. I knew he would make sure our baby was safe for the remainder of the night. Master Leo had his issues, but he could be trusted to defend our family members, even though I knew he would never call that fucking radio station and tell them to cut their shit.

I couldn't push my luck any further by sticking around to yap with my Master for another few hours. I knew the flesh couldn't take another beating for a few days. I had not even healed up yet from the last one at the hands of Master

Jonas and Master Malfred tag teaming the three days before.

Then that backhand party the Vampire threw on my head earlier that night only managed to make matters worse. I was starting to resemble the rotten apple just as I had during the days of Julius and Grisham's assaults.

I managed to get back into bed without discovery. I wasn't there five minutes though when the Vampire awoke and grabbed me. He hauled me across the mattress clutching me back into his cuddle. I held my breath in terror that he had noticed my absence but in another few moments he went back to snoring.

I closed my eyes and went back to breathing normally in relief. The rest of that night I fantasized about my Annette and our imaginary haus in the mountains. Der Makellos and my lambs were there, and Master Leo our friendly neighbor.

In that world of green fields and blue skies, there is no such a thing as special services, Masters, collars, cells, nor chains. If only I could find that place for truth, I would go dare and never come back.

Someday, Meine Liebe, we are going to seek it out together, ja? It must exist.

Otherwise, how could Annette know so much about it? You break my collar and we find it.

I nodded and smiled while imagining this perfect world the submissive called Nobody had told my Master about.

I had finally found my restful sleep when Master Leo's alarm went off. The Vampire come up out of the bed as if he had been shot. I let out a yelp and covered my head fearful he would hit me having also been ripped out of my slumber from this sudden noise.

He glared at me cowering next to him. "Who the fuck set an alarm? Gott dammit. I near pissed the bed from that startle, Christian Axel. Well, get up. Apparently, we are supposed to be somewhere according to the annoying announcement."

I whimpered a bit feeling fatigued. "Master Leo had that set to remind him to feed my lambs I think. They are with their family now, so it is no longer necessary to be awake Master." I closed my eyes seeking out my slumber once more.

Master Jonas shook me harshly. "I cannot sleep once I am up. Get the fuck up and fetch me coffee, boy. Then you get in there and attend your shower and hygiene. You will meet with Peter later this morning for your training."

I groaned but sat up with my eyes still closed "As you wish Master. I do beg the mercy of skipping the shower though. That water is foul. I don't wish to be radiated."

He scoffed. "Oh shit, not this fight again. Christian Axel, if I tell you to take a shower in horse vomit you will do well to move your ass fast and thank me for the kindness of it. Now, out of this bed. Move it. Why the hell are you so tired? You are young, and we have had plenty of sleep. Hell, more than eight hours' worth."

I got out of the bed still groaning in stiffness and fatigue. “That radio of yours kept me up all night again, Master. I would beg you to turn it down, at least at night.”

Master Jonas roared out, “There is no radio, Christian Axel. I already told you this. It is all in your empty head. Go get my coffee and shut your fucking mouth. I mean it.”

I flinched at his screaming at me but moved my ass to follow his orders. There was no reason to push him further on that subject. I knew a backhand would follow if I didn’t hurry to calm his anger. Master Leo was already in the kitchenette moaning to himself about how uncomfortable his sofa was to sleep on. He stood there in his robe by the coffee pot rubbing his face appearing most irritated.

I was grateful the java was already made, saving me from taking longer than I believed the Vampire would tolerate. I didn’t say a word as I grabbed a coffee cup and went to pouring the liquid. Master Leo stopped grumbling and watched me in silence. I flashed him a look of gratitude over the small mercy of having the liquid ready.

He smiled back. “Well, despite my deplorable resting situation, I must admit it is nice to wake up to such a glorious vision. It is not every they I get to watch a beautiful naked boy pouring coffee in my kitchen. My Maus used to say it is the simple things in life that make it worth living. Damn if she wasn’t right.”

I nodded as I took off with speed to attend my Master. “I am grateful to be of service to you, Master. Forgive me for not being capable to attend your visual pleasure further but I have to run. My Master is in a foul mood, and I do not have the protection of clothing as you pointed out, to offer any mercy from a thudding."

He laughed at my high protocol response then yelled after me, "Ah, damn, if only you were mine. I would throw away all your clothing and never allow a single bruise to mar up my gorgeous boy. I would stare at you all day in total bliss like the idiot I am. Everyone would have to call me Lucky Leo. Don't forget, the lamb has sent your breakfast. Finish your service then come eat it for her please."

I nearly tripped as I closed my eyes to silently thank Geraldine for saving me from the outrageous hunger I was suffering. I hope she sent seconds. I was starving.

I entered the room to find the Vampire sitting on the side of the bed waiting for his coffee and dressing service. I handed him his cup then dropped to my kneel beginning the task of getting him clothed. I secretly crossed my fingers that he would forget to make me shower, or at least let me eat my lamb's breakfast first.

Master Jonas sipped his drink and watched me with silence as I provided his wake up services. He didn't appear to be in as foul a humor as when he first awoke but I wasn't pushing my luck. I made damned sure to offer to do everything from brushing his hair to attending his teeth. The man had me attend all them, even the shaving of his face. Thanks to that, it took almost an hour to get the Vampire ready to face the world outside Master Leo's apartment.

When at last I could do nothing else, beside maybe wiping his ass. He is a damned lazy motherfucker. I dropped to a kneel to await his release. He sat there looking me over with a small smile on his face. I felt a little nervous wondering what his hold up in letting me get to attending my own dressing and hygiene needs.

He blew out his breath. “I will remind you I told you to shower and attend all your needs to be ready for any service I may require of you today. That said, I would like to take a moment to warn you about Malfred. Christian Axel, I know you are not the fool. Though lately I do worry you’re a bit daft. That man will be looking for retaliation and trying to catch you out without the protection of your man would be just his style. Normally, I would have no reason for concern. I merely would keep you locked up in our apartment until his anger subsided a bit. However, you must attend training down in the torture rooms daily or you will never pass your final sections for Dominant testing. I accepted your father’s offer because I do believe the man can hold his own against his former associate. That said, I am giving you a directive. When you are not in my sight, you are never to leave Peter for any reason. Do you understand me?”

I nodded. “As you wish, Master. May I please have my breakfast first? I thank you for the mercy of it in advance.”

He growled. “You hear me say that Malfred is gunning for you and your response is can I have breakfast?”

I shrugged. "So, someone wants to rape or murder me, Master. That is usual. I will require enough energy to run if I must or fight if cornered. I won't get far if they come after me on the empty stomach though."

The Vampire broke out in loud laughter. "Ah, you are amazing, Christian Axel. Fearless as they come. Ja, go eat your breakfast then get back here and do your tasks as I commanded."

I stood up to rush for that plate Geraldine sent for me but stopped briefly to say, "I am not fearless Master. I am helpless. There is a difference." I then took off down the hall to enjoy the thrill of my pup and a full stomach at last.

I found both those items waiting for me, I am happy to say. I stuffed down the huge breakfast food my lamb mercifully sent. My little pup watched me eat wagging his tail, drooling in hope that I would share with him or at least drop something in my haste to eat it all at once. I slipped him several bites of my sausage until Master Leo caught me.

He berated me for giving Der Makellos food that was meant for the humans. I didn't argue with him. I simply waited until he wasn't looking and snuck another bit to my best friend. The way I saw it, if my pup was a prisoner to his Masters like me, then the least I could do is offer him some comfort.

I could tell that he was happy I understood him like I did. He gave me many kisses for my efforts to smuggle him the thrill of a taste of the forbidden food. Master Jonas come into the living area and broke up this return of service I was getting from Der Makellos.

He glared at me with much irritation. "Did I tell you to get in that bathroom and attend your cleansing and other hygiene, Christian Axel? I do believe I did. I come in here to find you playing with your pup and defying my commands. Perhaps, I take you back to our apartment where there are no such distractions to prevent you minding your Master?"

I quickly put Der Makellos to the floor and took up my kneeling. "Nein, Master. I beg of you don't take me back there. I was going to do as you commanded right away. I request another punishment for my failure and thank you for the mercy of it in advance."

Master Jonas growled out. "Substitution punishment denied. You get your ass in there and get to your tasks before you anger me any further." He didn't even finish his sentence before I was running down that hallway for the bathroom.

I pulled the antidote from under Master Leo's sink and did my best to spray it all over me. I turned on the water and near screamed. It was greener than ever. I swear Meine Liebe they must have been pumping that shit right from the radiation canister itself that morning. No matter how much I wanted to stay with my little hound, I couldn't talk myself into getting in that horror.

I paced back and forth watching that foulness roll out of the facet. I had to find a way to appear clean without risking disease and eventual death from this nightmare. It was then I recalled the alcohol that Master Malfred had me use.

I left that shower running as I dug under the sink until I found a bottle of the astringent. I took a rag and soap then used this sterilized liquid to wipe down the boy. It irritated my skin a great deal, but better to be a bit itchy and raw then dead. I decided that I would trade my special services with Master Leo for bottles of this or even hydrogen peroxide. Either of them would wet my rags and lather the soap enough.

The only problem was the enema. I couldn't use the water, but alcohol was out of the question too. Such a thing would result in more than irritation. I sat there on the floor for some time trying to solve that issue when I recalled that often they boil water to sterilize it for the baby bottles. I wondered if I could do the same for the enema bag. I decided there was only one way to find out.

With much stealth I went to the kitchenette. I ran enough water through the coffee pot to fulfil my task. I noticed as I collected that heated liquid that green crap was forced to the top. I used a coffee filter to scoop it off and found to my relief this effectively removed the problem. It was useless at providing a full shower but with a little effort I could collect enough for my basic hygiene needs.

I rushed back down the hallway with my decontaminated water when I heard the Masters speaking in whispers. I stopped my wild run and held my breath to see if I could make out what they were discussing in secret.

Master Jonas scoffed. "I am calling my lawyer today Leo no matter what you say. The boy has no family of worth. I am willing to extend my protection and look after him for all my days. You would have this important task left to the likes of Peter or that horrible Agnette maybe?"

Master Leo responded. "Nein I do agree they must be prevented from taking this responsibility. However, Jonas, you should realize your age. The boy needs a guardian for all his life not just a couple decades. You will be growing grass over your grave, and he will be left to the mental institutions or worse, the streets. I am just saying seek out one that could give him more time in their care than either of us could."

Da Vampire sounded angered. "First of all, the second he finds his Frau, I will have all the time in the world, fool. She will cure me of death. That said, I do agree one thing even a female Priceless cannot do is save one if they, say slip off a banister and fall. I will make this deal with you brother. I take the guardianship and name you my second if anything ever were to happen to me, or I had to be away. Will that change your mind about going to Gretta with this information?"

I held my breath in shock when I heard Master Leo say, "Ja, brother. You do that and I will drop the subject. Hell, I will even help you with the cost of the lawyer and paperwork. However, I demand you put into writing you never take my rights for his favors away from me for any reason. I will always respect your place as his man, but Jonas I cannot live without holding him in my arms often. I have done all I can to deny my desire for that boy, but in the end I am the selfish bastard, much to my regret."

Master Jonas chuckled. "Ah, there is the truthful Leo at last. Welcome brother, it is a pleasure to meet you. Look, I will do all you want and even accept your coin in this venture. I will warn you though, once he has that Frau of his, he won't be too eager to put up with two old men pawing at him. You may find him full of fight against you over it in fact."

I felt the tears welling in my eyes when Master Leo responded, "You said his selection will be full of the beast schizophrenia too. In fact, I happen to know you plan to make damned sure she is. Therefore, he won't be capable of ignoring any commands from his guardians. I know what you are doing Jonas. You plan to dangle his access to his mate in front of him like he did the sausage for Der Makellos. Well, Gott damn, you do the same for me. I cannot stop you, so I have decided to join you. I am not so dumb as to believe in fairy tales Jonas. I realize Christian Axel can never live outside this Haus and that you have the power to make him comfortable or destroy him at your whim and any female he chooses too. Allow me to at least offer him some kindness in this brutal world he is trapped in for all his days. As long as I have life to live anyway."

Master Jonas chuckled. "Fair enough Leo. You keep your trap shut and I agree to all your terms. we will be his sole owners and only real family. Since you have no interest in the female I keep that little beauty for myself, but I will agree to share Christian Axel with you as long as you manage to stay alive anyway."

Master Leo scoffed. "And you put that in writing. I mean it."

Master Jonas growled. "I heard you the first time. Ja, I put this in writing and file it in the Hall of records. Happy now? If so then I ask you to take the boy to Peter when he finishes his dressing. I am going to head out and get that lawyer started. I would be a fool to mess around. I am sure Peter has thought of this shit too, If not he will soon enough I believe. I need to beat him to this punch, ja?"

Master Leo gasped. "Shit. Ja, I bet you are right. Get going then. I got the boy handled. See you later. You better have that contract on hand for my signature when next we meet."

I heard the Vampire grunt, then the apartment door open and close. I took off to the bathroom praying neither of them knew I had heard their sinister planning against me. I got into the steam filled bathroom and quietly shut the room off for privacy.

I fell into the floor weeping with a full-on crying jag. I couldn't believe that the Vampire and Master Leo were planning to take over my life even after I broke my collar. I knew what a guardianship was. Another word for collar is what it is. There wasn't anything I could do about it. I was trapped in that hell Haus, and the shady lawyers would grant these buggers the right to keep doing exactly that to me for all their lives.

It was then that Christian slipped out of the shadows to stare at me weeping in the floor. "Get off the floor idiots. What the fuck do you care what that Vampire or schwuler do? You break that collar, then break their necks, ja? No more Guardianship. No more trying to steal our Frau. Goodbye motherfuckers, right?"

I sat up and glanced at the anger/lust shard feeling better immediately. "Ah, you are right brother. I had not considered once the metal is gone I can kill them both without breaching prime directives."

He nodded. "Uh huh, you need not worry over their illusions that as the freeman they can control you any further. Once that collar is buried in the yard, we are our own Dominant. You worry about studying for the doctor college, getting the job and finding our Frau. I will handled these no nothings that think they can hold us prisoner past the sacred bolt cutters."

I smiled at that. "I can hardly wait Christian. Just think, the sun on our face, the grass at our feet, and the sounds of our girl telling us she wants us for all her days. Only a little longer, than our dreams come true."

Christian crossed his arms. "Damn right. Now, get up and deal with that nasty father of ours. Oh, and do take one thing that Vampire man said seriously. Watch your back brothers. I sense trouble is afoot. That tasty Elsa is hanging around waiting to take a bite, and to be honest I expect

Malfred to be gathering his forces as we speak. Don't let your guard down, and never be anywhere without Leo, Peter or Jonas."

I nodded. "I hear you brother. Maybe you need to stay close just in case, ja?"

He slipped back into the shadows. "I am never far away brothers. I am always ready for a fight. All you need do is scream." He disappeared as quickly as he appeared.

Without further hesitation I completed my hygiene tasks with my modifications that is. When I come out dressed and ready to go, Master Leo was holding his camera. I thought that odd but ignored him. He bum rushed me out the door before I could engage my sleepy pup in another round of playing.

I was irritated when he asked me to pose there in front of his door for a photo just in case the Vampire cut him off from visiting with me. I already heard that deal he made with Master Jonas. I knew he was full of shit. To this day I have no idea why he was playing like he was afraid. The Vampire was many things, but he tended to keep his word when he agreed to put it in writing. Master Leo had nothing to worry about. Christian Axel on the other hand had many things on his mind.

As Master Leo snapped his photos, Master Malfred come out of his apartment smiling. He lived next door in Barnim's old apartment, remember? I glared at him with hatred as he jumped in front of the lens and wrapped his arm around me. The man was dressed for the work out room. I realized he had seen Master Leo and I alone on his way to his destination and decided to take advantage of the situation.

Master Leo stopped his photography immediately. “Malfred get the fuck out of here. This is none of your business.”

Master Malfred laughed as he reached out and ruffled my hair. I pulled away and shot him a go to hell look). “Ah, so I cannot even be in the photo shoot with the Priceless without his man’s permission? I thought I was told I can do whatever I like with my forbidden metal but fuck him? How is smiling in a picture breaching my legal rights to my own collar Leo? I am all ears, tell me.”

Master Leo grabbed my leash and pulled me along behind him. “Ficken dich, Malfred. Stop being a pest. I am busy with the Priceless at this moment and have no time for your tomfoolery.”

The Dominant followed us with a mischievous expression on his face. “Tomfoolery? Ah, My name is Malfred, Leo, not Tom. where you headed?” He giggled at his stupid statement.

Master Leo didn’t stop his march for the stairwell. “That is also none of your affair, Malfred. Bug off, I mean it. Go away. You have no right to be trailing us.”

Master Malfred shot a look of confusion around him. “Huh? I didn’t know you owned the hallway and stairs too, Leo. Wow, you think your powerful enough to enforce me to stop following you. I will go wherever the fuck I want and you, my dear, cannot stop me either."

Master Leo sped up. "Fine, you can walk anywhere you like. You keep your fingers off the Priceless while you do it." I shot looks behind me watching with much anxiety as Master Malfred kept the pace with us smiling at me with evil in his expression.

He said nothing as Master Leo pulled me along behind him all the way to the steps that led to the torture chamber below. I nervously turned around as my Master began his decent down them. Master Malfred made a kissy face at me. I narrowed my eyes and flipped him off. That made him chuckle wickedly.

"Love that fight in you, Mad Maxx. Makes you even more attractive you know." He smiled with humor at his statement.

I snorted at that and kept my protocol with Master Leo following my three paces behind without missing a step. I noticed Master Malfred did the same never breaking off his passive aggressive chase. Then just as we reached the bottom of the stairwell Master Leo halted so suddenly I nearly ran into him.

There waiting for us on the last step was Olaf, Vilber, Karl, Louis, and Alexie. Master Leo turned and shot me a look of fear. I turned around to see that Master Malfred had been joined by Anna, Mila, Elsa, and another large Dominant male I knew only as Volf. We neither could go forward nor back. Master Malfred's pack of supporters had us surrounded.

Master Leo was visibly trembling but shouted out with force. "Move the fuck out of my way or find yourselves in chains for daring to block the path of an Elder."

I looked to each of these foul creatures to see them all humored by his worthless words. I watched helplessly as they moved forward and from behind. Alexie grabbed Master Leo with speed while Karl, Olaf and Louis come forward to snatch me. I turned and took off ready to attempt to fight my way through the mostly FemDom behind crowd.

Master Malfred and wolf come toward me ending that idea quickly as they were huge men. I turned around letting out yells for help as Karl and Olaf grabbed me by my upper arms like a falcon picking off a sparrow from a fence post.

I searched in total desperation for Master Leo. He was being blocked from aiding me by Vilber and Alexie. Anna and Mila rushed to aid their brothers to keep him from passing them at the bottom of the steps while I was being dragged up them by the brutes. Master Malfred, Louis, Elsa, and wolf took off ahead of us and pushed anyone coming down out of the way. There was no one capable of stopping the hijackers as they took off with their prize.

When we reached the first floor, Elsa broke off from her male counterparts. She blew a kiss to Olaf, and he returned the affectionate behavior. I felt my blood turn to ice as I realized she was his girlfriend. Sonofabitch. She wasn't there to kill me over her lost parents. The girl was playing the bitch wolf for her lover Olaf.

Oh, by the way, Meine Liebe, I forgot. You don't know what I mean when I called Elsa the bitch wolf. Well, that is a female wolf in heat that will leave the pack to hunt dogs. She finds her weaker brothers by sending off her scent of invite for a couple.

Once she has attracted one or two lust driven male dogs, she lets them chase her. She is actually leading them into an ambush set up by her wolf brothers. The unsuspecting canines walk into the trap thinking he is about to get some love. Instead, he is met by the gang of wolves hiding out waiting on him. At that point he is beaten to death then eaten for their dinner.

I turned around with my eyes wide in terror. "Wolves do that to dogs. Why Master?"

Master Maxx shrugged, "The wolf needs to eat Meine Liebe and the dog is not only easy pickings, but he is their competition you see. Like the moron Mad Maxx, the dog is eager to find affection wherever he can get it. Over the centuries the wolf found a way to exploit this weakness. Olaf wanted me dead as did Vilber. When he found no success with his brute force he realized using the softer tactic would likely result in an easy kill. However, thanks to my feeling guilty about being the one that killed both her parents, I didn't believe her desire for me honest. You see, only Master Malfred, Master Leo and the Vampire knew I killed Evelyn. While Olaf and Vilber did know I killed Felix,

I would find out later that Elsa didn't even know he was her father. This was one time when my feelings of regret saved my ass. Well, from an outright murder that is. The truth was Elsa was working to gain revenge for Olaf only. She didn't think she had a personal quarrel with me in any way. Does that make me feel any better about her attempts to have me assassinated? Hell no. She had just made my shit list along with all the other names I mentioned. It no longer would have even matter had I been rescued, which I was not, thank you very much."

I shot a look of disgust at him. "Uh oh. Not good Master. You and Leo had no chance to fight them all." I already had a pretty good idea of what this move of Master Malfred's was all about.

He nodded. "You can say that again, Meine Liebe. I normally would cane you for guessing ahead of my story, but in this case, you are maybe one of the few people on Earth that can guess what Malfred was up to. Not only is his intelligence in your blood but your life with Debbie has allowed you to see into the darkest heart with alarming clarity. Your ability to size these foul criminals up with your keen mind not only impresses me but scares me too. Maybe you can read minds. I sure as the hell can hear their thoughts at times. I wish I had been listening that morning let me tell you."

I nodded then leaned back to settle in to hear the rest of this horrific tale.

“As you already guessed Master Malfred had designed a plan to attempt to blackmail the Vampire into relenting his denial of my special services. The Dominant was very careful about how he handled this attack. He selected his most loyal men and women to act as witnesses if he required any. He made sure to call on too many of them to ever hope to control, bribe or murder them all before he could get even one to speak out.

I had assumed when he left the Great Hall he had gone to thrash my father Peter. Well once again, wrong. He had stormed off to call on his acolytes and make his plans to retaliate in a way that assured him success in reclaiming what he believed was his rightful property.

I didn’t go along with these men without fighting with all the vigor I could muster. I yelled, bit them, kicked, pulled, dragged my feet and let my weight fall to the floor several times. Nothing I did even slowed down their progression. I admit I was terrified which kept me energetic enough to keep up the attempts to stall them.

When they hauled me to the dungeon stairwell, I doubled my efforts. I had no idea where they were taking me or what the hell Master Malfred had in mind but whatever it was, I knew I may not survive it. Especially with old Olaf involved. Trust me, you could hear my wailing for aid for miles as they dragged me down those rock steps.

Once down in the dungeon the brutes pulled me along to a torture cell with only a set of chains and a table full of thudders inside. Olaf and Karl dragged me kicking and screaming inside while Master Malfred, Louis, and Wolf came in after them. The four of them stood there glaring at me while I yelled for help with all my lung capacity.

Master Malfred stepped inside and shouted. “Shut the fuck up, Christian Axel. No one is coming to help you. You are giving me a headache. Karl, make him be quiet, please.” I braced myself best I could as that motherfucker punched me in the stomach, knocking all the air from my lungs. That effectively forced me to mind Master Malfred’s command, let me tell you.

I hit the floor, on my knees, gasping for air while Master Malfred laughed. “Thank you Karl. That is better. Okay boys remember what I told you. Be careful not to injure him severely. If you kill him I will have your hodensack on a hook by dark fall. Just do as we discussed, then get the fuck out of here. I will deal with the blow back.” The brutes all chuckled and shot glances at each other.

Master Malfred looked out of the cell down the hallway as if nervous. “Get to it time is wasting.” He stepped out and slammed the cell door behind him.

I led out a moan of terror as I looked up at the four big men standing around me. It was at this moment I realized what the hell was going on. Master Malfred knew rape of the Priceless carries a death penalty for the silver or traps him in his metal. If it is ever reported to the Head of the Voting Council that is. Sure, the last time only the offenders got sent to the yard, but this time there was no chance I would not be left behind by the Guard if Gretta found out about it.

As Wolf and Karl grabbed my upper arms and Olaf knocked all the thudders off the table to the floor, I let out a loud wail of despair. The brutes dragged me to the emptied table bent me over it and held me down with strength. I struggled with all I had but they were far too powerful to even budge an inch.

Louis come up behind me and pulled my breeches down. He began the gang rape with much brutality. I was helpless to do anything but cry out in agony as the brute took his pleasure with me. The others egged him on causing him to become even more harsh in his intercourse. I was blubbering like a kid by the time he was finished.

My worst nightmare come to truth with my next rapist. Olaf took his turn without mercy. He finally got his taste of the forbidden metal with much vigor. I did my best to try to get away from that horrific scene of pain and humiliation but there was no escaping the wheel for any of us.

The chants of the men around me and the sounds of their lustful grunting filled my ears to deafening. The pain caused by their foul acts on the flesh sent me into near animal frenzy to try to escape it. I screamed and wailed until I was hoarse from it, and that was before Olaf was finished.

Wolf had Louis take his spot holding me still so he could take his turn "throwing it to me." Just like his brothers, he held nothing back. I had started to go numb by this time. There was a strange sound of rushing water in my ears that made me think I was drowning. This caused me to find the strength to engage in a violent struggle against my oppressors.

Louis and Karl had to smack my head into the table several times to end my panic driven thrashing. When Wolf reached his apex, Olaf come forward and took Karl's place. I laid there near insane, panting, and weeping as the black collar brute pushed me harshly back to the table when I tried to take advantage of the man change.

He leaned down into my ear and said, "Gotcha Mad Maxx. I waited a long time for that. I promise you for the rest of my days I will be remembering that moment with a smile on my face, you cocksucker. Mostly because I know you won't be able to forget that Olaf fucked you and made you love it. Next time though, I expect you to finish that blow job you started." He laughed with evil glee as I closed my eyes unable to deal with anything anymore.

Karl took up his mount and began his turn in this nightmare sexual assault. I heard him yelling he was doing to me what I intended to do to his little girl. He kept asking me how I like it and saying he was teaching me a lesson in empathy about fucking his family.'

I turned around and flashed a look of terror at Master Maxx.

He smiled with bitterness and stroked my cheek. "It is okay Meine Liebe. I don't blame you for the evil another does if that is what you are trembling about this moment. Truth is that the day I hurt you trying to stop that Darrell from taking what is mine, his statements during this nightmare crossed my mind several times. You can thank him and this very incident for quelling my anger before I went too far. I could have injured you for truth. I was so damned mad I had lost control of myself. The cruel memory reminded me of what it is like to be helpless when another is taking their pleasure from you when you are too little to fight. You do belong to me, meine Frau, and that means finding my lust with your flesh is my right. That said, there is no excuse for my being brutal, harsh, or unloving about it. I am your man and for now your Master. I swear to you I never wanted to be your rapist too. I vow that if you can break my collar, meine heart, I will never lay another finger, thudder, nor my own manhood on you if you say nein. Even if that means you and I will never be lovers from that moment on. You have no choice right now, but one day, I give that back to you. That Meine Liebe is a promise."

I shook my head. "I thank you for the mercy of it but Master that is not why I looked at you that way."

Master Maxx appeared shocked. "Nein? Then what caused this alarm in you over this story?"

I frowned. "I was upset that my dad hurt you Master. If he is still alive, I will kill him along with Peter, Debbie and Russell. No one hurts my man and lives to brag about it. I would help you kill that stupid black collar asshole, but I already know you killed Olaf a long time ago."

Master Maxx hugged me tightly, appearing overwhelmed with affection. "You are simply too good to be the truth. I certainly don't deserve such a treasure. I tell you about this dishonor of my being unable to prevent a theft of service and you are willing to kill your own father to avenge the worthless Mad Maxx. How can I not love you more than my own life? Not possible. Wait, how do you know I killed Olaf? I never said that."

I hugged him back with pure adoration. "Because Master, you are a man of your word, and you promised him you were going to do it. I bet he is buried next to Vilber outside the Haus door."

He laughed out loud in glee. "Ah, you know me too well Meine Liebe. I suppose you don't need to hear the rest of this story then since you seem to think you know the ending?"

I shook my head then turned around to settle back in. "I apologize for my ignorance Master. I had no right to assume anything until you told me what to believe. I await your mercy or punishment, either of which I am truly grateful for."

My Master feigned indignation. "Ah, you ruined the fun of swatting you with my cane, Meine Liebe. If you are grateful for the thud, then I must deny it. As for my mercy, what the hell is that? I know nothing of it and neither do you. I seem to notice we sit on a stinking mattress, in a cell, and right upstairs are two of the foulest people on Earth waiting to fuck you and me too if they get half the chance. Where the fuck is the mercy in that?"

I shook my head. "You are right, there is no such a thing as mercy Master. At least not for us there isn't. We can't even escape our nightmares when we go to sleep. I finally understand what you meant when you said you can never grant it to me. Even my Master cannot give me what doesn't exist no matter how much I beg him."

There was a long silence and then he kissed my head gently. "Damn. I better start slapping those big brains out of you quick or prepare myself for you murdering me one day. That kind of intelligence in one so young is both awe inspiring and fucking scary as hell. You are correct, but I didn't think you would understand until you were much older."

I shrugged., "You are not going to slap me to stupid, and I am not going to murder you Master. We love each other so much. I suppose that will be the thing that will mess up our plans the most. I can't kill you then run away like I wanted, and you will have trouble training me because of it. I guess we will just have to be together until we die. Nobody else would have us anyway."

Master Maxx swatted me with his cane making me yell out in shock. "Okay you need to stop creeping me out, meine demonseed Frau. Shut up and listen to the story. If you say another wise fucking thing to me tonight I swear I will forget myself, try to run off with you, and end up fucking us both over when the authorities catch us. I go to jail, and you get sent back to this hell hole without your man to protect you. You are only nine. Think like a fucking kid will you please."

I sighed then nodded. "As you wish Master."

He shuddered a moment then said, "For the record, ja we will be together until we die but not because no one will have us. Meine Liebe, nobody can understand us, nor will they be capable of handling a Priceless. In fact, I believe there are few that even deserve the gifts we can offer them. Now on with the story, shit, you really freak me the hell out Meine Liebe. Do you believe in past lives? Don't answer that. Okay, where were we? Oh hell, that's right, that little temper tantrum Master Malfred threw at my expense."

When Karl had his fill, he reached down and pulled back up my breeches. Olaf and Louis pulled me off the table then held me to face him. He tried to get me to look him in the eyes. I could do nothing but silently weep and tremble. I was a bit stressed out and in too much pain to give a damn about anything he was desirous of saying to me.

The men all chuckled while he bobbed and moved his head all around trying to catch my gaze. He tired of his game and grabbed my chin forcing my face to look at him. I refused even then by keeping my eyes to the floor.

That made him laugh. "What's the matter Mad Maxx? Feeling a bit sheepish about being the easy piece of ass? Ah, well don't let that bother you. None of us think less of you for it. Hell, we never thought much of you to begin with, did we boys?" The others all snickered and nodded their heads while grumbling he was correct.

Karl held up his hand to silence them. "You better get over it. You see Malfred told all of us to chase you all we like. Whenever any of us get the chance, alone or together, we are going to hold you down and fuck you until you wish for death. You are nothing but a stupid silver whore boy. I see nothing special about you. That Master Jonas and the other Elders act like you are made of platinum or something. Well, I just tasted that metal of yours and while I did enjoy your favors greatly, I find nothing worth insulting a Dominant of my brother's caliber over it. In fact, if I have my way, you'll be fertilizing the fields by spring. My daughter deserves better, and I have just the boy in mind for the job of Priceless that soon will have an opening. I be seeing you soon little nothing. We'll all be visiting you soon."

I looked up at him then forced the words through my swollen vocal cords. "Go fuck yourself, Karl. All of you can. I will kill every Gott damned one of you. One at a time or together. Makes no difference to me." I then spit into his face. *Probably not a smart move there, but as I said, I was a little stressed. I guess I wasn't thinking so clearly, ja?*

That pissed Karl off. He punched me in my stomach again. Olaf and Louis let me go and I hit the floor on my knees as I did before, unable to catch my breath. He kicked me with all his strength sending me to my back. Within moments all them were on me kicking and hitting me. I covered my head and gasped for air unable to fight any of them back.

I assumed they were going to keep on until one delivered the killing blow. Wolf came to his senses first. It took him a few attempts to call off his buddies in their attacking me. Karl kicked longer than the others, but finally relented when Wolf loudly reminded him that Master Malfred said not to kill me.

Olaf laughed then said, "Well, the boy isn't worth being sent to the yard over that is for sure. In fact, I wouldn't give my piss for him."

Karl led out a gasp then smiled as he undid his pants. "You are so wrong, Olaf. I intend to give meine to him." He immediately began to urinate on the boys flesh.

The other three men howled in laughter, then they joined him in relieving themselves of their water on me. There was nothing I could do. I was too beaten to even attempt to move. I had to lay there and tolerate this indignity. I closed my eyes and attempted to get to my fantasy world with my Annette. I was startled out of my plan to go stupid when I heard a crash at the door.

I groaned in agony when suddenly Olaf fell forward right on top of me. I pushed on him trying to get away. Then in the same quickness as he came down, he was lifted up. I tried to rise but found myself too injured to do anything other than moan and barely lift my head.

I almost fainted at the sight my eyes reported back to the wheel room. All around the cell men were engaged in hand to hand combat. I gasped as I saw my father Peter punch Karl in the face, sending the Dominant to his knees with blood gushing from his nose.

My attention was called to the left of me when once again Olaf fell to the floor. His attacker was Master Leo. The prissy schwuler had one mean right hook. He come at the black collar brute when he tried to rise. He promptly knocked him back to his ass.

Wolf was battling with the furious Vampire. *Look, I couldn't make that shit up if I wanted. A man calling himself Wolf fighting a bat. Had I not been there I wouldn't have believed that shit either.* Both big men were bloody as hell as they punched and threw each other around the cell. A Dominant called Byron was beating the hell out of Master Malfred and to my shock, Egon was smacking Louis around like a red headed step kind.

I laid my head back down and took a deep breath bracing against the pain. I forced myself to sit up, then to stand. Master Leo, who had sent Olaf running for the hills, rushed for me and caught me just before I collapsed back to the earth.

He snuggled me close but with much gentleness and whispered in my ear, "Be still, meine hase. Lean your weight on your Leo. I will get you out of here." I saw Master Peter slam into Karl which caused him to retreat right behind the black collar brute.

Master Peter looked over and saw Master Leo trying to slip me out of the cell. He came at us with speed and used his own flesh to block me from further injury that could be caused by the battling men all around us.

Once we got out the door, Master Peter turned around and picked me up into his arms like the bride. "Leo, get in front. I got the boy. Head for your place, I will follow. Hurry, he needs a doctor. He is busted up bad. Shit, I don't know if he is going to make it." I heard his voice, but it seemed so far away.

I giggled as I watched the ceiling rushing over my head. I wondered what he was speaking about, I felt fine. I was hardly injured at all, or at least I couldn't feel the pain of it anymore if I were. My father carried me with speed trailing behind my Master Leo. That strange sound of rushing water filled my ears again. I felt sick to my stomach. I tried to stop it, but I vomited all over my chest and Master Peter, yikes. He didn't seem angry, weird.

I looked at my chest to see that I was wearing a crimson colored blouse. Funny as I thought I was wearing a white one earlier. My memory does slip sometimes you know.

Thankfully, Master Jonas finally turned down that fucking radio of his. I no longer heard it though I couldn't seem to hear anything else either except that angry river. Or maybe that was a train coming.

Chapter 62: Close Call

Master Peter looked down at me with an expression of fear. “Christian Axel, my boy, can you hear me? Speak to me. Stay awake I beg of you. We are getting you help, little one. Listen to your better and do as you are told.” He said gently as he rushed behind Master Leo.

I felt dizzy and sick to my stomach. There was a strange silence falling over me like the kind you experience during a heavy snowfall. I noticed the sweat was pouring off my face, and I was unsure where the hell I actually was located. Nothing was making sense. I heard my father’s instructions and did my best to do as he said.

I smiled at him without the ability to recognize his identity to me. “Sure thing. I am happy to have the sausage. Did you bring enough for my hound? Why is the river so angry? Can you hear that water? Do you think it is contaminated? That is why it flows with fury, ja?” I suddenly felt panic rising within me.

Master Peter and Master Leo had managed to get me to the apartment. As the schwuler Elder unlocked his door, I began to fight with all I had against Master Peter. I thought he was trying to hurt me like those men did. It was the only thing I could seem to remember, that I was being attacked you know. For some reason, I was terribly confused and beyond faint.

My father was careful not to strike me back as I began hitting, punching and spitting at him. I wailed loudly, begging for aid. Master Leo turned around in a fright to see Master Peter keeping me restrained from getting out of his arms.

He gasped. “Peter. Put him down. He is freaking out. You will hurt him if you continue to hold him like that.” He come to help me get out of my father’s arms.

Master Peter shouted out in anger, plus he had to yell louder than me to be heard. “Leo, Gott dammit. The boy is dying. I suspect those rat bastards have ruptured his spleen. You see this bloody vomit. That is internal bleeding, fool. If we don’t stop the hemorrhaging soon, and get him a blood transfusion, he is finished. He is demonstrating confusion caused by his injuries. Stay the fuck back and pay no mind to anything he says. You must allow me to handle this. I am a surgeon. I know the seriousness of what I am look at here. Call that new doctor, tell him to bring every fucking thing he has to prep for surgery and his blood pressure monitor. I need a bed that the boy can say in for weeks if need be. Hurry the fuck up. We are running out of time to even have a chance to save him. Do what I tell you without wasting time with questions or bring me a fucking shovel to bury him. Make up your mind, Leo.”

Master Leo recoiled as if struck. “Dying? Oh Gott, nein. Please save him Peter.” He turned around and nearly kicked in his own door leading Master Peter down his hallway to his bedroom.

I wailed incoherently in terror, sweating like a field worker as Master Peter attempted to lay me on the mattress.

I come up to a sitting position feeling sicker than I had ever felt in my life. I held on to my father as I leaned over and vomited that bloody crap uncontrollably on the floor. Master Leo gasped with tears in his eyes at that sight. He rushed off to make the phone call to the Haus doctor.

Master Peter held me up as I emptied my stomach. He appeared unaffected by the foulness of it. When I finished I noticed the pain was horrid in my abdomen. I moaned in agony as he helped me to lay on my back.

He pulled up my shirt and attempted to press on my belly. I immediately tried to block him from touching me anywhere near my left shoulder or left side of my stomach. I would wail and panic, even tried to hit him, when he got close to touching those areas. I wasn't afraid he was molesting me, I just unconsciously knew to protect that area at all costs, you know. Not sure how I knew this, but I did.

Master Leo come back into the room to find me struggling against Master Peter getting a look at my tummy.

He stood there staring at me, his eyes wet with tears. "His color is bad Peter. The doctor is on his way. Were you able to find out if he is…"

Master Peter growled out. "Ja, I already told you. He is likely going to die, Leo. I cannot take him to the hospital and even if I did, it is too late. He would die on the way there. It is so far away. I was right. His spleen is ruptured, see that lump? That is the blood collecting in his abdomen. If that hole in him is large, he will not survive unless I can get his spleen removed. Trouble is, that to do surgery here in the Haus would assure death later from infection or shock. Right this moment I need to give him a blood transfusion or he will be dead within a few hours if that leak is not too bad. If it is, then there is nothing I do which is going to save him. I need him to be still and remain calm. When the doctor gets here, Leo, I intend to induce a light coma in him. He will need twenty-four-hour monitoring for up to two weeks if he lives. Otherwise, he will die in the next couple hours when he goes into shock or bleeds to death." He wiped his forehead appearing most agitated.

Master Leo covered his mouth with tears breaking out heavily. "You think he is going to die, don't you, Peter? Be honest please. I cannot deal with lies at this moment."

Master Peter nodded as he reached out to stroke my cheek lovingly. "Ja, Leo. He probably isn't going to make it. There is no way for me to even know how bad the injury is without the x-rays." He sighed sounding saddened.

I felt sick to my stomach again. I could hear what they were saying, but to be honest it was not sinking into my brain for some reason. I was feeling like I couldn't breathe again. I gasped and trembled, while gagging. Panic was making me her bitch for truth.

I tried to sit up to see if that would aid me in getting more air. Master Peter gently pushed me down to my back. "There now, meine heart. You are feeling afraid, that is normal. You cannot breathe better sitting up. This is the blood putting pressure on your lungs. Where is that fucking doctor? Shit."

I moaned in pain. “Please mercy, Master. I cannot breathe. Where is my puppy? Somone get my pup before he is injured. They are coming. Do you hear them? Help. Please someone help me. My stomach hurts. I am going to be sick.” I yelled out in my terror as I again began to gag.

Master Leo ran from the room to the sounds of knocking at the door. Master Peter helped me turn and vomit more blood. The Haus doctor come rushing into the room to find my father returning me to my back gasping loudly with a clear rattle in my breathing sounds.

The doctor looked at the blood on the floor, then went back to Master Peter. “Oh shit, this is bad. Okay, uhm, Leo, I need you to call my assistant, here is her number. Tell her to hurry. Leo tells me you are a surgeon, Peter? Have you assessed the situation?”

Master Peter nodded as Master Leo took off to make the phone call. “Ja, he is demonstrating symptoms of dizziness, confusion, sweating, guarding of the left upper quadrant, shortness of breath, a rapid pulse, change in mental alertness, nausea with blood vomit, complaining of abdominal pain, has observable lump under rib cage, weakness, and recently suffered a traumatic blow to his abdomen. I believe he has a ruptured spleen with internal bleeding of an unknown severity. The boy is fourteen years old and weighs about one hundred and twenty pounds. I cannot be sure, doesn’t show fever yet. I would like to check his blood pressure but am willing to bet it is dangerously low. We will need to do an emergency blood transfusion, possible surgical repair, and the patient needs to be induced into a catatonic state for his own safety. Before you say a fucking word doctor, it is too late to send him for aid, and I know this boy. He would rather die than be locked in that collar. The Haus law is that he leaves for aid, he is trapped in his metal. We must do whatever can be done right here in this room and bed. All we can do is hope for the best. Oh, and welcome to Das Kaiser Haus."

The doctor's eyes went wide. "You wish to do surgery here? Uhm, the boy will die of infection if we don't kill him outright from lack of the proper tools. A blood transfusion? Are you insane? I will call for the ambulance myself."

Master Peter stood up and glared at that doctor with fury in his eyes. "You get your ass over here and aid me in saving this kid or after I bury him, I will come to add your corpse to keep him company. You will learn that the human being can survive longer than you ever imagined. In the war not so long ago, there were no fancy hospitals or operating rooms. Doctors were forced to save the injured soldier in the bloody mud right where they fell. This bed and room are a sight better than all that. I will call a favor and get us all the things we need for this boy's care, which is if he lives through the next few critical hours. Give me your blood pressure machine now."

The doctor let out his breath. "Alright, I hear you Peter. I admit I am new to this Haus. You need not call any favors. I will get all the supplies we need without quarrel." He come forward with his doctor bag and the two of them worked together to take my blood pressure.

Master Peter kept me from pushing the doctor and pressure cuff off me. He gasped when he read the numbers. Then reported I needed that blood transfusion right away. My father gave him my blood type and specifics. Master Leo come back to the room only to have to lead the doctor to his phone.

I felt faint and things were getting pretty dark by this time. I could barely breathe. I caste a glance at Master Peter and smiled weakly at him.

"I suppose this is it, ja? Not going to escape that pale rider this time am I, Master?" I felt my eye lids starting to feel heavy.

He rubbed his eyes then took my hand. "Christian, listen to me. You need to fight. I don't want to lose you, my boy. If you cannot do it for me then do it to keep Malfred from winning."

I closed my eyes with the sensation of falling within myself filling me. "I want to tell you a secret Master. I don't care about any of you or the games you played. I only wanted to be left alone. Do you hear my lambs? They are such beautiful animals. Tell Master Leo to take loving care of Der Makellos. I think I am going to nap for a while. I am going to see my Annette and Ryker too."

I heard Master Peter sniffing. Huh, he was crying for me. I admit things are a bit fuzzy for these last moments before the doctor put me in the light coma. It is not something I can ever prove or even believe.

Just before I went into the silent void I thought I heard Master Peter say, "I love you Christian Axel. I never told you this, but you have made me proud all your life. No matter what terrible thing has happened, you endured it with silent strength. You are beyond magnificent. Far too good for me, or any of these sonsofbitches here. Though I am unworthy, I would beg you grant me one more proud moment by beating death. I confess to you, it is my dream to sit at your graduation from medical school and tell the man next to me with a prideful smile on my face that beautiful, intelligent, young man right there is my son. Someday I would like to bounce my grandchildren on my knee."

I slipped away to the place between life and death at that moment. I heard nor saw another thing for two weeks.

Long after I had broken my collar, Master Leo would tell me what happened during the time my life hung in the balance when I was inpatient at that hospital I told you about.

THE STORY TOLD TO MASTER MAD MAXX REGARDING THE TWO WEEKS AFTER HIS SPLEEN RUPTURED WHILE HE WAS IN A COMA

"According to Master Leo he came back into the room to find Master Peter and the Haus doctor working hard to prepare me for the blood transfusion. He said I was no longer responsive, and that Master Peter told him I likely would never awaken.

Despite their certainty I would not pull through, they continued the effort to save me any way possible. Master Leo told me my father granted his own fluids for my first blood transfusion (there were many over the next few days). The doctor's nurse arrived along with his medical supplies (IV stuff, blood for transfusions, surgical tools if it came to such a thing) within the hour.

He said he felt very useless and frightened as the men and the nurse worked non-stop for hours trying to stop the internal bleeding and stabilize my condition. He was never able to tell me what exactly the two of them did, but it is possible they opened me up and repaired the spleen with stitches. I say he may be correct since I do have a scar in the right area that I have never been able to explain.

Master Jonas, Egon, and Byron arrived at Master Leo's apartment after Master Leo was run out of the room to allow the surgeons to work without an audience. He told the three of them of the seriousness of this situation.

The Vampire apparently lost his temper. He went next door and kicked in Master Malfred's door. He dragged the man back to Master Leo's apartment. He had Byron and Egon "sit on him" while he went to Master Claus's apartment to report the sad news that Mad Maxx the Elder's Priceless collar was on his death bed.

The oldest of the Elders came running with tears in their eyes and broken hearts, or so Master Leo reported. All the sixth floor, minus Mistress Cora, with Byron and Egon sat in Master Leo's living room together waiting to hear the announcement of my final breath.

Master Leo told me that the Vampire, Master Claus and Master Bladrick told Master Malfred the second it was announced I had expired, Malfred was going to join me. They also said that Vilber, Olaf, Anna, Mila, Volf, Louis, Karl, and Elsa would be joining him for their part in the crime of "killing the Priceless and thieves of special services of the Elders." I was told that Master Malfred trembled in terror and even prayed for my survival though dough it was only to save his own hide.

I was told that all the Elders sat in solemn silence for a long time, many of them in tears at my sorry predicament. Master Leo said he held Der Makellos and cried like a baby many times the several hours that the two surgeons worked to save my life. He said he never cared if any of the others saw it either. He blamed himself for not heeding the sinister behavior of Master Malfred before the hijacking.

Master Claus asked during that long wait to hear the details of how I had ended up in such dire straits. Master Leo told him that he was being held by Vilber, Anna, Mila, and Alexie and then Elsa in short order. Master Peter come out of the thudding room to find out why my Master and I were running late. Peter hates when anyone is late to anything, as you are aware Meine Liebe. I nodded while blowing out my breath at this most true statement.

He found Master Leo in his most desperate situation. Master Peter immediately attacked Vilber while the schwuler Elder took on Alexie. The FemDoms ran away and so did Alexie the second the tides turned out of their favor. Master Peter managed to capture Vilber.

The two angry Dominants took Vilber to the thudding room and beat the holy terror out of him until he told them where Master Malfred and the others had taken me. It was a good thing they were able to get Vilber to spill his guts too. Otherwise, with that Haus being so full of hiding spots the Dominants would never have found me in time to save my life.

Master Peter knew that he would need strength to handle the five strong men. He found Egon and Byron standing in the hall of the torture chamber and asked them for aid. Egon readily agreed without quarrel. Bryon was also happy to assist for a price. That we will discuss later, ja?

The four of them were rushing to rescue me from my dilemma when they ran into Master Jonas. As luck would have it, he had been headed down to the torture chamber to tell Master Leo he had found a lawyer willing to do as they wanted, but he needed some information from him first. The Dominants and Egon told the Vampire of my kidnapping by Master Malfred.

They all ran fast as possible to try to end the horror but as you already know the damage had been done. The only good thing is the group of "heroes" did manage to thrash the criminals before they scattered to the four winds and found me before it was too late.

I was severely injured when Karl punched me in the stomach as ordered by Master Malfred. The cruel Voting Council Member, your father Meine Liebe, managed to get a shot right into my spleen. That ruptured the organ mildly. Had that been the end of it, I would have still been ill but not as significantly.

What caused the deadly internal bleeding, as I had always feared would happen one day, was their rough intercourse with the boy. As they took their turns showing off their brutality to each other while bullying me they slammed my abdomen into that wooden table just right. That constant thrusting opened that small wound to a larger deadlier one. That is why I heard that water rushing in my ears when Olaf was raping me. You see my blood pressure was already rapidly dropping thanks to the bleeding inside my chest. My confusion, a symptom of internal bleeding, caused me to mistake my racing heart for panic, and the blood in my ears for water.

Then when they beat on me, well they really set off that internal bleeding. By the time my Masters arrived to beat down my rapists I was already half-way across the river Styx. My father witnessed the ashen color of my flesh, blood vomit, and could feel my irregular heart rate. He could see the bruises and cuts from the beating and realized the brutes had busted one of my organs up in their harsh thrills with me.

You must remember I was only a little fellow back then. I couldn't have been more than five foot six and as you heard earlier, barely over one hundred pounds. These brutes were full grown, huge males. Two of them were over two hundred pounds, and the other two damned close to that weight as well. I was too fragile for them to assault me without any mercy or care taken, not to mention beating the hell out of me like they did. I am still shocked they didn't kill me outright when kicking the shit out of me on that floor.

Well, he may be a perverted child molester fiend, but your Master Peter is also an amazing surgeon. He recognized my symptoms immediately as those of someone with life-threatening internal bleeding with a likely hemorrhage in the spleen, stomach or intestine. Had it been any other of my organs, I would have died no matter what they tried. I actually was lucky it was my spleen though I didn't feel so damned blessed at the time.

Master Leo said Master Claus listened to the story without saying a thing. When he was finished reporting the events and those there acknowledged this is indeed how it all happened. Only Master Malfred didn't agree that is what happened. He was outvoted since four of my rescuers were there and only him to represent the rapists. Master Claus let out an angered wail.

He, with Master Bladrick egging him on, informed Master Malfred that his brother Karl, Olaf, Vilber, Alexie, Volf, Louis, and the three FemDoms would all be put to the yard if I did indeed die for truth. Allegedly, he told Master Malfred he would have him castrated and sent to the dungeon for life and he'd make sure it was a long terrible one.

If I were to survive, there was no way that Gretta was to hear of the raping of the Priceless from anyone. The Elders all agreed amongst themselves, this time even Master Malfred agreed, the incident never happened.

Malfred would be forced to pay all my upkeep and medical charges, and to add to insult his brother Karl, and his soldiers Mila and Alexie, were demoted from the Council. Byron would be raised in Karls place. Master Peter, because he aided in saving the Elders' collar, would name the other two that would fill the final two slots.

The two powerful Elders told Master Malfred if he had a problem, or any of the others named did, with his punishment then they could take it up with Grisham and Gustov. That was his way of warning them all any opening of their mouths about their theft of service would result in them going to the yard right behind the Priceless.

It was crystal clear that Master Claus intended to break Master Malfred's and all the Krauses' power in that Haus for all time. He had been dealing with that fucker's cruel maneuvering for over fifteen years. This latest attempt to gain the upper hand had very likely cost him the only thing that brought the old man pleasure. Do recall they thought I would die. He had enough at last. That Elder, or so I was told, was out for blood this time. He wasn't playing around with that idiot Uncle Malfred of yours anymore.

Vilber was taken to the dungeon for a month and joined shortly thereafter by his buddy Olaf. That brute black collar was happy to do his time next to Vilber after Master Jonas finished beating the holy fuck out of him. He feared the Vampire would kill him if he saw him anytime soon. He was also told if I died they both would be disemboweled by the Vampire and Master Leo before the Guard came for them, yikes.

Oh, hell, did I forget to tell you that Master Jonas didn't beat Olaf up right away? First, he selected four huge fellows of much vigor to rape him soundly. Ja, my man did indeed, ha. I may not always see eye to eye with Jonas, but this was one time that I have to say he did right by me. Olaf was the only black collar involved. Had any of the other rapists been lesser he would have done the same to them as well no doubt.

While it didn't erase what Olaf did to me nor grant my dignity back, you can sure believe it made me smile with satisfaction when I was told about it. After I was well enough for excitement that is. The Vampire reported Olaf screamed like a girl and he was a virgin to bottom sex with a man unlike your idiot Mad Maxx. Ah, you can bet old Olaf was not the happy bride in white that afternoon of his consummation, ja?

"I apologize, Meine Liebe. I don't mean to stop here but I need to laugh for a minute." Master Maxx began to howl at his memory of Olaf losing his anal virginity by gang rape.

I giggled wildly with him for several minutes as I imagined Olaf crying like a little girl and his butt bleeding for days after that punishment.

Master Maxx hugged me tightly. "I love you so much, meine Frau. You understand me so damned well. No matter what I have endured, you were worth the pain of it. I would do it all again too if I knew you would be here waiting on me on the other side. But hey, let's not do it all again, ja? I say we hurry your agony the fuck up and then we both can be smiling over nice things and forget all the bad."

I nodded while calming my laughter. "Your pleasure is mine Master." I smiled as he put me back in my spot on his thigh and began his story once more.

QUICK NOTE: I would apologize for the two of us demonstrating such cruel behavior as laughing at someone being gang raped but you know what? I am not sorry for it. That motherfucker was a rapist that Christian Axel had never hurt in his life.

Olaf was over two hundred pounds and over thirty years of age. What the hell was he doing raping a little boy of thirteen (that blow job scene at Drexel's), then again at fourteen (the gang rape).

He even tried to kill him many times because Christian Axel had "spooky eyes." Really? Who does that? Olaf had that coming and as far as I am concerned, so did Vilber. Though, Vilber was smarter than Olaf and didn't join in the gang rape.

Dare was one other black collar involved in this whole mess. I suppose the three of them weren't thinking about the repercussions of fooling around with the Elders' only silver. You know of course I am speaking of the beautiful Elsa.

Well for her part in this fiasco, she was exiled for good. The girl was new to the Haus and that made her vulnerable to the fiercest of punishments available. Once it was discovered she was Olaf's betrothed, yeah more than his girlfriend but his bride to be, the Vampire decided to really fuck the black collar brute up his tailpipe (figuratively this time). He had Elsa sent away to Das Kaiser Haus's sister Haus. Ja, that's right, the same one Master Malfred's Tamina had been sent to.

You see Master Malfred and Karl had a half-brother. He was hot shit at this sister Haus. Where that place is I still don't know to this day. They sent that girl to serve Master Malfred's brother called Jipsum for all her days.

Elsa was a black collar. She could have dropped her collar status and lit out on her own away from the Haus rules. Then she could still marry the brute and have his ugly kinder. To Olaf's surprise, she didn't cut off her dark color. The girl took the exile and left him at the altar. The rumor is that she immediately married a door guard brute from the new Haus.

When the dust settled, many lives were changed or even ruined by this horrible gang rape. Olaf and Vilber wore many scars from their beatings. Olaf was no longer nonempathetic to anal rape and lost his fiancé. Alexie, Mila, and Karl were booted back to the first floor with the young Dominants. Elsa was sent away to never be seen again. Master Malfred lost his bid to gain back his special service rights and owed a huge bill for his part in this scheme.

Master Malfred's power in the Haus now was clipped like a pet birds wings. His only hope was the tiny little blue eyed beauty that called his brother her father. He took his punishment with quiet honor, much out of character for him by the way, thinking he would be patient and wait for a better day. I wish I could say he learned his lesson, but men like Master Malfred never do. I would have to deal with the Krause curse several more times before I finally got those sacred bolt cutters in my paws.

So, what about Louis, and Anna? They were the only two that got nothing for the part they played, but both would get their comeuppance another day. For now, do remember their names Meine Liebe. They both were young Dominants looking to make their names in the Haus. With black hearts and revenge in their minds, I was sure to have to deal with them soon enough as well. And deal with them I sure did. That is a story aways off though. We will get to it in time.

While all this was going on, Master Peter and the Haus doctor were working tirelessly to save my sorry life. I was told by my father I had to be resuscitated three times, the second one, they were sure I was done. They even called it over and reported my death to the awaiting Elders.

Then to their shock I began to breathe once again. I was told there was much celebration after moments of vailing in grief. Even Master Malfred was seen weeping when they thought me dead. For many days I was more dead than alive according to the reports from everyone there.

To Master Peter's credit, he never left my bed side the entire two weeks of my peril. Neither did Master Leo. The two of them guarded my near comatose flesh with fierceness. The doctor reported I was not to be moved, awakened or stirred in any way or I could count the roots growing from my tree.

I was told I did awaken on occasion but that I was not logical or even coherent. I apparently didn't know who or where I was. When I did manage to find consciousness, Master Peter and Master Leo made sure I was gently restrained from tearing out my tubes, which apparently I tried to do several times. They took turns carefully attending my nature calls, feeding and changing all my dressings. I was beaten to shit with many stitches required apparently. Like I needed more scars.

The new Haus doctor was skilled and well learned, unlike the last motherfucker. He did an amazing job, with my father's aid, at snatching me from the clutches of that reaper. Death had to return to his place of darkness empty handed, likely cursing their names for doing what he was sure impossible.

On the fifteenth day, I awoke to find Master Peter sleeping in a chair on one side, and Master Leo gazing out his bedroom window behind him. I was startled to see all the tubes, and an IV bag above my head. I had no memory of anything. Yet sadly, that shit did return. I wish it hadn't but sucks to be me, ja?

I tried to speak and found my throat sore and voice barely audible. I had been intubated on a ventilator which was only removed a few days before. The clever fucks brought in one used in the war for field doctors. Master Leo heard my rasp and looked over with fear. He thought I was choking).

"Meine hase? Honey, you are awake," he yelled out in thrill when he realized I was looking at him with recognition this time.

I nodded. "Ja, can I have something to drink? Thank you for the mercy, Master," I croaked out.

Master Leo near ran over the top of Master Peter that had been pulled from his slumber by the squealing schwuler. "Of course, meine heart. Peter, look, Christian Axel is back with us at last."

Master Peter looked worn and had deep dark circles under his eyes. He smiled with pleasantness at me.

"Thank the Gotts. My boy, you scared the shit out of everyone," he said as he leaned forward and patted my hand with the tubes in it.

I narrowed my eyes. "I apologize for whatever I did, Master. Am I going to be thudded?" I trembled a bit thinking I may have tried to commit suicide or even hurt someone by the looks of it.

Master Leo laughed sounding relieved. "Hell, nein. Honey you didn't frighten everyone on purpose. Do you not remember anything?" He leaned forward and helped me to drink a glass of tea.

I gulped down the soothing liquid and thought hard to see if I could recall why I was laying in his bed ill. Then I remembered the cell, the sounds of those men, and the smell of piss. I closed my eyes and laid my head back shuddering.

"I remember what happened now, Master. Are you alright? I mean, did they hurt you too?" I didn't open my eyes trying to block out the flooding memory of that horrid gang rape business.

Master Leo let out his breath. "Nein, meine hase. I am fine. I escaped serious injury. You on the other hand have been playing cards with the boatman for the last fortnight."

I opened my eyes in a startle. "Two weeks? Oh nein, I will never catch up on my lessons at this rate. Shit, I need to get up and get back to work. Thank you for the mercy, Masters." I tried to sit up.

Master Peter rushed from his seat and pushed me back to the bed gently. "Oh no you don't, little man. You need at least another two weeks of calm, slow moving. You need to heal completely this time, Mad Maxx. I didn't work my ass off to save you only to have you throw it away being too quickly industrious. Your Masters will understand. They will not bother you until you have a full release from the doctor and me. In a few more days, you may get out of bed.

Then slowly you can get back to your tasks of service, but not today." He pulled out his blood pressure cuff and checked my vitals telling me to be still.

I laid their staring at the man. I remembered him beating up Karl, and his carrying me to the bed. I even recalled his telling me he loved me and was proud of me too. I heard him admit to being my father, desiring I graduate medical school, then giving him a chance to know my children. I took a deep breath to ask him about this, but at the last second stayed my tongue.

I also remembered him bonding me, then raping me as a little boy of twelve. I recalled his laughter at my cries of humiliation and agony. I thought of his forcing himself on me in the dungeon to pay for his aiding me to escape the clutches of the man he helped put me in that very bed. I could not forgive any of that, nor forget it either. He was just as responsible as my mother for my sorry station in life.

I swore right then and there, the second I finished my medical school, found my Frau, I would kill this sonofabitch. He saved my life, sure. I was not that foolish kid Maximillian though. I was the experienced Mad Maxx. I knew my old man kept me alive for his own sick desires and dark games of power. That shit he said was driven by guilt when he thought all his dreams for a future he had invested his own blood into was coming to an end.

The last thing I wanted was this child molesting cocksucker anywhere near my kind Frau or our children. Shit, then he could fuck us all, ja? I mean he already has called his special services rights with my Frau of nine. I wasn't wrong to see him for the monster he is that day so long ago. Master Peter has his good qualities as long as you are not one of his own. He likes keeping it in the family you know. Yuck!.

My glaring at him was interrupted when Master Jonas come barging into the room. I saw the man and immediately whimpered in fear. I knew Master Peter told me not to be out of that bed, but I knew the Vampire would be pissed as I hadn't served him in more than fourteen days.

He looked at me and a wide grin, full of those pointy teeth of his, broke out on his face. "Christian Axel, he lives. Ah, this is a wonderful day. Does this mean the danger has finally passed Peter?" He came rushing for the bed and I cowered a bit despite myself.

Master Peter put out his arm preventing Master Jonas from coming any closer. "Ja, the danger has passed. He will live unless he is overused too fast. This boy is neither to be excited nor molested in any way for at least another two weeks Jonas. If I had it my way, never again by any of you."

Master Jonas's smile melted to one of anger. "Oh? Is that so? Well, for starters you have no power to stop me from enjoying my man anyway I wish, Peter. Furthermore, I don't like you insinuating I am abusing him, or any of his Masters for that matter."

Master Peter growled with a frown. "You know I have held my tongue all this time, but I will not any longer. I want the boy to hear what I am about to say to both of you. When this Priceless was under my roof he rarely carried a mark on him outside his proper thudding areas. I cannot speak for what Xavier did, but I did notice since you stole him from me the boy is always a mess. I have never seen the likes of the bruises, cuts, marks, welts, handprints, and broken bones he has suffered since your submission, and yours too Leo. I trained this beautiful submissive with my own hands. He is graceful, mindful, and talented. He will do whatever you ask without beating him or at least used to. Am I to assume you ask something so bad the boy feels compelled to fight you over it? Perhaps, you all enjoy beating him up then? Nein? Ah, then I think maybe none of you know a Gott damned thing about the protocol of D/s relationships. You simply command the boy to service you and if he does it without quarrel or you thud him in a way that causes pain with injury. I don't know what the fuck you all are doing to him, but you would be wise to stop it now."

Master Leo crossed his arms and shot a look of indignation at Master Jonas then responded. "You motherfucker. How dare you accuse any of us of abusing or neglecting the Priceless? I have news for you, the marks Christian Axel wears as of late you helped put there. He was not the schizophrenic when you held his collar Peter. He is one now. Your friends have harassed, bullied and stressed the fuck out of him. This has caused seizures, self-abuse, and I dare say that fucking gang rape with a severe beating he just barely survived. That is not on us, fool. Whatever issues we have within our ranks is not your business to discuss with your better. For that matter, how dare you undermine us in front of our collar."

Master Jonas put up his hand demanding silence from the railing Master Leo. "Let this go brother. Peter saved our Priceless and ward. If he wants to insult us, let him get that out of his system. Do we really care what he thinks? It is not truth he is sharing, but what you say sure as the shit is. Christian Axel now belongs to you and me for all our lives, even after he breaks that metal. Don't let Peter get you into a pissing contest over the thing he threw away, not once, but twice now."

I shot a look of terror at the Vampire not understanding his words. "I belong to you and Master Leo for all your lives even without my collar. I don't understand this Master. I thought when I am the Dominant no one can own me."

Master Jonas smiled with thrill. "Ah, ja, normally that is truth, but you are ill with a debilitating brain disease my boy. You will need a guardian for that."

I shook my head. "Nein. I don't have schizophrenia. You cannot lie to the courts and get a fake paper on me Master. That is illegal."

Master Peter sucked in his breath and looked at the floor. "You motherfucker. I would say I cannot believe you did this but that would be bullshit. I do know you are capable of doing this horror. What did you do, bribe the judge? How did you manage to get it done without any records? Hell, when did you do it. I have been waiting for weeks to hear back on my own court date to take guardianship. There is no way you got in before me."

I jerked my head to stare at Master Peter. "What? You were trying to do this to me too? Why? I have earned the right to be free. None of you have the right to stop me."

Master Jonas yelled out causing me to stop my complaints immediately. "We do have the right and you are schizophrenic, Christian Axel. For your information Peter I needed not bribe anyone. I had the records from the late Haus doctor Briton. I admit I took advantage of your compromised position here attending the boy to jump over you in the court date. Oh shit, I just can't do it Leo. Sorry brother, but this is too good not to just, well grind it into Peter you know?" The Vampire shot a wicked smile at Master Leo.

Master Leo looked at the floor appearing suddenly shameful. "Nein, Jonas, please not right now. Not in front of Christian Axel I beg of you. This discussion can wait."

Master Peter narrowed his eyes in suspiciousness. "What the fuck is going on here. Leo, Jonas. one of you better start speaking. I mean it."

The Vampire laughed. "Well, I was going to wait to announce my good news until the boy was back on his feet, but this is a fine day for it. I went and got myself married, Peter. The lovely lady could barely wait to get my wedding ring on her finger. That is because she couldn't wait to get into my pants, for my wallet. That was okay though. I didn't really want her either. I was interested in what came out of her rather than putting anything in. Her son was the reason I offered to share a bank account with that crazy bitch of meine. Ah, the second she signed the papers, she granted me the son I always wanted. It was amazing too, since most of the time you have to wait nine months. Not my gal. She gave me one already bonded to me by blood. I filed the paperwork to terminate her rights to him and took him for my own. Agnette is quite thrilled that her boy brought her a fortune twice in his short lifetime. Christian Axel now is legally, legitimately, and unbreakably my own son, and I am officially his lifelong guardian. My brother Leo, well a few false papers and he became my blood brother on paper. Shit I managed to find a family in only two weeks, can you believe it? A wife, a son, a brother, oh and a man too, amazing, ja?"

I sat up with a startle as his words echoed in my ears. "What, nein. This cannot be. You cannot be my legal father," I wailed out in agony realizing that my mother was just the kind of woman that would do exactly that.

I gasped. "Wait, Master? Jonas is your daddy. So, does that mean Peter isn't anymore?"

He nodded. "Ah ja, Meine Liebe. He got Agnette to fill out papers claiming him the father since she never did such a thing for Gerard nor for Peter. She sold me out to the Vampire for an undisclosed amount and promptly left town, as usual for that bitch. That is why I have two last names. I have to use my legal one, the one Jonas Weiß holds, in my practice and professional life but privately I use the one I was born to, Schmitz. Jonas isn't my real father any more than that Steve fellow Debbie married, or Russell is yours. Karl is your real father and Peter is meine. The real difference is that Jonas managed to get Agnette to sign away her rights as my parent to the false father of her son. She then abandoned me to the Vampire's clutches for all time. I have never seen that woman since, nor has Peter. Good riddance to her. If I ever see that bitch again, I doubt I will be able to keep my hands from around her throat for what she did to me both times."

I groaned. "So that means Master Jonas can tell you what to do even though you broke your collar, Master?"

He nodded. "Well, kind of. It is complicated Meine Liebe and maybe you are too young yet to understand. Just know the man has his fangs in my neck for now. I have a plan to escape him when you are done breaking your own metal. We won't have to worry about having a bat in our bed. Now, Leo, which is a different story all together. He took advantage of Peter's being busy too. He is forever recorded as Jonas's brother. So that makes Leo my Uncle on paper. He also can sort of tell me what to do. Ah, if this a bit over your head we come back to it when I tell you about my life after medical school, ja?"

I smile., "As you wish Master. I am here for your pleasure."

Master Maxx giggled. "Gott damned right you are. Shit, I am starting to think about checking out that pleasure again real soon. Maybe I better get back on that story before I forget I am trying to teach my Frau, not fuck her to death before she is old enough to have lived, ja?"

My eyes went wide, and I turned around fast making sure to pull his arm around my little chest to keep him from taking special services.

That behavior made him laugh with much humor. "Ah. You are fucking adorable. Okay, I won't attack you for now. Beware meine little Demonseed Frau, I plan to get you later and often too."

I nodded. "I thank you for the mercy of it Master." Then I winced when I realized that was maybe the wrong canned protocol statement to give.

He really howled at that mistake. "I thank you for the mercy of it too, Meine Liebe. Though we both know that the kind of sex we have right now is not the fun kind for you, is it? Next time better think before you speak, ja? Where the hell was I? Ah ja, that bat found a way to make me a Vampire for truth."

Master Peter had to come restrain me to the bed I was throwing such a wild fit over this horrible news. He yelled at Master Leo to give him the sedative shot that was preloaded and sitting on his dresser.

Within only a few moments I found myself stabbed in the backside by a needle. Another few second passed and I found myself unable to get upset over anything. I bet I wouldn't have been anxious even if I had been set on fire. *Damn, that was the good shit, you know?*

I heard Master Peter yelling at the Vampire for stirring me up like that, but I really am fuzzy about the next few bits of information. I was laying there smiling and calm while the Dominants shouted at each other in full on fury. I found the whole thing funny at the time, but believe me, there was nothing humorous about this nightmare.

I heard Master Peter scream out, “You rat bastard. You took advantage of Agnette and me. How dare you, motherfucker.”

Then Master Jonas scoffed. “I took advantage, really Peter. That woman has waited for almost fifteen years for you to ask her to marry her and claim that boy as your own. Well, since you didn’t man up, then don’t be angry that this one did.”

Master Peter shot a worried look at me. “Watch what you say in front of the boy. He doesn’t know and he better never know.”

Master Leo growled out sounding disgusted. “He won’t remember any of this Peter. He is high as the kite. You sicken me. That is your beautiful boy right there and you brought him to this Haus, then you, oh fuck. I cannot even say it because it is so revolting.”

Master Jonas nodded with a smile. “Ah, ja I agree with you brother Leo. I thought I was a nasty bastard Peter. You, however, take the cake. I guess though now that I think on it, I am not any better. I am married to my own legal son and intend to sleep with him too for all my life. Guess he should be used to it though. I mean didn't you only recently brag that you trained him well? That you did."

Master Peter snorted. "You use my words against me, asshole. For starters we don't know that boy is really mine. Agnette slept with everyone. She lies too. How can anyone believe a fucking thing that bitch says. Hell, she married you for money and sold off her son twice. Maybe this kid is not even meine."

Master Leo and Master Jonas laughed bitterly, then the Vampire said, "Who you trying to lie to Peter? Funny that you can donate blood to that boy. Neither me nor Leo can. None of the other Elders can, I noticed. He also bares a strong resemblance to you, especially around the eyes and cheekbones. What do you think Leo? Is Agnette lying about the father?"

Master Leo shook his head still chuckling. "Hell no. Peter, give it up. That boy is the spitting image of you, and everyone can see it. They talk about it behind your back. Agnette always denied it, but his face tells on you. You may as well accept that Jonas taking credit for paternity and the responsibility of guardianship will end the tongues wagging about you. No one will dare to challenge Jonas. This was for the good of the son you have always denied. If you had cared even a bit for him, you would have done what he did to make the boy yours a long time ago. You hesitated and you lost your chance. Now you can just deal with it. What is done cannot be undone."

I giggled which startled the bitching Elders and Peter. "Can I see my puppy? My father has fleas. Can you loan me enough money for a flea collar for Der Makellos, Uncle Leo? I am happy to give you the blow job for it. My family fucks me over. Many say that, but Christian Axel is telling the truth of it." I laughed wildly at that. *Look don't judge me. I was higher than a hippy at a Grateful Dead concert, you know. Never heard of that band? Not my favorites. Kind of a cult group. Wait we are getting off topic.*

Somone brought my eager hound buddy into the room. However, I was nodding off from time to time by then. The sedative was working its magic with much vigor. I eventually went back to the quiet darkness of drug driven sleep. I barely remember even petting my playful friend.

The next two weeks I spent in that bed trying to come to grips with the horrors that began the month earlier. It was a lot to accept. The latest set of gang rapes had made me even jumpier than ever. My near death experience made me painfully aware that my fear of the Dominants in the Haus was all too real. Learning of my mother's disappearance and the Vampire's permanent relationship to me was more than a little disturbing.

Der hound was still missing. Christian had not come to aid us when we screamed as he had promised. I was more than a bit depressed. I felt overwhelmed by my task of learning all there was to know about thudding in only the five months I had left before I went before the vote.

Then dare was the cryptic words of Karl that echoed in my ears in the darkness of those long nights. He told me that all the men had been granted permission to hunt me for their lust in the hallways of that Haus. I assumed Olaf and Vilber had been neutralized but Karl and the others had been punished, but not severely.

There was no doubt in my mind that I should take that man's words to heart. He had nearly killed me, and he had admitted that he was looking to replace me with a boy of his choice. Things were looking as bad as they ever had in all my time in that fucking bat collar. I was no longer so sure I could beat the Haus at this game they all played with me.

Master Peter and Master Leo had to work hard to keep the Vampire from molesting me during the time I convalesced. It seemed, especially that final week, every time I turned around, he was on me, touching and saying lustful thing in my ears. I won't lie, I was terrified to go back to my services with him, or hell anyone.

I liked not enduring the sexual assaults a lot. That last one had been so horrid I didn't even think I could take another session of being the pincushion without losing my shit. I would close my eyes at night and try to imagine it, to brace myself, you know. I would immediately break out in a sweat feeling like I couldn't breathe. I was messed up bad after that pool room incident then the blood bonding in the Great Hall for truth.

However, the cell rapes set me right to pleasure submissive hell. I was healing in the flesh, but my psyche was severely damaged too, and that sonofabitch was not getting better. The day before I was to be released to return to my services, Master Peter was checking my vitals appearing deep in thought.

I didn't want to speak to Master Leo, because I thought he betrayed me at that time, was not so but that is another story. I never could talk with Master Jonas nor the other Elders about anything without them sticking a cock in my mouth for it. I felt compelled to try discussing my issues with the man that brought me across to this horrible existence in the first fucking place.

Master Peter had been most wise in the past. I prayed that he could say something to fix my latest issue before I ended up trapped for all time dealing with the very thing I thought I could no longer endure.

I looked at the floor while he mumbled my blood pressure was good for a change. "Uhm, Master can I speak with you for a moment?"

He flinched then looked at me with surprise. "Huh? About what Mad Maxx?"

I took a deep breath. "You taught me all I know about the special services. I have a problem and cannot seem to find a solution."

He sat down in the chair next to the bed and sighed. "Oh? Well, I need to hear what you're wrestling with before

I can say if I would be of any aid in your dilemma. I warn you. Talking about the bedroom habits of your betters is forbidden Mad Maxx."

I shook my head. "I know better than that, Master. I am not a novice. Nein. The problem is the same one you dealt with in your reign."

Master Peter chuckled. "Ah. You never learned to enjoy the penetration sex then?"

I winced with a grimace. "Nein Master. I still hate it. Yet, worse now. The things that, uhm, happened downstairs. I think, I am sure, I cannot do this anymore, Master. If I cannot get over this, then my Masters will beat me."

He nodded. "They sure as fuck will. Mad Maxx, you are excellent at enduring what you must. What happened to the boy that yawned in Xavier's chains? I confess I am shocked to even be having this conversation with you so close to your collar selection date. What the hell, boy?"

I shrugged. "Something went wrong in my head, Master. I cannot tell you why. I can only say I cannot handle this anymore. I think I may, I don't know, lose it if I have to put up with the special services with a man ever again."

Master Peter pursed his lips. "I think your nervous because those brutes stole service and did it most brutally. What you need is a soft touch for a bit is all. If you lover is careful, the first few times you will overcome this fear enough to make it to that vote."

I glared at him. "I don't think so, Master. Gentle or rough, I don't want to do it anymore. I never did."

He scoffed. "Perhaps you prefer the tawse then?"

I rolled my eyes. "Really, Master? You ever hung by hooks from the ceiling? How about been violated while paralyzed but alert? Need I mention blood bonded five times in two days? That tawse of yours looked like a fucking children's toy compared to those things."

He nodded. "Exactly. Maybe you should look at the special services the same way. That Vampire? The prissy Leo? Ah, old Claus? Are they as scary as Malfred? Or Karl perhaps?"

I shook my head. "Nein, I see what you are saying, Master. That is not going to stop my anxiety though. I won't be able to stop them from seeing my panic, nor do I think I can just lay there and take it. It has been a month on top of that. I will be healed a bit too far. That means, well you know what that means."

He frowned. "Surely your Master is considerate and able to think of that."

I scoffed. "You live in a fantasy world, Master, if you think that any of them give a shit about my comfort. I am just a fucking hole for their pleasures. I am not even the human being that is allowed to heal, grieve, or be afraid."

He looked at the ceiling and sighed. "Ah, I know you tell the truth. I have had to nearly put a muzzle on Jonas to keep his hands off you, and Claus no better. That Malfred also has tried to get in here without anyone looking. I must say I am shocked that these so called Elders are no more in control of themselves then the primary school kid on a playground. I taught you to do your duty with elegance, grace, and rightful equal service. I have been witness that other than Leo, you are not given the same respect in return."

I nodded. "You got that right, Master. Well, thank you for the mercy of attempting to answer my questions. I guess I will do as you say and hope that my anxiety won't send me screaming like the kid that saw a boogie man under the bed."

He chuckled. "I have missed our discussions, Mad Maxx. You are one smart young man. After you got ill, things have never been the same. I think of our time together as the best in my life."

I chuckled. "I bet, Master. I beg your forgiveness if I cannot lay claim to the same thrill over it."

Master Peter sighed. "Nein, I realize that. Mad Maxx, I have the right to special services with you per our agreement. You are always a man of your word. I am calling them right this minute."

I looked up with a startle. "What did you say Master?" I began to tremble in terror.

He stood up and locked the door then approached me. "I am going to solve your issue this minute, boy. You are well enough. The answer is very simple. I will help you get through this frightening first time back on the job after that terrible trauma. I am also quite skilled in handling the breaking in to keep the pain to a minimum. I will be patient, gentle and careful. Once you get back into the saddle so to speak, you will be capable of enduring these other fiends without problems. So, I say again, I am calling my rights with you for the special services. Get to it Mad Maxx. I am waiting."

I sat there staring at the floor feeling I may start weeping any moment. "Why are you doing this, Master? I trusted you enough to talk to you of my fears and you use this against me? I guess the fool is me. Why should I have expected better out of you. You are the one that put me in this path, and of all the liars I ever met you're the biggest."

Master Peter snorted then nodded. "Mad Maxx, I am not going to fight with you over this. You know better than this behavior. You are trained far better. This is your job. I could just leave you here if you wish to refuse. I will let the Vampire know you're back up to one hundred percent, or maybe you rather Malfred? Do you think they will be gentle with you or calm when you get anxious? Nein. They will beat you down and rape you as brutally as those men did. No matter to me. You will have to perform special services or there is no hope for you. I told you I can demonstrate you can and will handle this like the forbidden metal I know you to be. Make your choice boy. I don't have all day, and neither do you."

I nodded. “As you wish, Master. I already am aware I cannot fight you all.” I dropped to my knees and began my services as the pleasure submissive he had trained me to be.

The oral services didn’t cause me too much panic. I don’t like them, but not the end of the world. Given the choice I would dispatch all my unwanted same gendered lovers this way. I am not usually granted such a privilege and certainly wasn’t in this encounter with your Master Peter.

The moment he was ready for a mount he commanded me to brace for his intercourse with the boy. I stood up to disrobe and do as he told me, but he stopped me from my task.

“Nein. You just bend over the bed. I will remove your beeches.” He smiled and stroked my cheek softly.

I trembled. “Uhm, I would rather you allow me to take off my own clothing, Master. I thank you for the mercy of it.”

He shook his head. “You were not permitted such a thing during that attack were you? What if one of your Masters decided to grab you for his lusting while you’re bent over attending other services? You will panic, cry, and get yourself injured. I see the way they beat you up and I know you deny them nothing. I am going to get you over the possibly of anxiety if you are completely out of control Mad Maxx. I know you don’t trust me. That is perfect for this testing of your nerves. You have no idea for sure what I may do or if I will attempt to harm you correct?" I nodded feeling the tears welling up.

Master Peter caught one with his finger. "Ja, you're afraid, good. Now I told you to bend over the bed and await my pleasure. You keep your hands out of my way, or I promise you I make this hurt more than it needs to."

I took a deep breath then followed his order. He came up behind me and grabbed me harshly around the hips. I let out a yelp and tried to crawl across the bed in a blind panic. He held me tightly not giving me any quarter. He allowed me to paw and thrash until I was fatigued from it. I was blubbering like a little kid, and he had not even taken my pants down yet.

Once I gave up my struggle he snatched my breeches and pulled them down with a harsh quickness. I again flailed and vailed out in terror. Master Peter calmly pinned me by my hips but didn't attempt to molest me further.

As before he waited until my fit of terror calmed down. I gave up my fighting him and laid my face onto the mattress crying with all my might. Master Peter stood there silently, making no move to force his intercourse. To my surprise he allowed my crying jag to go until I had no more water to release in my despair.

I sniffled and shuddered but stopped sobbing. It was then he let go of my hips. Then I felt him preparing me for his entry with lubrication. *I guess that sex fiend carried the stuff around with him. Where the hell did he get it?* I very briefly became nerve wracked over this behavior but then closed my eyes and braced for his penetration.

He took much time engaging me in his entry allowing for my slow gaining of comfort rather than just forcing his way in. *You know Meine Liebe, the way I do with you ja? I glared at him for a moment but then nodded. I was aware he could be nasty about it, but truthfully he always gave me time to adjust to the pain*. It was painful but it wasn't as bad as I knew it could be nor as I thought it would be.

To my surprise he told me to relax, to breathe, and then didn't proceed with his thrust until he got my nod that the discomfort was minimized as much as it ever would be. After I gave him that indication that I was good to go, the bastard went to his intercourse without further hesitation. I kept my eyes closed and controlled my breathing as he had taught me the two and a half years earlier.

Then his thrusting became rapid, and he moaned out in thrill. I was pleasantly surprised I had made it through this horror of special services without getting my head beaten in nor my metal locked tight around my neck. He reached his orgasm with much vigor but managed to not cause me to hear that terrible water rushing in my ears or puncturing anything that wouldn't heal without medical aid.

He uncoupled pretty quickly after he found his apex. I yelped when he pulled my breeches back up with a chuckle.

He patted me on my back and told me to rise. "See, Mad Maxx, you are still the perfectly trained pleasure submissive I know and adore. I am a Dominant that is most satisfied with the service you have provided me. You are ready to go back to work without difficulty. If you panic, just focus on this intercourse session and not the one before it, ja?"

I kept my eyes to the ground while he adjusted his pants. "I see the wisdom in what you say Master. What if I panic again like I did in the beginning with you though?"

Master Peter shook his head. "Meine heart, you won't. You are rebroken in, but make sure the cocksuckers use proper lubrication. I will leave some for you to carry in a pocket in case. Focus on your breathing and relax. Fall back on your training. If you focus on doing your task for only that moment, then you will beat this fear before it becomes a dangerous phobia. If nothing else works, think of those sacred bolt cutters. You are almost there."

I scoffed. "Am I? My mother has run off, and Byron has risen. I don't even know the other two Dominants that you chose. I maybe pass the test but fail the vote."

Master Peter laughed with much humor. "Oh, meine Gott. I thought you smarter than that Maxx. The men that were raised and Byron are my men. They do what I tell them with your vote because I pay them to vote ja. They will not get their money until after. Well, except for Byron. I had to trade a leash with you to get his vote, and money too. No big deal though since he has been of amazing service and loyal to our cause since the beginning."

I gasped. “Wait Master, I think I may be hallucinating. Did you just say you traded my leash with Byron for his vote in the collar selection?”

He shook his head. “Nein, you are not hearing dings. That is what I said.”

I sat down on the bed and covered my eyes feeling I may get sick to my stomach. “Christ, do I have to let everyone in this Haus fuck me to get my Gott damned collar off. If that is what it takes, then go use Master Leo’s phone and get the lot of them lined up. We can just settle this by letting them all ride the Mad Maxx train this very afternoon. Hell, I am almost a fucking pro at this gang rape business. I can ever thank them for the Gott damned mercy of it. I am really sick of this. I mean it.”

Master Peter laughed hard at my frustration. “Cut that out, Mad Maxx. You have been around Leo far too long. You are becoming histrionic like him. I didn’t say you have to leash with all three new members. Only Byron demanded this in partial payment. The other two will vote ja without tasting you metal. Do you wish I go tell Byron nein and we can just leave it to chance that he will not vote nein? Say the word and I will break the new to him that you will never be breaking that metal.”

I yelled out in fury. “Nein, I will do what I must. When do I have to endure that cocksucker? For the record, this is bullshit.”

Master Peter nodded. “I know, Maxx. Remember, it is almost done. Now I must go. I see you tomorrow morning below. We will have to work hard to catch up on your thudding lessons, ja."

I waved him away without uncovering my face. "Ja, Master. I will be there. Thank you for the mercy of your aid on my problem, I think?"

He howled at that but left me alone in the room. I sat there a bit longer wondering if I could take another five months of this shit when I heard him come back to the front door. He must have locked it on the way out. He began to knock with strength.

I got up and went to let him back in still mumbling in anger at my bad situation. I opened the door and to my surprise it wasn't Master Peter standing there. I then let out a loud scream as the identity of the visitors struck me at last. Standing there staring at me and smiling with much wickedness were Wolf and killer Karl, and I was all alone in the apartment.

Chapter 63: Dangerous Distractions

Karl smiled at me real big, I could see all his teeth you know. “Hello there, Mad Maxx. Is your Master Leo home?”

I shook my head and yelled, “Nein,” as I tried to slam the door on the two of them.

Wolf blocked the it with his flesh, giggling with thrill. “Oh no you don’t, boy, we are coming in.”

I used all that I had trying to close the door to keep the brutes from getting inside the apartment/ “Help, someone help. I am being attacked,” I screamed at the top of my lungs.

Karl grabbed me by my upper arm pulling me off my labors to keep them out. “You stop that yelling. You are coming with us, but not too far, just a few steps. Wolf, I have heard tale this Priceless has amazing powers. I wonder if one of them is the ability to fly?” He pulled me into the hallway and Wolf grabbed my other arm before I could even get a single punch at Karl.

Wolf chuckled with much humor. “I don’t know Karl. I say we test it and find out.”

Karl nodded. “I agree with you. Come on, Mad Maxx. Save that flailing for catching the air. Maybe you will manage to escape death yet another time.” The two of them began hauling me to the banister.

I was shouting bloody murder, but no one was coming to my aid, as usual. I pulled and dug my feet into the carpet of that hallway with every ounce of strength I could muster. The big men had little difficulty hauling me despite my best efforts. They got me to the edge and bent me over the banister.

Karl laughed loudly. “Say goodbye, Mad Maxx. I for one will not miss you.” I screamed in terror as he put pressure on my upper half threatening to send me spiraling to my death below.

Wolf gasped out suddenly. “Wait brother. Before we kill this useless silver, let me have at him again. Maybe he will be more willing this time. You know, in exchange for a few more moments of breathing?”

Karl stopped his pushing me. “Huh? Now? Wolf you are the pig. This boy’s favors are not worth a bargain.”

Wolf scoffed. “Maybe not to you Karl, but I am a lonesome man. Give him to me for my thrill. When I am satiated, then we can end him, ja?”

I whimpered. “I will do whatever you want, Wolf. Please, let me off this banister, Karl. I beg of you.” I was weeping pretty hard by this time, nearly paralyzed with fear.

Wolf let out a sound of joy “You hear that Karl? The boy is willing. Let me have him just for a few minutes.”

Karl groaned. "Fuck, fine, but Wolf, hurry up though. The boy's Master will be back soon. You better hope no one comes by and catches you."

Wolf pulled me up and clutched me from behind around my neck. "No one going to be home for a least an hour. I can find my fun in less than seven minutes. Mad Maxx, you drop to your knees and suck my cock. You give me what I want and maybe I talk Karl into letting you live another day."

Karl shook his head. "I doubt that. Hurry up, Wolf. Maybe I want a taste too, then we kill him."

I nodded. "Ja, I can satisfy you both, no problem. Let me go Wolf so I can get to your pleasure. I cannot do what you want with you holding me like this."

Wolf chuckled. "Well, you could but I would rather have that blow job before I fuck you. Get to it Mad Maxx." He let me go and I turned around acting like I was resigned to doing what he wanted.

I watched Wolf start to undo his pants. He looked at me and hand motioned that I kneel. I nodded keeping my eyes to the floor. I pretended I was going to mind him, but then like a shot I took off running with all the speed of a frightened kid.

I heard the two brutes shout demanding I halt. That was not going to happen. I tore down that hall then down the back staircase like the Devil himself was chasing me. I could hear Karl and Wolf behind me doing their best to catch the panicked Mad Maxx.

The brutes were fast, but I was faster. I made it down the steps onto the first floor of the Haus. I didn't stop my wild race. I jumped the kneeling silvers and pushed the cowering black collars out of my way as I continued to outrun my pursuers. Karl and Wolf kept coming, keeping pace with my rapid retreat.

I was desperately seeking any Dominant that could aid me in thwarting the two killer ones chasing me. I finally come across a FemDom walking along speaking with a young male Dominant headed for the torture chamber stairwell. I dropped to a kneel in front of them sweating and panting.

The FemDom gasped. "Holy shit. Will you look at this Fritz. It is the Priceless collar. What do you want submissive," asked the stunned woman called Audrey.

I turned briefly to see Wolf and Karl still coming. "Uhm, I was seeking to brush up on my conversation skills, Mistress. You are renowned for your quick wit. Would you do me the mercy of allowing me to practice such a service for you?" She let out a yelp of joy.

"Ah, this is our lucky day, Fritz. Grab his leash please. I accept this offer. You will come with us Mad Maxx." Mistress Audrey grinned like a lottery winner while her companion grabbed my chain.

I shot a look back behind me and saw Wolf and Karl stop dead in their tracks. They glared at me with anger. I smiled and waved a goodbye while following Master Fritz in high protocol. The brutes didn't attempt to come any closer. They realized that an attack on me at that point would yield two witnesses they didn't desire.

Master Fritz looked back at me with curiosity several times as he and Mistress Audrey strolled down the hallway. I was a bit startled when they bypassed the entry for the torture chamber, which they had obviously been originally headed for, but I was not too worried yet.

To my dismay, in another few moments, I understood Mistress Audrey was headed for the Great Hall. I sighed with the knowledge that like all the others, this FemDom was in a big hurry to show off her prize. I rolled my eyes as the two of them stopped at the Hall entry waiting for the black collar attendant to seat them. These Dominants are all alike, hot air with no substance..

I followed behind Friz with my eyes to the floor feeling every Dominant in that place staring at me as we were being led to a table. I was most unhappy about this public display. but it beat the shit out of flying off the banister or sucking Wolf's nasty cock.

For a change, I was willing to get over this milder humiliation and likely thudding that would follow when Master Jonas found out about my being seen with these two nothing Dominants in the Great Hall.

I pulled out the chairs for both Mistress Audrey and Master Friz then waited for them to sit down. I took my place kneeling on the floor between the two. I could hear the two young Dominants speaking excitedly at this unexpected honor of being served by the infamous Mad Maxx. I saw Mistress Audrey looking at me there in my protocol position.

She took a deep breath. "Fritz, I have heard tale that a Priceless is allowed to sit at the table if given permission. I think I want to exercise such a display of power and cause a little jealousy from everyone. What do you think?"

He chuckled and nodded. "I was wondering what the hell you were waiting for. Mad Maxx, you pull up a chair and sit between us this minute."

I winced. "As you wish, Master." I got up and grabbed a chair to do as ordered thinking of how bad that Vampire's thudding was going to hurt.

I sat there as the two of them looked me up and down with stupid grins on their faces. I kept my gaze to the floor in submission saying nothing. I was miserable, no doubt. It bothered me a great deal that even these two young adults of barely twenty-one had the power to treat me worse than a pet dog.

Mistress Audrey was a young heiress of much wealth with no beauty. Her stringy hair was reddish brown, and her mousy brown eyes were set far too close together. This gave her the appearance of poor symmetry that was continued by a huge hawk-like nose and crooked mouth. She was rail thin without any female attributes of worth.

Despite her lack of physical attraction, she had managed to gain the attention and promised ring for marriage from her male companion Fritz. He too was not much to look at. The man was thinner than his Frau, with dark brown hair. His face sported many pock marks, with a weak chin, and heavy eyebrows. The man resembled an awkward rat, and his fiancé the scarecrow.

I do not say these things to be cruel to either of them. I simply give you the facts of their lack of good looks. What I can also say about this couple is that their attitudes matched their appearance.

Even at that young age, they were not well liked among their peers. Mistress Audrey was notorious for starting obscene and untruthful rumors about any FemDom in that Haus she felt was smarter, prettier, or more popular than her. This was almost all of them, to be honest.

Master Fritz was well known for his tendency to bully anyone he perceived as being weaker than himself. Which means he was cruel to silvers, black, and newly entering Dominants. He was also rumored to have been sent to hide in the Haus due to his molesting a six-month-old baby niece. If that shit I had heard about this man were truth, even a tiny bit of it, then I thought perhaps one day I would send the sicko to the yard.

Both of these waste of space were good examples of how money can buy even the most disgusting of creeps safety from the justice they surely deserved. I was starting to re-think my choices for escaping Karl and Wolf rather quickly. That feeling of regret was exacerbated when after several minutes these monsters were still staring at me like I was on the menu for their dinner.

Mistress Audrey flashed a glance at Master Fritz. "You know what I have heard about this submissive? They say to couple with him will kill you. I have heard it whispered his lovers all die from the overwhelming pleasure of the orgasm he causes them. Can you imagine."

Master Fritz snorted. "Kind of like having the Midas touch. Only instead of turning everything he touching into gold, he turns them into corpses."

She giggled at that. "Ja, exactly. Come on Fritz, aren't you the least bit curious to know if that rumor is truth?"

He shrugged. "I know it isn't true, Audrey. The four old buzzards and honorable Malfred still live, don't they? If he killed everyone with his couple, they would be dead too."

Mistress Audrey covered her mouth and chuckled. "Uhm, I heard there are protections that can be taken to keep the reaper at bay. You know Xavier, Drexel and Barnim, they all found themselves buried. That surely proves there is some truth to the stories."

Master Fritz narrowed his eyes and looked me over like he was searching for something. "Maybe. you, submissive.

Answer your Mistress. Is there truth to the tales talked about you?"

I shrugged. "I beg your pardon, Master, but I cannot speaking of the private services of my betters with anyone. I thank you for the mercy of it."

Master Fritz growled. "Shit. The thing is too well trained. I suppose I should have known better than to ask the whore for a list of his clients, ja? Well Audrey, you will just have to believe whatever you want to. I would have to assume this silver is judged priceless because his sexual artistry is above the mark. Should be too with the impressive list of those that can lay claim to conquest of his metal."

I winced at that cruel statement as Mistress Audrey giggled. "You are bad, Fritz. Ja, the list is long but the names on it are famous in this Haus. This thing was the favored collar of the vicious Xavier, and at this moment is bedded by that mysterious Jonas, and that gorgeous Malfred. I have heard the Elders fight each other day and night to hold him for their lusts. That means there is something special about him, though I cannot see it. Maybe it is hidden from view?" She sat forward a bit trying to look into my eyes.

Master Fritz scoffed. "Don't be stupid. Of course, you cannot see it. They are not arguing over his hair or fashion style Audrey. This thing obviously is amazing in the sack to cause so much fuss over it. That I can believe. See his mouth? That creature was made for oral pleasures. His backside is a pretty thing too. I imagine without all these clothes, he is a real beauty to look at while you fuck him."

Mistress Audrey gasped. "Do you think? I have heard he is covered with scars like this one on his face. See there on his neck and hands. Ah, it must be truth. The tale is that there is not a single stretch of his skin unmarked by them. How thrilling it would be to see them for truth. I wonder, do you think he is as well-endowed as I have heard? They say he is gifted in his manhood but that it is forbidden to touch or even see. To lay sight on its cock would curse the FemDom to stupid is the gossip, you know."

Meine Liebe, I have to tell you, this was a most uncomfortable discussion I was privy to. You know in life you assume others say things about you behind your back. It is easy enough to ignore such tall tales, and gossip, unless you ever hear what they are actually saying.

It was not that anything Mistress Audrey or Master Fritz were saying I had not heard whispered a thousand times in the hallways by everyone. What was making me uncomfortable – besides being called a thing, it and spoken about as if I were not sitting there in from of them – was their focus on such foul and private topics.

Being the pleasure submissive means you are viewed by the Dominants as the trained sexual artist. That said, no one, not even one of our kind, wishes to be seen as nothing more than a piece of meat without feelings or other fine qualities such as intelligence. I was painfully aware I was believed to be the sex doll of the Elders but let me tell you I sure as hell didn't appreciate being reminded of this bullshit that morning in the Great Hall.

Master Fritz laughed. "Ah, Audrey, you know what they say, curiosity killed the pussy. Maybe we eat our meal then take this thing somewhere private and make him strip down. Then you can find the answer to your questions, ja?"

I shot a look of anger at him. "Pardon my intrusion Master, but such a command is forbidden one of your station. You would dare to attempt such a grievous theft of service from my Masters?"

He frowned. "Is it? I don't understand how looking a theft of service is."

Mistress Audrey growled. "You will be silent submissive. Say another word without being commanded and I will demand justice for such disrespect from your Dominants. If Fritz wishes for you to sit here naked you will do as told without quarrel or be sorry for it."

I put my gaze back to the floor. "As you wish Mistress."

My ears burned with my anger, but I knew she was correct that as long as neither of them touch me. Truth was that by Haus Law I was without recourse to stop them without gaining a brutal punishment for it. I had to mind any and all commands of Dominants in that place if the order was non-servicing in nature.

Service is defined as anything that requires I handle the Dominant's flesh or personal items/tasks or vice versa.

Demanding I strip down would be one of those things that could not be defined as a real service since looking isn't taking anything other than my privacy, which is not valued by Haus Law for the submissive.

The way this works is if they wanted to see me naked they could command I remove my clothing. That would be the extent of their right to order such a thing. Any Dominant could look upon all my flesh all they liked as long as they didn't go any further. If they attempted to take photos, touch me in any way, or even paint a nude of it, then they would be subject to a violation of my Elder Master's exclusive rights. This was an old rule designed to allow for a Dominant to get a closer look at any silver they found of interest.

Usually such an order to strip down was only used before the Master or Mistress interested approached the collar owner to bid for a leash or go after that submissive if they came up on auction. It was well known that I had five Masters and would not be going up for auction nor was it likely the Elders would be granting any leashes to low Dominants such as Audrey and Fritz.

Therefore, if these two even threatening to demand I strip it could be perceived as an attempt at thieving services from my many Masters. I sat there waiting for one of them to be so stupid as to push this issue.

I was prepared to demand the punishment if necessary, that was for damned sure. The way I saw it if they wanted to see a nude boy, they could go buy a fucking magazine full of the willing nudists like a normal person does. Mad Maxx wasn't going to grant them the thrill of invading my privacy.

I say this because as you know, Meine Liebe, I am no prude. In the Motherland there is not such a focus on modesty when it comes to nudity of either gender as there is here in the USA. Germans think nothing of the naked flesh, and do not make such a big deal of a woman going topless when prudent, such as at the sunny beach. I merely was unwilling to take off my clothing in this incident over the principle of the thing. These low Dominants thought so little of me to call me a thing. Well, I was going to be damned to do anything that would make them smile.

"I sat there enduring more of this open discussion of the many rumors surrounding my legendary prowess in the couple, the culprit of my heavy scars, and the craze to obtain a demonstration of my sexual artistry that most Dominants of the Haus seemed to demonstrate.

I rolled my eyes often, where the two of them couldn't see it, as I listened. These idiots were as uneducated about the truth as most of the silvers and blacks were in basic schooling. I realized if they represented most of the so called betters in the Haus (believing outrageous and mystical rumors like I heard them repeating) then there was no wonder why so many had been acting like they won a great prize when I approached them. Helga and Heidi are two good examples.

It was not lost on me that I would need to be cautious with my future interactions with any Dominant or be prepared to suffer for whatever rumor they had chosen to take for honest reports. I admit I was not only horrified that grown people believed such flotsam, but that all that time I had been ignorant of the growing pile of bullshit being heaped upon my name.

Master Maxx turned me around to face him. "As I have told you, never let another's vision of you be taken to heart. You should be you without apology nor fear of what others think of you. This is important for you to learn Meine Liebe, or you will never survive long as the Priceless pleasure submissive that you are. Normals will call you whore, prostitute, trash, scum, and worse. Ignore the ignorant belief systems of the society that put you in this situation in the first place. They don't come to save you from this pathetic existence, so you should never ever feel shame in doing what you must to survive like your Master Mad Maxx is not shamed by his past ja?

Also recall I said it is most important you be aware of the belief systems of those around you. If they think you are the whore, they will attempt to treat you like one. Now, the trick is to keep the honest truth in your mind to battle their lies. If you believe their assessment of you, then you will become their victim. Do not let them define you. You are not the whore. Unless they are between you and your freedom they have no right to your favors, nor to treat you as their property.

When the they come you are out there in the land of the normals. You hold your head up in pride no matter how much they try to run your good name through the mud. They wouldn't survive a single second in our world, meine Frau. They are the weak prairie dogs trying to bring down the lion. We are of the few on all the Earth that can honestly say they have had their Metal Tested. One day you will do something only the best in the whole world can do. You will break that hold of oppression with your own hands. Like your Master Maxx, ja?

You remember that meine love when the no nothings call you names and make sport of you. You are not less than them, you are more than they can handle. Do what your Master Maxx does when they pull that shit.

I smile at those dumbasses that are not even worthy for me to stomp on. I took Xavier's and Barnim's torture. I endured five Elder Masters, and several fucked up fetishes. I rose from the dungeons of the Haus, stood my ground, and fought my way to the sacred bolt cutters. I sit here as the Dominant with my dream on my lap here tonight.

You meine little one, already have endured all I went through and in some cases more. You sit here beautiful, calm, and adorable this night on my lap, despite all the attempts to send you to the afterlife. I am in awe of my tiny Frau that has survived attacks from giants and can still laugh with me. You have so much further to go, and you are aware there will be much agony in it. Yet, you have not given up nor shirked from your tasks.

I want you to listen to me closely, Meine Liebe. I am proud of you beyond words. I love you for all you have endured and will suffer. I can never thank you enough for your service to your unworthy Master Maxx. You aid me to become a better man every second you take a breath."

I sat there staring at him letting his words sink into my childish brain. "I love you too, Master. I won't lie. I am scared but I'm not going to let you down. I will break my collar like you did."

He smiled then kissed me on my forehead. "Now we go back to the story."

I giggled and nodded as he flipped me back around.

"Mistress Audrey and Master Fritz continued their cruel gossiping about me for some time before another pair of Dominants approached the table. The appearance of the young Master Oswin and his partner, Mistress Fiona, finally shut them the fuck up.

Master Oswin and Mistress Fiona were like these two idiots, first floor nothing Dominants of barely twenty. He was a heavy set, dark haired, and bearded man of around twenty-five and his girlfriend Mistress Fiona a short brunette that wore thick glasses and was oddly shaped with a big bottom and a willowy top.

They were apparently friends of the ugly pair that held my leash for that moment. I groaned when they asked to sit down at the table and were quickly granted permission. I kept my eyes to the floor while the new beastly pair looked me over with the same fascination as I had already endured for the last thirty minutes from the original low Dominants.

Master Oswin spoke first. "I told Fiona that Audrey and Fritz had somehow managed to snag the Priceless, but she didn't believe me not even when she could clearly see this is the thing sitting right there. Ha, Fiona, you owe me that five dollars. This is not a look alike. This is the creature itself. That scar doesn't lie."

Mistress Fiona fawned with her eyes wide. "Ah, I gladly pay the five dollars, Oswin. Audrey, sister, tell me how did you manage this amazing feat? How long do you hold the leash for? If I were you I would not be here at this table. I would have that Priceless back in my apartment to explore the incredible skill he is rumored to possess."

Master Oswin snorted. "I have to agree with, meine Liebling. What the hell are the two of you doing here? Hell, if you don't wish to taste him then give his leash to us. We will do it for you and give the report tomorrow." He laughed as Mistress Fiona nodded in eagerness.

I shot a look of concern at Mistress Audrey that was staring back at me with her eyes narrowed. "Well, Fritz and I would indeed be doing just that, but you see that service permission was not granted. Sadly, we were only offered conversation."

Mistress Fiona's smile melted to a frown. "Only the conversation services? That is a shame. This thing I hear has quite the tongue, but his ability to use it for speaking is not of interest to me nor to Oswin. Who granted the service right? Go see that Elder and see if you can get a full leash. Oswin and I will be happy to pitch in the cash to aid you in obtaining such a pleasure, if you are willing to let us take a taste too."

I flinched as she said that. I unabashedly glared at this idiot with my mouth open at that insult. I wanted to tear her face off and stomp on her skull. They spoke of me like I was nothing but an animal; nein, a rubberized sex doll, which was around only to fuck at their leisure. It was truly sickening.

Mistress Audrey didn't have a chance to answer that nasty woman before three other low born Dominants approached seeking to join the fast growing group. Master Bruno, Master Valintin, and Mistress Hedy, all giggled with glee as they received the approval to take a seat.

Once again silence reigned at that table as the new sets of eyes lustfully searched my flesh. I was starting to wonder if the entire first floor Dominant group would end up sitting around me like a pack of hungry wolves.

Oh, you see the first floor Dominant is the teenager, young adult in their twenties, or the low-born of no worth for their whole life. They all have apartments on the main floor of the Haus. These apartments are not very big and consist of the largest population of Dominant residents and biggest consumers of silvers. They go through those poor collars like tissue paper. Sadly, Master Stefan was one of these creatures, ja?

The second floor has slightly larger apartments. There you find the Dominants above thirty, low-borns that earned a special favor from a Dominant above them, and those that entered the Haus as the Dominant from another Haus.

The third-floor rooms are reserved for the Dominant who only visits for a season but lives outside the Haus most of the time. There are not many apartments on this floor and often it is devoid of residents.

Thanks to the fear of depreciation, which happens when no one is around for upkeep in a home, the Elders and Voting Council used these empty rooms as a type of currency. Often you will find, for a moment, one or more of the apartments occupied by black collars that have earned special favors from high ranking Dominants. Olaf and Vilber were commonly housed in these rooms if you are wondering what a black collar could do to get on that floor.

The fourth floor is where all the high born or those of great worth reside. These apartments are as large and richly decorated as anything found on the Voting Council level (fifth floor) or the Elders sixth floor apartments. The richest, most deeply entrenched Dominants could be found there. This included, until they rose, Master Leo, Mistress Gretta, Mistress Cora, Master Malfred and Master Karl (that last cocksucker had been busted back down to the fourth floor after that gang rape shit).

I had of course begun my career as the Priceless pleasure submissive to Master Peter on the third floor. He was fourth floor material but thanks to a lack of available apartments he had been granted the largest empty apartment the level below his ranking.

With all that in mind, understand that thanks to my real father being Peter and Agnette, I should have qualified, not only to automatically break my collar, but at least a third or fourth floor apartment if I choose to stay in the Haus.

I was originally fucked out of the honor by Peter's denial of his paternity. That meant I would at best be on the second to first floor. The second floor was possible because of my legendary status while submissive as the Priceless. Because Jonas had rushed to claim his relationship as my father and Master Leo my Uncle that boosted me right to the fourth floor by proxy.

You, Meine Liebe, are a Krause by blood. Your family is one of the founders of that horrid place. I don't say that to hurt your feelings. I say it because it is the truth and that grants you special favor within the ranks of that foul place. You are High Born silver by your paternity but only half thanks to the mother of yours. Therefore, you are sadly not granted the privilege of automatic collar break assurance.

That doesn't mean that in every other way you are not viewed as the High Born you really are. If you do break that collar you are fourth floor Dominant even if you are poor as the church mouse. You must understand being that high a ranking Dominant means that you qualify, like your man Master Maxx, for a seat on the Voting Counsel, and if you serve time as the Dungeon Mistress, qualify for Elder when you're of age for it.

I narrowed my eyes, then turned around. "Not going to happen. I am burning down the Haus, Master. I will never hurt kids, not ever. I don't care about any stupid power over child murdering molesters."

He laughed. "I should thud you with my cane for interrupting my story but what you say is too damned wonderful punish. Good, that is what I wanted to hear come out of your heart. Then it is agreed. You break that collar. Then we accept our fourth floor apartment and torch that fucker."

I nodded. "Your wish is my pleasure, Master."

Master Maxx nodded. "And your pleasure is my wish." He ruffled my hair and continued his story without swatting me for a change, thank God.

Now I told you all that to demonstrate my truest disgust at the treatment I was receiving from these nothings that morning at their table. Though I wore a collar, and even that was above them since the collar belonged to the Elders. I technically was too good for the likes of any of them.

I told you I don't believe in one person being better than another by birthright. That is truth, Meine Liebe. That said, when it comes to the Haus, and the protocols that I had to follow or be beaten for it, this bullshit of being surrounded by the low level trash was not acceptable for a submissive of my level.

Not a one of them had the right to sit there and speak such evil about my private matters nor treat me less than an animal. Especially, when in only a matter of five months I was going to be miles above them all in ranking as the Priceless Dominant.

Besides all that, I had earned my right to be a respected free man unlike any of that garbage sitting around bad mouthing my name. What the fuck had any of them ever done of worth? Ah, that is right, they were born blessed, wealthy, and fucked six-month-old babies, at least that Fritz bastard had. Nothing but a pack of disgusting criminals if you ask me.

I was painfully aware Master Jonas, and maybe all my Masters, were going to take serious offence to this dishonor of being seated at this table with them. I had to find a way to escape this fast sinking situation without being too disrespectful as I could still get thudded if openly insolent. I also need to avoid running into the hunting Wolf and Karl.

Two more low level Dominants, Master Roland and Master Magnas, approached the group. They too were granted permission to take a seat. My rising fear hit the roof at the appearance of these two well-known schwulers.

I realized with much terror, the scene was fast turning from embarrassing to downright dangerous. Master Roland and Master Magnas were known not only as purely interested in boys, but for their brutality with the poor silver collars in their grips. They were also quite large fellows for their youth of barely twenty. I was not in the mood for another tag team rape that could be incited by dangling the temptation of easy target out there like it appeared I was doing.

It was time for Mad Maxx to get the fuck out of there. The problem was I had been rapidly surrounded by nine of them. I looked around the Hall with panic praying that a single member of the Voting Council or any associate of Master Peter was there enjoying breakfast.

To my dismay, I spied no one that could aid me in a polite dismissal from this horrifying situation. I was on my own, as usual, to pull my metal out of this mess. I braced for the likelihood that Mistress Audrey or Master Fritz were going to demand my punishment for behaving without manners. Oh well, sucks to be me.

None of the low born Dominants had been talking. They continued to sit there shooting looks of curiosity at each other. Each was grinning and focusing their main attention to the stupid Mad Maxx sitting there with his eyes to his lap. They often would glance at my leash held tightly in the sweaty grip of Master Fritz.

I leaned forward without looking up at my eager audience and whispered to Mistress Audrey, "Forgive me Mistress, but my time is up. I must return to my Master Jonas this moment. I thank you for the service of your conversation."

She shot a look of anger at me. "Nein, I didn't get but a moment's service out of you. I do not desire to release you just yet."

I shook my head. “My deepest regrets at my insult of not serving you to your full satisfaction Mistress. However, I do not have a choice in this matter. My Master’s directives override my desire to service you to your fullest thrill with it. You will have to take up the matter of my shortcomings with my Masters. I thank you for the mercy of the punishment they will enforce over my failure.”

Master Fritz frowned. “Audrey, ignore this thing. He has to mind us as long as we hold his leash. I will pay the fine for theft of extra time of his service from his Master Jonas. Do not grant his release.”

Master Oswin spoke up “Ja, I agree with Fritz, Audrey. Hell, I will kick in some of the fine money if you keep him here for our pleasure to look at him.”

All the low born Masters and Mistress’s then broke out swearing their coin to Mistress Audrey if she would refuse to grant my release and thieve the Priceless’s service (steal time in this case) from Master Jonas. She sat there mulling over her resolve to anger such a powerful Dominant just to suit the thrill of her friends.

I admit I trembled in growing anxiety over this seemingly innocent situation that was getting out of control. I recalled Master Jonas and Master Peter’s warnings that I was a target for almost every Dominant in the Haus. Both had told me many of the residents were gunning to get their taste of my metal before I was no longer within their grasps.

You see if I gained the sacred bolt cutters I would be protected from sexual assaults by the Haus law as the

Priceless Dominant. The belief was I would end my life if I didn't break my metal which also would put me beyond their reach. Which I would have, that I can assure you.

The legend of the Priceless dictates no other can rise while there is a male of the forbidden silver alive. That is allegedly the truth even if the Priceless is no longer a submissive. The general belief was that I would be selected the first Priceless Dominant ever in the Haus's recorded history.

Most realized that if this did happen, they would not live long enough to see another Priceless collar rise. This assumes my life would be long and healthy. The Haus residents were in no hurry to see me break my metal for that reason alone. Many would be happy to see me dead rather than on the fourth floor in my own apartment.

I had become a legend in my own time. As you just heard, there were many rumors about my magic abilities and mystical skills. The time left for me to serve on my knees was fast coming to an end. This sent many a Dominant to fear they would never get to hold or a coupling with a Priceless collar for the rest of their lives.

This all had led to a universal threat to me from almost every single one of the Haus residents. For the first time since I had been leveled Priceless, I understood the truth of my terribly compromised position.

I sat their listening in shock to those motherfuckers offering a minor fortune just to keep me sitting there so they could stare at me. Fear overcame me as I realized, finally, how dumb I am, that they likely would be willing to push the limits to taste my metal just as my Masters had warned me. Maybe even risk the most severe of punishments just so they could brag they had survived a couple with the infamous Mad Maxx.

The time had come for me to take extreme action. I was not a slave. I could demand punishment for disobeying if I were unwilling to follow a command. I decided a beating was better than risking another gang rape, by a long shot.

I jerked my chain out of Master Fritz surprised hand then stood up abruptly, immediately silencing all the chatter at that table. "I told you I am due back with my Master. You refuse to grant my release. I take the punishment Mistress without quarrel for leaving your leash this moment to attend my services to him that owns my collar." I pushed back my chair and headed for the Great Hall entry.

Master Fritz stood up and yelled out in fury. "Catch the Priceless. He is trying to escape his leash to Audrey."

To my complete terror, every Dominant at that table and several from others come running after me. I let out a yelp and took off fast as my legs could go. I would have attempted to scold them for breaching proper protocol and Haus Law of not allowing me the right to leave, but I believe the lot of them were not going to listen to reason.

They came at me like I was a rabbit and them hungry dogs. I screamed for help at the top of my lungs as I flew down the hallway. Doors all around me opened with curious Masters and Mistresses poking out their heads to ask about all the commotion. I could barely believe my eyes but many, when told by my pursuers of their attempts to capture me, joined in the chase.

Behind me a small swarm of low born Dominants grew into a huge breathing mass of these first floor apartment owners. This was like a nightmare come to truth. Many times, when trying to slumber, I had dreams of being hunted like a beast by a crowd. Well, this was no illusion, I was being hounded and if I was caught…holy shit. I was sure to be ripped to pieces.

I am sure I sounded like the emergency ambulance coming down that hallway at full speed. I was screaming nonstop begging for aid from everyone, even the Devil himself, to save me from this pack of monsters. I swear it was the only time in my life I would have been thrilled to see my Vampire man.

However, there was no Master Jonas, Master Leo, Master Claus, nor even fucking Master Malfred, anywhere to be found. I ran blindly headed right for the Haus front door. I feared heading back to the sixth floor after that whole Karl and Wolf incident, you know. I didn't even care that Vilber and Olaf were standing there guarding the only route to my escape from the sure destruction right behind me.

The look of shock on the door guards faces would have been funny had this not been such a serious situation. Vilber and Olaf backed toward the door, their eyes wide and mouths on the floor. They both appeared frightened. I am sure they were too. I myself would not have believe such a scene had I not been there.

I can only imagine what went through their minds as they saw the huge number of Dominants that were charging with force only a short distance behind the wailing Priceless collar roaring toward them. I didn't give a damn what they were thinking at that moment. I only knew the brutes were in my way and I needed to go out the door.

Olaf and Vilber blocked my attempts to reach the doorknobs with their huge frames. Each time I tried to push my way past them, they would push me back. I let out a long shout of frustration and fear when I realized I was cornered if I couldn't get through that entryway.

I turned around to see the crowd almost upon us. "For fucks sake, let me out, Gott dammit. Those sonofabitches are going to tear me apart," I screamed at the black collar brutes.

Olaf laughed. "Good, I hope they kill you, Mad Maxx."

I glared at him. "You better hope they do motherfucker. If I live I make sure my man does more to you than a little tease and tickle foursome game."

He took on a look of fury. "You cocksucker. I am going to kill you myself." He came out swinging at me and I ducked but tripped to my knees.

Vilber come forward and grabbed me around my back lifting me to my feet. I struggled in his grip while he backed up to the door. He was holding me from behind. I was forced to face the crowd that was silently spreading out surrounding us on every side.

Master Fritz come to the front sweating and almost out of breath. “Give the Priceless to me, Vilber. He is on Audrey’s leash. I demand you turn over what belongs to her this minute.”

Olaf backed up as the swarm began to come closer. “Fuck this shit, Vilber. Give Fritz that little bastard. This is not our fight. I am not willing to take another thudding or worse.”

Vilber snorted. “Shut the fuck up Olaf. I am through listening to you. All you ever do is get us into trouble. I will handle this on my own for a fucking change.” He gripped me more tightly, though I had stopped struggling thanks to being paralyzed by fear.

Master Fritz nodded. “That is right, shut up Olaf. Vilber, give me that thing. It doesn’t belong to you. You mind your better or find yourself in deep shit over it.”

Vilber nodded. “Oh, I will give him to you Fritz, when you give me something worth the beating and dungeon time I am going to get for it.” I let out a gasp of terror when he said that and nearly pissed my pants to be honest.

Master Valintin standing next to Master Fritz yelled out, “Name your price, Vilber. We will see that it is paid in full.”

Vilber looked to a frightened appearing Olaf. “I think this time this collar’s Masters would kill two black collars for getting involved. My starting demand is to know how you plan to protect us from that."

Olaf nodded. "Forget it, Vilber. I will go find the dumb bastard's Masters. We get our reward for saving his worthless ass."

I nodded, almost stupid from the fact that for a change I agreed with Olaf. "JA, go get my Masters. They will pay you handsomely for saving their Priceless."

Vilber tightened his grip until I was nearly smothered from the squeeze. "Both of you shut the fuck up. I say again to all of you. Tell me how you will defend Olaf and me from his Masters, then you can have this bastard. My price is you kill him when you are finished with your thrills. Take your time so you can make fucking sure it hurts a lot."

I let out my breath in full on fury. "Vilber, I will fucking kill you. I swear it. Let me go motherfucker. Help! Master Jonas, Master Leo, please someone call my Masters." I struggled with all my might, kicking and trying to bite Vilber.

Master Oswin laughed, as did many of the low born Dominants in the crowd. "No one here will tell you handed him over will we? Everyone nodded in unison. The Elders cannot punish all of us, Vilber. You hand him over and I swear that his tongue will never utter your or your brother's name again. The dead cannot speak, ja?"

Vilber laughed with an evil tone, as did Olaf. "Then come take him from me Fritz with my blessing." I screamed even louder as Master Fritz approached and grabbed my leash.

Vilber held me back as I attempted to kick the Dominant as he wrapped that chain around his hand securely.

He turned to Master Valintin and Master Bruno. "Come hold this thing from attacking me please. If you do, then I assure you I will be in a sharing mood regarding this collar's skills." The two of them come forward with smiles and quickly tore me from Vilber's tight grip.

I fell to the floor refusing to walk. They dragged me along behind Master Fritz as he and the rest of them turned around headed back the way we had come. Half the group took up the back and half led. I was surrounded and restrained. This was a disaster unlike anything I could describe.

I began to openly weep when I realized that at this point even if Master Jonas, hell all my Masters, came to my aid, they could easily be overpowered by the sheer number of persons in this hoard of low born Dominants. This innocent attempt to keep from being murdered by Karl and Wolf got out of hand rapidly. I had fallen from the frying pan right into a raging fire.

It was then I saw Christian running right through the crowd. The boy nearly was knocked backward by the force of his jumping inside the flesh. He come at the three of us trapped on the wheel. Without a word he kicked the mind wall with all his strength.

The flesh jerked and spasmed for a moment. This caused Master Bruno and Master Valintin to stop their march and stare in confusion at the contorting boy in their grips.

"What the fuck? Hey, this thing is having a seizure I think," said Master Bruno as he flashed a glance at Fritz.

Master Fritz was forced to stop when he hit the end of the leash held back by his stronger brothers. He turned around to examine the reasons for this hold up.

"Why have we stopped? Do you think I care if he is seizuring? Bring him along anyway. Besides, he is not having a Grand Mal. See his eyes are open. I think he is alert." He approached the spasming flesh.

Taube, Maximillian, Christian and I all shot smiles at each other as the dumbass got within our kicking distance. Without hesitation we kicked him right in the hodensack with all our strength. Fritz led out a high-pitched scream. He fell to his knees letting our leash go as he reached between his legs gagging and sputtering.

Master Valintin was shocked so badly by our sudden move he unconsciously let his grip ease on the boy. We turned the wheel and sent him to his face with a busted bag of family jewels as well. The crowd around us was unsure what to do as was Master Bruno.

He let the boy go and backed away as I began to laugh manically. "What's the matter cocksuckers? I thought you wanted a taste of my metal. Well, here we are. All of us are going to kick your asses. We kill the first one for fun, then the rest of you better run. Eeny meeny, miny, Brono. Catch that cocksucker by his toe. When he bleeds he will know what a fine tree he's going to grow. Come and get it love. None of this group needs to question the rumors any longer. I am ready to show everyone for truth why the level me the Priceless." With that we turned the boy and ran headfirst into the hallway wall.

The boy stagged backward for a moment, then laughed as he rammed the wall once again. The crowd was terrified by this display of insanity. No one knew what to make of my strange rhyming, head banging, and wild laughter.

You may recall the universal fear in the Haus that crazy is contagious. Well, Christian knew we could never beat all those people in a fist fight. He wisely decided to use the secret weapon of inciting fear in them by making the object of their desire appear contagious.

This was a real risk since any of them could easily call the Guard and report me hopelessly mad. The way I saw it, better to be shot to death then fucked to it. I watched with humor as all the low born Dominants shot looks of confusion at each other. They continued to back away.

Master Valintin was aided to his retreat by Mistress Hedy. Master Fritz crawled away still gagging loudly on his own power. Though no one approached me, they also didn't unpack or leave. I continued to howl, rant, and smack my head into the wall. I had busted my forehead open pretty bad by this time and still the dumb fucks stood around blocking my escape.

I shot a look of fear at my brother shards when we all realized another head butt and the boy would go limp. An unconscious state was not a good thing to be at that moment. Christian stood there looking at the three of us shrugging his shoulders unsure what to do.

Taube scoffed. “A lot of good you are Christian. Shit, I say we run.”

Maximillian nodded. “I second that idea. Just tear through the lot of them.”

I shook my head. “Do you see that wall of nothings, fools? What the fuck? Maximillian and Taube, stay off Christian. Give him a moment to think will you?”

Maximillian frowned. “Sure, Mad Max, because we have all fucking day? You know I am almost sorry we won’t live to see the Vampire desex the whole lot of them. Oh, and that Claus, wow, I almost feel sorry for them when he is through with that medieval shit he going to torture them with.”

Mistress Fiona yelled out of the crowd, “Holy fuck, this collar is insane. Do you hear him? Who is he even talking to?”

I was startled at her words. I had not realized us shards were speaking to each other with the boy’s voice, oops. I smiled at them with a shrug which made the crowd back up more. I thought I was finished for sure over that madness, but I noticed this more than anything I had done unsettled the group. I narrowed my eyes then spit on the floor.

"Which one of you bastards is singing? Stop it. That song not only sucks, but you also cannot sing it worth a shit. I am going right this minute to complain to the manager. Maximillian, make a note. We will call the fucking police to report this noise infraction. Christian, you handle the transmissions. Taube, well, you just keep your ass handy. Come on, Mad Max, time to get the fuck out of here." I began to walk toward the right side of the surrounding crowd still yelling orders at my brother shards.

The FemDoms and Dominants moved out of the way to allow the boy to pass as we had hoped and suspected they would. I continued to speak out loud to myself. I was just nearly free of that horrible nightmare when I felt a large hand clamp down on the boys upper arm.

I let out a loud shriek. "You will unhand the King's entertainment, you fool. Who the fuck do you think you are to dare such an insult." I turned my head to get the identity of the fucker I planned to kill.

A low born, tall Dominant with dark hair called Matz stood there smiling at me. "You may frighten these other idiots, but I care not if you are as insane as the march hare Mad Maxx. Magnas and Roland, come on boys, I got the Priceless." I got several nasty punches into the man but was quickly subdued by the brutal schwuler pair from the table earlier.

The three of them were rapidly joined by another foul low born called Bernt. The four of them dragged me down that hallway kicking and screaming for all I was worth. It was lucky that none of the other large crowd decided to overlook my perceived mental illness.

That didn't make me feel any better as these four nasty brutes hauled me away. I was painfully aware they were trying to seek a hiding spot where they could enjoy their prize without fear of interruption.

I struggled for the third time that day against my abductors. They tore at my clothing all trying to grab my flesh even before finding a quiet spot to enjoy their sport to the hilt. Magnas yelled to his brother Dominants that he knew the perfect spot to get their taste of my metal.

Matz and Roland held me tightly by my upper arms dragging me along. Magnas led them and Bernt took up the rear to push me along when I tried to dig my boots into the floor. I continued to yell, wail, threaten, scream and even cry, but nothing I did or said stopped the progression to what I knew was going to be another gang rape.

I was about to fall into a catatonic stupor when I saw that they had taken me to that fucking storage closet that I hate. I couldn't believe my bad luck. I decided that if I lived to break my collar, the thing I would do right after killing Olaf and Vilber was to destroy that fucking room.

Magnas opened the door and turned around with a smile. "After you boys." He motioned them to pull me inside.

I closed my eyes and braced for the horror as they started to enter the closet. I was startled from my resignation of this nightmare by the sound of Bernt letting out a loud grunt of agony. I turned my head just in time to see Byron and another middle aged man called Friedrick beating the shit out of the low born Bernt.

Magnas saw the two men too. He let out a yelp of fear then took off running down the hallway leaving his brothers to suffer the beating without him. Matz let me go first and tried to run but Byron knocked him into the wall outside the closet sending him sprawling to the floor. He joined his groaning brother Bernt rolling around in pain.

Roland took a left hook from Friedrick. This sent the young Dominant right to unconsciousness in one of the fastest knockouts I have ever seen to this very day. *Well, you would have had to see Friedrick to know why. The man was a huge, burley brute physically built like the Clydesdale horse. Hell, his hands were almost bigger than my fucking fourteen year old head.* Within mere moments I was rescued from that horrid four man hijacking by the two High-Born males.

I dropped to my high protocol kneel as Byron was a Council member and trembled with relief that the two had come along when they did. Master Byron and Master Friedrick glared at the two low-borns that still had their alertness. Roland was busy in the pea patch with the sandman, ha.

Master Byron then growled out. “I sure hope we didn’t just catch a bunch of nothings trying to steal from our honorable Elders. However, I do believe that is what was going on here. I think we have problem with thieves. How do you suggest we handle this situation brother?”

Master Freidrick shook his head then said in his booming voice. “Well, by Haus Law we can have these criminals sent to the chains for a lashing.”

Master Byron laughed. “That is truth. I know that one that escaped us. I will send the Guard to have him hauled downstairs later, if the Priceless wishes to press charges that is.” He cast a glance at me quietly kneeling there.

I nodded. “I thank you for the mercy of it, Master.” I shot a look of hate at the three men.

He smiled. “Smart boy, Mad Maxx. You cannot allow this to go without punishment or next time instead of four, there will be eight. These nothings must learn their place. You idiots look upon the Priceless for the last time. This collar he wears belongs to another. There are laws in this Haus that dictate you keep your filthy paws of things that do not belong to you. I will send for each of you later this afternoon for the chains and whipping. Get the fuck out of my sight.” Bernt and Matz stood up and staggered off openly weeping.

Master Byron approached the unconscious Roland. “Shit Friedrick, did you kill this one?”

Master Friedrick shrugged. “I forget my strength sometimes brother. That dumbass ran right into my fist you know?” he chuckled as Roland stirred as if on cue.

The young male groaned as Master Byron leaned down into his face. “You go home, boy. I am sending for you soon to join your co-thieves for a well-deserved lashing. You got a problem with it, then we go see if this boy’s man Jonas wants to do worse, ja?”

Roland nodded. “That won’t be necessary. I go and await your call. Thank you for the mercy of it.” He slowly got back to his feet and headed off holding the hallway wall to steady his dizzy head.

The big Dominants watched Roland limping away chuckling with much humor. Then they turned their attention back to me still waiting for a release to return to my Masters. For a change I was most happy to go back to the sixth floor.

Master Byron looked me up and down. “Did any of those fools injure you, Mad Maxx?”

I shook my head. “Nein Master. Master Friedrick and you came to my aid before they could do anything more than frighten me.”

He laughed. “You scared? Never. My older brother was there the night your couple killed Xavier. He told me he saw you yawning at the end of that sadist’s chains. I have to admit, I was impressed to hear his tale.”

I shrugged. “That was a long time ago, Master. There was only one Xavier as well. These four men were far more upsetting.”

Master Byron let out a surprised gasp. “Did you hear that Friedrick? The boy just referred to Xavier as upsetting.”

Master Friedrick raised an eyebrow. “Amazing. I swear to Gott brother I have dreamed of this boy a thousand times since hearing the rumors of his prowess. Seeing him in the flesh up close, Well it is more than a little awe inspiring.”

I looked to the floor with much confusion in my expression. “I apologize, Master, but I do not understand. Had you not come by I would be crying like a little bitch in that closet unable to escape the lust of though four low-borns. How the hell is that anything to be impressed with?”

Master Friedrick chuckled. “If I had been a little man like you and in the same situation my pants would be soaked with piss and shit. You though, kneel in proper protocol and wait with patience while we dispatch these foul would be thieves. Your actions are remarkable. I tell you Byron, I think the rumors I have heard are understated. This silver is something else.”

Master Byron nodded with a smile. “Ah, don’t I know it. That is why when Peter come to me a couple weeks ago and asked me to aid him in recouping his property from Malfred’s gang, I lobbied for a leash with him. I want to enjoy the demonstration of his skills before the time for such an honor runs out.”

Master Friedrick let out a gasp while I winced at his words, while verifying what Master Peter already told me. "Holy hell, you managed a leash with the legendary Priceless. You fucking lucky bastard. I hate you Byron, I really do."

Master Byron reached down and took up my leash. "You say the kindest things to me brother. I am not a fool. Peter was in a tight spot. He would have promised me anything to get me to save this forbidden silver. I was lucky indeed, and thoughtful enough to request such a pleasure." He motioned me to stand, which I did immediately.

Master Freidrick looked me over wantonly. "How could I get as lucky as you, I wonder? I would give anything to have a night with this silver."

Master Byron took off walking toward the back staircase with Master Friedrick strolling alongside us. "Fool you may be a big cuss, but you are dumb as the post. You are a Voting Council member now. This boy will be going up for collar selection in five months. You want a leash with him, then turn around and say, 'you want my vote of ja, then you give me your special services for it.' I mean that is the perk of being on the fifth floor Friedrick. You can get a leash with any silver looking to be judged Dominant, even Mad Maxx the Priceless."

I shuddered as he said those words even as I felt relief to see he was escorting me back to the safety of my Elder Masters. "I beg your forgiveness, Masters. Master Peter told me that only Master Byron had lobbied and received such a promise. You Master Freidrick, gave your word for another thing of value I was told. A deal is a deal. I would think it dishonorable to break your agreement by demanding more than already granted." I cowered assuming I would be backhanded for insolently interrupting my betters in their discussion without being recognized.

To my surprise they only chuckled, then Master Friedrick turned to look at me. "I will never break my word to vote ja, Mad Maxx. I am honorable and loyal to Peter to death, like Byron here is. However, I can change my mind about the price. I will contact Peter immediately to tell him to keep his money. I want a leash with you instead. I would hope you are not insulting me by denying me the right to negotiate when something so valuable to you is at stake."

I dropped my eyes to the floor and blew out my breath with disgust. "Nein Master. Of course not. I will offer no quarrel with you if you desire the leash right. However, I am unsure how either of you think dealing with Master Peter is proper protocol. He is not my owner."

They both stopped in their tracks with looks of shock at each other, then Master Byron looked at me. "Shit Friedrick, the boy is right. We have to get permission from the Elders for a leash. No wonder Peter wouldn't give me a time or date for this exchange to take place."

Master Friedrick narrowed his eyes. "Do you think Peter is planning to screw us over maybe?"

I shook my head. "Nein Master. Master Peter will pay you since he told me it would happen after the vote is caste.

The special services leash though, not his right to grant you."

Master Byron huffed. "Well fuck it then. I will vote any way I want. That bastard. He knew this and misled me."

I shot a look of terror at him. "Wait Master. It is true that Master Peter cannot grant such a privilege, but I can. My services are mine to grant any lover of my choice. My Masters couldn't order monogamy on anything other than my own penetration of another. You can obtain my favors for your vote of ja and I will deny you nothing if you would be willing to provide another service as well."

The Dominants glanced around nervously to assure themselves they would not be overheard making a deal with the Priceless collar of the Elders. They moved in closer to speaking quietly. I trembled as the two of them towered over me like giants.

Master Byron blew out his breath. "I am willing to hear what you offer and what you desire in return for my vote." Master Friedrick nodded in agreement with his brother's statement of interest in making a deal with me.

I closed my eyes and swallowed hard to keep down the bile in my throat over what I was about to say. "Dis Haus is looking to rip me apart. I need protection as much as I need your vote of ja. I realize it is better to provide for the lusts of two rather than two hundred. If you both would be willing to guard my dignity I will grant you full access to my skills within reason. I will never breathe a word to

Master Peter of our secret deal, or anyone else for that matter. You will get his money and my favors in abundance until the day I break this metal. If you agree to this deal then I want it put into writing. I have a place to hide it where it never needs to be seen unless you try to betray your oath to me."

Master Byron smiled with glee as did Master Friedrick. "I sure as hell take this deal, Mad Maxx. It would be my honor to protect a lover of your caliber from anyone else taking what is meine by agreement."

Master Friedrick slapped Master Byron on the back with a yelp of joy. "I couldn't have said that better myself brother. You have yourself a deal Mad Maxx. You grant us your favors and we return the service with our own, and grant ja at your selection without anyone being the wiser for it."

I grimaced. "I will want our contract in writing immediately, and Masters I remind you that this is only for the five months I have left in this metal. After that you will let me alone for the rest of my life however long or short it is."

The Masters chuckled at that, then Master Byron nodded. "Fair enough. I suppose we will just have to get our fill fast as we can. In fact, I say we return to the closet and start this agreement right this minute."

I looked up with a startle. "Huh? Nein. I want this in writing first, Master. I give nothing until that is done."

Master Byron jerked my chain and began hauling me back toward the storage closet ignoring me. “You will get your fucking contract, Mad Maxx. Friedrick and I are men of our word. However, I want to see what I just bought, and I happen to know your Masters have not come around seeking you yet. I am aware you serve four already. That is a lot of cock to wait in line behind. One would be a fool to let a chance to start this bargain off on the right foot when the chance comes up. Come on brother. You may as well get used to sharing with me. The next five months looks like we are partners, ja?”

I was helpless to stop the strong Dominant as he dragged me along by leash behind him and the giant Friedrick following to assure I was not backing out of this deal with them. Christian let out a scream and jumped from the flesh as the door of that horrid storage room came into our view.

I looked at my brothers Taube and Maximillian with a shrug. “Well, I guess that will teach us not to answer the door when the Master is not home.”

Maximillian frowned. “Mad Max, has it not bothered you maybe a little that none of our Elder Masters have been around all morning? Where the fuck do you think they have gone. Even Leo and Malfred are missing.”

I groaned. “Shit, you are right. We have been so busy fighting for our lives I didn’t think of it. Where did they go?”

Taube let out a gasp. “Brothers, I think for this minute we have more to worry about, look there.”

I swung my head to see Karl and the monster Wolf standing there outside the closet door with Wolf’s half-brother, the one born in America, the fellow you know as Russell.

Chapter 64: Closeted Hell

Master Maxx turned me around to face him. "Now a quick warning, Meine Liebe. Don't ask me what Russell was doing there or what his role in this story is all about yet. At this time, I had no idea who he was, nor the importance of him at all. I will ask you to remain patient and I will explain all of it when I get to the place I found out. Do you understand me?"

I nodded. "As you wish, Master." I said then looked away from his gaze.

He appeared confused. "No arguments? Am I to assume you are not curious to know what was going on."

I shrugged. "What you think is up to you, Master. You told me that Ryker is my brother. Karl is my daddy. Malfred my uncle. I am a Krause from a family of child killers and monsters of the worst kind. You are the son of Peter and of a Vampire. You are my husband who has slept with all those people I just mentioned and with me too. I am told I have to marry and fuck that Vampire and human dad of yours soon. We both were ordered to be borne by one man, who obviously didn't get what he wanted from it. So, to be honest, if you told me Russell is my brother, uncle, or hell even the Easter bunny, I wouldn't be surprised. I know you will tell me what I need to know when I need to know it. I trust you and I also kind of don't want to know."

Master Maxx laughed hard at that. "Well, I have to say I agree with you on the absurdity of it all. However, when you lay it all out there like that, makes me feel sick to my stomach. Okay, then you sit there and be still. I will tell you why Russell was there, and how he fits into this nightmare we call life when I found out, soon." He kissed me then turned me back around to start his tale.

I gasped loudly and began to tremble. I was certain I had made a major blunder trusting these two brutes. I felt my heart speeding up while the sweat beads stood at attention on my forehead. The entire morning had been a bit more than trying.

From the second the sun rose, I had dealt with my father's unexpected lusting, followed by a near spill from the banister aided by two rapists. I thought I had escaped only to end up being the show pony in the Great Hall by a couple of nothings.

In an effort to end that tanking situation quickly, I got myself chased by a mob through the Haus. To my horror I was then handed over to said mob by two would be killer guards. I was black and blue in the face from ramming the boys head into a wall to literally save my ass, only to be hijacked and near gang raped anyway. I was saved by two huge men from the Voting Council, only to have them attempting to manhandle me into something I wasn't ready for yet.

To top off this shitty series of events I found myself being haul right into the clutches of the very two cocksuckers that started the entire nightmare. You know

Meine Liebe, I admit I was thinking to myself that some days it doesn't pay to get out of bed, ja?

I flashed a look of horror at Master Byron, who shot a look of concern back at me then looked at his partner Master Friedrick. "Shit, what the hell are these motherfuckers grinning about, brother? They are blocking our thrill to boot. I think you better be ready for a battle."

Master Friedrick nodded. "I always am brother, but I will point out we are out manned if this becomes a fray."

Master Byron sighed. "That is the plan no doubt. Karl and Wolf will engage you and me in the fight then that cocksucker Russell will grab the Priceless with us busily engaged in blows. We should just forget this. Let's turn around and take the boy to his Masters. There will be another day to sample the joys of his skills, ja?" He looked back at me with wanton frustration.

Master Friedrick nodded. "I am with you brother. I think I could take them both, but the Priceless's safety comes first. We fight them another day when the odds are even."

To my surprise, pleasant surprise by the way, the two brutes turned tail and began to head back for the stairwell. I kept my eyes behind me watching the three criminals. They stood there glaring in anger but didn't move to follow.

Just as we approached the back stairwell a very tall man of near six foot three came walking by. He had a beautiful FemDom on each arm. The three of them were laughing and the ladies were gazing at this handsome fellow with adoration in their eyes.

Master Byron let out a gasp, then yelled out to this Dominant, "Rolf, just the man I was hoping to run into. Are you busy, brother? I need your aid with something."

Rolf stopped his journey, and a big smile went across his face. "Byron, Friedrick, what are you two dogs up to? Getting into trouble maybe? What do you need? Rolf is never too busy to aid his friends when they are up to no good. Gisela and Sigard are always down for a little mischief aren't you ladies?" The two FemDoms giggled and nodded at his statement.

I fell to a kneel behind the massive Master Byron and humongous Master Friedrick. I peeked with eager curiosity around their tree trunk sized legs, eyeing those gorgeous FemDoms. Both of them were likely the most beautiful in that whole fucking Haus at that time. I found myself forgetting all my problems while admiring their fine forms. As usual the idiot Mad Maxx was dumb struck by the sight of the thing he wanted most in the whole world, besides his freedom that is.

Sigrid was a blond with huge brown eyes that sported long eyelashes. She was a perfect hourglass shape and knew just the right way to wear her dresses to show off her amazing figure. The woman's hair reached her waist and legs went on for miles. The girl was twenty-eight, and hitting her apex of perfection that to this day is legendary among the FemDoms that ever walked the Halls of that place.

Gisela's dark chestnut mane shined with a supernatural glow. Her eyes were large and blue as the sky. The woman was slightly shorter than her taller sister Sigrid, but she was nothing to sneeze at herself. She boasted a bosom that could make a man desire a hug anytime she would honor him with such a pleasure. Her soft features were enhanced by an unblemished milky white complexion that made one think of the royalty of the olden days. Her heart shaped lips could be seen for miles thanks to their pink contrast to such a lovely skin tone.

I found my breathing coming in shallow, rapid bouts for like the hundredth time that morning, but this time it was not anxiety driving it. Those women were making me remember I was male and straight. I found myself having to adjust my breeches when my manhood hit the end of my chastity device. I swore under my breath at that fucking Vampire father of meine. Gott damn him. I couldn't even look at a girl without risking permanent injury.

Master Rolf approached our group still leading those stunning FemDoms holding his arms. I looked at him wondering what the hell he had that made two of the most desired ladies in the Haus fawn over him like he was the rock star.

Master Rolf was huge in stature, like Master Byron and Master Friedrick, but unlike them he was not as brutish appearing. He was strong looking, don't give me wrong. He was merely more symmetrically proportionate with a square muscular chest and somewhat narrow in his hips.

I figured that was my answer. Master Rolf had to be a FemDom favorite being the perfect specimen of male form with his wavy, thick brown hair and box like jaw. I assume his natural appearance of appearing about to burst out laughing added to his desirability among the females. That and his deep set dark blue eyes.

You see, Master Byron had a large chest too, but he was just massive in every area with heavy legs and muscled arms. He was a brunette but always appeared in need of a haircut. This made him appear younger than his thirty-five years. He had the boyish face with a brutish build. His fresh appearance was deceiving. Master Byron was a clever and well educated man that was famous for his loyalty, to a fault, to those he called his friends.

Master Friedrick, like Master Byron, was built like the farm hand. Heavy in muscles and with a huge shoulder span and as I told you, hands bigger than my head. His hair light brown hair was prematurely greying and his hairline receding at the young age of thirty-five. His face had the appearance of a wise middle aged man, but in truth, Master Friedrick was not well educated or even smart man. What made him likeable was his honest, down to Earth ability to know that fact. He never carried on airs, nor denied he was not the sharpest knife in the drawer. Master Friedrick was also widely known for his fierce loyalty to those that he claimed alliance to.

Master Rolf was a close associate to these two ex-lovers. Ja, the brutes had been an item in their youth. The relationship ended more than a decade before but their affection for each other as the best of friends never has to this day. The three had all been friends since their days of being the children of very wealthy German families with deep roots in the Motherland's long history of monarchies.

You see, these three Dominants were unusual Haus residents in that none were criminals nor embarrassments to their kinfolk. They had not been sent to live in the walls to keep them out of prison nor did any of them have a history of unwarranted cruelty.

What these three men had done to end up being sent here was to be the youngest of many "spare sons." Their parents wanted them out of sight of the public to keep from pulling the spotlight off their much more celebrated older brothers.

It likely bothered all these Dominants a bit that their heir older brother could claim only the luck of birth that caused them to be more successful than the three of them. If it did though, they never told a soul about it.

Master Byron smiled with wickedness. "Well brother, Friedrick and I are looking to start a fight. However, we are currently outmanned. You feel like scrapping?"

Master Rolf let out a yip. "Does a dog lick his hodensack? Ja, hell ja. You point out the motherfucker you desire me to pummel. I am so there." He appeared thrilled to be asked to battle, which surprised me a great deal. Why the fuck anyone would desire a possible black eye was beyond my comprehension, you know.

Master Friedrick chuckled. "Ah, then follow us brother. We point you in the right direction."

The two huge brutes turned around ready to head back for the storage closet which was still within view by the way. I got up to follow since I had no choice. Master Byron still clutched my chain leash tightly. It was at that moment Master Rolf and the two beautiful FemDoms saw me there. I was so little they had missed me kneeling behind the big men all that time.

Mistress Sigrid let out a yelp. "Holy hell. Look there, Gisela. That is the Priceless."

Master Rolf stopped along with his companion's with an expression of confusion overcoming him. "Wait, brothers. What the fuck? Is Sigrid correct? This silver you are hauling by chain, oh meine Gott. That is the Forbidden Metal. How?"

Master Byron and Master Friedrick halted their march and shot each other smiles as Master Byron responded, "His metal is ours if we keep him protected, brother. That is what we are doing, earning our taste. You in or out of this task? We don't have all day. The cocksuckers we wish to teach a lesson about fooling with what is ours by agreement will get away if we fuck around much longer conversing like a bunch of old ladies."

Master Rolf and the FemDoms stared at me in shock as Gisela said, "You get a taste if you defend him from others trying to get such an honor? Holy shit, I want in on this deal. I will fight too. Sigrid you in?"

I smiled with joy at that statement as Sigrid nodded. "Hell ja. I would beat up my own mother to get the thrill of tasting the Forbidden. Let's go brothers. Who are we killing?" I liked these girls style you know.

Master Rolf snorted. "Wait a fucking minute. If I go then I want in too. This is bullshit that everyone else gets the good stuff but Rolf."

Master Byron shot a look of fear to Master Friedrick then back at me. "Wait, none of you can just hit one man and get what belongs to Friedrick and me. This contract is with us and the Priceless. Not him and the three of you."

Sigrid scoffed then looked at me with a sweet smile. "Tell me little silver. Will you let my sister and me enjoy your favor if we beat up the bullies that dare to threaten such a treasure?"

I nodded so hard my head almost fell off. "Ja, I am happy to leash with your honorable sister and you, Mistress. I would marry you both right this minute."

My childish response caused the group of Dominants to break out in wild laughter as Gisela responded, "See, he Priceless says ja. Let's go. I am ready to seal this deal. A finer marriage proposal I never have had." Sigrid nodded still laughing.

Master Byron put up his hand to silence the crowd,. "Ah, well, we can work this all out after we have beaten the foe. You see though three motherfuckers hanging around that closet? We have to remove them to enjoy this beautiful boys skills. Otherwise, I bid all you a fine morning and see you later."

Master Rolf grunted. "Wolf, Karl and who the fuck is that other asshole? Well, okay I am good for running the sonsofbitches off, but I want the Priceless to give me the same agreement as he offers all of you for it." He looked at me, searching for my answer.

I stopped smiling and looked at the floor. "Uhm, nein. I cannot give you the same as I grant Master Byron and Master Friedrick."

He frowned. "Why the fuck not? You are willing to let these girls taste you and my brothers. What the hell?"

Master Byron pulled me behind him. "He has a long-term agreement with us brother. This is not a one-time service in either direction. We have his favors for many reasons other than this single fight. I think you misunderstand him."

Master Rolf rolled his eyes. "Shit. Okay, then if he cannot give me the same as you two I wish to have what he offers our sisters. One taste for one service. If I cannot get that at least, then I am not willing to risk getting a busted head."

Master Friedrick looked at me with a shrug. "That is a fair request, Mad Maxx. You should take his offer."

I shook my head in disbelief. The brutes wanted me to agree to allow this Dominant to join in their two-man tag team to get access to a room to fuck me over. Oh, hell no.

I winced. "I would rather go back to my Master Leo's apartment now if you don't mind, Masters."

Master Byron growled. "That is too bad Mad Maxx. We are going to get what we are earning this very morning. You can hope Freidrick, and I can beat those three men alone, or you can be fair to our brother Rolf and assure we vin. If we lose this battle, then hard to defend you from their designs with you when we are unconscious, ja?"

Sigrid leaned down to look at me with a kind smile on her face. "Say ja to Rolf, little silver. Me and Gisela will be there too. Like a big happy family, ja?"

I narrowed my eyes still looking at my boots. "Mistress forgive me, but five of you. That is not possible."

That made them all laugh again as the gorgeous FemDom sung out. "Not all at once silly. We take our turns. You will not be overwhelmed."

I looked up at her in surprise. The idea of getting to be with the two gorgeous women was worth putting up with one more man, or so I thought at the time. I was starving for the interest of the female.

"I am in a chastity device, Mistress. I cannot uhm, be with you and your sister like a man should be." I closed my eyes and blew out my breath in frustration.

The FemDom didn't appear upset. "Ja, I am aware. Your being chaste is not a secret in this Haus, little silver. We work around that, devices can be removed." She winked at me with wickedness.

I smiled and swooned at her. "Are you trying to trap me in my metal Mistress?"

She giggled. "Would you mind so much if you had my sister and me to satisfy all your days?"

I felt myself floating in the air as I said in a trance. "Nein, I would not Mistress. I would thank you for the mercy of it." Fucking hormones. Being a teenage boy is not fun, Meine Liebe, let me tell you.

The FemDom reached out and run her hand through my sweaty hair making me shudder. And it required an adjustment of my caged cock too. "Well then, tell your Master Rolf you take his offer for service in return for his taste of your metal, ja?"

I nodded with a stupid grin on my face fully hypnotized by the gorgeous woman. I was unable to think straight nor resist her commands at that moment. The promise of a willing couple with that Goddess and her sister was far too much for this stupid boy to resist. No matter what other foul thing I had to do to get it.

Master Rolf's sudden yell of thrill snapped me out of my seduced trancing. "Well hell, ja. Let's get this ugliness out of the way. We then party boys, oh, and girls."

Master Byron nodded then took off dragging me behind him. The group of females and his brother Dominants were fast at our heels. Wolf, Karl and Russell saw the crowd coming back toward them. I noticed they all took up the stance of aggression.

I guess I assumed they would turn tail and run away. Well, nein. Their faces made it clear, they were ready to fight. I shivered in fear realizing that if my champions failed, I was going to be nothing but a rumor by sunset.

That second we were almost within striking distance of the brutes, Master Byron turned around and handed my leash to Mistress Sigrid.

He looked at her sister then to his brothers. "Sigrid you and Gisela stand back and protect the Priceless with all you have in case we fail, ja? Do not let him go. If we miss then others in this Haus will be looking to attack too. You run with him fast as you can back to his Masters on the sixth floor."

The FemDoms nodded as Mistress Sigrid took my chain. They then stopped their march holding me hostage with them only a short distance from the oncoming fight. I dropped to a kneel and watched the show unfolding as nervously as my Mistress's appeared to be.

At this point, I wasn't so sure the three of us wouldn't end up having to flee as Master Byron told us we may.

This was one scary moment being unsure if I had not made a huge mistake offering my special services to these brutes in an effort to end the constant hounding of Karl, Wolf, and apparently others in their family. Once again, I thought maybe I should have stayed in bed.

Master Byron shouted out at the scum. "You boys seeking something?"

Master Karl yelled back. "Ja, we are. That Priceless you hold. Give him to us or there will be trouble."

Master Freidrick chuckled. "There is already trouble, cocksucker. That collar is under our protection. You want him, you come through us first."

Master wolf sneered. "Call your boys off, Byron. There is no reason for the honorable Dominants at our levels to fight over that little nothing. Be reasonable. Hand over his leash and walk away. We never saw any of you that we swear to."

Master Rolf chuckled with evil in his tone. "I wouldn't give meine piss for any oath your give Wolf, nor you Karl. Both of you are nothing but crooks. Trying to steal from the Elders. Shame on you."

Master Karl put up his fists. "That is an insult I will not tolerate. Come on you brutes we settle this shit right now."

With those words the battle began. I shook in terror as Master Byron come forward his fists flying right into Master Karl's face. The two big brutes slammed each other into the wall with enough force to shake the floor beneath my knees.

Master Friedrick went after Master Wolf with the same violence. The two began to exchange punches like the prize fighters, sweat and blood splattering all over the place. The sounds of their knuckles colliding on each other's skulls echoed down the hallway.

Master Rolf took on Russell. The two of them exchanged a couple of punches then Russell attempted to pull the Dominant into a hug to prevent further assault. Master Rolf would have none of that. He forced his arms outward and broke Russell's hold on him. He then laid into his face and chest with a rapid fire series of blows. This sent Russell into the wall his air rushing from his lungs with an explosive sound.

The FemDoms yelled out words of encouragement to their teammates in the fray. I was surprised by the blood thirsty comments both were shouting for all to hear. I was never aware of how brutal the female could actually be. If their Dominant brothers had done half of what these ladies were suggesting, wow, the black collars would have had their hands full mopping up that mess for years.

I knelt dare in silence my eyes wide in both fear and awe. These Dominants I had contracted with were amazing fighters. They were far too advanced in their skills of battle for any of Master Karl's boys to handle. Each man threw punches in an organized fashion. They obtained the most damage possible with the least amount of effort, making each blow count. I watched this scene recalling a professional boxing match I had seen on Master Claus's television once. Master Byron and his crew were good enough to have been capable of holding dare own against the best prize fighter. At least I thought so anyway.

To be honest, the fighting was nearly over almost as quickly as it began. The clear winners were my men. Master Wolf, Master Karl and Russell were bloody messes, barely able to stand in only a few minutes. The first to run was Wolf.

Master Friedrick hit him in the nose, breaking it, and that was enough for him. He fell into the wall, then rapidly fled holding his face in silence. He nearly fell several times in his retreat. Russell saw his brother hauling ass and wisely decided to do the same. Only Master Karl remained.

Master Friedrick and Master Rolf leaned over their knees catching their breath chuckling while their brother Master Byron made short work of his foe. Master Karl saw that he was outnumbered when he fell to the floor after a painful blow had been delivered to his chest. He looked around and an expression of terror came over his bloody face.

Master Byron was coming to aid him back to his feet so he could hit him some more of course. Master Karl decided he wanted no assistance from his opponent. He growled out in fury then got up and turn around fleeing down the empty hallway to join his defeated brothers. Surely, to lick his wounds. He was not getting to throw the Priceless from the banister that day, ha.

Oh wait, not a time for celebration for the Mad Maxx. True, I was out of danger from those brutes looking to kill my ass. However, that same part was in peril from three that were humongous and capable of beating the Karl group to a pulp like that. There was no one around to see either the fighting nor hear my scream for help after it when these fellows demanded their payments from me. I was alone, left to the mercy or lack of it, from the toughest three men in that entire Haus.

I trembled in sheer dumb terror as the three brutes all slapped each other on the back congratulating his brother for a great win in battle The FemDoms were squealing in thrill and clapping for their hands. The ladies shouted out many praises and gave each other high fives over their brothers' victory.

The men caught their breath quickly then come back toward the three of us. I kept my eyes to the floor as the girls give each of the Dominant's a kiss, while continuing their flattering words. I didn't have to look up to feel their eyes on me with smiles on their faces. They towered over my kneeling frame like ancient trees do a mouse.

Master Byron shot a look at the others. "Well, the closet is ours brothers and sisters. To the victors go the spoils, ja? I am taking my taste first since I got the leash rights with the Priceless before any of you did." He snatched my leash from the startled hands of Mistress Sigrid.

Master Friedrick nodded. "Sounds fair to me brother. Make sure to leave something for the rest of us though." He chuckled with a bit of bitterness at that.

Master Rolf looked at me with his brow furrowed. "How long do we fucking have? Shit, if I have to wait in line behind all of you maybe I go read a book and do my laundry first. I say we go in groups. You take Friedrick with you Byron and I join the lovely ladies in my own taste. That would solve the time issue."

Master Byron frowned. "What the fuck Rolf? Do you hear yourself? It won't fucking matter if we go one at a time or all at once. This is a little fellow. I don't care how skilled he may be, no way you can go faster than nature will allow."

Master Rolf scoffed. "Don't be stupid brother. That boy can handle two at a time. He is built for it. If he were female three. Ja, ladies?"

The FemDoms blushed but nodded with loud giggling.

He snorted. "Ja, see. You and Friedrick take him for your taste then the three of us go next. we will stay out here and make sure there are no interruptions, then you boys do the same for us. Deal?"

Master Friedrick smiled. "That makes sense too, Byron. Let's do what Rolf says. I don't mind sharing at the same time. It would go faster too."

Master Byron looked at each of the others and sighed with frustration. "Fuck. I suppose I am outvoted. Okay, fine. Come on Friedrick. You stay out of my way though. I don't need you cock blocking me." He pulled my trembling ass after him toward that fucking storage closet with Master Friedrick following to the sounds of laughter breaking out among the three left behind.

Not once during that horrible discussion of sharing my favors did any of them ask me what I wanted, which was to run away or rethink going over that banister to be honest. There was nothing I could do about it. I needed protection, and worse they were big enough to kill me with one blow if they wanted to.

If all five had decided to gang up I would have had to comply like it or not. I did my best to brace for the coming humiliation but there really is nothing that ever can prepare you for the harsh tag team of two huge fellows like Master Byron and Master Friedrick.

As Master Friedrick closed and locked the door behind us, Master Byron walked over to clear off a table for their lustful acts. I closed my eyes and reminded myself of two things. The first is that my dignity would buy me a ja vote for freedom in only five months.

The second thing I thought of was if I could survive this hellacious two-man sodomy. Then the luscious

FemDoms would remind me of why I bothered to keep fighting for a better day. I decided to forget Master Rolf was with their group for that moment anyway.

Master Friedrick was looking me over with curiosity as I stood there with my eyes to the floor wringing my hands in nervousness, okay fucking terror. "He is so little, brother. I am worried I will hurt him you know. It will be like the Saint Bernard on the Pomeranian, ja?"

Master Byron laughed. "Jesus Friedrick. You are dumb as the post sometimes. The boy can handle you, long as you don't try laying on him. Fuck you act like a virgin. Mad Maxx, to your knees boy. Show this stupid brute your skills and be quick about it please. I would like to spend more time getting to know you better but that will have to wait. Time is near up I believe. Let's go."

I nodded then dropped to my knees as told. The big brutes undid dare pants without wasting any more time. I was ordered to demonstrate my oral skills on them both at the same time. This was not something I had not encountered before. Master Jonas and Master Malfred had already forced me to become quite talented at this juggling act, no pun intended there, yikes.

What was new and horrifying was that these fellows were a sight larger than anything I had ever encountered before. The sad fact was that both fellows were proportionate in every way. Big men meant big everything. I gasped and nearly ran screaming when my new lovers gained full interest in my abilities. My expressions of terror appeared to humor the men a great deal.

Master Byron chuckled. “Calm down, Mad Maxx. We will be kind lovers, I promise. You get over there on that table and I will go first. You keep your Master Friedrick happy while I taste your metal. This will all be over in no time. Easy for you and just think no bruises, busted spleen or being pissed on for your efforts, ja?”

I groaned as I stood up to do as commanded. “I beg your mercy to be gentle Master. I have the lubrication please use it liberally.” I reached in my pocket and handed the tube to Master Byron grateful that Peter had visited with me earlier that morning for the only time in my pathetic life.

Master Friedrick chuckled. “Damn, I am impressed. He is so fucking good at the special services he carries the good stuff on him. Now that’s a professional there. I admit I have never been so thrilled in my life. Not even with you brother.”

Master Byron slapped Master Friedrick’s shoulder playfully. “Shut your mouth, Friedrick. You loved it and you know it. What I want to see is the sight of this boy’s flesh. I have heard rumors about it. Mad Maxx, before you get on the table, strip down please. Let us see the real Priceless in his entirety.”

I shrugged. “As you wish but not really necessary to finish this service and wastes time, Master.”

Master Byron nodded. “Ja, it does but I have to see it. I have always wondered. Go ahead and strip, then get on that table but sit up and don’t get like the dog. I don’t care for that impersonal shit. I like to look in the face of my lovers.” He pointed at the spot he intended to engage me.

I let out my breath at them words. Shit. Bad enough I had to tolerate his penetration with that fucking huge cock of his, but he wanted to see the look of horror on my face while he forced himself on me. Damn, I hate it when they do that. The whole scene was getting worse by the moment. I took off my clothing wishing I would die before either of them got around to touching me. I must say at this point, the Vampire, Leo, and even that fucking Malfred or my father Peter were looking better and better to me.

When I was completely without clothing I walked over to the table to do as commanded but was startled out of my walk of shame by the men’s loud gasping. I turned around to see what the hell was the issue to find them both staring at me with their eyes wide in fascination.

I dropped my gaze feeling suddenly more upset than I even knew possible since I was already pretty freaked out. “I beg your pardon, Masters. Are you displeased? I can put my clothes back on if you wish.”

Master Friedrick let out his breath and shot a look of amazement at Master Byron. “I don’t believe what I am seeing. How the fuck is he walking around and speaking to us? If I bore the torture that left marks that heavy on my flesh you would find me drooling and shitting my pants in the nuthouse for truth. This little man is the toughest sonofabitch I ever seen. Look at him. He isn't even afraid of us about to sexually assault him. Shit, I bow in respect to this boy. If he grows up, I wouldn't want to be an enemy of his."

Master Byron smiled and nodded. "He is magnificent. I think I am in love. I never have felt so lucky in all my days. This beautiful boy is about to be in my arms. You can stand here and admire him all day if you want. Byron is going to consummate this contract with vigor and make this wonder meine." He come rushing toward me causing me to cower in terror.

He grabbed me under my arms and lifted me in the air placing me on my backside to the table. I gasped and trembled while he prepared himself and me for his entry with the lubrication. He continued to assure me he would be careful. I closed my eyes and nodded bracing for what I was sure would be a nightmare couple.

Master Byron was not lying to me. He did take his entry slowly. That didn't help much considering the amount of Master Byron he was trying to penetrate me with. I confess I wailed and white knuckled it as he attempted to give me time to adjust to his manhood. The pain was unimaginable. Well, I suppose you are aware of it aren't you Meine Liebe? I nodded with a groan recalling my first few times handling my six foot five Master's very proportionate sex organ myself. I definitely had empathy for him in this case.

Nothing I did aided me in this most uncomfortable matter. I tried to relax (good luck with that), gritted my teeth, wailed and ignored the tears that streamed down my cheeks while he started his slow but strong intercourse thrusting.

When my worst screams of agony were dying down a bit, you eventually go numb from the pain as you well know, Master Byron began to kiss on my neck and chest uttering sexually charged thrills regarding how much he was enjoying his couple with me.

Master Friedrick approached, and I was commanded to engage him with my oral skills. He reminded me I need to keep him ready for his own mount the second Master Byron found his orgasm. That was tougher to do than you think. The brutal thrust and overeager adoration he was heaping on my flesh with his mouth made it difficult to attend to both of them without losing my mind. This was a true test of my ability to endure this pathetic existence as a pleasure submissive.

Somehow I managed this balancing act to the completion of Master Byron's apex. It seemed to go on forever but soon I noticed his increased panting with harsher mount. I confess. I had to stop my blow job with Master Friedrick to scream out in torment as the man suddenly went into a brutal bucking thrust. Master Byron yelled out many praises of joy as he reached his loud climax.

Master Byron's statements and wild behavior at his completion incited near explosive excitement in Master Friedrick. The brute was drooling, I swear it, as he watched Master Byron breath out in relief then fall forward to kiss my chest a few more times. He loudly demanded he uncouple and get the fuck out of his way so that he could have his turn with me.

I whimpered that I needed a moment to rest, but Master Friedrick was not going to hear of it. He pushed Master Byron off and took his place before either of us knew what the hell was happening. I wailed out in agony as the big brute forced himself into me without the mercy of adjustment.

Master Byron yelled at Master Friedrick while trying to redo his pants. "Animal. Christ, can you not control yourself. Let the boy have a minute before you go fucking him like a mindless cock."

Master Friedrick stopped himself and looked into my sweating, tear drenched face. "Oh, shit. I apologize, Mad Maxx. Where the hell are my manners. I lost myself there. We wait a moment before I continue, ja?"

I screamed out full of pain and terror. "Just hurry up and fucking cum, will you Master. I want this nightmare to be over so I can finally go home."

He nodded then went to work with his brutal thrusting. I wailed and clawed the tabletop doing my best not to beg for mercy. The man was bigger than Master Byron and he had not stopped to think to use the lubricant. It was not completely a dry sodomy situation thanks to the liberal use of it by Master Byron, but a fresh helping of that slick stuff would have been most appreciated. Hell, this was a bad scene.

I had a secondary humiliation of having to endure the creepy voyeurism of Master Byron. He stood there watching his brother bugger me with a look of being the star struck fan. I did my best to ignore his unnerving gaze of awe, and his brother's loud piggish grunting and panting. That wasn't too hard given the fact that I was pretty sure instead of busting my spleen, these two brutes were going to bust my uhm, well you know, my meal ticket. *Master Maxx and I howled in laughter at his calling his backside such a truthful name. Okay we are sick puppies to find that funny but to be honest what else can you do but laugh when shit gets that real.*

Lucky for me, Master Friedrick was more heavily primed to reach a fast climax. The brute reached his orgasm relatively quickly in comparison, though it still seemed too long at the time. He bashed into me so hard the back of my head smacked into the wall near knocking me the fuck out.

Unfortunately, I maintained my consciousness. He fell over panting burying the boy under his huge frame. I could barely hear him mumbling his gratitude to me for granting his taste of my metal thanks to the mounds of flesh all around my ears.

I moaned in pure despair begging him to get the hell off me. I could barely breath with his weight on my chest and cock in my nether region. That was simply more Master Friedrick than the Mad Maxx could handle. Master Byron come forward and pulled the brute off me. He loudly reprimanded him for forgetting I was a little thing that shouldn't be cuddled without thought for his size advantage over me.

I was shaken and weeping silently on that table but more than grateful the horror was over for now anyway. I was already thinking I was going to have to find a way out of this bargain. I barely made it through that session and was sure I could never do that. Nor did I want to again.

I had briefly forgotten I still had three more to go but shuddered harder as I suddenly recalled I wasn't done yet. Though I didn't mind the FemDoms so much, after that shit, I was kind of fucked out you know.

The two brutes patted each other on the back with satisfied smiles on dare faces as Master Friedrick said, "Damn. That was amazing. This is the best deal I think I have ever made. Mad Maxx you are the Priceless. I swear I never cum so hard in my whole life. Vow, where the hell did you learn that shit you do with your tongue?"

I moaned. "I was trained by Master Peter, Master. You surely know that."

Master Byron laughed loudly. "Ah, maybe so but that cold fish didn't teach you that. I should know I was in a threesome with him a couple years back. Worse experience of my life. That bastard couldn't blow out a dying candle. Nein, that artistry you demonstrated for us, that shit is natural. You were born with those remarkable skills to pleasure no doubt. Come on Friedrick. We must give up our beloved treasure to damned Rolf and the harpies. The good news is we can enjoy this boy anytime we have the chance. Mad Maxx, we see you in a bit. You have my oath of loyalty and vote of ja for truth. You are worth all of it and more." He slapped the smiling Master Friedrick on the back.

Master Friedrick nodded. "Ja. What Byron said goes for Friedrick too. You need anything, call on me. I will come running without hesitation. You will be out of that metal the moment you come before me at collar selection. You have meine vote ja." The two of them walked to the door turned around smiling another moment then left, closing it behind them.

I groaned and tried to reposition on that table but let out a yelp of pain. They were big guys. I heard speaking outside the door and female laughter. I wiped my tears away as I got off the tabletop. I dropped back to a kneel wondering if I should dress or wait for the next group's commands. I tried to assuage my horrid feelings of self-hatred by thinking of how wonderful the couple with the beautiful FemDoms was going to be.

I no longer even cared if they tried to blackmail me over giving up my penetration virginity to them. Hell, I hoped they did. I would be most happy to couple with them both on command until the day I got those bolt cutters. What a wonderful punishment it would be, ja? *I rolled my eyes and somehow, he saw me, though my back was to him.*

I let out a squeal when his cane swatted my naked thigh. I didn't say a word as I wondered if one of his shards was watching and told on me. Probably that tattle tale Christian did it.

The door come open and in walked Master Rolf with the gorgeous FemDom's at his side. They all stopped and led out a collective gasp when they saw me kneeling naked in the floor by that table. I didn't look up to see what caused that sound of shock coming from them. I was used to that noise by this time. My heavy scars always upset people when I have been unfortunate enough to be viewed in my entirety.

I am not the prude, but over the years I have learned best to keep as much of my flesh hidden as possible from prying eyes. The normals don't handle the sight of it any better than the many Dominants and collars of the Haus did back then. I do not care for the rude staring nor the even less mannerly questions about my appearance.

You know, I often have wondered how they would feel if I were to approach them as a stranger and demand they tell me of the most horrible experience of their life. I imagine they would take offense and maybe even slap me for it.

Well, this is what it is like to have the unthinking person gasp, ask how this happened or just gawk. People are the pigs in general, Meine Liebe. Those nasty scars you already bare, and all them you will amass thanks to your mother's cruelty, best learn to hide them like your Master does, or pay the price of being the survivor that others insult without care.

Master Rolf finally spoke after several uncomfortable moments of my trembling under their startled gaze. "Well, that proves as truthful at least a few of the rumors I have heard about this collar. If you believe your brothers doe eyed expressions, the rest is truth too. I am the straight man my honeys, but I am unwilling to pass up my chance to taste this forbidden silver just so I can boast that I survived it. You must accept if everything else they say is to be believed, then coupling with this kind results in death you know."

Mistress Sigrid let out a gasp. "You are completely straight? I mean I knew you preferred the FemDom's company, but surely you have enjoyed the company of one of your own gender before today."

Mistress Gisela nodded. "Ja, sure he has. He is fucking with you sister. Tell her Rolf. This Priceless is not your first boy."

Master Rolf nodded. "Oh, you heard me correctly ladies. I have never been with a male in my life. Nor have I ever known an urge to do such a thing with all the lovely girls running around. I am the pussy hound, meine beauties. I have no interest in some foul, hairy man."

I let out a sigh of relief thinking this was my luck at last. "There is no reason to break such a healthy habit, Master. You need not bother with me, and I will swear you did for truth. I am happy to service the Mistresses and swear to your honor without dispute."

Master Rolf and the FemDoms chuckled at my childish statement. He approached me looking over my scars with an expression of curiosity. Then he motioned me to stand. I did as commanded while he circled me examining the boy without touching. I kept my gaze to the floor but began wringing my hands in anxiety unsure what his game was about.

He stopped his pacing in front of me with a smile. "You meine boy are neither foul nor are you hairy. You flesh is firm, and form very attractive despite your obvious male status. I never seen prettier eyes, not even on the sexiest female. If I were to lust after one of my own gender you certainly fit the bill. I think I am going to give your skills a try. Maybe I find no interest, but I sure as shit am going to find out. To your knees and see if you can excite me boy." I sighed and dropped to a kneel while the FemDoms giggled behind him.

He turned around to address them as he undid his pants. "You ladies joining in or leaving me to handle this boy all by my lonesome?"

Mistress Sigrid chuckled. "We must confess we never been entertained by a two man intercourse situation. If you allow us we watch, then when you finish granting such a voyeuristic thrill, we take our turn tasting the forbidden, ja?" Gisela nodded with a sly smile on her pretty face in agreement with her sister.

Master Rolf blew out his breath. "Okay, but if you watch me attempt to handle this as the clumsy virgin for same sexed couple then I get to watch you two take your bite shortly."

Mistress Gisela and Mistress Sigrid agreed in unison to his offer. I groaned as he pulled his manhood free demanding I give him the blow job. I began my oral skills on him crossing my fingers that like me, he was truthfully the straight man. If so, then this would be a short humiliation then I would finally get into the wonderful parts of the correct gender for a change.

I wasted no time assuming that Master Rolf would lose interest quickly. Well, I never was the lucky bastard. Turns out, the man wasn't as straight as he thought, and I prayed he was. I do believe he gained erection faster than his openly bisexual brothers Master Byron and Master Friedrick.

He appeared as surprised by his response as I was disappointed by it. I quickly realized there was only one hope left to pull my ass from the fire, literally and pun intended. I worked more vigorously and eagerly attempting to get him to come to climax without getting to full intercourse.

The Dominant was completely entranced in thrill and paralyzed from commanding more within only a few more moments. I began to believe my ploy had worked when he began panting and thrusting without ordering me to take a submissive stance or get on that fucking table. Likely, I would have gotten away with this hedging of services had it not been for the sudden audience calls of foul ball as the FemDoms also recognized Master Rolf was nearing the point of no return.

"Rolf, you better get that boy in position before you blow your load in the wrong hole. If you don't couple you can never lay claim to survival of it," shouted out Mistress Sigrid.

Master Rolf panted out. "Shit I think it maybe is too late. I cannot hold back." He grabbed my head and I braced for his climax, closing my eyes in relief that the worst was almost over.

Then Mistress Gisela grabbed him around the chest and pulled him back out of my grips with force. "Stop, damn it. You are about to lose you chance, fool. Boy, take your position over that table for your Master's pleasure," she yelled at me.

Master Rolf let out a growl of frustration. "Gott dammit, I was about to cum. What the hell, Gisela. You're a cock blocker. I could get blue balls doing that you know." He shrugged her off more than a little angered.

Mistress Sigrid come forward glaring at me with sternness. "You better follow that command. Get to it this minute or suffer for it." She pointed at that table.

I shot a look of resignation at Master Rolf. He was like his brothers if I forgot to mention it, a big man. "How do you desire that I position for your intercourse, Master."

He took short shallow breaths and wiped the sweat from his forehead. "Uhm, I don't know. Like a dog, I guess. I never thought this far about this thing. Is that the typical way to do it?"

I winced. "There is no typical way to do the unnatural, Master. If you wish that way then so be it, I would ask you grant me the mercy of the lubrication. The bottle is there on the floor next to Mistress Sigrid. I thank you in advance for this kindness. Oh, and you will find it more pleasant as well I believe."

He shot a look of surprise at the FemDoms. "Lubrication? Huh? Why would I need that? I don't turn the boy on is what he is saying?"

The Mistresses began to cackle at that ignorant statement as Mistress Sigrid reached down and picked up the lubricant bottle. "Wow, you really are the virgin to anal sex Rolf. I thought you were funning us. That place you plan to penetrate doesn't make its own. Wouldn't matter if you made the boy hot as the firecracker. The boy is correct. That hole wasn't meant to be fucked. You use plenty of this and you won't be able to tell the difference though. You'll see." She threw the lubricant at Master Rolf.

Master Rolf groaned but prepared himself as I took the position of submission taking shallow breaths in preparing myself for the agony of this oversized virgin about to tear me apart if he was not careful. As he took his place behind me for his mount I called back to him.

“I would ask you to go slow and be gentle please. This is not a vagina you are thumping. I can guide you through this process if you would grant me the mercy of it Master.” I braced for his blow for speaking to him as if he were the novice. *Though he openly admitted himself to be, you never call a Dominant out without risking being punished for it. I was willing to take the smack to avoid a worse pain when he punctured me in a way that would never heal.*

To my surprise he not only didn’t strike me he sounded relieved when he said, “Ja, you tell me what to do and I will do it. Thanks for the help, Mad Maxx.”

The FemDoms enjoyed the show as I instructed the Dominant on the most comfortable way to sodomize me. I have had a lot of humiliating and uncomfortable situations in my day. This was right up there near the top of the list. It was like giving someone directions on how to murder you in a way that doesn’t hurt as bad as it could.

By the time the man reached his screaming orgasm I felt about as low as the snake’s belly. If it had not been for my hope to reconnect with my manhood by coupling those two gorgeous girls, I may have been tempted to slit my wrists right then and there.

When he finished, thankfully in record time for my only real luck that fucking day, he uncoupled quickly appearing somewhat embarrassed himself by this weird bi-curious experience. I let out a breath of relief and when to rise but Mistress Sigrid come up behind me before I could.

She wrapped her arms around my chest and whispered in my ear. "Wait a moment, Mad Maxx. You have two more to go." I furrowed my brow at those words in confusion.

I tried to lift up and she put her weight on me. "What? I don't understand Mistress I cannot grant you service in this position." It was at that moment I learned what the word pegging meant.

I let out a gasp, "Oh no, Master she didn't."

Master Maxx swatted me quick as a flash, then while I yelped in pain he said, "Fucking right she did. Gott damned bitches thought this very funny too. While I was busy dealing with those big brutes Mistress Sigrid rushed back to her apartment and got their strap on apparatus. In all my days I had believed the female to be the better of the genders. That day in the closet, I got educated. I learned that even the most beautiful girl could have a heart of stone. They took turns hurting me and laughing while one held me down. They both were larger and stronger than me too. Never assume that someone is kind based on how they look, or weak as they may appear, meine Frau. Evil knows no boundaries. The most handsome can be the most brutal and the ugliest the angel. What matters is neither the physical nor even the charm. You can only tell a soul good or bad by their actions. Watch, listen, and never make up your mind about another until they have demonstrated the truth of what they hide within."

I nodded but sniffed back a few tears thinking of how awful that must have been to be fooled into such a horrible situation. I loved him already more than you can know. Hearing that those women attacked him so cruelly when he never did a damned thing to them to deserve that, well they both better hope I never meet them. That is all I will say about that.

"I had no idea when the FemDoms made the deal with me to taste the Priceless they meant like their brothers had. It took Master Rolf pulling that fucking Mistress Gisela off me, then several threats to stop that cruel behavior of the FemDoms.

I was on the floor weeping like a kid by the time he got them to stop sodomizing me with their fake cock. I was more than a little grateful to him for his empathetic standing up for me in this horror. I would not soon forget that favor. Many, if not most, of the Dominants I ever knew would have laughed and jeered while the evil women took out their brutal joke on me.

Not Master Rolf. He scolded them both saying that he would not allow this abomination to continue. That neither of them had been honest with me when they got my approval for services. He also noted that the ladies had done nothing to earn such an obviously upsetting sexual act on the Priceless. He helped me off of the floor after sending the angered FemDoms from the closet with threats of backhanding them to ugly.

He looked at me with an expression of apology. “I am truly ashamed of the behaviors of those bitches, Mad Maxx. You are a man of honor that deserved better. I appreciate you kept your word and never shirked your duties, despite the fact I realized your straight like me.”

I sniffed back my tears but looked at him with a startle. “How do you know that, Master? I mean I did just allow the couple of three men, and I suppose two women.” I almost broke down crying again as I said that.

Master Rolf chuckled. “The cock doesn’t lie. You wear that chastity device, and I noticed you never had any issues with it. If you were the schwuler, well things would have gotten painful and tight, ja?”

I nodded as I grabbed my scattered clothing to dress quickly. “You are correct. I am going to break my collar, so I never have to endure this shit anymore for the rest of my life Master. I say that with respect.”

Master Rolf smiled. “Well, I for one will celebrate when you do. I even bought an expensive bottle of champagne to drink the day you walk out the front door a freeman at last.”

I stopped buttoning my blouse with a gasp. “Huh? Why would you do that Master? I mean why do you even care? You come in here to taste my metal for bragging rights when you are the straight man. I would think you would be like all the others and hope I trip and fall into my collar for all time.”

Master Rolf chuckled. “You see that is why I came in here and tasted you metal though. I want to see history made by the boy I have heard amazing things about. If half the rumors about your struggles are truth, now that I have seen and been with you I more than believe they are, you have earned your right to cut that shit off your neck. Your skill was not hype, and your manners are above the mark. I give you not only my respect but my lifelong loyalty and friendship if someone of your caliber would bother with a nothing like Rolf. Just know, I would be the first to welcome you as my brother. In fact, you come see me the second you are done with the bolt cutters, and we drink that bubbly together, ja?”

He reached out his hand offering to shake my own. I stood there staring at it like it was something from outer space for several moments. He cleared his throat in that uncomfortable silence.

I took his hand and shook it still feeling nervous about this weird exchange. “Ja, ja, I will share that drink when I am judged Dominant. If I live that long. Thank you for the mercy of it, Master.”

He laughed out loud and long. “Ah, you are too much, I swear to Gott. You know what? I am joining my brothers in their plan to keep you safe in these halls until your selection date.”

I looked at my boots with a shudder. “Okay, I suppose one more won’t matter. I offer you the same deal, but you cannot offer me a ja vote at the selection so maybe you don't force my couple? I only give you the blow jobs?"

Master Rolf nearly fainted in shock. "Oh hell, I apologize. I had no idea what my brothers got. I thought they were doing this for the one time. Nein, I give you my vote for Dominant and my security for your friendship only, Mad Maxx."

Now that near sent me to my own faint. "What? I don't understand. You give me your vote, what vote? For nothing you grant security. How can that be?"

Master Rolf giggled. "You didn't know? I was raised to Voting Council just this morning by Peter. That is where me and those awful girls were headed, to celebrate my good fortune. Ja, I give you my vote and my protection but not for nothing. I desire your friendship, I think you don't value that because you don't realize just how rare a treasure it truly is. In this life you can only count real friends on a single hand. Friendship and love are the two things that are like you, they are Priceless. So, do we have a deal?"

The door opened suddenly, Master Byron and Master Friedrick came inside appearing upset before I could answer. Master Byron looked at me with worry in his expression.

"What the fuck happened in here? Sigrid and Gisela are super pissed at you Rolf. They have been out their cursing your name for the last five minutes. I had to force them to move on, but I fear they will be waiting to cut your throat at your apartment later," said Master Byron while looking me over as I finished re-dressing.

Master Rolf scoffed. "The dirty bitches took liberties with the Priceless that he never agreed to. I made them be honest. If that makes them angry, tough shit. I will thrash their asses if they ever do that shit again."

Master Byron let out a gasp and rushed at me. This caused me to cower to my kneel. I whimpered as he grabbed the back of my hair pulling me to me feet so he could examine my flesh. Master Friedrick also appeared upset as he watched his brother poking and prodding me. Master Rolf crossed his arms and sighed.

Master Byron looked into my face. "Did those bitches hurt you, Mad Maxx? If they did, say so and I will see them in chains for it."

I shook my head. "They only injured my pride Master. Thank you for the mercy of your concern. I will be okay. I am the wiser for my stupidly believing they are women of their word like the three of you are men of yours."

I gasped as Master Byron pulled me into a tight hug. "Oh, thank Gott. I thought maybe they hit you or worse. Well, no matter. I will punish them anyway. No one hurts meine Mad Maxx and gets away with it."

Master Friedrick growled "Your Mad Maxx? Wait a minute. He is meine too, and Rolf's."

Master Rolf chuckled. "That boy doesn't belong to any of us. We are not good enough for him. Now are you done acting like the mother hen or do you wish to offer him a suckle, Byron? I do believe we better be getting him home. The Elders will be back from their meeting with that lawyer by now."

Master Byron let me out of him embrace while I narrowed my eyes at Master Rolf. "They were with a lawyer all morning. All of them Master? Do you know why?"

Master Rolf grinned. "Sure do, little man. You see there was this boy that died in 1966 named Christian Axel Schmitz. It is my understanding that death certificate is in error. The young man didn't die, he was in a coma."

I let out a huge gasp. "Huh!. The world thought me dead. But I am not dead Master. Who the hell did they bury."

Master Byron frowned. "Probably some unlucky collar of eight that was culled right away. Most of the children that come here have no family nor history outside these walls. You on the other hand were not a throw away. The Haus Elders had to cover up your disappearance. So, they claimed you dead and buried you."

I trembled in terror. "Are you saying I don't exist, Master? Then how can I live outside these walls? This cannot be true. Master Jonas told me he recently took paternity of me. That he married my dishonorable mother to do this. I must have an identity, or I cannot go to medical school, get a driver's license, nor marry my Frau."

Master Rolf shrugged. "That is why they been with the lawyers all morning Mad Maxx. No one expected you to live this long much less break that collar. They all have a lot to answer for and almost no time left to fix this issue. It will cost them a fortune to bring you back from the dead if they even can. I guess they are the ones getting their pants ripped down and fucked for a change, ja? Come on, we will take you home. I think you have had enough for this day."

I nodded as Master Byron took up my leash motioning me to follow them. I walked along in silence while the three of them quietly spoke of their thrill with their elevation and their experience tasting the forbidden silver. I kept my head down with my heart sinking in my chest. My spirit felt crushed, and my wind had been knocked from my sails.

I was leashed to three men besides my five Masters. Only Master Rolf had backed out of a demand for on call special services rights. I had no idea how I was supposed to service the Vampire, Master Leo, Master Claus, Master Bladrick, Master Peter, Master Byron and Master Friedrick to their satisfaction without falling apart. Then I was to understand most of the Haus was gunning to do what the cruel FemDoms had done and worse. I had Master Karl and Master Wolf, plus his family, looking to murder me without caring where they had to go to do it.

Now to learn I had been legally dead for over seven years was simply too much to bear. No wonder no one had ever come looking for me. They thought they knew exactly where I was, in the cemetery.

I realized Christian Axel could never be brought back from the dead. That was not what my Masters were doing. They were working to create a new person, a false one. The son of a Vampire, and nephew of a schwuler lover. My collar had cost me everything. My childhood, my education, my dignity, and even my name. There was nothing left of the boy that once wanted to be a doctor to fix the broken. He had been killed and the dead don't come back.

The three Council members returned me to Master Leo's apartment to find it still devoid of my Masters. They watched me until I was safely inside with the door locked. I took up my thrilled baby hound and sat down on the floor with him. Der Makellos licked my face and did his best to console me while I wept until no more tears would come. My chest was aching with the weight of my sorry lot in life and fear that I could never overcome all I had left to endure to find my way out of this hell.

When I could cry no more I put my sleepy hound to bed, then I went to the bathroom. I turned on that shower and watched that contaminated water flow. I no longer cared that I would die from getting into that radiated shit. I wanted to die, Meine Liebe. I just no longer had the strength to do it outright. I got into that foul stuff and scrubbed away all the horrors of that morning along with a few inches of my flesh for good measure.

I put on a fresh pair of breeches and a blouse, then crawled into Master Leo's bed. I covered my head with the blankets deciding I was never getting out of that bed for the rest of my life. I was done. I simply couldn't take any more of the hurt, the humiliation, the setbacks, the fear, and the noise.

As that terrible morning turned to late afternoon at last I heard the door open. Master Leo and Master Jonas were speaking in whispers, but I didn't care. I refused to move, listen in, or acknowledge either of them even when they come into the room.

I closed my eyes as I heard the Vampire say, "Christian Axel. Get up, meine Liebling. We are going to the Great Hall tonight to celebrate."

It was then Master Leo let out a wail from his bathroom. He come running holding the bloody sandpaper screaming. Christian Axel is at it again Jonas. Boy was he ever wrong. This time I did something different with that sandpaper than he assumed.

Chapter 65: X Marks the Spot

Master Jonas glared at the sandpaper with an expression of confusion. “Christian Axel is at what again, Leo?”

Master Leo held up the bloody, wet sandpaper for the Vampire to clearly view. “He has scoured his waist to his knees. I thought we had beaten this dangerous obsession but here is the fucking sandpaper and blood is everywhere in the tub.”

The Vampire bellowed out, “Fuck. Christian Axel, you get out of that bed this minute. I want you out of your clothing. I need to see how much damage you have done this time. Leo, call the fucking Haus doctor. We likely will be in need of medical assistance again.”

I didn’t move a muscle nor respond to my Master despite his apparent fury. Master Leo started for the bedroom door but stopped to look back. He noticed I had not minded my better’s command. The schwuler stood there staring at me in shock at my insolence.

Master Jonas also stood there unsure that he was witnessing my lack of response. “Are you fucking deaf, Christian Axel? I told you to get out of that bed. Strip now,” he yelled a second time.

I continued to ignore his orders. I heard Master Leo gasp as the Vampire come rushing me. I didn’t bother to offer any resistance to his pulling me from the mattress. I let myself fall limply to the floor making not a sound. Master Jonas stood over me taking deep breaths his dark eyes on fire with anger.

Master Leo come running and caught his arm before he managed to backhand the shit out of my head. I still refused to move or even acknowledge the two of them. I laid there on the floor, trancing caught in the place between life and death full of despair.

I hate to confess this, but I had given up my fight. There was nothing left to keep me dreaming of a better day. Master Rolf had told me there was a grave that bore the name of my birth. The boy laying on that carpet, he was not someone I wanted to be, that was for damned sure.

With the real Christian Axel dead, it only seemed natural that the flesh should be where his name said he was. The dead do not come back to life, Meine Liebe. I now understood that the last seven years of my life had all been a lie. That little boy that was hell bent to get out of his metal, shit he wasn't even a real person.

More than that I finally realized they all had been lying to me all along. They only said what I wanted to hear to get me to do what they desired without too much quarrel or having to beat me too much. They might pull a muscle, you know.

None of them, not Peter, my Elder Masters, nor even the Vampire ever planned to see me break my collar. The proof was this late appointment with a lawyer. Their scrambling to try to undo what they intended to do forever was too much to bear. I had sold out my dignity, My soul, hell, my everything for something that was fantasy.

Master Leo calmly stated while still holding Master Jonas back from striking me. “Christian Axel, honey, get up. You are not in trouble. Your Masters just want to see what your hygiene ritual has done. You get up and strip off though breeches please.”

I glared at him. “You can go fuck yourself, Leo. Jonas, you can go fuck yourself too, and each other for all I give a shit. Kill me if you like. I wish you would. Otherwise, shut the hell up, both of you. You make too much racket, and it gets on my last fucking nerve.”

Master Jonas nearly blew a vein in his forehead at my open defiance. “You little bastard, get your insolent ass up. I am taking you downstairs to the chains. We will see how fucking smart mouthed you are after a few hours dancing at the end of my tawse.” He kicked at me but missed thanks to Master Leo pulling him back and restraining him from extreme damage to the boy.

Master Leo shot a look of terror at me. “What has gotten into you, Christian Axel? Holy hell. Are you trying to get yourself sent to the yard?”

I snorted. “Christian Axel? Who the fuck is that? You must be in the wrong apartment, cocksucker. There is no one by that name here.”

Master Leo gasped as the Vampire railed, “You see, Leo. You go to easy on these submissives, they get unruly on you. Let me go. We take him downstairs together. We strip him in the thudding room and there we find out what damage he had done to our property."

I got up suddenly and flashed a look of hate at that rat bastard. "Necrophiliac motherfucker. You lay claim to a corpse. All you make me sick, you wealthy freak. I would vomit, but since you never fucking fed me there is nothing to bother with, ja? You know I find it rather humorous you never forget to feed the hound, but this idiot you manage to miss every time. That is the joke, like me, nothing but a fool. I realize you value the dog's happiness more than my own, but he need not work for it. I paid for what I never got with my ass, didn't I? Well, the way I see it, I have a few years credit built up by now. I am going to spend my earned free time in this bed alone. Both of you, get the fuck out of my sight before I kill you in your sleep. You touch me again, I swear by the Gotts I will cut your throats for you. Watch me." I crawled back into the bed and covered my head with the blankets leaving the stunned Dominants standing there with expressions of disbelief on their faces.

Master Jonas come out of his shocked stupor first. He rushed the bed growling with intense ferociousness. I felt his claws close on my waist under the blanket in a move to pull me off the mattress once more.

Fast as lightening I come out of the covering and punched him right in the nose. He staggered backward knocked nearly stupid from my sneak attack. I shot a look of threat at Master Leo waving my fist.

"I fucking mean it. You leave me alone. Bring a gun and shoot me or be ready to be thumped. I will not allow another Gott damned finger to touch my house. None of you bothered to pay your rent. Consider yourselves evicted motherfuckers. This idiot is condemned. Bring the wreaker or stay the hell of the property." I slipped the cover back over my head sure that they heard that shit.

Da Vampire was beyond livid. He let out a roar that sounded a lot like the angry lion. I didn't care. I braced myself for the oncoming battle with him. I was sure to lose to this much larger man, but that was fine by me. I had decided to die with the honor I had thrown away for more than the last three years of my life. The last penetration from a man on this worthless boy would be with his fists, not his nasty cock.

There was a loud and intense knocking at the door. This caused the Vampire and Master Leo to pause a moment before engaging further with their insubordinate submissive collar. I heard them arguing about who should get the door and who should pull Christian Axel out of bed to haul down below. Even Master Leo was thinking it was time for a tune up of the reminder why I better mind my Masters.

The pounding on the door got more urgent. Master Jonas let out a bellow and took off to answer, likely to tell the visitor to fuck off. Master Leo approached the bed clicking his tongue.

"Oh, meine Gott, meine hase. You are in deep this time. I will not be able to stop Jonas from whipping you for this shit. Get up please. Don't incite more wrath in him than you already have. Think of Der Makellos. Of our haus together. You are only a few months from freedom, meine Liebling. You would throw all that away over what? Something has happened. Please speak to your Leo. I cannot help you if I don't know what is wrong," he plead from the side of the bed.

"I can tell you what is wrong with him Leo." I heard Master Malfred chime out. Apparently he was the fellow at the door.

Master Leo scoffed. "Jonas. What the fuck? Why did you let this bastard in here? I already know it is likely tied to your bullshit, Malfred. That last incident would set anyone over the edge."

Master Jonas growled. "I let him in because of what he told me just now Leo. It seems our Priceless was chased through this Haus by half the first floor this morning while we were away. Christian Axel, what the hell were you doing out of this apartment downstairs."

I stuck my hand out of the blankets and flipped him off then pulled my arm back under the covers. I heard the three Dominants gasping in horror at my over the top attempts to piss them off. Master Leo shouted out to Master Jonas to stay put.

It was then that the Dominants pulled out their big guns. I heard Master Jonas let out his breath then say,

"Alright, you stay in that bed. You need not show us what you did to yourself, nor explain why you were downstairs this morning to be chased around like a fucking hase by wolves. Don't matter to me, Leo or even this bastard Malfred. Since you no longer work here, then there is no reason to keep the tools of your trade around or the perks of it. Leo, you go pack up Der Makellos. We send him to the Guard for good. If the boy doesn't wish to earn his pet, then he forfeits that animal back to where it came."

That shit dare caught my attention.

I come up from under the covers. "You leave my puppy alone. I will kill the first man that lays a hand on him."

Master Jonas smiled with evil. "Oh? With what? Your bad breath from that shitty hygiene we all have overlooked for months now? Come out here and defend that hound if you think you can. There are three of us and one of you, little man. However, we make it fair. You only have to beat me. You do that, then I cut off that collar myself and send you and that pup right out the front door with my blessing."

I glared at him. "Fuckin liar. I cannot ever go out that motherfucking door and you know it father. You killed me. All of you murdered me. I am dead, motherfucker. Out there in the world, I am worm food. I hate all of you more than you can ever know."

Master Malfred sighed loudly. "Ah, I know what this shit is. That teenager angst I have heard so much about. The boy is hormonal, and puberty can be such a bitch, ja?"

Master Leo grabbed his chest dramatically. "Oh, meine Gott. Really, Malfred. This boy is flirting with death, and you think it related to getting a skin break out and wet dreams for the girls? Fuck this is insane. Christian Axel what the hell are you speaking about we murdered you? Boy, you are breathing sure as the sun rises. I hear you, we all do. The dead cannot talk."

I scoffed. "This one can. I am coming for you, Vampire. I am dead already. You better watch out since I cannot feel pain anymore and you can. I send you to wherever the hell your kind go when they turn to ashes. Even your fleas will burn up. I suppose you think you can turn into a bat and escape me? Not this time." I climbed out of that bed with my fists up ready to do battle with Master Jonas.

Master Malfred covered his mouth appearing in pain, then suddenly let out a loud laugh. "This would be fucking adorable if I were watching it on the television. Look at him. He thinks he can beat you Jonas. The boy is insane. I stand corrected Leo. This is not driven by puberty. The boy is the psychotic. Listen to him speaking of being deceased and killing vampire bats. Shit. What you need is a sedative."

I growled out in anger. "What you fucking need is a muzzle and a group of six with rifles at dawn, you rapist cocksucker. Shut the fuck up unless you want some of this ass whipping I am ready to hand out."

Master Malfred stopped laughing. "Oh hell no. I will not stand here and be insulted by a fucking silver nothing. Let me have five minutes with this little bastard. I will fix him up right back to quiet on his knees where he fucking belongs."

Master Bladrick bellowed out from behind, startling everyone to silence. "None of you lay a fucking hand on that beautiful boy or I will throw you from the top of the stairs myself. What the fuck is going on in here. I have five people come knocking on my door speaking of Mad Maxx nearly being torn to pieces while we were away. I come to see what the hell happened, only to find the door wide open and all this yelling. The boy is obviously upset over something. Mad Maxx, what is going on?"

I laughed. "Nothing but a return of services, Master Bladrick. You go on home, and I be along shortly to check on you."

Master Leo gasped "Wait, you show Bladrick respect but none of us? What? Why?"

I shook my head. "That man has never fucked me once. He keeps all his words to me and never has taken more than earned. Master Bladrick never calls me by a name that is not mine, thanks to you other lying motherfuckers. He has Mad Maxx's respect for all his days. The rest of you greedy fucks couldn't live long enough to pay back what you have stolen from me."

Master Leo ignored my statement, as usual. "Bladrick, the boy will listen to you. Please, he has injured himself somehow but will not allow us to see the damage. Will you do us the honor of ordering he shows what he has done to himself with the sandpaper?"

Master Bladrick's eyes went wide. "What? Sandpaper? Mad Maxx? Did you hurt yourself with sandpaper boy? If so let me see this injury this minute. That is a directive."

I smiled with wickedness. "Ah, your pleasure is my own, Master." I undid my breeched then dropped them to my knees and ripped open my blouse without hesitation.

I demonstrated to all them the deep, bloody scouring I had done with that amazing sandpaper tool. I had scarred a huge letter X into the boy's flesh.

As you are aware Meine Liebe, it reaches from my belly to my upper thighs.

I turned around to steal a glance at the scar he was talking about. I had noticed it long before that night. It had seemed odd that it seemed to resemble an X that surrounded his boy part, but I dared never ask him about it.

Master Maxx shot a mischievous smile at me.

I gasped in fear over being caught looking and quickly turned back around.

He giggled then squeezed me tightly in a hug as he went back to his tale.

I sat there wide eyed in fascination as he told me the story of his attempts to solve his problems by using an X.

The Dominants in the room gasped collectively including Master Bladrick as he yelled out, “Mad Maxx, what have you done to yourself.”

I giggled full of demons. “The Vampire has been hiding from your view my cock with this metal cage. But now we have it clarified, ja? I am a fucking man. Stop treating me like I am the female. I am built to do the penetration, not the other way around. X marks the spot you should be paying attention to, motherfuckers. It is there so you can stop missing that I have a cock and a hodensack.”

Master Leo wailed out. “Holy Christ, Christian Axel. You have desecrated your beautiful skin.”

I shook my head still smiling with evil. “Ah, ja I did, but no worse than any of you. It is my flesh, but you all seem to forget that too. I will rip it to shit all I want. You cannot tell me what to do anymore. I am going back to bed. Get the fuck out and leave me be. I am tired of this discussion.” I pulled up my breeches and crawled back into the bed returning to my hiding under the blankets.

I heard Master Bladrick chuckling, sounding quite humored. “Well boys, I am headed back to my apartment. The boy has made his points. He is indeed the male, and it is his temple to do with as he pleases. You are all merely visitors, but he must live there. I think he has let you all know that you’re not attending your services fairly. That is his right to call all you out when you are not meeting your end of the bargain. I may not agree with his outrageous way of doing it, but I know all you too well. You are hardheaded, deaf assholes. You only listen when your feet are held to the fire. He knows that and does what he believes he must to put you in your places. Alright, enough of this insanity. Mad Maxx, I will see you later, my boy."

I called out from under the cover. "Ja, Master. I come attend your turn down service later. Rest well and don't forget to take your medicine."

He snorted with much humor. "I do love that boy more than I can say. I see you dirty bastards later. Jonas, I will be passing on your offer to have dinner at the Great Hall. I am too worn from that long meeting with stuffy thieves that call themselves the lawyers today. Enjoy your meals though and I thank you for the generous offer." With that he left the apartment.

Master Malfred, Master Leo and Master Jonas stood there quietly for several moments after the oldest Elder left the room. They appeared unsure what to do with my railing ass. That wouldn't last long though.

Master Jonas came to his senses more rapidly than his brothers. "Christian Axel, you get out of that bed. I am taking you below for punishment. You cannot beat me, and even if you could, Leo or Malfred are my backups. I suggest you come along without quarrel or suffer worse for your attempt to avoid what you have coming."

I yelled out, "Do your worst freak. I am not afraid of any of you."

Master Jonas calmly called back. "Fair enough, boy. Leo, you go pack up that puppy and send him away. Malfred and I will wrestle the Priceless out of the bed."

I got out of that bed immediately rushed forward and dropped to a kneel at the Vampire's feet wringing my hands. "Nein. I come with you without further argument. Leave Der Makellos alone. He has done nothing. You dare not punish the innocent for meine own willing behaviors."

Master Jonas scoffed. "That is fucking bedder, but you still show disobedience. First of all, you don't fucking tell me what I will or will not do. Secondly, address me as your Master or find that puppy of yours served up on a platter in the Great Hall."

I looked up at him with a hate filled glare. "As you wish, Master. I beg of you to leave Der Makellos in peace if it pleases you." I spit out the words full of fury at his using meine baby hound against me like that. He is a rat bastard, not that it surprised me though. That Vampire is the worst kind of brute, you know.

He reached down and snatched up meine chain leash with vigor. "It does for as long as you stop your shit, Christian Axel. I warn you though one more insult, refusal to mind my orders, or even nasty look, and that dog is history. You understand me, boy?"

I looked to the floor sneering as I said, "Ja, Master I understand more than you realize. thank you for the mercy of it."

Master Jonas scoffed. “You are pushing it, Christian Axel. I don’t like that tone. You come with me this minute. I am going to remind you of your place. Leo, Malfred, you are welcome to join me.”

Master Leo shook his head. “I want to say that I don’t wish to go but I better. You are too angered, Jonas. I wish you would give yourself a bit to calm before correcting, Christian Axel. He is only just healed up from that dreadful near miss attempt on his life. He needs medical attention for that latest self-injury.”

Master Malfred, to my surprise, nodded. “I agree with brother Leo. I think you maybe bond him or do something that is less physical for the punishment Jonas. He needs more bruises like Denmark needs more rocks. He is the psychotic and not always capable of even knowing what he says or does is wrong, ja?”

Da Vampire groaned, sounding as if he were in pain. “You two Fraus are giving me a headache with your excuses to allow this insolence to slide. That is the problem you know. The boy is given too much freedom and treated too equally to his betters. It has caused the lines to blur in his mind over who is in charge. He thinks that he has the choice to disregard the commands of his betters. You heard him. He even thinks his flesh is his own. That is bullshit. You listen to me, Christian Axel. I own you, boy. I am your man, Master and guardian. If I want to fuck you or hand you over to be fucked by the entire Haus you will do it and thank me for the Gott damned pleasure of it. Your comfort, lack of it, even your right to breathe exclusively belongs to me. You hear me?"

I scoffed. "Ja, I am listening, Master."

He smiled at that. "Good. Then you stop acting like an ass and get back to work, ja?"

I nodded still refusing to look at him nor end my hateful voice tone. "As you wish Master. As you say, I have no choice."

Master Malfred snorted. "That is the truth. What I would like to know Jonas, is what the hell was Christian Axel doing downstairs this morning while his Dominants were out attending business."

Master Jonas narrowed his eyes. "Leo, go call Peter and tell him to bring his medical stuff. I want him to look at this mess the Priceless has made of himself before I take him below for his punishment. Malfred is right. You tell us why you were out of this apartment, Christian Axel. I warn you, lie and the hound will pay for it."

I smiled with wickedness. "I dare not lie to you Master. I was pulled from this apartment by Master Malfred's brother and Master Volf. They come to visit me this morning."

Master Malfred and Master Leo gasped while the Vampire jerked my chain harshly. "I told you not to lie. Why the hell would you leave with Wolf and Karl. That makes no sense."

I nodded. “Oh, I didn’t go willingly, Master. They knocked on the door. I answered unknowing who was coming to call.”

Master Jonas growled out. “Bullshit. You say they come to this apartment on the Elders’ floor to see you? You lie.”

I shrugged my shoulders. “I swear it on my honor, Master. They come to visit me saying they knew the Elders to be out of the Haus for the morning.”

Da Vampire shot a look of anger at Master Malfred. “Oh, they said that did they? I wonder how they knew we were in town. Humm, so they come here, and you just left with them and got yourself into trouble downstairs? I find that even harder to believe then their being here in the first place.”

I chuckled. “Well, Master nein. I didn’t leave with them. They come by to offer a flying lesson. I told them I was busy but there were two of them and only one idiot Priceless. I decided I was disinterested in their generous offer, but they pulled me out the door as neither was willing to take nein for my answer. I was blocked from returning home thanks to their insistence that I tour the Haus from the sixth-floor banister. I found myself the unwilling guest of the honorable Audrey and Fritz. They decided to throw a party in my honor and invited the entire first floor. It was indeed quite flattering, but I told them I felt I had to decline their most generous offer as well. The two of them were of the same eagerness as Master Karl and Master Wolf to see that I did as they desired despite my interest in doing other things. It seems that today not many were of the mood to accept my saying nein. Kind of like my own Masters with my choice to stay in the bed, ja? Anyway, I was lucky enough to find kindness from the new Voting Council members. The three of them minus, Master Peter and Mistress Gretta, made sure that my wishes to return home be respected by the many in this Haus that seemed to want to theft the services of the Elders from me."

Master Jonas's eyes went wide at my statement. "What is this you say? You were hauled out of this apartment by Wolf and Karl, then hijacked by Fritz and Audrey that offered you up to the first floor scum?"

I nodded. "Ja Master, and saved by Master Byron, Master Friedrick and Master Rolf. They beat up and punished the hijackers Magnus, Matz, Valitin, and Roland that would not back off when I threw a fit over this horror of the first floor attacking."

Master Malfred gasped. "You swear on your honor that my brother and Wolf started this mess, meine taube?"

I glared at him with hate. "If I lie then may lightning strike me where I kneel, Master. Master Karl and Master Wolf dragged me from this apartment like they were hauling out the television as sneak thieves."

Master Jonas shot a look of anger at Master Malfred. "You expect us to believe you are not behind your brothers attempt to end the Priceless this morning? You act shocked, but I imagine those thugs were acting on your own orders."

Master Malfred growled back, “I did nothing of the kind. I was not told of this dishonor. That motherfucker did this shit on his own. I was with all of you. Think Jonas, why the hell would I want my collar sent to the grave? This boy says they tried to end him.”

Master Jonas snorted. “I put nothing past your sorry ass, Malfred. If you didn’t command them to do this bullshit then what the fuck were they thinking. Killing the Priceless would end your holding any power in this haus.”

I cleared my throat. “Forgive me for interrupting my betters Master, but I was told by Master Karl they intended to end me for a reason.”

Master Leo gasped. “Well speak up then Christian Axel. Why?”

I turned my hateful glare at the schwuler Elder. “I would respectfully request you stop calling me that Master. Christian Axel is dead, and you all know this. Master Karl told me he wanted to put Wolf’s boy in my place as the Priceless.”

Master Malfred let out a furious howl. “What the fuck. That motherfucker. He is trying to betray me, his own kinsman. Nein, I know this boy they are speaking of. That sonofabitch is the killer psychopath. I see what he is up to. He plans to put that boy in the Haus to kill all of us and take the seat of power for himself and his men. Gott damn him.”

I nodded. “They had another man with them too, a man Master Byron called Russell.”

Master Jonas shot a look of fear at Master Malfred. "Holy shit, Malfred. If I find out you are involved in this plot I swear to Gott I will kill you with my bare hands. Wolf is calling in all his brothers and kinsmen to join up with Karl. This is an assassination attempt on the Elders, plain and simple."

Master Malfred put up his hands shaking his head wildly. "I swear it on my honor, I am not involved in this horror Jonas. That fucking brother of meine has gone rouge. I will attend to it if you allow it. I cannot believe he would dare to fuck me over."

Master Leo scoffed. "Really Malfred? It is obvious betrayal is in your bloodline. Doesn't surprise me that nothing, not even kinship, would prevent your family from doing whatever it takes to steal something that doesn't belong to them. It is all your fault even if you didn't order this latest threat. You called that sonofabitch in to rape our Priceless in the first fucking place. I not only agree to allow you to handle this but demand you do it. Otherwise, I will join Jonas in ripping you apart. I have had enough of you and yours bullshit. This constant drama is too much for me. I cannot imagine the stress it is putting our Priceless under. The boy is already dealing with too much. He doesn't need more."

Master Jonas's expression suddenly softened. "Ah, you are right brother Leo. That is what has caused this outburst in our boy. He is behaving like an ass because he felt let down by his Masters. Well, that is understandable. I also much agree with him on his other complaint. We all should stop calling him Christian Axel. He is no longer that boy, he is correct."

I glared at him. "I was told today by someone who knows that the Elders buried Christian Axel in 1968, Master. You all lied to me. I am not able to be that boy that rots in a lonely grave."

Master Jonas looked to the floor and took a deep breath. "I think that whoever told you that should be whipped for sharing information that was not theirs to udder. However, they did speak the truth. The boy Christian Axel is long since dead. We have been fighting with the lawyers all day trying to argue that this was an error. We were unsuccessful in resurrecting that poor lost boy. That said, we did manage to prove the boy had a brother born in Denmark to Agnette a year after his own birth. His legal father Jonas testified that this young man is alive and well in my home. The government allowed for this birth to be recognized as legitimate. That is what we were going to celebrate tonight in the Great Hall. My son Maximillian Weiß is now eligible to become a German citizen."

I scoffed. "Maximillian is my name, Master, is this what you wanted to celebrate?"

He nodded "Ja, Peter suggested we call my beautiful son the name he has been known by for seven years already. I thought this was very fitting and would be easy for you to assume without adding more stress. I wanted to call you Heinrick, but in the end Peter's advice was wiser."

Within the wheel room I shot a look at the stunned Maximillian, as did Taube. The Max boys had won control of both the flesh and even its identity. None of us knew what to say to this total abomination of the fucking truth.

That day February 2nd, 1973, I was officially resurrected from a living death. Master Jonas had arranged that I would be known to the outside world as Maximillian Heinrick Weiß. He told me that he claimed I was his "love child" born at home and therefore unrecorded, to Agnette in an obscure little town in Denmark.

This meant that I would have to apply, then take the citizenship test, to become German. This was pure insanity since I was a native German already. I had only left my country once in my whole life and as you know had been held hostage in it almost all of it.

The absurdity was too much for me to bear. I realized that trying to grant me back the identity the Haus had stolen was out of the question but to not even give me the right to the name Christian Axel Weiß nor admit I was born in the Motherland, well, it really didn't matter did it? I was the pathetic Priceless pleasure submissive of the Elders at Das Kaiser Haus. As far as Master Jonas and the others were concerned, I was lucky to have been allowed to live long enough for my legality being a citizen in any country to be an issue.

Afterall, they never intended for me to break my collar for truth. They were indeed all lies they fed me to keep me on my knees, reaching for a dream that wasn't going to happen. I have always wondered what they planned to do when my collar selection test came, and I failed. I suppose they expected I would attempt to kill myself.

If I accept that as their belief, then I can assume the Elders were planning to lock me in a dungeon cell leashed to the wall after my fifteenth birthday to keep me from escaping their lusts through the grave.

As I knelt there listening to Master Jonas report his good news of his win in the courts to slip me past the questions of a boy that should not exist, I realized what I just told you. I shivered as I thought of how they would have retrieved me for their pleasures, then returned me to my horrifying nightmare in the bowels of that Haus. Until I finally broke down and gave up my bid for freedom if I ever did.

Right then and there I decided Maximillian Weiß beat the hell out of the alternative probability. It also occurred to me that if Master Jonas and the others were going through all this trouble to answer for my existence to the government, and if I could make it the five months, I was a free man.

All I had to do is survive. I took a deep breath to calm my nerves. I was no fool. Making it another day would be harder than it should be. It was clear that most the Haus was looking to rape me and some of them hoping to end my days above the ground.

The main thing to come from this disappointing and bittersweet hopeful information, was that this idiot submissive better stop acting the ass or face the possibility of ending Master Jonas's attempts to grant me a future outside the walls. It was no longer important what the world wanted to call the boy, as long as he was out there to be recognized at all.

I settled my insolent behavior down immediately. It wasn't going to be fun putting up with the contracts I had made with my father and the Voting Council for the special services. Especially those three big fellow, yikes. I really had no choice now that it was a true probability I would indeed be handed those sacred bolt cutters. More than ever before, I needed protection. They had proven, including Peter, they would give it to me.

You must always understand everything has a price, Meine Liebe. When it comes to freedom I had to be willing to give up all I had, even my name and country. I had knelt for the Vampire to save the life of Der Makellos as a dead boy that called himself Christian Axel.

When Master Jonas told me to rise, I did so as Maximillian, the future Priceless Dominant, surgeon and eventually the man of Meine Leibe, the female Priceless of the legends. I accepted my fate without any further quarrel that very moment.

To this day, I am the man created by the Vampire's lies. You know me as your Master Mad Maximillian for that very reason.

My Master sighed as I turned to steal a glance at him.

He winked and pushed in my nose making me giggle. "What is in a name, meine Frau? Nothing. In meine heart I will always be the boy Christian Axel Schmitz, ja?"

I nodded then turned back around. I was glad he finally explained to me why he had two names, but I did feel pity that he lost his name in his struggle to escape his metal.

Little did I know I too would suffer that same fate not more than six years later at the exact age my Master had, fourteen, but that is for another story.

Master Malfred left the apartment to seek out his traitorous brother, while Master Leo called down to the fifth floor for my real father Peter's aid in my medical treatment. Master Jonas read me the riot act and told me the second Master Peter released me, he was going to take me downstairs for torture. I sighed with bitterness but accepted that my outburst couldn't go unpunished. I asked for that nasty moment in Master Jonas's chains, and I knew it. Oh well, sucks to be me, ja?

Master Peter arrived rather quickly. He too scolded me for scarring myself up like I had. He treated the wound with antiseptic and offered the Vampire to take me for punishment in his place. I winced when Master Leo talked Master Jonas into allowing for this third-party thudder.

It wasn't that Master Leo was trying to be a bastard to me. He was worried that Master Jonas was so angered by my disobedience he may lose his cool with me in the chains. They both knew Master Peter to not only be a levelheaded thudder, but he was more than trained to inflict much pain without much permanent damage. The fact that he had also been the one to break me into my metal in the first place was the added bonus to the two fed up Elders.

Master Leo knew that Master Peter was in on a secret plot to aid me in obtaining the bolt cutters. This is why he was not worried that my father would hand me over to any enemies we may encounter on our way down to the torture chamber below. I admit I wanted to kill the three of them for punishing me no matter who was doing it. I still think to this day I had the right to stand up for myself that afternoon, but in the end being justified didn't save my ass, trust me.

Master Jonas handed meine leash over to Master Peter and told him to move fast. He and the four other Masters, minus Master Bladrick, still intended to haul me with them to a dinner celebration in the Great Hall. He wanted time for me to get dressed and ready to attend them in a few hours.

I followed Master Peter without saying a word from Master Leo's apartment. He chuckled under his breath appearing quite thrilled at getting a chance to thud me as he had back in his heyday of holding my collar. I wrung my hands and did my best to brace for the coming pain. I swore to myself I would not beg him to stop no matter what he pulled on me.

To my shock, he hauled on the fifth floor and stood there waiting. I said nothing but looked around wondering if maybe Master Jonas and Master Leo were idiots to trust this man (me too, of course). Then I saw why he had paused our trip to the chambers. Master Rolf, Master Friedrick, and Master Byron come down the fifth floor hallway in a pack.

I shot a look at Master Peter, trembled and backed the fuck up. I was in no hurry to encounter these three big brutes for a second time in the same day. Master Peter smiled at my appearing afraid, then crossed his arms.

"What is the matter, Maximillian? You worried these boy will try to haul you to the storage closet again?" He chuckled at my startled behavior at his statement.

I shook my head. "I assure you I don't know what you mean, Master."

He scoffed. "Ah, you practice discretion. I did teach you well, my boy. Good. I know nothing and you say nothing. Come along quietly and continue your silence at things that the Elders need not know. All will continue to go well for you. Open that mouth of yours and find I won't be as kind a Master as your first go round with me, ja?"

I nodded and cast my eyes to the floor. "I do whatever you wish, Master. You get no quarrels from this idiot."

He laughed. "You are a lot of thing Maximillian, but you are not in the least an idiot. You choose your men well. They come no better than Rolf, Byron, and Friedrick. You treat them right and you will find yourself in safe hands for all time. More loyal hearts you will never find, at least not around this place of scum."

Master Byron had rushed to beat his brothers to approach us. "Ah, you are right on time Peter. You have the

Priceless with you. How marvelous. Can I hold his leash?" He looked me over with eagerness.

Master Rolf arrived and heard that weird statement. "Jesus Byron, you act like a fucking kid. Can I hold the Priceless's leash? What the hell. He is not a fucking dog that needs walking, you know."

Master Friedrick arrived last. "What? Did someone bring a dog?"

Master Peter rolled his eyes. "Maximillian, do know that while these men are reliable, maybe they are not the brightest bulbs, ja?"

Master Rolf scoffed. "Damn, you are a bitch today Peter. What is with the insulting? You keep that up then maybe we won't share the fun with you."

Master Peter scoffed. "Cut the drama, Rolf. Here Byron, you take the leash if you are going to pout about it. I am not worried. In five months, this boy belongs to me again anyway. Enjoy him while you can fellas. Time is almost up." He handed meine leash to the thrilled Master Byron that was practically drooling on me, for truth, yikes.

Master Byron smiled like a happy kid. "Well for now he belongs to us, Peter. I intend to enjoy every second of it too. Friedrick you with me?"

Master Friedrick grinned and nodded. "Hell ja. I am happy to have this treasure even if only for a short while. Life is short. You take what you can get." He walked over to stare at me, causing me to cower and tremble before his huge frame.

Master Rolf come forward and grabbed the huge brute. “Get the fuck off the boy, Friedrick. Hell, you’re scaring the shit out of him. Poor boy. Look, Peter we need to get going if we are to finish this business in a reasonable amount of time. Shit we have six customers to attend you know.”

That odd statement really caused me to tremble. What the hell did he mean six customers? I started to cry thinking that the brutes intended to hand me over for a gang raping. Master Byron saw my face breaking up and tears starting. He came at me causing me to really panic.

“Nein, nein. I never agree to this. Let me go. Help, someone help me,” I yelled out as I rolled into a ball at Master Byron’s feet.

Master Rolf yelled out, “See, I told you dumbasses. You have scared that kid to death. You are a bunch of assholes.” He knelt down next to my quivering, weeping flesh.

He reached out to pat my back causing me to flinch and yelp as he said softly, “Calm down, Mad Maxx. I won’t let anyone hurt you. I told you this already. We are going downstairs to punish those that did hurt you. I wanted you to see that Magnas, Matz, Valitin, Roland, Gisela and Sigrid pay for all they did to you, our brother.”

I stopped wailing and looked up in shock. "What? You are taking me to witness you punish my betters Master. I don't understand."

Master Rolf chuckled. "Your betters? I think not. Boy, you are so far above these nothings it is a wonder you don't have a nosebleed from it. Now get off that floor and come with us. We have a lot of work to do. I pray that me and these other unworthy brutes can punish them all to your satisfaction, ja?"

I shot a look of confusion to Master Peter. "Master, I beg of you to tell me. Is this Master Rolf saying the truth? I thought you were taking me below for punishment, not to witness such a thing on another."

Master Peter smiled with humor. "You, meine boy, need training in the art of the thudder I believe? Well, no time like the present to begin your lessons. Especially since my brothers here have found such worthy volunteers for your cane." This made all the Voting Council laugh with much wickedness in their tone.

I narrowed meine eyes. "Then you want me to thud the low Dominants that attacked me this morning? What of the FemDoms and my own insolence to my Master Jonas?"

Master Peter scoffed. "Rolf will handle the FemDoms since their level is higher than we dare allow you to attend, but you will watch that this punishment is completed. As for your own alleged insolence, I was not there when these so-called bad behaviors happened. I found a compliant, mindful Priceless submissive when I came to that apartment. I am not convinced you were disobedient. Besides, my Maximillian would never dare such things Jonas accuse him of. Get off the floor. We need to go. You are wasting our time acting the fool." I wiped my eyes and took Master Rolf's hand that he offered to help me back to my feet.

The group of them took off with speed headed downstairs hauling my surprised ass behind them. Master Byron looked back with a coy smile several times as we traveled. I would look at the floor and wring my hands in nervousness. I wanted to believe they weren't walking me into a horror gang raping, but to be honest, I didn't really believe any of them. There was nothing I could do but brace for the oncoming nightmare that surely they had planned for me.

We arrived in the torture chamber in record time. There in a line in the hallway were the four brutes that had tried to pull me into the closet earlier that day. They all had their eyes to the floor and three of them sported bruises or black eyes from their earlier encounter with the three Voting Council brutes.

I stood there quietly shaken on my leash as Master Peter unlocked the thudding room door. He and the four of us entered leaving the awaiting victims to take their turns on the chains. I was shocked when suddenly the two vicious FemDoms come pushing through the door, both bitching loudly the Master Rolf had no business calling them down to be punished for nothing.

I watched in stunned silence as Master Rolf grabbed Sigrid by her long, beautiful hair and dragged her to the thudder table. Her sister Gisela began to punch on him demanding he let the girl go.

Master Rolf not only ignored Mistress Gisela he grabbed a big pair of scissors from the table. I let out a gasp of terror as Master Peter, Master Friedrick and Master Byron laughed when the big brute used the tool to start cutting off Mistress Sigrid's locks.

The FemDom wailed and began to beg. Her sister Mistress Gisela decided she wasn't willing to stick around for her turn with Master Rolf. Master Friedrick grabbed the woman before she could escape through the door. I almost fainted when he hauled her over and aided his brother in giving both evil females a short haircut.

The ladies screamed, cursed, and clawed the two, while Master Peter and Master Byron laughed their asses off at this scene. I couldn't believe my eyes, Meine Liebe. The men didn't stop until both were nearly bald.

When they finished, because there was no more hair to cut off, Master Rolf glared at the weeping FemDoms and said, "What is the matter ladies? You are not injured. You both wanted to behave like a man earlier. I assumed you would appreciate sporting the markings of that gender you were most happy to mock when hurting that little boy over there. You see he thought you both females, but you fooled him. Not anymore, ja? He can plainly see you for what you truly are. Let this be a lesson. You keep your word when you give it, or you shut your mouths up. Now get out. I never want to see either of you again." He kicked Mistress Sigrid in her pretty hind side.

The FemDoms ran from the room, swearing that Master Rolf would pay, to the sounds of all the Dominants laughing at their empty threats. I huddled close to Master Byron in fear as the women stormed past me glaring with hate in their expressions.

Master Byron smiled at my closeness and reached out putting his arm around me. "Don't be afraid little one. Those bitches will never bother you again. If they dare to, I will put out their eyes for them. That is a promise." He squeezed me with much affection causing me even more anxiety. Yikes, this guy was acting like he was in love.

I watched the door with trepidation in case the FemDoms returned. Another shock went through me when Egon come through it instead of an angered woman. He flashed a smile at me then looked at Master Peter.

"I am here Peter. Who you want first?" He stretched his arms as if warming himself up.

Master Peter snorted "They are all the same to me. Grab one and I get the boy set up with the thudder."

He nodded. "You bet. I get that fucking Roland first. I hate that motherfucker more than any of them. Any objections?" Egon looked to the other men in the room and found no complaints.

Master Byron turned to me. I watched unable to believe my eyes as he wrapped, as best he could, the chain into a tight ball. He then reached into his jacket and produced a carpenter's apron. He told me to hold still as he tied did thing around my waist. I watched him drop my wrapped leash into the pocket. For the first time in years, I was free to move without fear of my chain tripping me or getting in my way.

Master Peter commanded me to join him at the thudder table. He aided me in choosing a tawse, then waited until Egon had gotten the weeping Roland clipped into the chains. The young Dominant saw me standing there holding that thudder and began begging for mercy before Egon even started his task. That made all the Dominants and Egon to laugh loudly.

Master Rolf shot me a look of humor. "See Mad Maxx, this idiot realizes at last he fucked with the wrong man, ja?"

I nodded with a smile, though I was thinking at this point I was hallucinating this whole thing, "Ja, he did Master. He messed with several of the wrong ones I think."

Master Peter chuckled "Well, he won't soon forget this shit. Come here Maximillian. Now you stand here and let's begin this lesson. Egon, you come aid me in instruction will you brother?"

Egon smiled at me with great joy. "You bet Peter. Just remember our deal. I get to go last." The men all laughed even harder at that as I stood there in sheer disbelief at this unexpected situation.

The next hour I handed out my punishment thuds to each of the four men that tried to rape me that morning. Master Peter and Egon criticized my form, made sure I followed the rules for proper safety of the victim, and instructed me in the art of the proper swing.

Master Byron, Master Rolf, and Master Friedrick watched the show and clapped when I finished leaving my welts on each of the guilty. All the young rapists wailed and begged like little bitches after only a couple of my swings. Master Peter bragged to all of them “his Maximillian” could take more than thirty minutes of heavy thudding before even the first call for mercy.

The fellows loudly discussed among themselves their belief in what Master Peter bragged of me. They all based this on the scars they witnessed upon my flesh earlier that day in the closet. The huge Dominants in that room praised me so much that for the first time since I come to the Haus, I was proud of my damaged skin rather than shamed by it. I hadn’t felt this assured of my strength at endurance since the day that doctor patched me up after Gerard cut me to ribbons.

When the last young male Dominant was punished by my cane, Master Peter had me use a different thudder on each man, Egon eagerly took his place in the chains. I used my favorite, the cane, to reward my old friend for his assistance and undying loyalty to me throughout my entire journey towards my freedom. I gave him a well-practiced and artful thudding until the man was in tears thanking me for the mercy of my swing.

Even Master Peter was impressed by meine grasp of that particular thudding tool. He had no idea I had been training with it since the days in his household. I was a professional already with the cane, but I needed a lot of work with other torture devices such as the quirt, tawse, flogger and electro play. My work to prepare for my final testing was cut out for me.

I admit I was still worried I would not learn it all in time to pass but I kept my fears to myself. I had never been treated to any kind of real friendship nor even been treated like a man before. I wasn't about to ruin it. I was enjoying being a part of this group of strong Dominant males so much I didn't want to appear the whinny bitch, you know.

While Master Peter unclipped the grateful Egon from the chains, Master Rolf approached me with a smile. "You did wonderful for your first time little man. I am proud of you. Those rat bastards will think twice before they fuck with you ever again."

I nodded as I put the thudders I held into the used bin to await the black collar collectors for cleaning. "Thank you Master for the mercy of allowing me to punish those that did harm."

He chuckled. "Well, it is a start but not near enough to make up for the damage I have done to you. I will find a way to repay my debt to you though, I swear it." He looked at his boots appearing ashamed.

I shook my head in total confusion. “Pardon me Master but I don’t understand. You have done nothing to me. You don’t owe me payment.”

Master Rolf shot a look of worry at the other men and saw they were busy speaking to the enraptured Egon.

He leaned in close and said quietly, “Ja, I did Maxx. I am the straight man and so are you. I had no business letting those harpies talk me into the madness earlier today. I mistreated you to show off to them. That was wrong of me. Now I have to live with that horrible memory and so do you. I am a sonofabitch for it. Do remember, I told you I desire your friendship, not your services, special or otherwise. I want to make you my brother not my lover. I will not beg your forgiveness because there can never be any for what I did. Instead, I will do what it takes to repay what I took that I didn’t even want. One day, if you call me your truthful friend and trusted brother, I will know I am finally worthy to accept the only title I desired from you in the first place, ja?” He kept his eyes down and turned bright red with shame as he said this.

I gasped. “You mean you were being serious, Master? I thought you were only trying to make yourself feel better about your showing interest in that couple.”

He shook his head and groaned. “I didn’t want to do intercourse, nor receive that blowjob. I found myself capable of both only because your skills are above the mark. I never want to do that shit again. Not with you and not with any man. I only desire the female. When you are free of that stupid collar we can chase the girls together? I always wanted to have a partner to go hunting for the fairer sex. They can be so fucking dangerous a prey. Having a brother, I trust to have my back would be a dream come to truth. I do the same for you, ja?" He flashed a nervous smile at me.

I stood there with my mouth open sure that I was hallucinating at this point. "Uhm, ja I would be happy to chase the women with you, hell anyone. I would just be happy chasing them mindlessly, uhm, Master."

Master Rolf laughed. "Maximillian, which is your name right? (I nodded) You call me Rolf instead of Master. Five months are nothing. You are almost there. I am your brother not your better."

I nodded still stunned almost too stupid. "Ja, okay Mast, brother Rolf. So, you will not be aiding Master Byron and Master Friedrick in my protection then?"

He smiled. "I will be more than aiding brother Maximillian. I am always going to be there at your side. You need me, I am there no questions asked."

I narrowed meine eyes. "What am I supposed to pay you with then? You are willing to wait until I have a job?"

Rolf smiled even brighter. "I told you Maximillian, the best things in life have no limit to their worth. Neither of us can afford the other if we were to try to put a price tag on friendship. I tell you that from the moment I ever heard the tales of your journey I have admired you. I am honored to stand here tonight speaking to the only person I have ever hoped to call me a friend in all my days. You more than earned your right to walk among the living, despite all that so many have done to steal that from you. You need not believe me, and I understand why you wouldn't. That is okay. I am not going anywhere. My offer stands until the day they put my worthless ass in the ground. I will never touch you again like I did today. In time you will see I speak the truth. I will wait. You take your time. I forfeited the right to be angered over however much of that it takes the second I took advantage of you."

I admit I was impressed if half of what this man said was truthful. "Fair enough Rolf. We shall see if you are funning me or not. I will warn you, if you are trying to fuck with my head, I have no problem sending you to visit with others that thought they could hurt me and get away with it."

He put up his fists with a huge grin. "Now, see that is why I adore you Maximillian. I tell you I want to be your friend and you threaten to kill me. You are my kind of people."

I laughed at his teasing. "You may as well drop those fists Mast, errr, Rolf. I do not scare that easy."

Master Friedrick saw me speaking to his brother Council member. He came over to stare at me with a goofy grin of his own across his face.

He watched Rolf mock spar at me then frowned. "You know I been thinking."

Rolf groaned. "Oh, hell that is bad." Then he laughed hard as Master Friedrick pushed him playfully.

"Fuck you Rolf. I mean it. I was noticing that Mad Maxx is so little, but his feet, look at them. They are huge. This boy is going to be a big man or should be one. He needs aid in reaching his size I think. This stupid Haus doesn't take care of her silvers like she should. I say we feed this boy up with proper protein and take him for work outs in the gym with us. I bet in a year he will be big enough to whoop anyone's ass that fucks with him, ja?"

Master Byron had arrived by this time and heard Master Friedrick's discussion. "Ah, ja. I cannot believe I am saying this, but Friedrick has a great idea. Of course, it is only so he can fuck the boy without squishing him I believe, but still, we should do what he says."

I looked down at the floor with a frown. "So, you two will not back off the payment of meine special services for your protection services like Master Rolf is?"

Master Byron looked stunned, as did Master Friedrick. "Huh? Nein. I am not about to give up meine deal with you, nor is Friedrick. In fact, I have that contract you wanted on me." He reached into his back pocket and handed me a rolled-up piece of paper.

I looked at it with a grimace then took it to read over. It clearly spelled out what the two Dominants expected of me in return for their votes of ja at collar selection and protection until that time. It also included that our agreement would end forever upon meine successfully breaking my metal. I sighed as I noted they both signed the paper at the bottom in blood.

I rolled the paper back up quickly and stuffed it in my jacket inner pocket as I saw Master Peter approaching. "Ja, it looks correct Masters. I accept the arrangement. I do not have a choice. I need the help."

Master Peter snorted as he walked up. "No need to use discretion this time Maximillian. I am already aware of your bargain with these brutes. All of them. I wrote that fucking contract you just tried to hide from me. I wanted to praise you for being smart enough to get the details in writing."

My mouth flew open in shock yet again. This was as weird an afternoon as that morning had been, you know. "Huh? You know about this arrangement and are not angered? You plan to tell my Masters about it then?"

Master Peter snorted. "Hell, no on both questions Maximillian. I am fine with sharing services with my brothers. I would have suggested it myself had I thought of it. You need defending and while I can hold my own, if I learned anything from that bullshit Malfred pulled last month, I figured out we need you surrounded with strength. These boys are the best in the Haus. No one is going to fuck with you with them around. I didn't expect them to work for free. You and I will work out our own provision of service around their own, ja?"

Rolf shook his head. "I cannot do shit about any of you taking advantage of Maximillian during this dangerous time, but I want to tell all of you I think your animals of the worst kind for it."

Master Byron and Master Friedrick shot looks of irritation at Rolf while Master Peter scoffed then said, "You are correct Rolf, you cannot do shit about it. So, I suggest you shut the fuck up. Keep your opinions and knowledge of this arrangement to yourself or find yourself sorry for it."

Rolf nodded. "Peter you know better. I never betray my friends. I say nothing if none of you hurt this boy. If any do, I wouldn't want to be him. Brothers or nein, he is honest in this deal. You all better remember that. I won't stand by and see more taken than earned by any of you. That is a fucking promise."

Master Peter growled. "Long as you stand aside and keep out of it, there will be no trouble. We all must work together for the next five months to keep Maximillian safe and prepare him for the day of his release from servitude. There can be no fighting amongst ourselves, nor drama or he will not make it. You understand me Rolf?"

Rolf spit in the floor and nodded. "I told you already, I won't get in the way of what the boy agrees to. I also will not be a part of it. You need me to defend any of you and your rights you can count on me. If Maximillian is the willing and not being forced, what he or any of you do is not my business. Nor do I want to hear about it either. I voiced my belief about what I think of it, that is all."

Master Peter nodded back. "Fair enough Rolf. Now that I have all of you here together I wish to address this very arrangement we all have with Maximillian. I will like to remind you boys that he has four Masters calling on his services already. He is spread thin for time, and we need to not wear him out. I see that look in your eyes Byron, you too Friedrick. I happen to know you already extracted payment earlier today. I have as well. I want an agreement this minute that only once a day, and only in the morning or early afternoon do any of us take our rights with the Priceless. If he gets caught by that vicious Jonas, then we are all out of our pleasures with the boy."

I let out my breath in both shock and relief when Master Peter said that. "Thank you for the mercy of it Masters." I understood if they desired to all force my favors again before taking me back to attend to Master Jonas and Master Leo I couldn't stop them.

Master Byron whined. "Only once a day? Shit. That doesn't seem fair. We had to fight twice today. Why can we not collect a couple in return?"

Master Friedrick nodded. "I agree with both of you, Peter. I don't want to lose my services from the boy, but I also think if we fight twice we get rights twice."

Master Peter glared at both of them. "You will have to settle for making your once a day fucking count. Some days you won't be fighting or doing shit for the boy. That will make up for the days you do more. Use your fucking brains. There is only one Priceless and three of us and four of his Masters. Can you boneheads add? If so then you do the math. The boy will fall over dead if you overuse him. That is not protection, now is it?"

Master Friedrick's eyes went wide. "Seven a day? Ah, hell. Okay, I agree to what Peter says Byron. That little man cannot handle more than that. Fuck, I wouldn't be able to handle the three of us."

Master Byron sighed. "Well, I guess we can all say with certainty that Friedrick can add. Sheesh. Okay, okay, I agree to this caution too Peter. I see your point even though I think it sucks."

I stood there wringing meine hands at the number, but then recalled I didn't handle all four Masters at the same time. Master Bladrick couldn't even engage in the penetration sex to boot, though his services were beyond gross. I wasn't about to correct Master Peter though. I knew he was aware he was hedging but I also realized he just literally saved my ass from those two large, overeager cock hounds. I was a little more than grateful, I admit.

Master Byron had me undo the carpenter's belt and give the pouch back to him. He took up my leash as the four of them took off leading me back to Master Leo's apartment. Rolf, Master Peter and Master Friedrick took up the front as Master Byron hung back with me behind the others.

As we started up the stairs to the apartments he fell back and turned around looking at me with a coy smile. "Here Mad Maxx. I got you something." He handed me a small box wrapped in fancy paper.

I looked at it as he took off walking with speed to catch us back up to the pack of Voting Council members. He turned around smiling like a love-struck Frau from time to time. I dropped the present into my inner pocket wondering what the fuck was wrong with this guy.

Master Peter left the three big brutes on the fifth floor and took me the last flight. My Elder Masters were to never know of the situation that occurred in the torture chamber below. Master Peter told me to tell the Vampire he used electricity for my punishment. It doesn't leave marks, ja? I kept my smile hidden behind my hand and my head down as he gave a "blow by blow" false description to Master Jonas about all my begging and screaming.

When the Vampire would glance at me while Master Peter told him of my pain, I sniffed loudly as if I'd been weeping recently. Master Jonas nodded with a smile of approval as he was assured I would give him no more insolence.

He looked at me with sternness as Master Peter finished his tale of punishment. "Well, you ready to mind your manners now Maximillian?" The Vampire took my leash from Master Peter.

I sniffed loudly and nodded. "I am Master. I apologize for my shortcomings. It will not happen again. I have learned my place well."

Master Jonas smiled with all his pointy teeth. "Good, then you get into that bedroom and prepare for the celebration dinner and specials services later with your man."

I took off for the bedroom cursing the Vampire for showing off in front of Master Peter by saying that last thing. I found Master Leo sitting on his bed when I entered which nearly scared me to a faint. He looked up at me appearing quite sad.

I stepped inside and closed the door. "Is there something I can do for you Master," I said while taking my kneel at his feet.

He reached out and stroked my cheek lovingly. "Nein, meine hase. You cannot fix what is wrong with your Leo. I fear I have failed you."

I looked at him filled with confusion. "I don't understand Master. How have you failed me?"

Master Leo shot a worried glance at the door then cast his eyes at the floor. "Jonas he had you judged incompetent and unable to care for yourself. He turned the evidence that you are the schizophrenic to gain this dishonor. He has told me as long as you do whatever he tells you then he will keep this information on a need to know basis. Otherwise, he will block you from everything, from medical school to a career outside of this Haus, meine hase."

I gasped and felt meine heart stop in my chest. "He did what? Oh, meine Gott. That means…" I couldn't finish my sentence.

Chapter 66: Wolf Killer

Master Leo nodded as he said what I could not bring myself to speaking aloud. "That means even if you break your collar he will control your every move. In fact, I believe it is his plan to make sure you never live outside these walls. He has trapped you for all your life to require someone, be it him or another he appoints, to be at your side wherever you try to go."

I closed my eyes with a grimace. "Is there nothing I can do about this, Master? I am not the incompetent. Even if I were, that pervert would be the last person on Earth the court should be granting such power over another to."

Master Leo sighed. "That is why I worry. Jonas is the selfish bastard. He cares only about this crazy notion of the Female Priceless, Christian Axel." I interrupted him.

"I say this with respect Master, but don't ever call me by that name again please. That boy is dead. I must forget about him. I can never start meine life over trapped in a dream that will never come to truth. I think that is the answer. I will not concern myself with this bullshit the Vampire has pulled. Not yet anyway. When I break meine collar I will hire a lawyer of meine own. Then I prove to the judge that Maximillian is not the schizophrenic, ja?" I opened meine lids and smiled bitterly at the schwuler.

He frowned. "Christian, errr, Maximillian, honey, you are the schizophrenic. There is no doubt of this. You will require a Guardian for all your days to look after your affairs when the cycles come on." He stroked my cheek with sadness in his expression.

I scoffed. "That is a lie, Master, and you know it. However, if that judge will not listen, like you never do, then maybe you can be meine Guardian instead, ja?" I took his hand and kissed his knuckles causing him to shudder with thrill.

Master Leo's expression became one of happiness. "You would allow me to do this for you Maximillian?"

I nodded. "Ja, Master. You are the best choice if there must be one. I warn you though, I will find a good lawyer. That fellow will tell the judge the Vampire is mistaken. This could work, ja, it will work." I let out my breath with relief thinking this was the answer to all my troubles. *I just needed someone to fight for me legally, is all. Maybe I even get my name back. That is what I thought at the time anyway.*

Master Leo chuckled. "Sure, it will work, meine hase. You can show that you can function with only light care."

I frowned. "Are the lawyers expensive, Master? I heard many Dominants complain they are thieves. How long do you think it will take for me to afford the best one?"

He gasped. "Ah honey, you would never be able to afford one better than Jonas has. Not without aid."

I looked at the floor. "Then I am finished Master. There is no reason to fight anymore. I cannot stay here in this fucking Haus. I want off meine knees. I don't want to suck anymore cock nor take any more of this sex with the man. I demand you send for the Guard right this second. I won't do this bullshit anymore. I mean this."

Master Leo put up his hand demanding silence. "Thats enough Christian, Maximillian. I don't want to hear another fucking word about dying come out of your mouth. Stop it. It is true you cannot afford the best legal team, but your Master Leo can. I will hire a lawyer for you meine hase. We will battle that Vampire's grip on you together."

I narrowed meine eyes. "You would do that, Master, to free me from your lusting. I find that hard to believe. I say that with respect."

He glared at me with anger. "You still don't trust me? I say I will aid you in this struggle and I mean that. You must learn in the real world you sometimes need help from another. If you don't start trusting someone then you not only will end up very lonely, but you'll eventually may also find yourself on the streets without any hope of survival."

That caused me to shrug. "I would have hoped even on the street knowing that I am the dead man that I would die free of the grips of those that destroyed meine life, Master. I would like to trust you, but you already betrayed me once. I say that with respect and with truthfulness. If you are offering to help me beat the Vampire you must be expecting something from the arrangement. I am not a fucking fool, so stop treating me like one, I beg of you. Maybe your lawyer works hard to get Maximillian as the property of Master Leo instead of Master Jonas, ja? Then my lonely

Leo never has to worry about me getting away from him all his life. That sound about right?"

Master Leo's eyes went vide and he gasped pulling his hand to his chest. "Maximillian, how dare you accuse me of trying to hijack you the way Jonas has."

I sneered at him with a nasty smile. "I accuse you of nothing, Master. I know you is all I am saying. You tell me of this dishonorable behavior of Master Jonas when it was unnecessary to do such a thing, not now anyway. Your timing is interesting, ja? I told you once to look in your mirror and admit your truths, Master. I offer that sound advice one more time. You hire that lawyer if you wish. I cannot stop you, any of you. Not yet anyway. If I really do break my collar, then all you better watch your asses. I won't be showing any mercy to those that misused me when I was helpless. I hope you are listening to me Leo. The terror I am going to unleash on everyone that ever took advantage will be epic, painful and unforgettable. The one fucking thing I have learned expertly from this horror show childhood I have suffered in this Haus is how to provide equal service for what I am given. I really do love you, but if you cross me ever again, I will kill you like all the others that are on my list. I may do it with tears in my eyes, but I will do it. I am going to collect from those that owe me. I dare you to piss on me any further."

Master Leo gasped. "Maximillian, that is the cruelest thing I ever heard you say in all the time I have ever known you. This is not the heart of the boy I know and love.

Maybe the schizophrenia is changing your personality. I admit this is frightening to me."

I grinned with wickedness. "Ah, schizophrenia, psychosis, puberty, stress, blame any or all that shit if you like Master. You and the others never will take the responsibility for what you have done. I have always served all you with honesty but got none of it in return. You knew the Haus claimed I was dead, didn't you Leo? Yet, you said nothing. Far as I am concerned, you all killed that poor little boy Christian Axel equally. Well, that is fine. I happily embrace the identity of Maximillian, the son of his mother Das Kaiser Haus and father Brutality. You better hope he doesn't decide to embrace you back, ja?" I began to chuckle with demons as Master Leo covered his mouth dramatically as if in shock.

The Vampire came into the room to find me kneeling at Leo's feet with him still seated on his bed. "What the fuck, Maximillian. I told you to get ready for dinner. Instead, I find you in her giving Leo head? Did you learn nothing downstairs in the chains about minding your Master's commands," he growled out in fury.

Master Leo gasped. "Jonas, Gott damn you're nasty minded. Maximillian is not granting me the special services. He was speaking with me only. I ordered him to kneel and converse."

Master Jonas suddenly broke out in laughter. "Ah, okay. I see now that you would have to be amazingly skilled to do more than speaking with his zipper up, meine boy. Shit, I apologize Leo for thinking you were calling in his favors before his doctor's release tomorrow. I thought you the fiend for not being capable of controlling your urges, but hell, not like it has been easy for any of us, ja?"

I glared at Master Jonas over that foul comment. "I would respectfully request if Master Leo is done with his demand for the conversation service I be released to attend to your orders Master."

Master Leo nodded. "Ja, Maximillian. I am pleased and you are released. Jonas, before we go to the Great Hall, please allow the boy to go attend to Bladrick. I don't desire to have to let him leave after we get back to the apartment late tonight. I am nervous about what happened today, and maybe it is not a good thing to let the Priceless wander alone when most are in the bed."

Master Jonas nodded. "You make an excellent point brother. Maximillian, when you're dressed for the Hall, hurry to attend to the ailing Elder. I expect you can get all this done within an hour and a half, ja?"

I nodded as I stood up to head for the bathroom for dressing. "As you wish, Master. You will not be in need of dressing service I am to assume?"

He shook his head. "Nein. I am going back to our apartment to do that. We will stay the night here once more, then tomorrow we return home. Leo and I have worked out a schedule to allow you to see your pup if you mind your manners. I warn you though, anymore shit like you pulled this afternoon I will end that dog for good."

I turned around as I was shutting the bathroom door, "I do believe I heard you clearly the first time on this threat Master. Though I thank you for the mercy of repeating it so that I never forget how cruel my man can truly be." I closed the door ignoring his flash of anger at me for nearly crossing the line of insolence in my statement. *Ah fuck him. It was unfair to threaten meine baby hound like that and he knew it.*

I rushed through my preparations. I made sure to get the flesh ready for the possibility that Vampire would not wait until the next day to call in his rights. I only had to refresh a bit and throw on my jacket, boots and a little makeup. I ignored the stinging of my latest scouring the best I could. I was starting to think that sandpaper business was not one of my better ideas. *Master Maxx and I laughed pretty hard at that obvious statement, yikes..*

I left Master Leo attending to Der Makellos to look after Master Bladrick. I had been attending him pretty regular for the last several months by that time. His health was taking a turn for the worse with his cancer starting to really cause him much pain. I made sure to check on him every late afternoon when I was capable of it.

I never forgot his ending the torture of Master Barnim. That old buzzard may have been the criminal to others but to Mad Maxx he always demonstrated a soft spot. I could depend on him to offer me sage advice and a fair deal whenever he was well enough to stand up for me that is.

Master Claus had given me a key to their apartment. I found the oldest of the Elders sound asleep, full of his prescription medications. I checked his pulse, pulled up his blanket to make sure he was warm enough, kissed his forehead and bid him a good night. Master Bladrick didn't stir from his slumber. He was deeply unconscious, and I was grateful he was out of pain for a bit. I was sure he needed that break.

I quietly left the apartment as swiftly as I had entered it. I didn't see Master Claus anywhere. I assumed he was in his own room dressing up for that sham celebration of meine dishonor of losing the name Christian Axel. It really pissed me off how much trouble my Masters were going through to celebrate their giving me a submissive's name in return for the proud one they took. As I have said, there wasn't shit I could do about it.

I started to head back to Master Leo's to await Master Jonas when I spotted Master Rolf headed down the stairwell. I watched him from my perch on the Elders' floor from the banister. This man's weird statements and promise to never demand to taste my metal again made him a bit of a curiosity to me.

I smiled as I noticed the naturally pleasant Dominant appeared to be singing to himself as he traveled down the steps. I started to return to meine own journey when a movement behind him as he passed the fourth floor caught my attention. I gasped as I noticed the Wolf and Karl had been waiting in silence for him to pass them.

In pure horror I saw the two of them slip up on Rolf. Wolf pulled out a knife and stuck it to his back before he even knew the bastards were trailing him. I couldn't hear what they said to him from meine distance, but I could see the look on Rolf's face. He was frightened as the brutes pushed him along. They were kidnapping him.

I took off like the panther to follow the three hoping to find out where they were taking him. Doing this without being spotted was harder than you think. The brutes were nervously looking all around them to see if anyone was noticing them absconding with a Voting Council member.

However, I managed to keep up without being spotted. I near fainted when I saw them haul him into that cursed storage closet I hate so fucking much. *I mean does every fucker in that Haus do all their dirty deeds in there. I think there should be a huge caution sign on the door and a Gott damned camera in there too.* The three of them went inside and closed the door.

I stood outside across the hallway unsure what the hell to do. If I went to tell the Elders Rolf was in trouble, Wolf and Karl would have time to kill him if that was their plan. I decided there was no time to go seeking aid. If I didn't attempt to help meine protector, then surely he was finished.

With as much care as possible I turned the knob and found the door locked tightly. I glanced around to notice the hallway devoid of people. I reached into my inner coat pocket and dug around until I found the hairpin I carried.

I always kept one handy in case I got into a situation that would require lock picking. I learned that shit from my long eighth month stint in that fucking dungeon you know. Such a thing would have made all the difference had I thought of it in advance.

Anyway, I used my tool with speed and skill. I had that lock undone in moments. I admit I had not thought of what I would do after getting entry. Without a weapon of any kind, I was merely asking to hand the would be killer brutes not one victim but two.

This dumbass didn't even consider this likely fact. I burst through that door yelling like I was seven-foot-tall and weighed five hundred pounds. I was shocked to near stupid at the sight of Rolf bound and gagged. His face was bloody indicating the brutes had been beating the fuck out of him while he was helpless to fight back. I stalled my charge unsure what the hell to do next.

Wolf and Karl had stopped their physical assault in a startle at my abrupt appearance and shouting like that. They at first seemed as stunned as I was. Neither made a move from their spots of pummeling Rolf.

Karl came to his senses first. "Well look what we have here Wolf. The Priceless has come to us. This must be our lucky night. Two cocksuckers to choose from. Grab him before he changes his mind about joining the party ja?"

Wolf come at me with vigor, I tried to turn around and run but tripped over my fucking leash. I went sprawling face first to the floor with a loud groan. The brute laughed as he grabbed me by my upper arms and lifted me like a feather. He kicked the door shut. I was useless to push him off me as he wrapped his left arm around my struggling flesh. I gasped in terror as I heard him relocking the fucking thing with his free hand.

Karl chuckled with much humor as Rolf's eyes went wide in fear. "Bring that little bastard over here Volf. We finish him and this motherfucker Rolf too. If we are careful it will look like he killed the boy, then himself, ja?"

Wolf laughed loudly as he covered my mouth when I had started yelling for help. "Sounds like a great plan. Shit, this is too easy. I thought for sure it would take weeks to hunt this shithead down to send to the yard."

Karl nodded. "Me too brother. Doesn't matter now though does it. Get that knife. Slit his throat and that will shut him up."

Wolf nodded then dragged me over to a storage shelf to retrieve the knife he held on Rolf to get him there without quarrel. I saw that weapon and silenced my attempts to wail immediately. The man glared at me with a wicked smile noticing my attention was drawn to his killing tool.

"Ah, you are not so brave now are you Mad Maxx? Well, it is a pity to have to kill you before I got to enjoy your favors to the hilt. Fine silver is hard to come by, ja? Too bad, really too bad." He feigned sadness as he dropped his hand from my mouth to put that knife up to my throat ready to slide it across the boy's jugular.

I whimpered, “Nein, Wolf. Stop this. I can grant you a Priceless favor right this minute. I do whatever you want.”

He scoffed. “You mean like you did this morning? I think not Mad Maxx. You had your chance. I say goodbye to you. See you in hell boy.”

I closed my eyes and trembled. “I will do whatever you want this time Master. You have a knife, ja? I won’t try to run nor give you any quarrel I swear it.”

Wolf hesitated but held the knife tightly to me skin. “What do you think Karl? The boy swears he will give me his services this time if I hold off cutting off his head. Is he to be trusted?” He chuckled and pressed the knife harder making me wince.

Karl sighed. “Will you stop thinking with your dick, Wolf. Kill the fucking boy and come over here and help me end Rolf. If you want to fuck something that bad I will pick up a silver on the way to the apartment later.”

Wolf snorted. “I don’t want a silver. I want to fuck the Priceless, Karl. After we kill him there will not be another for maybe my whole life. You know my boy is not the real thing and he is my son to boot. Mad Maxx’s death will be it. No more fine metal in this Haus for Gott knows how fucking long.”

Karl rolled his eyes at that. “You really believe that legend of the Priceless bullshit, Wolf? Come on man. I thought you were smarter than that. It is all a fantasy made up by the Elders of the past to entertain the residents. That motherfucker is not any better in the sack than any other submissive in this place. I have fucked him too, and I couldn't tell the fucking difference between common or forbidden silver."

The brute Wolf sneered. "That was because we were taking his services against his will, fool. If the Priceless grants them willingly then you can be assured he knows secrets the low silver doesn't. I want to taste his metal the proper way. What the hell do you care anyway? So, he dies in another ten minutes versus right now without my ever knowing what makes a Priceless special. No difference to you but a world of it to me."

Karl crossed his arms then looked over at the table that only hours before I had already been manhandled on. "Okay, but you give me that knife to hold on him while you get what he swears to give. Otherwise, slit his throat and be done with this argument."

Wolf grabbed meine collar holding it from the back as he handed the knife to Karl. "You heard the man, Mad Maxx. You do what you promised, or Karl here puts that knife in your skull."

I nodded. "Ja, I give you no trouble Master. I will show you why they level me Priceless."

The brute laughed. "Karl, hold his leash tight so he cannot run away this time. On your knees boy. You get me ready for my taste then we will see if the legends are truthful."

I dropped to my knees as Karl took meine leash and held that knife over me. Wolf, of course, wasted no time to undo his breeches and demand a blow job. I went to it without hesitation pulling out every trick I have in my book to keep this man happy.

While I endured this unexpected servicing, in the wheel room the three of us attempted to come up with a plan to save the boy. There were two of these brutes and it was unlikely that we would be able to catch one off guard to attack without his brother putting an end to our struggle for good.

Maximillian looked at me with disgust. "This is simple Mad Max. Get Karl involved in the special services at the same time. You know tag team them like earlier. With both interested in their cocks, their eyes can have the wool pulled over them."

I shot a glance at Taube that was nodding as he said, "It is the only way. Rolf is tied up. No one knows where we are. That door is locked. You have to distract them both, then wait for a chance to strike. Not fun, but if you don't, then the second Wolf is sated we are history."

I let out a long sigh. "I hate that you boys are right. Okay, Maximillian do your stuff. Seduce this rat bastard. Taube, be ready with me, to find a chance to kill them."

Maximillian smiled as he took over the boy's mind pulling out of his oral engagement with Volf. "Master Karl, perhaps you wish to join your brother? I can handle two at once. I am well trained in that art and happy to demonstrate this for you." I shot a coy smile at the stunned Dominant.

He looked with confusion at his sweaty, panting brother. "Do you hear this crazy shit? This whore is not satisfied sucking one cock. He wants more."

Wolf smiled with a dreamy gaze back at Karl. "You are a fool to deny the offer, Karl. This boy is amazing. You are wrong about his being no better than common silver."

You know what they say, Meine Liebe? Curiosity killed the cat or in this case the Karl.

Your father couldn't deny such a challenge. He undid his pants with eagerness and thrust himself into the ongoing special services his brother Wolf was getting. I attended the new man in the situation much more vigorously than Wolf though I was careful to not neglect my first customer too often.

With silent patience I watched that knife Karl held, waiting for the moment of his letting down his guard even a little bit. The men didn't take long before they became deeply enthralled in their lustful interests. I completely focused my attentions on Karl, at that point hoping to send that man over the edge. If I could bring him to climax, he would for a moment be vulnerable.

Wolf was unhappy with my sudden withdrawal of oral attentions. He loudly demanded I take the position of submission. I nodded but didn't stop meine skills on his brother Dominant. I leaned forward giving him no fight as he got behind me and pulled down meine breeches for his intercourse.

I was unhappy about this London Bridge situation but realized that if Wolf were busy with penetration I could take out Karl then him before either of them even knew what hit them. I gasped and shuddered as the brute began his sexual assault on the boy without allowing any mercy. It took only a moment for me to refocus my efforts to get that fucking knife, but it was a most uncomfortable few seconds let me tell you.

Wolf had begun to moan loudly in his thrill when I saw Karl do what I had been waiting for. He closed his eyes and groaned out in his rapture. With the speed of the cat, I reached up and snatched the knife from the orgasming Dominant's paralyzed fingers.

It appeared he didn't even feel the blade in his groin for a brief moment. Wolf sure didn't notice his brother's peril. The man continued his harsh intercourse with the boy as I sunk the blade into Karl's gut with a second thrust of my own. Karl led out a loud cry of agony, but Wolf thought he was merely announcing his climax.

Wolf yelled out, "Hell ja, brother. I am right there with you." Then before I could turn around to stab meine sexual offender in the eyes Karl fell to the floor with blood flowing like a river from his stomach and cock.

Wolf uncoupled immediately and tried to stand seeming stunned by the sight of Karl twitching in his death throws and his own blood. He come to his senses quickly. I struggled to get away from him, but he was too fast as my pants were around my fucking knees. He rolled me to my back. I swung the knife at him, but he caught me by the wrist.

As your father Karl groaned out his final breath, Wolf wrestled the weapon from my hand. I closed my eyes to await the slashing from that blade when all the sudden I heard Wolf let out a gasp, then a loud wail. I opened my eyes to see the brute fall to the floor with his throat opened and torrents of blood flowing from the wound.

I was stunned as I watched the man try to hold his neck closed without any luck. He started to kick, slash the air wildly with his blade, and gurgle in his final struggle to avoid the coming reaper. I nearly pissed myself when Master Malfred come forward and grabbed the knife from the dying Wolf's grasp.

I couldn't find meine tongue as the Elder Master stood over me shaking his head. "Gott dammit Karl. You stupid sonofabitch. Why the hell did you join up with this trash? Look at you. Dead as a doornail. Why fool? You never learned to avoid this fucking criminal. I told you he would kill you one day. Fuck, you chose this stupid cocksucker over your own brother." He walked over and kicked the near dead Wolf in the forehead while weeping silently.

Just then the man you know as Russell come through the door. He took one look at his half-brother Wolf with his eyes opened and fixed to oblivion and led out a wail. Master Malfred turned around to see him standing dare.

Master Malfred pointed at him with fury in his eyes. "You, this is your families fault. You filled my brother with false words and hopes. I am going to kill you next motherfucker." He took off with his knife posed to strike.

Russell didn't stick around to ask Master Malfred why his brother and Karl were lying dead on the closet floor. He didn't want to find out either. He ran like the scared rabbit right back the way he came. I come out of my startle and pulled up my pants.

As Master Malfred chased Russell down the hallway with murder on his mind I rushed over to the battered Rolf. I shook like the newborn calf as I worked out the knots of his bondage. I could have grabbed the knife from the hand of the dead Wolf, but I was sick to meine stomach from the flood of blood around the two corpses. *Amazing how much the brutes had bled before their hearts stopped, you know.* I didn't want nothing to do with either of the dead men.

I pulled the gag from Rolf's mouth, and he sputtered, sounding excited. "Oh, meine Gott. You saved meine life Maximillian. I never seen anything so brave in all my days."

I shook my head. "I didn't feel brave Master, errr, Rolf. Master Malfred will be back. He is going to end me the second he finds out that I killed his brother. I don't know what I was thinking." I began to feel the tears welling in my eyes as I finally got the last knot undone and freed Rolf from the ropes.

He rubbed his wrists and caressed his blackening eyes. “Nein. I saw Wolf kill Karl with meine own eyes. That was crazy you know? He sure got jealous over having to share your affections didn’t he. Oh, and I told you to stop calling me Master. I am your brother Rolf, forever now whether you like it or not.” Rolf winked at me with a mischievous smile.

I gasped. “What is this you say? I killed Karl and you know that Mast, err, Rolf. Master Malfred will know I did it.”

Rolf laughed then stood up pulling me to meine feet with him. “There are only two witnesses that saw you do that. One lays there silent for good, and the other sears he saw Karl killed by Wolf. On meine honor I will swear to that until the day I join these rat bastards in hell. You keep your mouth shut Maximillian and let me do all the talking. You need only to nod in agreement, ja?”

I grimaced. “I have nothing to pay your with for this favor Rolf. One day I will get a job. Otherwise, you can have whatever services you desire from me.”

He frowned at that. “Maximillian, you saved meine fucking life boy. You even endured that horrid sexual assault from those brutes to do it. Then you stand here offering to pay me with your dignity or other subservience to me. Hell, this is the other way around. I wonder what service I can ever provide in return for what you did for me. Can you put a price on life? I think not. However, I will say this, if ever you can come up with a way for me to return this amazing thing you did, I beg of you to ask it. It will be yours or I will die trying to get it for you."

I sniffed back meine tears and looked at the floor. "If what you say is true Rolf, I ask only that you keep your promise to never tell Master Malfred I killed his brother Karl. And one more thing."

He smiled with glee. "Anything, Maximillian. You name it."

I nodded. "I would ask you to be meine friend for truth, the way you said you would earlier today."

Rolf stuck out his hand in an offer to shake. "Brother Maxx, that you already had the moment you didn't hate me for being the idiot brute I truly am. I swear to you from this day forward we are no matter our bloodlines. I would die for you and you for me."

I looked up into his face to see honesty in his eyes. I smiled with truthful joy as I took his hand and shook it with strength. He chuckled then winced as he looked behind me onto the floor at the mess of blood and dead flesh.

"Yikes. This will be awful to clean up ja. I am glad tonight I am no black collar." He and I were startled by the sudden reappearance of the red-faced Master Malfred.

He walked into the storage room unable to take his tear stained eyes off his dead brother Karl. "Did you see what happened here Rolf?"

Rolf nodded and shot me a look of caution. “Ja, I did Malfred. Fucking Wolf wanted to rape the Priceless before Karl there murdered him. The two of them abducted Maximillian and I off the sixth floor while we were chattering about his thudding lessons you know. Anyway, so Karl told Wolf he had no time for nonsense such as sex with the boy. Wolf got angered and well the two fought. I was tied up and Maxx here too little to do anything to stop that fucker when he stabbed Karl in the stomach. Then the sick bastard pulled down his pants and nearly cut his cock off. I swear had you not come when you did, well he already raped the forbidden silver, and I think he was about to silence him from telling anyone about it and for murdering of Karl. Did you get Russell?”

Master Malfred shook his head openly weeping. “Nein, the motherfucker got away. I thought Wolf may have done something like you say. Meine Taube, are you injured from Wolf's rape, or did he manage to cut you?”

I sniffed and wrung meine hands with anxiety. “I am not too injured from the theft of service Master, just a bit sore. You saved me from being cut or worse by the brute. I thank you for the mercy of it.”

Rolf scoffed. “Shit you missed killing Russell. Malfred, that is bad news brother. That sneaky bastard saw you kill his brother. If I were you I would watch meine back. Those Hirsch's are known for their vengefulness. There is your own lying cold in his fluids to prove that.”

Master Malfred nodded. "Ja, I am aware. I am not worried he can get back into the walls with his ticket about to grow grass. It is Karl's daughter Rachel that is in the real danger from that coward. I imagine since Russell is not the member here in the Haus he will attempt to attack meine family through our most vulnerable member. He is a fucking American like meine niece's mother. I was recently upset when Karl told me he had come to Germany to offering to purchase the girl's vaginal virginity. He tried telling my brother this Debbie offered to sell it to him while she is less than a year old. The fucking nerve of that pervert to speak such nasty lies. That trash was told to leave our Female Priceless alone. I will get Jonas on this dangerous situation right away and have that child moved to the Haus for her protection. Maximillian, your future Frau will be here for you to visit whenever you want. That is maybe some good news among so much sadness today, ja? Karl would want it that way I am sure."

I turned to look at Master Maxx. "Guess he wasn't telling lies was he, Master." I frowned with bitterness.

He shook his head and stroked my hair. "Nein. He was sent by Karl and Wolf to look after their precious treasure originally. That sicko and Debbie began an affair shortly after he took the job. Russell is a well-known child molester here in the USA with three prior arrests for sexual assaults on children under ten. Well, Wolf put the fox in charge of the henhouse. Debbie apparently did sell your virginity to that bastard behind Malfred's back."

I startled. "You mean Master Malfred is still alive? You didn't kill him Master?"

Master Maxx smiled with evil in his expression., "Not yet. I will get around to him though. I have a list you know; Gretta, Cora, Peter, Malfred, Jonas, they are all on it. I need all them as of yet for your own collar breaking. I kill them right afterwards. Maybe you help me do it?"

I nodded with a nasty smile. "Right after I kill Debbie and Russell, Master. Oh, Jasper, Whiskey, and Sonny too."

Master Maxx poked me in my belly making me giggle. "You know the year you were born that group called the Eagles wrote this song called 'Witchy Woman.' I wonder sometimes if the band met meine Demonseed Frau and were inspired, ja? You are simply frightening, Meine Liebe."

I kissed him on the nose making him smile with much humor. "I thank you for the compliment Master. I love you too. I wish though you or my Uncle Malfred had killed Russell before he killed Rachel, oh well sucks to be me."

Master Maxx sighed. "You borrow meine own words, Meine Liebe. I tell you there are so many things I wish I could take back. I would do anything to breathe life back into several and steal that same thing from others. Russell is number one on that list, followed very closely by both meine father and your Uncle. It is one cruel world when most of the people you wish dead are related to you."

I wrinkled my nose. "Well, we have each other, and I don't want you dead anymore, Master."

He laughed loudly. "Ah, well, then I can sleep peacefully once more, ja? So, I ask you again. If I let you out of this cell tonight what would you do?"

I smiled full of demons. "I would burn this fucker to the ground, Master."

Master Maxx's mouth dropped. "Huh? I thought you said you didn't want to see me die. If you did that I would burn up in the basement."

I shrugged. "Only if you were stupid enough to stay in the basement Master. I told you I would burn down the house. So, if you let me out you better run. Don't worry, I would say run Master run."

He laughed so hard at my childish statement he had to take a potty break before continuing his story. But I wasn't kidding, and to be honest it wasn't funny.

I glared at Master Malfred. "Fuck what Karl wanted and fuck you too Master. I don't say that with respect either. I will never marry any blood of yours. I don't care if she were the last woman on this fucking earth. *So much for that bullshit since I did marry you.* You motherfuckers took my virginity, childhood, freedom, and even meine name, but I will be damned if you will steal meine choice of a Frau."

Master Malfred reared back his arm to backhand me roaring in fury. "You insolent bastard. I am sick to death of you telling me no." Rolf rushed him and blocked his blow.

He held Master Malfred's arm with his brute strength. "You keep your hands off Maximillian. He has the right to say what he did. It is not insolence when it is truth. He is about to be a Dominant Malfred. You cannot tell him who to marry nor who to fuck soon enough. You better watch how you treat him starting today, you idiot. I would think if you want him to call you family someday, then demanding, striking and cursing him is not the proper way to win his affection, ja?" He pushed the man back with a grunt.

Master Malfred was strong but not strong enough to beat the determined Rolf. He dropped his aggressive stance toward me with a storm of fury breaking out behind his expression.

The Dominant glared at me. "He may become the Dominant soon but tonight he is still meine collar. You kneel you disobedient bastard right this minute. I demand you grant me special services for protecting you from Wolf's blade."

I shook meine head with open hatred. "Jour job is to protect and defend meine collar, Master. I owe you nothing for doing what you swore to do for meine submission. You have been blocked from such service by meine man, I do believe. I cannot defy the orders of the one that controls how I share meine sexual artistry. You gain Master Jonas's permission, I will do as I am told. Otherwise, you will have to fuck yourself, ja?"

Malfred started to come at me again with anger drawing out the veins on his forehead but again was blocked by the calm Rolf. "You cannot speak to your better like that. You are a nothing. A fucking submissive."

I turned around to head out of that horror closet. "Master you are wrong. I am not just a nothing submissive. I am the Priceless one and not for much longer. You are not better, you merely outrank me. That is also going to change soon enough. Thank you for the mercy Rolf. I see you later. I regret I must leave the two of you with this nightmare mess, but I have orders that supersede this situation. If I don't go, then I will indeed be owed the punishment my Master Malfred claims in error."

Rolf smiled as he held back the railing Master Malfred. "Okay Maximillian. I see you in the morning for that thudding lesson, ja?"

I waved and left without another word. I rushed up the stairs headed for Master Leo's apartment praying that I was not terribly late. That Vampire was sure to skin meine hide for this latest drama. I then recalled the story that Rolf gave to Master Malfred. I grinned as I thought of how wonderful it was to have a brother on meine side. His excuse was perfect to explain why meine ass was in that closet.

I walked into the apartment without fear for the first time since I came to that sixth floor. Master Jonas was there fuming. Master Leo was on the phone calling all around the Haus seeking my whereabouts. I dropped to a kneel as Master Jonas came off the couch and tried grabbing me in his anger.

He glared down at me. "Where the fuck have you been Maximillian. We have been worried sick."

I cast meine eyes to the floor. "I do apologize Masters. It was most unavoidable. I was approached by Master Rolf for a quick notification about meine training in the morning. While he relayed the message Master Karl and Master Wolf got the drop on us. We were hauled downstairs at threat of death. The brutes then proceeded to steal the services of the Elders."

Master Leo hung up the phone upon hearing those words letting out a gasp. "Another fucking rape. Holy shit. Jonas, this has to stop. I demand that Wolf and Karl be hauled out of the Haus by Guard right this minute."

Master Jonas bellowed out, "You Gott damned right that is going to happen."

I giggled, which made both of my Masters stand there speechless staring at me. "That won't be necessary Master."

Master Jonas growled. "Oh? You trying to tell me how to do meine job again Maximillian? If I were you I would choose my next words to me carefully. Why don't you think I should call the Guard on these two thieves."

I looked up at him with a huge demonic smile. "Because the Guard already cleans up the mess that once was Master Wolf and Master Karl. One killed the other to gain meine skills for himself and Master Malfred killed Wolf in the middle of his crime. He and the Honorable Rolf are downstairs right now securing the scene of the murders."

Master Jonas shot a look of surprise at the more shocked Master Leo. "Did you hear that? Malfred's brother Karl is dead by his comrade Wolf's hands. I am sure Malfred must be devastated."

Master Leo nodded as he threw his hand dramatically to his chest. "I can only imagine. Holy hell. What a fucking insult it must be to the Krause family."

I snorted with borderline hostility in meine voice. "Oh, and I am uninjured from the brutes' rape but thank you for asking Masters. We can go to the Great Hall when you are ready. I do believe Master Malfred will not be joining us though. I doubt he has much of an appetite for celebrating bring back the dead when he must bury his brother soon."

Master Leo's look softened., "Oh meine Gott. Maximillian honey, I apologize for not asking about your health after such a fright."

I glared at him. "I beg your mercy Master, but I think rape is more than a scare. However, I do understand why such a thing would be viewed that way by meine Masters. I suppose you all believe I should not despair such an insult to meine psyche and dignity, being the whore that I am. You are right you know. I am very accustomed to being used against meine will. I believe after three years of it nonstop I have developed a bit of a tolerance for disgusting affection heaped upon me by perverted men."

Master Jonas reached down and snatched meine leash jerking it viciously. "Enough of this underhanded insulting your betters, Maximillian. You are pushing your luck. In fact, I think you have said all I want to hear from you for the rest of this day. I order silence. That is a directive."

I silenced meine speaking and dropped meine gaze back to the floor. The Elders of course didn't take what I told them for truth. Master Leo called Master Claus. The four of us went down the stairwell together and they followed the gathering crowd to the storage closet.

They arrived to find Master Rolf speaking to the Haus doctor. He was giving the story he had already sworn to earlier. Master Malfred was weeping over the corpse of his brother that had been covered with a sheet. Master Leo and Master Jonas shot a look of shock at me, and I glared at them with a wicked smile on meine face but didn't say a word. I wasn't given the Vampire an excuse to have me whipped.

Thanks to that foul business, the three Elder Master's planned celebration feast was muted quite substantially. The three of them sat there mostly silent with me forced to sit between the schwuler and the Vampire.

When the food came I snarfed up the stuff on meine plate while they barely touched their own. I believe meine fine spirits, despite the loss of two high ranking Dominants, was unnerving to them for some reason.

Master Claus and Master Jonas were briefly called away from the table to speak to the Voter Head Gretta regarding what they desired she do, if anything, about their brother Malfred that had committed murder on a High born Dominant. Master Leo sat there with me appearing lost in his thoughts. I got bored with nothing more to eat, nor the right to speak.

I recalled that colorful box that Master Byron gave to me earlier. I stealthily took it from meine pocket and unwrapped it under the table. It was not bigger than the palm of meine hand. When I had the thing bare of its paper I peeked into meine lap to see what was in that present.

I nearly gasped in shock. There laid a tiny, white lamb figurine fashioned from high grade China with diamond chips for eyes. It was perhaps the most beautiful gift I had ever received besides the true animals themselves. I wondered how the hell Master Byron knew this particular gift would touch my heart.

I narrowed meine eyes at Master Leo with suspiciousness. I thought maybe he was in a conspiracy with these new Voting Council men, or perhaps more deeply involved with Master Peter then I ever assumed. I was unsure of his latest game, but to be honest, I didn't like it.

I dropped that pretty lamb statue back into its box. I stuffed it in my pocket with the promise of putting it with meine other treasures down the vent when the Vampire hauled me back to his apartment the next morning.

I sat there staring at Master Leo with seething darkness filling meine chest. I couldn't believe I not only had trusted this man once, but even had loved him. He was the worst of them all. At least the others didn't pretend to be something they were not.

Master Leo noticed meine looking at him with fury. "What is it meine hase?" He seemed curious to know meine thoughts.

I shrugged, but minded Master Jonas's order of silence. Master Leo sighed and took a drink of his tea but didn't push me further. The Great Hall stereo system cranked up and music began to play through the huge room.

Within two songs our song "Nights in White Satin" began to play.

Master Leo smiled with warmness to himself then looked at me with much kindness in his expression. "Ah listen to that, meine hase. No matter what goes wrong in the world, the music stays true. Would you do this worthless man the honor of dancing with him? For a moment can we forget the many errors I have made stumbling through the darkness I helped infuse into your heart?"

I shrugged once again which caused Master Leo to throw down his napkin in irritation. "Fine then. You insist that I behave like your Dominant then so be it. You will join me in this dance. Come here now," he said with sternness.

I got up from meine chair and took his arm allowing him to lead me to the dance floor without quarrel. He took the lead in the slow dance initially appearing quite angered at me.

As the next sad song, many slow ones about lost loves or shattered dreams I noticed, his fire of anger quelled to a slow ember of maudlin memories. He pulled me tightly to his chest and hummed with many of the sirens singing through the speakers.

By the third slow dance he looked down at me with an expression of pure love. "Meine hase, holding you like this brings back all the passion I could ever hope to hold for anyone in meine soul. I miss holding you in meine cuddle at night keeping you safe from the nightmares that plague you. I cannot live without your happy eyes watching our baby hound play his doggy games. I feel so lost on the right way to proceed in aiding you to find the comfort, affection and safety I promised you when you first said I love you Leo. Can you tell me what I can do to find meine way back into your fondest favors?"

I snorted then looked around to make sure the Vampire didn't hear me breaking his directive. "Ja, Leo. You can stop lying to me. I heard you scheming in the hallway about stealing meine future. You said to that Vampire bat you would aid him in taking Guardianship. Nein, you offered to help him do this to me."

Master Leo frowned. "Ah, so this is what all this has been about. You think I betrayed you with Jonas."

I nodded then spat out with hate. "I do more than think you did, I know you did, Leo. I heard you demand to have a part in this hijacking, and you paid for half that lawyer of his too."

Master Leo took a deep breath. "Ja, meine hase you heard right. I won't lie about that. However, understand I only did that so I could keep Jonas from stealing you away behind his apartment walls without anyone capable of legally doing shit about it. I had to act that all was good with me, or he would never have believed I am like him, looking only to keep meine bed warm with a beautiful boy for all meine days. Please listen and think on the wisdom of what I say to you. I pretended to be the Vampire's brother to keep meine foot in his door. I would never do anything to hurt you again, not on purpose. How can I make you believe that meine Liebling?" He stared into meine eyes with an expression of desperation that was honest, to my surprise.

I furrowed meine brow. "Leo, if you tell the truth then help me stop Jonas from controlling meine life after the collar break. I confess I want to hate you, but I cannot do it. I look at you ready to tell you to go to hell for all time, then something holds me back. You still make meine heart flutter and bring a smile to meine bitter lips. I damn you, me too, for this unnatural addiction I have to your affections." I groaned as Master Leo smiled with joy.

He stopped his dancing to lean down and pull me into a deep kiss. I felt myself melting into his embrace like the idiot I am. Meine knees went weak as I began to kiss him back. For a moment, it was as it had been before Malfred ripped our strange love affair apart with his cruel blood bonding scheme.

The song 'California Dreamin' by the group 'The Mamas and Papas' began to play as we examined each other's mouths, growing more heated by the minute. I was not finding any issues with a shrinking cock cage. Thank the Gotts I was no longer feeling lustful with this man, but I was not willing to stop his adoration.

The truth was it felt good to be loved, held with tenderness instead of brutality, and cared for by this man that no doubt loved me with his entire being. I hate to admit it, I didn't want his kissing on the dance floor that night to end.

Try not to judge me too harshly for that. I had one weird, hard, and stressful day. Master Leo, well he always seemed to know how to make me feel better. He was until those days the only person in meine life to truly care to know the real me. It was his tenacity to keep trying to do better, even though he made many mistakes since he is human, that kept me coming back for more of his affection despite meine lack of sexual interest in him.

Master Leo whispered into meine ear. "Jonas will be back soon, and I want you so bad I think I may burst. I apologize for meine lack of being able to control meine urges but you asked me to be truthful. There it is Christian Axel."

I glared at him as I whispered back. "That is not meine name anymore Leo."

He panted out. “Bullshit. Jonas may think he has the final say on everything, but he does not. The world can call you whatever they like. The ones that took the time to see the real person you are will always know your truthful name is Christian Axel.”

A smile broke out on meine face. “I do love you, Leo. Damn me. Come with me and I grant you what you desire before the Vampire gets back to block you from it.” I pulled out of his embrace and tried to drag him to the bathroom in the back of the Hall.

He glanced back at our table with anxiety in his expression. “Nein. Christian Axel if Jonas caught us he would shit a brick. Besides, you need not do this. I am not commanding you hand over your favors to me.”

I chuckled. “Good. That is what I want to hear. Sooner or later, you will be commanding I comply with your lusting. That always pisses me off. Better to let me offer meine services when I am willing to be generous to meine Master than to wait until I am forced, ja? Give me this control back Leo and watch how willing I am to see that you are the happy man you have earned the right to be.”

Master Leo smiled with sudden understanding. “Ah. I finally get it. You beautiful boy. Ja, hell ja. I come right this minute wherever you want me to go.”

I chuckled as he allowed me to pull him along rapidly for the restroom. “Oh, you will cum right this minute Leo, which is a promise. After you’re sated, I wish to go back to see Der Makellos if you would be so kind to grant me the request."

Master Leo shot a coy glance at me. "You know I can deny you nothing. You look at me with though big blue eyes and Leo's brain turns to mush every time. I am your helpless fucking slave, and you know this."

I stopped at the bathroom door and pulled him into a groping kiss. "You better never forget that Leo. You need me, but I do not need you. Be honest, fair, and equal, then I will make sure you needs never go without attendance from your skillful lover." I said to him just as I pulled the thrilled Dominant inside with me and locked the door behind us.

The only problem I have ever had with sneaking around to fulfil Leo's lust is that man cannot keep his calls of ecstasy quiet for shit. I ended up having to stuff his handkerchief in his mouth during our couple in the bathroom thanks to his damned intercourse racket.

If ever you end up sleeping with him Meine Liebe, take meine advice. Make sure you put something in your ears to drown out all the noise from his sexual wails. Yikes, the man is loud, believe me.

Anyway, the makeshift gag worked. No one in the Hall was the wiser to our lovemaking antics that night in the washroom. Leo had been without any release since my near death experience. He was most eager to find his climax and I was grateful to make short work of this special service to my Master.

He took his intercourse with me was as near perfect as I can ever hope for when enduring this sexual bullshit with men. He used lots of lubrication, performed gently, and it was over almost before it started. If only every Master was so fucking easy to please as my Leo was that night, I would not be as bitter about sleeping with them. Just remember I said, "as bitter." I did not say I would be happy to do it no matter how fucking kind or nice they are about that penetration sex business.

Once we had cleaned up our mess we sheepishly snuck back to the dance floor hoping no one spotted our brief absence. The two of us took up a vigorous dance to the song "Fortunate Son" pretending we had merely stepped off the floor to grab a smoke break or catch our breath between changes in the records.

Master Leo was glassy eyed and wore a huge smile of joy as he spun me and stepped around in his mock mating ritual movements. I giggled at his silly antics. He never seemed to care a fig for what anyone thought of his original dancing styles. The man danced to please himself without worry if others agreed that he was doing any steps correctly.

It was around the second song when out of nowhere Master Byron, Master Friedrick and Master Rolf appeared from the small crowd of dancing couples on the floor. They approached with solemn expressions even the usually humored Rolf. I saw them first and backed out of the gyrating Master Leo's embrace. He turned around concerned to see what I was staring at in apparent terror.

He glared at the three men “What do you boys want? Can you not see that I am busy with meine collar?”

Master Byron shot a look of irritation at his brothers then said, “Leo, Jonas sent us to retrieve you for an emergency meeting of the Head of the Council and the Elders. He said either you come willingly, or we are to drag you along.”

Master Leo stopped dancing and put his hands on his hips in defiance and disbelief. “Excuse me? He sent you brutes to manhandle an Elder if I said nein to a meeting of meine brothers and sisters? What the fuck is going on?”

Master Rolf sighed. “Leo, old friend, calm yourself. This is a good thing and one meeting you will enjoy I believe. The honorable Gretta wishes to speak to the Elders about Malfred’s possible demotion or even exile due to his killing of Wolf. Jonas said you need to be there, and he told me and meine brothers to make sure the Priceless gets home safely while you attend your Elder business.”

Master Byron come rushing forward grabbing meine leash, nearly sending me into a wild run from the startle of his sudden move. “I will hold his leash personally, Leo. You can be assured no one will fool with the forbidden silver as long as we are around.”

Master Leo frowned. “Demotion or exile, well now that sounds positively delicious but unlikely. I am to understand the killing was to protect and defend our collar from that brute Wolf. Bad as I hate to confess it, he wasn’t enacting revenge for the death of his brother Karl and therefore was in his rights by Haus law."

Master Rolf nodded. "True, true brother Leo, but nevertheless, the Elders are seeking your vote. We will attend Mad Maxx if you can trust us to do this with speed and honor."

Master Leo looked to me. "I leave that up to Maximillian. Honey, do you trust these men to take you home to our baby hound and apartment? I leave this decision up to you. I don't mind making the Council and Elders wait."

I glanced up at the creepy Byron smiling with that star struck look in his eyes, and the giant Friedrick also with a goofy grin. I then flashed a quick look at Rolf that stared directly back. He winked at me letting me know he had his brothers under control if I choose them to take me home rather than Master Leo.

I sucked in meine breath and prayed trusting Rolf was the right thing to do. "Sure Master. I will be okay with meine protectors. They are all honest men." I knew if I were wrong meine ass would soon pay for the error, literally.

Master Leo nodded. "Alright then I will leave you to these capable hands. You go home Maximillian and wait quietly with our hound. No sandpaper, silly antics nor sounding off to Jonas when we get home, ja?"

I nodded. "As you wish Master. I thank you for the mercy of it." He kissed meine forehead and rushed off to the fifth floor to attend his meeting.

Rolf rolled his eyes when Master Leo was out of sight. "Shit that was weird Maxx. Most parents when they leave the kid say, no parties with your friends, don't drink all our beer and stop smoking up our pot." That made all three of the brutes howl in laughter.

I didn't get that joke. I didn't even know what pot was, had no friends, and rarely drank beer. I stood there wringing meine hands, fearful I had just made a huge mistake trusting these guys. Then Master Byron came in closer with that odd look in his eyes.

He leaned down and whispered in meine ear. "I hope you liked meine present. You look beautiful tonight. I swear the moon and stars must be jealous that you put them all to shame."

Meine eyes went wide, and I stood dare unsure how to respond to that insanity. "Uhm, thank you for the compliment, Master?"

Master Friedrick come forward with a startle. "Hey, did Byron say something sweet to you Mad Maxx? That is not fair. He knows I cannot woo you with fancy words, poetry nor songs. I am not the skilled conversationalist. However, I can take you to the gym every day and change your diet. When I am done with you, I will help you find your strength in life as the muscled man that can hold his own in a battle."

Master Rolf sighed. "Ah, you know we sound like the three kings that followed a star from that bible. I can hear it now. Behold we have come bearing gifts for the young king of kings. Come on boys. I want to show Mad Maxx the gift I have brought to him from meine Eastern country."

Master Byron laughed at Master Rolf's clever comparison, but Master Friedrick seemed lost by it. I watched the two laughed hard at the huge brute with a good heart and few brains. I decided despite his harsh couple with me earlier, I liked Master Friedrick. He simply was too simple to be dishonest. I was happy to have this gentle giant on meine side.

"Okay, the one place Friedrick is not gentle is in the couple. Remember that Meine Leibe because Friedrick is one of your leashes when you come of age. All three of these men will leash with you. They are the Haus's Voting Council to this day and as you know, we need their vote of ja for you to break that collar. You would do well to make them happy."

I snapped my neck and stared at him in disbelief.

Master Maxx shrugged while looking sheepish. "I apologize Meine Leibe and believe me I don't like this shit of sharing meine Frau, but that is the way it is done. I did it and you will have to do it too."

I groaned as I turned back around to hear the rest of the tale.

I wouldn't be breaking my metal for six more years. Maybe the three of them would be dead by then or kicked off the Voting Council by then.

I decided not to worry about the eight leashes Master Maxx had to promise to various Council members and Elders to assure my freedom. Well not yet anyway, yikes!

The three brutes took off with Master Byron holding tightly to me leash, dragging me behind them out of the Great Hall. I was a bit overwhelmed by so much appearing to happen all at once.

Master Malfred was in danger of being sent away. Wolf and Karl were dead which meant no more threats of their throwing me from the banister. Master Leo and I had somewhat made up and our relationship was on a slow mend. I watched the three Voting Council members ahead of me that had sworn their allegiance to protect me with pure awe and wonder.

It seemed downright disturbing that as Christian Axel I could never do anything but lose. As the boy Maximillian on the other hand, I was turning out to be a fucking winner or at least I seemed to be for the moment. I had lived long enough by now to never trust a Gott damned thing I thought I saw, heard or believed. Nothing is ever as it appears on the surface.

As our group began to climb the stairs, Rolf did his best to explain to Master Friedrick who the three king of the orient from the bible were and what they did to become famous.

Master Byron, as he did earlier, fell back and walked next to me appearing dreamy. “Did you like the lamb I give to you,” he said practically drooling on me.

I nodded then wrung meine hands with vigor as I hazarded a question. “It is beautiful Master. I would like to inquire how did you know I adore the sheep and lambs? Lucky guess?”

Master Byron was swooning. “Nein, meine buddy Rudolf from the stables told me you had five of them not long ago. He said you sadly had to let your pets go be with the flock and it broke your heart. I never heard of such a kindness in anyone in this harsh place of cruelty. I was touched by your defending the animals even to the point that Rudolf said you risked your skin and life. I thought I would give you a lamb no one can take away from you Mad Maxx. I know she is not as warm and soft, but she is as hard to replace. I had her custom made.”

I stopped dead in meine tracks staring at him in disbelief. “Master, something like this was not made in a single day. How long ago did you order this be created for me?”

Master Byron smiled then looked at his boots with embarrassment. “More than a month ago, when you were injured, and I first laid eyes on you. I knew that day, I needed you in meine life. I adore you Mad Maxx. I want to make you meine truthful lover and partner the second you are judged Dominant. Say ja, and I will treat you right and spoil you with all this worthless man has in this world.”

I stood there feeling I may faint from shock. "This is not happening. Master, forgive me, but I uhm, can I have time to think over your most generous offer?" I wanted to scream hell no, I am straight, you idiot.

However, I told you I am no fool. I knew that if Master Byron was in love with Mad Maxx, and thought he had a shot to have such a relationship after meine metal was no more. Then I would be wise to keep him believing that.

Master Byron grinned so hard his face nearly broke from it. "Ja, ja, you have plenty of time, Mad Maxx. I have the contract with you for this next five months, then after you will be free to choose who is in your bed. That gives me plenty of time to prove I am the man you should allow to fill your home and heart."

I groaned. "Uhm, Master Byron, you are aware I am blood bonded to the Vampire Jonas. He may not be pleased to find you in a bed coupled with his man, ja?" I knew better than to lie about that well known fact. Like it or not, I had to be at least that honest with this crazy man.

He chuckled and to meine surprise so did Master Rolf and Master Friedrick. Rolf motioned me and Master Byron to hurry and catch up as they stood on the fourth-floor banister walkway waiting. I wanted to know what the hell the three of them thought was so funny about a jealous Vampire man, but I kept meine mouth shut. These guys were big motherfuckers and that alone commanded meine careful respect to keep them from becoming angered.

To meine surprise, when Master Byron and I got to the other two, they took off down the hallway with speed. Master Byron followed and hauled me behind him. None of them spoke until they reached the corner of the High-Borns level. They all stopped in front of the door of an apartment located there.

I trembled in terror as Rolf produced a key and unlocked this door. I thought the two of them, maybe Rolf too unlike what he promised, were taking me to one of their old apartments. They had recently moved to the fifth from this fourth when they were raised to the Voter Council, you know. I thought they wanted to have their way with me. I had wondered how they planned to extract their daily payment from me without being caught by the nosey residents of that Haus. I supposed this was their answer. Double sucks to be me, no pun intended.

Master Byron pulled my shaking, hand wringing ass into that place behind the brutes. Rolf flipped on the lights, and I gasped to see the place was empty of furniture, or any decorations. This apartment was devoid of a Dominant. I did meine best to calm my rapidly beating heart and hold back meine tears when Master Byron smiled with thrill and reached around meine waist.

I closed meine eyes and braced for his lust when, to my shock, he reached into the secret pocket and pulled out the small box that held the China lamb. He grinned as he held it for me to see then handed it off to Rolf.

I wanted to demand they give the gift back. I thought I earned that lamb dealing with that fuckers' big cocks, you know, and if I hadn't yet, I sure would. I dared not say a thing with no one around to stop them if they decided to beat me or even end my life. No one knew where they took me, and they were trusted by my Masters, even Peter. I thought it best to be still, endure and cry about it later when alone with Der Makellos. The hound doesn't judge a man for having hurt feelings, you know. I watched in disappointment as Rolf took the pretty little lamb from the box and then went to the mantle of the empty fireplace. He sat the small figurine on it then stepped back to admire his placing in this waste space of nothingness.

He then turned to me and said, "What do you think, Maxx? Does she look good there or would you rather have her on the right side?"

I shook meine head. "I think the lamb goes wherever you wish it to be, Master."

Rolf and the others began to laugh at meine statement causing me much confusion as he said, "Nein, Maxx. The lamb goes wherever you want it to go. This is your haus after all. I merely wanted the honor to offer a bit of decoration advice for our new brother in his very first home." He came over and handed me the keys to my fourth floor Dominant's apartment.

To Be Continued in Book 8: Broken Silver

About Author: Alexandria May Ausman

Alexandria May Ausman in her 16th year was diagnosed with Schizophrenia. She was quickly abandoned by her foster parents. While still only a teen, she was forced to battle this devastating illness alone.

Alexandria has struggled with lack of a support system, numerous psychotic episodes, exploitation, homelessness, and an uncaring mental health system.

Alexandria raised two healthy children. After obtaining her bachelor's degree in psychology she worked as a child abuse investigator and became a diagnostic psychologist while acquiring her Master's in psychology. Alexandria never forgot the experience of 'slipping through the cracks.' Her life's goal is to help people suffering abuse and/or mental illness have access to necessary services. By accident, she became a model of 'gothic attire' and the World Goth Queen.

She began writing a fictionalized account of her life experiences after a catastrophic return of psychotic symptoms. Today, Alexandria is retired, and homebound due to crippling symptoms of Schizophrenia. She currently lives in Tallahassee, Florida, with her loving husband and a loyal support dog.

www.ingramcontent.com/pod-product-compliance
Lightning Source LLC
LaVergne TN
LVHW020655110826
845149LV00012B/2005

* 9 7 8 1 9 6 3 3 3 5 0 2 6 *